Macabre Ink is an imprint of Crossroad Press

For information, address Crossroad Press at
141 Brayden Dr., Hertford, NC 27944
www.crossroadpress.com

ISBN 978-1-63789-177-3

No AI was utilized in the writing or the physical production of this book.

The House at
BLACK TOOTH POND

This novel is dedicated to my wife, Kimberly Ann Brugger,
for making sure I stay creepy.
Er, wait...
That my books stay creepy.

The House at
BLACK TOOTH POND

STEPHEN MARK RAINEY

THE HOUSE AT BLACK TOOTH POND

I. FRIDAY

Chapter 1

It was damn near thirty years ago, and Parrott's heart still ached at the memory of his dad saying, "I should be back in a couple of hours," and then never coming home. Bryce had been old enough at the time—eleven and a half—to understand that his father, as county sheriff, faced job-related dangers beyond what most folks ever thought about when they began their typical workdays. But George Parrott was *his* dad, and somehow, young Bryce had believed in the kind of magic that preserved life, preserved love, and that his father would always, *always* come home.

But magic didn't work that way.

No.

Magic simply wasn't.

That sad fact hadn't dissuaded him from becoming a law enforcement officer. If anything, it reinforced his decision to follow his father's path, especially his work ethic, which truly was to serve and protect. For George Parrott, that timeworn slogan had never been something trite or blithely tossed about, but a genuine job description.

A way of conducting himself, personally as well as professionally.

Anymore, such community-minded individuals seemed too few and far between, but Bryce Parrott intended to count as one of them. Enough of the local population must have believed in his commitment to service because, every election for the past decade and some change, they had voted him sheriff of Sylvan County, Virginia. Or maybe his last name struck a familiar chord and the voters jumped on it. When they went to the polls, people who knew nothing about specific candidates tended to fall back on names they remembered. It didn't much matter how or why.

Or maybe they thought that, with a surname like his, he tried harder.

"Sheriff!" Deputy Beamer's voice rang from down the hall, a little shriller than usual. "We got something here."

Parrott had expected "something." The odor he'd detected when they entered the tiny, squalid apartment did not come from a fresh flower arrangement.

"What've you got, Vince?"

Beamer—tall and bony, two decades younger than Parrott and only a few months in the department—stood in front of the single bedroom at the end of a short hall, his eyes so wide that white showed all around his coffee-colored irises. The deputy pointed to a deep red splotch the size of a quarter. From it, several dried rivulets streamed down the dirty white door jamb just below the strike plate.

"And in there," Beamer said, his latex-gloved hand pointing to the floor just inside the partially open door. Another splash of what could only be blood, this one saucer sized. Its dull color indicated the splash was probably several hours old.

"All right, Vince. Open it up."

With a tentative hand, Beamer pushed the door inward. It groaned like an arthritic old man.

"Oh, my God!" Beamer's voice cracked. "Oh, my God!"

Parrott stepped forward and peered around the frozen deputy, into the small, dimly lit bedroom.

To the right, a single window—its raggedy old curtains half-drawn—admitted enough late-afternoon sunlight to reveal pale plaster walls covered with chaotic splotches and streaks, which Parrott knew were not the result of some crazed artist flinging buckets of paint. Several gore-covered, fleshy masses of various sizes and shapes lay scattered around the room, some piled in the center of a sagging, full-size bed. The nightstand next to the bed lay on its side, and a cheap lamp lay broken on the floor.

The room smelled like a combination of vinegar, gasoline, puke, and something else Parrott couldn't identify. He took a deep breath, held it, and stepped past Beamer into the bedroom. After a few moments, the stench wriggled into his olfactories and forced him to lift his arm and cover his nose and mouth with his sleeve.

The sheriff took a quick inventory of the body parts scattered around the room. The torso—or most of it—and what might have been the head nestled in a pool of blood and offal on the bed. An entire arm and the forearm of another lay tangled on the floor underneath the window. A foot and the shredded remains of a leg occupied the seat of an upholstered easy chair in the far-left corner. On the floor at the foot of the bed, a hand, torn from its wrist and missing its little finger, resembled a huge, squashed spider.

"Oh, my God!" Beamer repeated, this time at a slightly lower volume.

The body had not been cut apart. It had been *ripped* apart, the pieces scattered with evident abandon throughout the room.

Parrott had viewed death—horrific death—all too many times. However, he'd never seen—or imagined he might see—anything this *wrong*. He ventured a few tentative steps closer to the bed and noticed that a glistening, transparent gel coated portions of the ruined anatomy—like wet shellac, he thought. All that remained of the decapitated head was a crushed bulb of blackened bone, partially covered by shredded flesh, with goo-filled depressions where the eyes, nose, and mouth had been.

"Okay," he said to Beamer. "Call the coroner's office. Tell them I want Doc Crawford herself out here. And grab your camera."

Beamer swallowed hard. "Maybe I could wait outside?"

"You'll be fine. Make the call. And grab your camera. I need you to take pictures."

Beamer stepped back into the hallway, and a moment later, Parrott heard his low voice calling dispatch on his radio mic. A first, he still sounded quavery, but after he had spoken with the dispatcher for a minute or so, his voice became steadier. Good. That little task would help him refocus. After a couple of minutes, the deputy returned, looking slightly more composed, the department-issue Pentax KP in one hand. "The ME is on the way."

"Thank you, Vince. All right, you know the drill. Let's get some pictures. And don't touch any of that gooey shit, even with your gloves. We don't know what it is."

"I think I feel a little ill."

"You'll be okay. I *need* you to be okay. Okay?"

Beamer half-smiled and nodded. "Okay." After taking a few deep breaths to steady his nerves and his stomach, he raised his camera and began clicking away, picking his steps with special care as he circled the bed. But when he came within a few inches of the ruined hand at the foot of the bed, he hopped away as if he'd stepped on hot coals.

This was the deputy's first death in the wild, but now occupied with his task, he appeared more confident. Even in a less horrific situation, the first corpse could knock a person pretty hard—so what a fucking initiation to the worst part of the job *this* must be.

As Beamer took his photos, the sheriff made a circuit of the bedroom. The first thing he checked was the single window. Behind the half-drawn, tattered curtains, the wooden sash was closed and locked. Apart from the toppled nightstand and shattered lamp, he didn't see any other displaced furnishings. A couple of lamps on tables, a dust-covered mirror hanging on the wall, an ancient TV set on a metal stand; apart from the blood spatters, all appeared undisturbed. On the dresser adjacent to the bed, he found a small pile of personal effects—wallet, keys, some change, an ink pen—probably just as the dead man had left them. No cell phone to be found.

The wallet contained less than a hundred bucks in cash, a very new Virginia driver's license, auto insurance card, and a couple of bank cards. Based on the ID, the wallet—and almost certainly the body—belonged to one Mr. Frank Lydell.

So, unless a phone or some other unknown item belonging to the dead man had been taken, he saw no evidence of burglary. The landlord, a stooped, chain-smoking septuagenarian named Richard "Dicky" Rudd, had unlocked the front door for them when they'd arrived. All the other doors and windows appeared secure. Parrott had asked Mr. Rudd to wait outside until he and Beamer finished checking out the place.

"All done, Vince?"

"Yes, sir."

"Bring up a roll of barrier tape, will you? Then you can wait outside to greet the ME when she gets here."

"Thank you, Sheriff." With obvious relief, the young deputy exited the apartment.

"Yo, Sheriff!" Dicky Rudd's ancient voice creaked from somewhere down the hall. "What the hell is going on?"

"Stay out yonder, Mr. Rudd," Parrott called back. "I'll talk to you directly."

"My afternoon's going to waste."

"Won't be long."

An hour ago, Dicky Rudd had called the department's non-emergency number, concerned about the sharp, "irregular" smell that tainted the air outside Mr. Lydell's apartment. There were eight units in the old Druid Hills apartment building, and Rudd lived directly downstairs from Lydell. No, he'd heard nothing unusual from upstairs last night or this morning. No footsteps, no television, no running water; just a lot of dead silence. Well, yes, Rudd sometimes had a little nightcap to help him sleep, and last night, he had enjoyed one or maybe several. Initially, Parrott had intended to send Deputy Dan Sykes and Beamer on the call until he remembered Sykes had taken a personal day for his son's first birthday. So, he'd decided to come out here himself. If nothing else, it gave him an opportunity to see how well Beamer was holding up in the field.

Under the circumstances, better than fair to middlin'.

"Sheriff!" came Rudd's sharp, grating voice, the closest thing to a roar the old man was capable of. "What the hell are you doing?"

"I'm coming right now, Mr. Rudd."

The old man stood in the sparsely furnished living room, just inside the front door, and he gave Parrott a withering stink-eye as he approached. "So, dead in there, is he?"

"Outside, please." Parrott stepped through the open front door and motioned for Rudd to follow him out to the balcony. The older man did so only reluctantly. Parrott pulled the door shut behind him.

Rudd's lower jaw protruded about a mile. "I'll ask you again. What the hell are you doing?"

Ignoring the question, Parrott drew a small notepad and a stubby pencil. "Mr. Rudd, we'll need to verify that the deceased is, in fact, Mr. Lydell, but for now, I'm going on the assumption that it is. How much do you know about him?"

"Not much, other than he paid three months' rent upfront—in cash—and didn't make much noise. He was gone a lot."

"How long has he lived here?"

"Maybe a month or so. What's happened to him?"

"Did he ever have visitors?"

Rudd's jaw inched out even farther. "Can't think of a one. Not when I've been around. And I'm pretty much always around. So. What happened to him?"

"For the moment, until I have reason to believe otherwise, we're going to call this a crime scene. That means you don't come in here without my permission. I'd appreciate it if you'd hand over your key."

Rudd's indignant glare would have devastated a weaker soul. "This is my property!"

"Believe this, Mr. Rudd, you'll thank me for not letting you in there."

"I will not."

"Do you know where Mr. Lydell lived before he came here?"

The glare didn't soften. "Can't remember offhand. Out of town, I think."

"Did he have a job?"

"I don't know. Like I said, he paid three months upfront. That was good enough for me, you know?"

"You said he was gone a lot. Like for a regular work shift?"

"I suppose. Plus, most evenings."

"Did he stay out late?"

"Usually no later than my bedtime. That's ten o'clock, to answer your next question."

Beamer came clumping up the stairs to the balcony carrying a roll of yellow tape in one hand. He handed it to Parrott.

"Thanks, Vince. Would you see Mr. Rudd back to his place, please—after he gives me his door key?"

With an angry puff of breath, Rudd handed over the key. "This is governmental overreach, you know."

"You can take that up with the mayor."

The old man turned and started herky-jerky down the stairs. "Don't bother seeing me to my place, Sheriff, I know the way."

"Thank you for your cooperation, Mr. Rudd."

Another unintelligible grumble, and Rudd passed out of Parrott's view.

The late afternoon sun had slipped behind the wall of tall pines that surrounded the old apartment building, and as shadows closed in, the air turned noticeably cooler. A swirl of dead leaves blew past the balcony railing and Parrott heard them rustle through the gravel parking lot below.

He was about to head back into the apartment when an unusual sound from the surrounding woods drew his attention. A distant, shrill, warbling cry.

A whippoorwill.

He hadn't heard a whippoorwill in years. Reclusive, nocturnal birds, they typically inhabited only the deepest woods, farther out in the county. Mighty odd to hear one this close to town. In fact, if he remembered right, they were damn near endangered.

The melancholy, almost eerie song continued for a few moments before falling silent. To Parrott, it seemed a fitting dirge for the human wreckage scattered inside the apartment.

Chapter 2

The little body of water nestled in almost perpetual shadow a couple of hundred yards into the woods off Old Beckham Road, seven miles out of Aiken Mill. To locals in the know, it bore the name Black Tooth Pond because the broken trunks of a dozen or so trees, burnt black from a long-ago fire, protruded like rotted teeth from the pond's farthest end. If a mere handful of Sylvan County's residents could claim to recognize the pond by name, far fewer could pinpoint its precise location. And no one alive would remember the fire that had devastated several hundred acres of the region's densest forest, even in the swampy lowlands that encompassed Black Tooth Pond. Still, if one were to examine a specific corner of northwestern Sylvan County on virtually any local map, they might notice the small, unnamed body of water amid an expansive, unbroken swatch of green in the valleys between Copper Peak, Mount Signal, and Thunder Knob. And then forget it existed.

A small town by any standard, Aiken Mill was still the largest and most prosperous cornerstone of a triad in Sylvan County that included the little communities of Beckham and Barren Creek. Early in the twentieth century, the natural contours of the land had steered the construction of the paved road between Aiken Mill and Beckham in a wide, sweeping arc around the lower slopes of Copper Peak, turning ten miles of straight distance into an almost twenty-mile drive. A newer highway provided a faster, more direct route between the towns, so that, nowadays, a traveler on the Old Beckham Road might drive its full distance without encountering another vehicle.

Apart from a nine-year stint in Richmond, Martin Pritchett had lived his forty-four years in and around Aiken Mill. He'd completed his undergraduate studies close to home at Beckham College and then moved to Richmond, where he earned his doctorate in Psychology at Virginia Commonwealth University. He subsequently set up a private research firm in the city with a couple of partners, but due to his own lack of solid business sense, things hadn't worked out quite the way he'd hoped. So, a decade after bidding adieu to Beckham College, things came full circle, but with him on the other side of the classroom desk. While this outcome hardly fell in line with his early career expectations, now that he'd been teaching at the small but prestigious school for going on thirteen years, he'd come to love it.

It was Martin's younger brother, Phillip, who introduced him to Black Tooth Pond. Phil owned a perpetually exuberant Golden Retriever named Rufus, whom he enjoyed taking on long walks in the most secluded locations he could find. Occasionally—like now—Martin accompanied him. Almost twenty years earlier, during his own tenure at Beckham College, Phil and a couple of his friends had discovered Black Tooth Pond while exploring the Sylvan County backroads, looking for a place to smoke pot. It was certainly private property, but since there were no nearby houses and no one else ever came out here, it became their go-to place to get stoned.

To the best of Martin's knowledge, Phil occasionally indulged in his old vices, but he was long past his days of living for his next altered state. Still, his regular walks with Rufus gave him a pleasant reason to revisit these old stoning grounds.

Around Black Tooth Pond, the towering columns of trees, most bearing thinning crowns of red and gold, extended into impenetrable distance in every direction. Deep layers of dead leaves blanketed the narrow deer path that paralleled the reed-choked banks of the pond, and Rufus took great pleasure in romping through them just to hear the loud crunches and crackles beneath his paws. Phil gave him plenty of slack on his long leash.

Martin walked abreast of Phil, hands thrust in his jacket pockets, for the late afternoon breeze nipped at him with increasing determination. Given Phil's work schedule at Studio 253, a local company of commercial and graphic artists, his walks were relegated to after four o'clock, and as the days grew shorter, so did the length and frequency of his outings. Happily for Martin, on Fridays, his last class ended at three o'clock.

The shadows had grown long and the daylight dimmer as the sun struggled to cast its rays through the near-endless processions of trees around the pond.

"Guess we ought to head back," Phil said, glancing at the black, broken trunks that rose from the water like groping fingers, only a short distance ahead. "I do miss the summer hours."

"Not me," Martin said. "Hate the heat."

"You have air conditioning. And only two summer classes to teach every day."

"My body doesn't tolerate heat and humidity as well as it used to."

"You sound like you're older than Dad. How'd you get to be older than Dad?"

"The price of gaining wisdom."

"That's ass-wisdom. You are a wise ass."

Martin had five years on his brother, and he figured that, by any objective standard, he was the far more handsome, cultured, and intelligent of the two. A good inch taller, marginally more athletic (he played golf regularly at Lynwood Golf Course and sometimes walked rather than drove a cart), and, though his forehead had grown slightly taller in the past few years, at least his hair wasn't growing prematurely gray like his younger sibling's. By the time he'd reached thirty-five, Phil's admittedly luxurious mane had gone from sandy to almost pure silver.

Despite his lingering youthful recklessness, which he seemed disinclined to outgrow, Phil had always been more or less all right. Quirky, but all right.

An artiste.

Rufus's boundless energy showed no sign of abating. He zoomed from tree to tree, sniffing, digging, running in circles, and tugging his near-helpless leash-bearer along wherever he went. At last, with a commanding, "Hold up there, buddy," Phil managed to settle the dog down enough to shorten his rein.

"How old is he now? Eight?" Martin asked. "He's got more energy than when he was a puppy."

"Almost nine. He'd run rings right around you."

"He's doing a pretty good job on you, too."

Phil snorted. "I might spoil him a little."

At last, with Rufus marginally more mellow, they started back down the deer path toward Phil's Toyota Tacoma, parked by the water's edge. The pond was a couple of hundred yards long and about half that wide, and when they had more time, they usually circumnavigated the entire thing. Black Tooth Pond, especially in fall, was beautiful, Martin thought. And yet, somehow, almost creepy. Despite a low breeze, the air carried no sound—no bird songs, no rustling of squirrels or other small animals in the layers of dead leaves. Even when the sun blazed overhead, its brilliant rays never filtered all the way down through the overhanging branches. Neither Martin nor his brother had ever encountered another person out here, not even a fisherman, which they found surprising since catfish, bass, crappie, bream, and others clearly thrived in the pond. Not to mention the unusual fact that not a single "No Trespassing" sign hung in view anywhere nearby.

"Got plans for tonight?" Phil asked.

"Dinner with Alana at seven."

Most of the civilized world had expected Martin to be the first to marry and, subsequently, produce a veritable herd of diminutive humans. But no. Although he and Alana Mendes—his "special friend," as his parents called her—had entered a relationship that showed signs of heading for long-term, for them, it was still early. Children were certainly not on their radar. Probably not ever. On the other hand, Phil, whom that same civilized world considered a nouveau Bohemian, had leaped with uncharacteristic aplomb into traditionalism by proposing marriage to a young woman named Carli Vaughan, a local real estate agent, whom he'd been seeing for over a year. Despite her questionable taste in men, Martin quite liked her.

Their wedding was coming up in just over a month. He couldn't help but wonder how Phil would adjust to cohabitating with—and being committed to—another human being for the first time in his adult life. It wasn't unfair to say that Martin had some reservations—unspoken, of course—about Phil's ability to uphold his end of the bargain.

"And what are you up to tonight?"

"Work, believe it or not. I got a contract to do a portrait. Tight deadline. I'll be at it all weekend."

"Really? A portrait?"

"You know Sam Edmiston? Town council guy?"

"Sure, yeah. But a portrait? And he contracted you?"

"Yes, he did."

Martin could see it now. A Phillip Pritchett portrait would be a stick figure with a big round head and a few splotches of paint for features. His brother's typical work leaned toward Neo-expressionism, more in the style of Peter Keil or Karel Appel than Andrew Wyeth or Norman Rockwell, whom he figured would never go out of style in Aiken Mill. He gave Phil a sidelong glance. "No fuckin' way."

Phil's jaw tightened, a sign that he was on the verge of becoming defensive. After a moment, though, he shot Martin a dismissive look. "You doubt. Sometimes, you are not a smart man."

"I've seen your work."

"Not lately. It's my job to *sell*, you know."

Martin offered him a conciliatory nod. Phil's profession had always stood on tenuous ground, and he knew all too well the threat that AI posed to his financial well-being. In a small town like Aiken Mill, Phil's unique personal style carried some honest-to-God weight; tech-based art would offend the sensibilities of those who desired and could afford artwork created the old-fashioned way—even if they considered its style crude. The local aficionados of fine art wanted—demanded—*real* art. And, almost to Martin's surprise, enough of them existed to carry substantial economic clout. Phil's biggest worry was his business clients. If those companies could create campaigns that cost only a fraction of Phil's custom work, they'd jump on the lowest-priced alternative in a heartbeat.

Still, Martin's appreciation for his brother's chosen style only went so far. A connoisseur of what he had always called "mop-and-slop" expressionism he was not.

"I hope Mr. Edmiston has a very open mind."

"Are you gonna go there? Really?"

Although the two of them had enjoyed a mock adversarial relationship since their youngest days, at times, Phil could become unexpectedly hypersensitive. Martin held up a mollifying hand. "I'm sorry. You know it's an older brother's sworn duty to give the younger one shit."

"You don't do it well."

"I'll practice harder."

"Fair enough."

Fences marginally mended, they walked the last hundred feet to the truck. As they reached it, Phil opened the driver's side door, unhooked the leash from Rufus's collar, and gave the dog's backside a little nudge, which was all he needed to hop into the back seat on his own. By now, it was dark enough that the pond had become a big, black, featureless pool of shadow that blended seamlessly with the darkness beneath the surrounding trees. As Martin opened the passenger-side door and started to clamber into the seat, a distant but clear sound stopped him. A sound he hadn't heard since his childhood.

A warbling, melancholy cry.

A whippoorwill.

"Hey," he said to Phil. "You hear that?"

"Yeah. I hear them out here from time to time. I love their song. Hey, check this out." He shot Martin a smug little smile, drew a deep breath, and pursed his lips. Then, adding a little extra vocalization in his throat, he whistled, producing a near-perfect whippoorwill cry. With a laugh, he said, "Pretty good, eh?"

"Impressive," Martin said, not without sincerity, though finding this talent perfectly superfluous.

"If you say so."

"I did." He scanned the surrounding deep, silent shadows. "You know, I don't think I've heard one since I was a kid. Somehow, they always unnerved me a little."

"How come?"

"Well, to a young'un, they sounded kind of scary."

Phil scoffed as he climbed into the driver's seat. "I find them soothing. A little sad-sounding maybe, but melodic. Beautiful, really."

"I guess it is kind of neat to hear one again after so long."

"Thanks."

"I wasn't talking about that racket you made."

Phil sighed, started the truck, and made a slow, cautious three-point turn at the pond's edge to head back out to the main road. Martin glanced back into the gathering darkness, roughly in the direction from which he'd heard the whippoorwill cry. For one brief instant, he felt the faintest touch of unease, the brush of chilly fingers on the back of his neck; a mild yet very real resurgence of the dread that a whippoorwill's voice had instilled in him as a child.

Thankfully, the sensation passed before Phil even began to maneuver the truck up the narrow, treacherous dirt road that led to the old highway.

THE HOUSE AT BLACK TOOTH POND

II. SATURDAY

Chapter 3

Melissa "Doc" Crawford looked like a fourteen-year-old kid, but she had been the county medical examiner for going on fifteen years. Short, slight of frame, uncannily youthful face. A pixie, Sheriff Parrott thought. Hell, when she'd taken the position, she'd looked ten, so at least she had the decency to mature a little over the years.

Right now, her eyes, typically wide, bright, and humor-filled, held Parrott's with uncharacteristic graveness.

Graveness and incomprehension.

"I wish I had some clue what I'm dealing with here, Bryce. I wish."

Parrott drew his gaze from hers and focused on the hideous almost-a-body, the myriad "reassembled" parts glowing like an incandescent, malformed mannequin under the harsh white light above the autopsy table. In this setting, the masses of dark gray flesh and bone, some still glistening with the enigmatic goo, appeared marginally less shocking to his senses than they had scattered in bloody piles in a dim apartment bedroom.

As with any visit to the morgue, which occupied the deepest subbasement of Travis Holsinger Memorial Hospital, the chilly air assaulted his sinuses with a mélange of odors, the most pungent being pine-scented disinfectant and some sharp chemical that only God and the ME could identify. Mr. Lydell's remains had occupied space here for almost twenty-four hours.

"So, nothing toxic? I've been afraid we might have breathed something that would boil our insides."

Crawford shifted her attention to the remains, which, in addition to the devastation it had suffered in the field, now bore numerous tool-made orifices wherever enough flesh remained to create one. "Not toxic. Unexplainable. You know that substance coating the epidermis? It's defied every attempt at analysis."

"What does that mean?"

"I mean it appears to not exist. There is more happening in a drop of distilled water than this stuff. Under a microscope, there's nothing to see. I mean *nothing*. It reacts with nothing. Our spectrometer registers nothing. Granted, it's not top-of-the-line—you know, budget and all. But whatever this stuff is, it comes up empty and inert. And once it's separated from the body tissue, it vanishes." She shook her head as if doubting her own words.

"It vanishes?"

"Gone. As if it evaporates in a very short time. A few minutes. As long as it's in contact with the victim's remains, it doesn't seem to go anywhere." Her eyes shifted to the reconstructed horror on the autopsy table and then back to his. "To make things even more entertaining, I have no idea how our victim came to be in this condition."

"No idea? Words you've never spoken, Doc."

"I hope I never will again. Now, as you know, this body wasn't cut apart. It was mauled. Torn apart. There's evidence of what might be claw and bite marks. Not from any animal I can identify, though. Not a bear, not a mountain lion. But something big."

"Jesus." He pointed to the autopsy table. "By all indications, it happened inside the apartment. What about some kind of tools? Something a perp might have used to inflict that kind of damage on a body?"

She pointed to the upper half of the partial torso, which bore several sets of long, very deep striations, like marks left by four, widely spaced claws. On the intact portion of the left thigh, two very different-sized, parallel gashes ran from top to bottom of the limb. "These sets of lacerations were not made by the same thing. Almost all the lacerations were made by different...somethings. And the sheer force required to do all this...." She gestured to the whole of the grotesque wreckage. "It would require superhuman strength."

"God, what a horror." Parrott's mind fled to the marginally more comfortable topic of their examination of Lydell's apartment. "We found no evidence of breaking and entering. No bloody footprints. No animal tracks, certainly not big ones. Violence did happen in that room. Whatever did this, whether human or animal, it had to have a means of getting in and out. We've found nothing of the sort. That place was locked up tight from inside."

Crawford nodded. "There was none of that goo left in there, either—except on the actual remains. Which, in its weird way, is consistent with my findings."

"What about the fumes in the apartment?" He crinkled his nose at the memory. "Fumes would indicate some kind of particles in the air. Wouldn't they?"

"They would. So, you can appreciate my bamboozlement."

"What do you do now?"

"I keep looking. I've sent samples of both tissue and that substance to a contact of mine at the FBI lab in Quantico. If there's any place to get some answers, I'd say they're it. At first, I thought this stuff might be saliva from some animal. But how could that be? It contains no trace of a single element. By all rights, this substance should have picked up residual matter from the body, from the environment." She shook her head and heaved a sigh. "There is none."

"Okay, so nothing 'natural' would have these properties. Could it be manmade? Something—what would you call it?—bioengineered?"

"It would still be composed of detectable organic or synthetic material."

"Jesus." Parrott produced the little notepad from his shirt pocket. "All right, let's switch perspective. From my end, we've determined that the deceased is, in fact, Mr. Frank Lydell. No known middle name." He squinted at his scribbles. "Well, there's a chance he changed his name at some point. His history appears to go back only so far. We're looking into that. According to his ID, fifty-eight years of age. No criminal record. Only lived in Aiken Mill for six weeks. Last address was in Providence, Rhode Island."

"Rhode Island?" Crawford's eyes focused on something far away. "Wonder why he ended up in this hole-in-the-wall town."

"So far, we can't find any record of family or acquaintances here. But it's way too soon to tell. We've still got plenty of people to question. Anyway, it doesn't look like he had a job here, but get this. Apparently, he withdrew everything he had from his bank in Providence before coming here. He'd stashed a couple of thousand dollars—in cash—in that apartment."

"At least your busywork has been paying off."

"We still have many, many questions." He gave a little snort. "So, yeah, there's a hell of a lot more to do. Mostly by you. You want to quit slacking off, please?"

"Fuck you, Bryce." Her voice was harsh but her eyes took on a gleam of humor.

"You're too kind."

"You have no idea."

"What are you going to do now?" Doc asked.

He glanced at his watch. It was just past six. "Dig a little more. Cook another pot of Juan Valdez. Go home when it wears off."

"Speaking of, don't wear yourself out. You're getting old, you know."

"Fuck you, Doc."

She drew back in mock offense. "Don't ever speak to me again."

"Trust me, I won't. Not until tomorrow." He pocketed his notepad, grabbed his hat from the nearby countertop, and slapped it on his head. "Till then, I remain ever silent."

"Goodnight, asshole."

He said nothing and did not look back as he exited the morgue. He found his mind drifting back many years, to the night his father failed to return home. Sheriff George Parrott had also been brutally murdered. The killer, who went only by the name of Ren, had been a depraved sociopath, a reputed Satanist or witch cultist or some such. He, in turn, had been killed by one or more members of his so-called "coven."

One could never say that Sylvan County wasn't home to some unique and bizarre violent crime. Not only that but, relative to other locales with comparable populations, an extraordinary number of individuals had vanished from this area without a trace—going back long, long before Bryce Parrott was even born.

Sylvan County, the Cold Case Capital of the World.

#

By the time Parrott arrived back at his office, the sun had set and most of the half-dozen deputies on duty were out on patrol. The evening staff of three didn't appear particularly busy, which he found a welcome switch from the barely controlled chaos of the previous evening. Although he hadn't eaten anything since early this morning, he didn't feel hungry. Coffee, though, he could use. At this hour, he decided there wasn't much point in brewing a new pot of high-grade Juan Valdez in his personal coffeemaker. So, he grabbed his oversized, overused Green Bay Packers mug and ambled into the lunchroom. It wouldn't be good, but a fresh, full airpot of some cheap generic brand awaited him, courtesy of Farley MacBane, the department's receptionist/gofer/occasional deputy. Standing before the airpot, Chief Deputy Dan Sykes, back after his apparently exhausting day off to celebrate his kid's birthday, had just topped off his mug.

"I hear I missed an interesting call yesterday," Sykes said.

"Indeed, you did."

"From the sound of it, maybe I got lucky for once."

"Don't go getting used to it."

Sykes half-smiled. "I know better than that."

Parrott returned an equitable micro-smile. He found Sykes an excellent chief deputy, if sometimes too brash for his own good. Early thirties, ex-army, never so much as a wrinkle in his uniform. He kept himself exceptionally fit, which made him Parrott's favorite for any job that required significant physical exertion. He gave Sykes a quick wave of dismissal and headed back to his office, where he closed himself in and sat down at his desk.

A handful of messages stared back at him. Nothing urgent, and absolutely nothing new regarding the late Mr. Lydell. A pair of routine traffic stops that resulted in drug busts. A domestic disturbance out on Henry Switch Road, the third in a month for that quarrelsome young couple. A suspect charged with grand larceny—robbing Lloyd's Jewelers a couple of weeks earlier—had decided to flee on foot from a pair of arresting deputies, only to be apprehended after he barreled through a plate-glass window at Avery's Ice-Cream Shoppe, two doors down from the jewelry store. The felonious klutz needed extensive stitchery but had suffered no other serious injuries.

Parrott's mind didn't linger on the day's more mundane business.

"It appears to not exist. There is more happening in a drop of distilled water than this stuff."

Parrott was no forensic expert, but the unfathomable substance found on that ruined body baffled him no less than Doc Crawford. Everything was made of *something*. Wasn't that an unbreakable rule of chemistry, or physics, or…whatever branch of science might apply here?

All that was Doc Crawford's purview. Right now, his focus was on the *other* part of the equation. Something had torn a living person apart, something with incredible strength. Something that left no other evidence. Something that by all rights should never have been able to get into, much less out of, that apartment.

Well, unless Dicky Rudd had opened the door for some ravaging predator and then bid it a fond adieu after it had completed its terrible business.

A ludicrous prospect.

Right now, Parrott needed information that could provide insight into Frank Lydell's life, not only since his arrival in Aiken Mill but prior to it. Especially any associations he might have made here in town. A brief background check—all they had managed so far— indicated that Lydell's otherwise unremarkable history went back only thirty years, when he would have been in his late twenties. Prior to that, there was nothing. No known family, no school records, no work history, nothing.

It was early, true. New—or in this case, old—information might very well turn up. Still, Parrott couldn't avoid dwelling on the possibility that, at some time or another, Mr. Frank Lydell, all-too-recently and inexplicably deceased, had been someone else altogether.

If so, he must have had good reason for changing his identity. Maybe a reason that had somehow led to his horrific demise.

Chapter 4

The road stretched before him, far into the dark distance, the headlights barely defining its contours. There were no lines on the uneven pavement, no road signs; only dark, impenetrable trees on either side. The tires rumbled on the asphalt with a deep, hollow sound. His hands, slick with sweat, clutched the steering wheel as if to prevent it from twisting itself from his grip and whipping the car off the road.

He knew this road. He shouldn't be going this way. He needed to turn around.

Now.

NOW!

#

On those relatively rare occasions that Martin Pritchett stepped inside the doors of Calaman House, the blended aromas of hickory smoke, seared beef, and seafood, so distinctive and familiar, brought with them a brief but intense pang of nostalgia. Many eons ago, whenever his dad felt inclined to take the family out for a "fancy" dinner, Calaman House was usually their destination. Since Vernon's, the town's only other semi-upscale restaurant, had closed its doors a few years back, finding any other comparable dining option required traveling to Roanoke, forty-five minutes away.

Since Alana had never eaten here, introducing her to the experience felt like a personal obligation.

The restaurant's dark, wood-paneled walls, warmed by the glow of small globe lamps, mounted just above head-high and spaced at regular intervals, provided the elegant ambiance of an earlier time, though the thumping bass and whiny, autotuned vocals of some current song he didn't recognize felt disagreeably anachronistic. At least the volume was low.

An obsequious young hostess led them to a table for two, candlelit and draped with a white linen tablecloth, nestled in a cozy corner. As they sat down, she presented them with menus and told them with exaggerated delight that their server, Joshua, would take care of them shortly.

Alana's eyes roved the room. Then she gave him a dubious look. "So, your mom and dad brought you here when you were a kid?"

"Once in a while."

Her hazel eyes glimmered in the soft, flickering light. "I guess they thought you were worth it. Parents tend to have a rosy-eyed view of their children."

He laughed. "Hell, yes, I was worth it. Now, my brother, Phil... not so much."

"Well," she said, her voice earnest, "I hope my rosy-eyed view of you is justified."

"I'm sure I have my work cut out." He barely glanced at the menu, since he'd perused it online. With equal earnestness, he said, "For that matter, so might you."

Her eyes had turned to her menu, and she did not look up. "Effortless."

Joshua, a burly twenty-something with a huge, bronze beard and oversized Buddy Holly glasses, materialized to take their drink orders. Alana ordered a glass of Viognier from one of the relatively new, nearby Virginia vineyards.

Martin and white wine had never gotten along, not since that night at Beckham, twenty-some years ago, when his PSY 470 professor, Dr.

Stanley, had hosted a wine and hors d'oeuvres soirée for his honor students. Near the end of the evening, most of a bottle of Sauvignon Blanc, along with the assorted remains of popcorn shrimp, stuffed mushrooms, and Swedish meatballs, had erupted from Martin's digestive tract onto Dr. Stanley's dining room table.

The next day's hangover achieved epic proportion. His only saving grace was that, at the time of the incident, Professor Stanley had already passed out in his bedroom, and—by some dark miracle—never learned the identity of the Mad Vomiter.

"A gin martini," he said to Joshua. "Beefeater, very dirty, and drop a sliced habanero into it, please."

The young man smiled, pivoted, and headed for the bar.

Alana knew the story of his most notable drinking disaster. "And you couldn't handle a little white wine."

"This is an old friend's recipe. He introduced me to it a few years ago, and now I can't do a martini any other way."

"What do you call it? Martini de Marty? A Martytini?"

"Martytini. I kind of like that."

"Go for it. There is no charge."

He smiled. Four months ago, just before the start of the school's academic year, Alana had become Beckham College's Admissions Director, and a couple of chance meetings on campus had led them to several enjoyable lunch dates. Having established an easy rapport, it wasn't long until they went on their first "official" off-campus date—at Willy's Downtown Tavern, which was pretty much Calaman House's polar opposite. She was thirty-three, but their age difference mattered not a whit to either of them. And now, as Martin read it, they had settled into a not-quite-but-damn-near-committed relationship.

Her family had come from Brazil. She'd lived there for the first couple of years of her life, but she'd grown up and spent her entire adulthood in Orlando, Florida. She'd held a couple of administrative positions in that city's school system, for which she was—to put it mildly—the very definition of "over-qualified." For her, relocating to this remote little community, regardless that it was a positive career move, meant an adjustment on a scale he did not envy.

"So, are you weary of this dark corner of the world yet?"

The face she put on suggested that, simply by asking, he had lost his sanity. "Don't be ridiculous. God, I hate Florida. You know that. It's a madhouse. It's too hot. Everywhere you go, there's either too many damned people or nothing but alligators and armadillos. At least here, it's beautiful. And there are actual seasons."

"I'll grant you that. I do love these mountains. Still, it's kind of an odd place. Sometimes it feels like if the world ended, we wouldn't know about it for a very long time."

"You'd start suspecting as soon as your internet went out."

He laughed. "No doubt. You know, I've lived here most of my life, but I've spent time in a lot of places. And this area feels…old. I mean, outside of town, people don't live much differently than they did a hundred years ago. They hang onto outdated ideas. Even superstitions. And out past Barren Creek, there's nobody but Mennonites and moonshiners."

"Oh, yes. I hear there's lots of moonshine around campus."

"Most of the students can't legally buy alcohol, so it's the spirit of choice." He grew serious. "You know, it was just a few years ago that one of my students ended up dead. He made some deal with one of the locals to run moonshine, didn't follow through, and ended up with his head blown off, stuffed inside his car, and set on fire. That was a pretty big case around here."

She stared at him. "Are you trying to run me off?"

He cracked a wry smile. "Not at all. From what you've told me, this must be small-time stuff compared to your stomping grounds."

"Well, we never had any Mennonites, at least that I know about."

Joshua reappeared to deliver their drinks and take their orders. For Alana, blackened scallops, roasted vegetables, and a house salad; for Martin, Chicken Cordon Bleu with grilled asparagus and mashed potatoes.

"No beef for you tonight? I'm impressed," she said as Joshua took their menus and sauntered away.

"I've had a lot of dead cow this week. Felt like changing it up." He tested his martini. His "Martytini." The habanero added just the right burn. He nodded his approval. "They build a good drink here."

She took a few sips of her wine and made a little face. "I think I'll stick to California."

He looked toward her but found his gaze extending past her. Deep darkness seemed to have swallowed the space behind her. The distinct impression of movement gripped him, as if he were seated in a careening automobile.

Her voice dispelled the odd sensation. "What's the matter?"

He dragged his focus back to her. "Nothing, I guess. Just felt a little discombobulated for a second." He masked his discomfiture with a little smile. "It happens when you get old."

"You're not that damned old. Don't start with that stuff."

"Just wait. You may change your tune. Anyway, that's the second time it's happened this evening. Since I got back from walking with Phil and his dog."

"You get along okay with your brother, don't you?"

"Yeah, we get along. He's kind of scattered, one might say. Never really made up his mind what he wanted to do in life. But he gets by well enough. He's very creative."

"You said he's an artist?"

"That's what he calls himself."

"I'd like to see his work."

"I'm not sure you would."

"Oh, come on."

"I told you he's getting married, didn't I?"

She nodded. "Good for him." Her gaze lingered on him for a time, searching, appraising. "So, you've never been married. I'm sort of surprised."

"Is that good or not good?"

"You're the psychiatrist. You tell me."

He laughed. "You know I'm no psychiatrist. I teach psychology to a bunch of college students. There's a huge difference."

"But you know psychology things."

"Sure, I know things. Like I know you're not married because the guy you divorced was emotionally abusive. A real fucking asshole. That, by the way, is my professional, scientific opinion."

"A not-exactly-masterful change of subject. I'm not pressing you on anything. Except, well, I do wonder what, precisely, is wrong with you that you've never been married and that you were 'available' when we first went out."

"That," he said with the slightest of smiles, "will remain my secret."

#

He had very much enjoyed his dinner with Alana. He found her easy to talk to—and to listen to. Despite having a reasonably extensive vocabulary and a better-than-average grasp of the English language, Martin knew full well that he tended to come up short when expressing his feelings and ideas, especially to anyone with whom he sought to develop a more-than-casual relationship. In his younger days, he had been more than proficient with that degree of sharing—to the point of oversharing—but for him, this inevitably went every way but the right way. He knew full well that he habitually overanalyzed; ascribed motives to others, oftentimes far too creatively; and acted on impulse, regardless of the consequences. So, in emotional matters, he preferred to remain reticent. He also realized that, as he'd grown older, he had settled into a state of cynicism that others sometimes found unappealing.

Not exactly the best recipe for building a relationship based on trust, mutual respect, and positive reinforcement. His years of education might have helped him attain a commendable level of self-awareness, yet this went only so far in mitigating his near-lifelong case of low self-esteem, the result of having expressed himself, too openly and too frequently, to exactly the wrong individuals, peers and adults alike. He had learned to cope by masking or denying his innermost feelings.

Physician, fuck thyself.

Martin lived in a small—Alana called it "cozy"—A-frame chalet on Knollwood Court, a wooded cul-de-sac at the edge of the Aiken Mill town limits, close to the newer Beckham Highway. It was one of four similar chalets, two of which also housed college faculty members. Both of those professors were married and had children—thankfully, not loud, obnoxious youngsters—and seemed to be gone more than they were at home, so Martin rarely saw much of them, either in the neighborhood or on campus. It might have been nice, he thought, to have neighbors with similar enough interests and schedules to get together for drinks or something on occasion, but still, he could never claim to be lonely or bored. Between his regular class prep, the occasional research project, spending quality time with his brother, and now building what seemed to be a promising relationship with Alana, he was beginning to wish he might somehow find *more* downtime.

So, what about these strange mental diversions his brain had taken?

Darkness. A road. The sensation of movement.

The first one had occurred as soon as he set foot into his living room after his outing at Black Tooth Pond with Phil. Then at dinner.

Whatever it was, it felt new and disquieting. Like a waking dream.

No. It was much more vivid than that.

Was he overtired? He didn't think so. It was only a couple of months into the school year, and—for the first time in a long time—his life on the academic front felt very much in balance.

Didn't it?

Well, every effect had a cause.

Oh, fuck no. It couldn't be.

Was he falling in love?

No. No way.

After dinner, he and Alana had sat and talked for a long time, so even before heading home, his two Martytinis had worn off. In the way of almost every college prof he knew, his home bar was anything but a trivial fixture. A couple of years ago, via Amazon, he'd treated himself to an honest-to-God bar console at a brag-worthy price. The modular construct occupied a corner of the dining alcove that adjoined his living room, its shelves of bottles and racks of glasses lit by timer-activated LEDs. Since—at home, at least—drink was rarely out of sight and/or mind, he had forced himself to establish a healthy self-discipline to avoid overindulging.

Still, while he'd enjoyed the restaurant's martinis, right now, a single, tall shot of scotch—Glenlivet 12-year single malt—seemed a fine enough dessert idea. No classes or office hours tomorrow. So, why the hell not?

He filled his double-size shot glass, took only a small sip, and went out the front door to the small, covered front porch. The air felt chilly but pleasant. Above, the waning crescent moon gleamed silver-gold as it crept toward its zenith. Martin very much appreciated these wooded surroundings, the quiet seclusion of the cul-de-sac. To his right, warm lights glowed in the windows of the two nearest houses. The house to his left hid in darkness beneath the trees. Only one streetlight burned out here, a couple of hundred yards up at the corner of the main road. From here, it looked like a lonely little beacon in the night, partially obscured by the silhouettes of pine trees. Beyond his short, gravel-topped driveway, the paved road extended only a short distance before it vanished in the black.

The sensation of movement. A dark road twisting and curving before him. A rush of apprehension—as if his body and mind had slipped out of his control.

"What the—?"

Knollwood Court reappeared in his field of vision.

But he knew the road that kept flashing before his eyes. He'd been on it with Phil and Rufus earlier tonight, on their way to and from Black Tooth Pond.

Old Beckham Road.

But it was just a road. One he had traveled more times than he could count over so many years of his life. Why the hell did it keep flashing before his eyes this way?

He tossed back the last of his scotch and savored its oaky heat on the back of his tongue, the brief warmth that flooded his bloodstream.

And he was done for the evening.

THE HOUSE AT BLACK TOOTH POND

III. SUNDAY

Chapter 5

For many years now, Sheriff Parrott had been anything but a regular churchgoer. Yet, out of some age-old sense of loyalty to the little congregation of Amber Hill Christian Church, he maintained his membership, came close to tithing each month, and maybe four or five times a year darkened the doors of the little white building near the summit of Mount Signal. He hadn't planned for this morning to be one of those times, but in the hour between 0500 and 0600, his body sent several texts to his brain indicating that further sleep was out of the question. At last, he decided that darkening those doors for the sunrise service seemed as good a plan as any. He dragged himself out of bed, brewed a pot of Señor Valdez, and fixed himself a quick cheddar cheese omelet.

Several times, he checked for messages that might alter his sunrise service plan, and each time he found none. Then, after going through his regular morning ablutions, he made several earnest attempts to convince his body that additional sleep might, in fact, be a realistic possibility, only to be rudely rebuffed. So, since his body and the rest of the world had failed to impose an alternate plan on him, off to church it would be. Ordinarily, he took Sundays off or went into the office only for brief spells, but he could not count on today being in any way ordinary. After the service, hi-the-fuck-ho, off to work he'd go.

He owned two decent suits: a light-colored one for spring and summer and a dark-colored one for fall and winter. He put on the dark suit, deposited his uniform and equipment in the Explorer, and set out for Amber Hill. He lived in a modest house his grandparents had once owned on Whittle Road, a quiet residential street on Aiken Mill's east side, halfway between downtown and Mount Signal. From here, getting to work was an easy drive, but getting up the mountain, not so much. For that, he had to thread his way to Amber Hill Road by way of a series of snaking, crisscrossing streets designed and engineered by some corps of absolute morons back in the nineteenth century.

No streetlights lit this remote stretch of Amber Hill Road, so his headlights cut a bright swath through near-total darkness ahead. Above, though, a few pale gold streamers crawled across the still midnight-blue sky to silhouette a portion of Mount Signal's huge, irregular hump, which towered over the road. The road steepened and the curves sharpened as the asphalt ribbon curled higher up the slope.

About halfway up the mountain, a hidden graveyard lurked at the edge of the woods. The very graveyard where his father had been murdered. Parrott had visited the site only once, a long time ago, and it had felt awful yet unreal, as if that little home of the dead had sprung from some nightmare he'd suffered as a child. After that, he hated even passing the half-visible, rusted iron gate to its entrance. He was only a few hundred yards shy of reaching that gate when his phone dinged. On his dashboard screen, he saw that it was a text from Doc Crawford. The nice, smooth-toned lady in his phone read it over the Bluetooth-connected car speaker.

"Are you coming in this morning? Got more autopsy results, and I could use some of your coffee."

He slowed the Explorer, found a nearby driveway on the right, and turned in. He paused just long enough to text her an affirmative. Then he backed out and turned his vehicle to head back down the mountain. He hated to disappoint God on this very lovely, very early morning, but now he could hardly sit and listen to Pastor Jack Hain without fidgeting and constantly checking for messages. A long day of little to no rest awaited him, and he figured it better to dive right in than put it off.

#

At 0730, Doc Crawford dropped into his office with updated autopsy results on the Lydell remains. The moment she shambled inside, face wan and eyelids heavy with fatigue, Parrott knew her world might be an even unhappier place than his.

Six of the original ten cups remained in his personal coffeepot behind his desk. He reached back and grabbed a spare mug from the shelf above the machine. "Juan Valdez?"

"Absolutely."

He poured a mugful and handed it over to her. "Late night, I see."

"Three o'clock and all is hell." She ignored the steam that curled up from the mug and took a too-long, too-fast swallow. Her face, if nothing else, suddenly sprang to life.

"There's ice in the lunchroom," he said.

She offered him a pained half-smile but ignored his remark. "It's obviously too early to get anything back from Quantico. So, nothing new on our mystery goo. However, I did find an interesting item or two that might provide some pointers."

"Do tell."

She held up a file folder she'd brought with her. "I've emailed you this stuff, but I figured we might as well converse." She glanced at the first page. "I've calculated that Mr. Lydell died twelve hours to fifteen hours before you found his remains. Most likely Thursday night, possibly in the wee hours of Friday morning. Now, both from the body and the bed sheets from the Druid Hills apartment, I found a handful of fibers. Looks like they come from a rug—a very old, moldy rug. Definitely not from his apartment. Also from the nails, a lot of dust. The kind of stuff you'd find in a very old place. Microscopic bits of brick, wood, plaster, even traces of decomposed plants."

"Okay."

"I'd say he was digging around some old structure. Again, not the Druid Hills apartment."

"So, you're talking about more than casually picking up crap from the environment. Searching for something, maybe?"

"It's a possibility."

"Anything else?"

"Bloodwork didn't show anything particularly unusual. No drugs or other toxins. He was borderline diabetic and slightly anemic. As you can guess, the contents of the abdominal cavity were a mess. What was left of the liver and kidneys indicated he probably drank with regular abandon."

"A diabetic and a drinker. Not a great combination."

"You're on your way to general practitioner." She almost smiled. "What about you? Anything new?"

"We've still got some neighbors to question at Druid Hills. So far, we've got nothing useful." He frowned as a memory toddled back to him. He reached for his notepad on his desk and flipped a few pages back. "I did speak to Mr. Dicky Rudd again yesterday. Always a pleasure. He mentioned that two nights prior to our finding the body, all the dogs in the neighborhood cut loose for an excessive spell. He only brought it up because it went on for so long. But you know, we do have dogs in Aiken Mill, and there's lots of woods around that area. So, we've got plenty of raccoons, possums, groundhogs, deer, coyotes, Bigfoot, the Fugue Devil. You know, woodland critters that dogs bark at."

"What the hell is a Fugue Devil?"

He snorted. "You don't know the old story about the winged devil that comes down from Copper Peak every few years to collect souls?"

"I do not."

"I guess you wouldn't, being a transplanted Yankee and all. It's one of our not-so-well-known-but-colorful local legends. Apparently, a very long time ago, some mad musician who lived up on the mountaintop played music that called up this demon from hell. And since then, every few years, it comes out on a certain night and does dirty deeds."

"Colorful, yes."

His mind's eye turned inward. "Funny thing is, my dad used to tell a couple of hair-raising stories about this thing. As a kid, I was pretty well convinced he believed in it."

"I don't suppose this Fugue Devil would agree to an interview so you could determine its whereabouts on the night in question?"

He laughed, but at that moment, the light in his office grew dim. Both he and Doc Crawford turned their gazes out the window. Just above the trees, the morning sun still shone brightly. Not a visible cloud in the sky, yet the shadows in the room deepened as if a translucent black veil had unfurled over the window.

"Under the circumstances," she said, "I'm not sure I feel like laughing. I'm serious, Bryce, I've never been so baffled in my life. This feels like something out of a bad dream."

He swiveled in his chair to grab the coffeepot. "How about we finish this? I'd say we both could use a good wake-me-up."

She held out her mug, and he filled it before emptying the pot into his. The two of them drank coffee in silence for a few minutes.

The sheriff did admire—and like—Doc Crawford. One of these days, he might go so far as to invite her to dinner. Or something. It had been almost five years since Tia had decided she couldn't go on as Mrs. Lawman for the rest of her life. A hard time that had been—a bitter separation and contentious divorce. But they were both better off apart. Nowadays, no matter the state of the world and the bullshit he had to deal with every damn day, at least he could sleep at night. He wished Tia no ill, even hoped she might find happiness, though he doubted her feelings toward him were anywhere near as generous.

Doc Crawford drained her mug and sent him a reproving look. "Your coffee's broken, Bryce. Do better."

#

After lunchtime, once most church-goers would have arrived back home, Sheriff Parrott had sent deputies Dan Sykes and Suzan Carter knocking door-to-door on the apartment building's first floor—careful to avoid Dicky Rudd's place, since he and Parrott had already shared a couple of acrimonious heart-to-hearts, and he sure as hell didn't need any more of *that*. His primary interest was interviewing one Mrs. Betty Lester, who lived in the apartment next door to Lydell's. She had not been home on his pair of earlier attempts to talk to her.

This time, when Parrott knocked on the door, he heard a low rustling inside, a slow creaking, and then a scratchy voice calling, "Who is it?"

"Sheriff's Department, ma'am. I'd like to ask you a few questions."

"I didn't do it."

"I know you didn't, ma'am. Just looking for some information."

"I don't have any."

"You might. Would you open the door, please?"

A long silence followed, but finally, with a long, slow groan, the door opened inward. A short, stubby silhouette materialized in the dim space beyond. "What?"

Parrott stepped forward so she could see his badge. "I'm Sheriff Parrott, ma'am. May we talk for a moment?"

"Parrott? I didn't vote for you."

"That's perfectly all right."

"I'm not sure it is."

"If you'd rather me not come in, we can talk out here."

"It's chilly out there, isn't it?"

"Kind of."

The short, gray-haired, bleary-eyed woman, late seventies, maybe early eighties, sighed with the sound of an old furnace starting up, took a slow step backward, and motioned for him to enter. Once he stood inside the entryway, she said, "What did you say your name was?"

"I'm Sheriff Parrott, ma'am."

"I remember Sheriff Parrott. You're not him."

"I expect you're thinking of my father. He died some years ago."

Dull brown eyes looked him up and down. "And you want what?"

"Is your name Betty Lester, ma'am?"

A long, suspicious stare. "It is."

"I'd like to ask you a few questions."

"Why?"

"Mrs. Lester, are you aware that your next-door neighbor, Mr. Frank Lydell, died under unusual circumstances a couple of nights ago?"

She sent a sour look at the wall that adjoined Lydell's apartment. "When I got back this morning, Mr. Rudd told me something bad had happened. And there's tape on that door. Is that your yellow tape?"

Parrott nodded. "That is our tape. Now, you say you just got back. I gather you've been gone for some time?"

"I've been at my son's since…." She thought for a very long time. "I went there for Thanksgiving."

Lord help me.

"Ma'am, it's six weeks until Thanksgiving."

"We ate turkey, so it had to be Thanksgiving."

"Where does your son live, Mrs. Lester?"

"Danville."

"Do you know how many days you were gone?"

Her muddy brown eyes turned hot for about two seconds. "Since. Thanksgiving."

He glanced up at the popcorn ceiling, hoping he might discern some message of wisdom in its textured patterns. He did not. "All right, ma'am. Do you know if you were home on this past Thursday? Specifically on Thursday night?"

Mrs. Lester continued to peer at him like an exasperated kindergarten teacher confronting a willful child. "Was that Thanksgiving?"

"No, ma'am."

"Then where would I go?"

Patience, Parrott. Patience.

He spoke in a soft, slow voice. "Mrs. Lester, do you remember the last time you saw your neighbor, Mr. Lydell?"

"Oh, it's been a long time. I almost never see Mr. Lydell."

"Thank you, that's good to know. Now, if you would, please try to think back to this past Thursday. At any time, maybe after midnight, did you see or hear anything unusual? Either from your next-door neighbor's apartment or maybe even outside?"

The old eyes turned questioning again. "Unusual how?"

"Did Mr. Lydell have visitors? Someone come to his door, maybe?"

She shook her head.

"How about any loud sounds. Voices? Sounds of a struggle? Anything like that?"

She shook her head.

"What about—?"

The old woman held up a hand. "I think Mr. Lydell bought a bird."

"Excuse me?"

"I heard a bird over there. One of those noisy, whiny things. Like a goddamned siren going off."

Mrs. Lester's sudden animation caught Parrott by surprise. "You heard a bird over there?"

"I did the other night. It was very loud."

"Do you mean on Thursday night?"

"Was that Thanksgiving?"

"No, ma'am."

"Then it might have been on Thursday."

A random memory tickled his brain. "A whippoorwill?"

"I guess so."

He remembered hearing a whippoorwill cry at his office the other night, after he'd left Lydell's apartment. Odd coincidence, maybe, but the only thing that could mean was that whippoorwills were venturing closer to town than usual.

"Oh, and there was a smell." She crinkled her nose and scowled. "Oh, a terrible smell."

He stiffened. "Can you describe the smell, ma'am?"

She thought again. "It was like fried chuck."

"Chuck?"

Again, her expression accused him of idiocy. "You know, vomit. Urp. Barf. Like somebody chucked into a hot skillet."

That smell: a combination of vinegar, gasoline, puke, and something else he couldn't identify.

Oh, God.

Mrs. Lester studied his face for a moment and then a faint smile brightened her sullen features. "Yes, Mr. Parrott. That's exactly how bad it was!"

THE HOUSE AT BLACK TOOTH POND

IV. MONDAY

Chapter 6

There wouldn't be that many more after-work walks in the woods this season, for darkness was falling earlier each day, and temperatures too cold for comfort lay in the foreseeable future. Martin knew that his brother would continue to take Rufus for walks, but mainly around his neighborhood, and neither Phil nor the dog enjoyed that half as much as venturing out to the country. For Martin, these late-afternoon outings provided both much-needed exercise and a welcome mental quietude—at least when his brother was in good humor. Lately, Phil seemed touchier than usual, which Martin attributed to his upcoming wedding.

Today, he did seem more mellow. Martin appreciated this, for it had been one hell of a day down in the mines. In theory, teaching advanced college courses presented relatively few discipline challenges because students chose to be there, *paid* to be there, unlike in the lower grades, where most kids had no choice in the matter of attendance.

Horseshit.

47

"And that means you, Mr. Sigmon."

"Say what?" Phil called back, trying to keep his footing on the path as Rufus darted endlessly back and forth, the need to sniff every tree having assumed control of his muscles.

Martin hadn't even realized he'd muttered aloud. "Nothing. Just grumbling to myself."

"What have you got to grumble about?"

"Just some daily work shit."

"Always and ever, daily work is shit."

Well, not always, but he saw no need to belabor the point. And he didn't want to poke any of Phil's recently hypersensitized nerves. So, he replied, "Amen."

The sun still hovered above the treetops, so they had at least an hour before they'd need to make their way back to the truck. To their right, the pond's surface rippled as a light breeze swept down from the surrounding hills, carrying a hint of the chill that would soon settle in for the season. Then, as if with the wind, a memory of those odd images and sensations of traveling Old Beckham Road in darkness flickered back to him. This was not another onset, merely a recollection from the other day. No thought of those peculiar episodes had even entered his mind as he'd ridden here with Phil and Rufus on that very road from Aiken Mill.

Interesting. Maybe.

Or not.

As they rounded the edge of a small cove, they drew to an abrupt stop, for a huge fallen tree now blocked the path ahead. A tulip poplar, probably blown over by wind—and quite recently, as it hadn't been down the last time they'd walked here. To the left of the trail, at the base of the trunk, a huge rootball protruded like a knobby fist from the muddy earth. The roots themselves looked spindly and shriveled.

Definitely not a healthy tree.

To the right, the poplar's skeletal upper branches lay half-submerged in the pond. A few yards shy of the water's edge, the half-rotted trunk had broken in two, and the gap between the sections offered easy enough passage through the unexpected obstacle.

The heavy bole had smashed down a cluster of saplings along the left edge of the trail. Peering past their wreckage, Phil pointed into the deep woods. "Hey, looky. It's another path."

Sure enough, with the now-fallen trees no longer obscuring

the view, Martin saw a narrow, winding path that must have once branched from the main trail. From its terminus just beyond the flattened saplings, it snaked into the distant shadows.

"You've never been back that way?"

Phil shook his head. "Never even seen it before. Kinda weird, considering how many times I've been out here."

"Yeah, stoned."

He laughed. "C'mon, I haven't been stoned in years. Wanna check it out?"

Martin glanced at the deepening blue sky. "We can't go very far."

"It's just now five. We've got time."

Martin gave a little shrug. "Okay."

As soon as they set foot on the path, dark shadows fell over them, despite the trees being mostly bare. Rufus now seemed more subdued than usual, but he continued to lead as they threaded their way into the woods. It wasn't long before the trees gave way to thick, tangled scrub, most of it above head-high, into which the path continued. It curled through the dense growth for maybe a couple of hundred feet. As they came to its end, Martin made out a towering, dark shape ahead, and he realized it was a massive magnolia, at least fifty feet tall and probably thirty in diameter, its lowest branches and boughs spilling onto the ground like scaly green tendrils.

Phil actually gasped. "That is one big motherfucker."

As they proceeded a few steps farther, Martin saw beyond the tree an expansive, tangled network of vines and branches with unnaturally sharp, angular contours. He realized then that he was seeing the roof of an old structure, draped with mostly dead foliage. From its apex, through a gaping, splintered maw, a giant, ghostly white sycamore had clawed its way *out* of the house and into the sky.

"You really didn't know this was here?" Martin asked.

Mute with wonder, Phil shook his head. He loosened his grip on Rufus's leash, but now the dog showed no inclination to advance another step.

In rural Sylvan County, ancient, abandoned structures were anything but rare, and in their early post-college days, both Martin and Phil had taken delight in discovering and exploring such places. So, taking care to avoid getting snarled in the briers and creepers that surrounded the house, they made their way toward a shadowy rectangle at the structure's nearest end. From a few feet away, Martin confirmed it was a door, partially opened inward.

"You coming?" he called.

After a long silence, Phil said, "Yeah." Then came the slow but chaotic crunch of footsteps as he and Rufus battled their way through the tangled barrier. Near the door, a small but sturdy ironwood jutted up from the brambles, so he secured Rufus's leash around its lichen-spotted gray trunk. He patted the dog on the head and said, "Okay, buddy, you stand guard, and don't let any marauding groundhogs get us."

Rufus responded with a nonplussed glare.

Carefully mounting a single, weathered concrete stair, Martin placed a hand on the filthy, peeling door and pushed. With an angry scrape, it inched forward and froze. He gave it a more forceful shove and, with what sounded like a sigh of resignation, it swung fully open. A cool, musty odor seeped out of the gloom. He did not find this smell disagreeable, for it reminded him of the earthen cellar of their grandparents' house in Barren Creek, where he and Phil had played as kids.

Still, as he placed one cautious foot on the interior floorboard, he felt a twinge of revulsion, though not from anything tangible. He slid his leading foot forward, testing his weight, until he felt confident the floor was secure. In the half-light that seeped in through the door and a pair of grimy windows, he discovered that he stood in a small living room, furnished with a disgusting, moldy couch, a few rickety chairs, a wooden coffee table, and the smashed remains of an ancient television set. Trash of all sorts littered the floor—papers, old drink cans, food wrappers, picture frames—some empty, some containing photographs of men, women, and children, their features too smudged and stained to make out—and even some nasty, ragged old clothes. Black mold and strips of disintegrating wallpaper adorned the sagging walls.

"What a treasure trove!" Phil's exclamation was anything but ironic.

Martin took a few slow steps toward the center of the room. At the farthest end, an open door revealed an array of broken branches and the half-visible trunk of the sycamore that had grown up through the roof. To his right, in front of a small brick fireplace, he saw two yawning holes in the floor, their edges jagged and splintered. And in the far left corner, a warped staircase with a half-collapsed banister ascended into impenetrable darkness.

He pointed to it. "Your penthouse is waiting. Gonna go up and take a look?"

Phil scoffed. "I'm not entirely stupid." But after a long, thoughtful scan of the stairs, he added, "Well, maybe."

Martin noticed on the coffee table a massive pile of dusty, yellowed envelopes. These turned out to be mail—some unopened—addressed, in various combinations, to Clarence, Harriet, Franklin, Maxine, and/or Theophilus Caviness. The delivery address was an Aiken Mill post office box rather than a house number. He thumbed through the lot of them and determined that the postmarks ranged from December 1952 to December 1975.

"The House of Caviness," he said, barely above a whisper.

"What?"

"This place. Must have belonged to a family named Caviness." He held up a stack of envelopes. "Letters, bills, advertisements. Damned peculiar."

It didn't take long to ascertain, by way of countless late payment and collection notices, that the Caviness family had accumulated a substantial amount of debt. None of the personal letters bore return addresses, though all their postmarks read Providence, Rhode Island. At random, he picked one and carefully withdrew a few sheets of folded, brittle paper. One leaf was a newspaper clipping, dated November 17, 1952. A bold headline read, "U.S. Explodes First Hydrogen Bomb in the Pacific," and the article beneath it detailed how the sky above the ocean blazed with the light of five hundred suns. Accompanying the clipping, a note scrawled in blood-colored ink read, "*HELL IS COMING. HELL IS HERE!*" The note was unsigned.

Every anonymous envelope he inspected contained one or more strikingly negative news story—from the assassinations of John F. Kennedy, Robert F. Kennedy, and Martin Luther King, to the 1964 Good Friday Earthquake in Alaska, to the 1968 My Lai Massacre in Vietnam. Inevitably, a terse, unsigned note accompanied each clipping, proclaiming that the torments of hell would soon plague the people of the nation, if not the world.

Phil studied these bleak epistles from over Martin's shoulder. "Looks like they all came from the same sender," he said. He pointed to a stack of unopened envelopes. "I bet the family got fed up with their overwrought compadre and just stopped reading. But why save all this mail—and pile it up here?"

"God knows," Martin said. "Maybe I'll take the letters with me. They make for a thorough and colorful catalog of very bad news."

"Complete with hysterical personal commentary."

He realized then how difficult seeing the pages had become. Good lord, it was already getting dark outside.

"This may call for a future visit," Phil said. "Who knows what else we might find?"

Ordinarily, Martin might have found the prospect of further exploration exciting, but that earlier sense of foreboding now resurfaced—probably exacerbated by these testaments to everything wrong with the world in the mid-twentieth century. He decided that, whatever their possible historical significance, he didn't care to keep any of these letters. Somehow, they felt *poisonous*.

"I wonder what became of the family," he said. "Looks like they just went away and left everything they owned here."

"Who knows? If they had no money, they might have ended up on the street or something."

"Yeah." He looked around the place a final time. "Can't help but think it was a sad story."

Beyond the open door, opaque shadows draped the brambles and trees. Before they could set foot back outside, a distinctive, warbling trill rang from somewhere nearby. Phil paused and listened.

"Ah, the whippoorwill," he said. Then, as he had once before, he drew a long breath, pursed his lips, and unleashed his near-perfect whippoorwill call. This time, as if in response, the bird outside sang its mournful song.

"Fun, eh?"

"I'm glad you're enjoying yourself."

With a self-indulgent grin, Phil stepped through the door and set about untying Rufus's leash. As Martin made to exit, a low rustling rose behind him.

Then, from *inside* the house, a sharp, shrill whippoorwill cry shattered the silence.

Stung by shock, he spun to face the gloom.

The rustling came again, unmistakably from one of the holes in the floor. In that deep darkness, he glimpsed—or thought he did—a smoky gray smudge, which slid in and out of view like a fast-moving snake. Another trill issued from the opening. This one soft. Almost mocking.

Jolted by surprise—and icy fear—Martin leaped through the door into daylight's last remnants.

Phil's eyes widened at his abrupt appearance. He must have thought Martin had stumbled because he threw out a steadying hand.

"Careful there! You all right?"

Relief swept over Martin like a balmy, cleansing breeze, and he waved Phil away.

Immediately, he felt stupid. Nerves had gotten the better of him. Some critter had taken up residence inside the crumbling house. Another whippoorwill, outside but nearby, had called out. Their cries could be loud, even disconcerting.

As they once had been to a certain child.

"It's later than I realized," Phil said. "We'd better get on."

They headed back toward the pond at a brisk pace. With every step, Martin felt more and more confident that, inside that house, he'd suffered a simple scrambling of impressions. The barrage of negativity in all those letters and the day's stress had supercharged his anxiety. This conclusion satisfied him.

Until he chanced a look back.

It wasn't what he saw or even heard, but what he *felt*. From the huge magnolia, which towered above the surrounding trees like a massive, black blob, a low whippoorwill song began to pipe with the same air of mocking purpose he had perceived inside the house.

No, it wasn't a real whippoorwill song. It was mimicry, like his brother's.

Exactly like his brother's.

Rufus picked up his pace, clearly anxious to leave, half-dragging his hapless owner behind him.

Phil had surely heard the same thing as he, Martin thought. He'd heard it, but he hadn't *felt* it.

Not yet.

Chapter 7

Martin hadn't been home five minutes before his dominant, rational mind reassembled his confused impressions from that disturbing experience into a sensible whole.

Anxiety. Stress. Bad lighting.

He had never been one to let his imagination run roughshod over him. Well, maybe in those years before the healthy development of folds and wrinkles in his teeny-tiny brain. Not that he wasn't still imaginative. Sometimes, usually late at night, his mind went on complex plotting binges and constructed bizarre, surreal scenarios, usually related to work stresses or other uncertainties, usually with unhappy or enigmatic endings. He had long ago made peace with the fact that, despite having never suffered severe physical or emotional trauma, he harbored a deeply pessimistic nature. Ever since early childhood.

This, perhaps more than any other factor, had led him down his chosen career path. To explore motivations, rationalizations, the evolution of human emotion and intellect over a lifetime.

There were always more questions than answers.

It was also the reason that, despite his parents having enjoyed a loving, mutually fulfilling marriage for going on fifty years, he had little interest in that fragile institution. In his experience, and to some extent by way of empirical evidence, Mom and Dad were the exception, not the rule.

"U.S. Explodes First Hydrogen Bomb in the Pacific."

"HELL IS HERE!"

The pervasive negativity of the news clippings and anonymous notes he'd discovered in that massive pile of mail in the House of Caviness still stuck with him. The impression that they were somehow *poison* had struck him with inexplicable intensity. And it lingered.

That movement under the floor. That gray *streak* in the darkness.

Just a critter. What else could it have been but a critter?

He sighed to himself. "No, I'm not imaginative. Not at all."

The atmosphere in that house, though. The deep shadows, the decay, the sense that actual insanity might have once resided there.

The whippoorwill.

Christ, it was a fucking whippoorwill. Nothing more.

Yeah, all these things *were* hard to stop thinking about.

Anxiety. Stress. Bad lighting.

From his honest-to-God bar, he took the bottle of Glenlivet and filled his tall shot glass. Monday night. Typically, not a drinking night. But he wasn't going to *drink*.

He was hungry.

Bachelor he might be, but Martin had never settled for microwave dinners, fast food, or going hungry. He enjoyed preparing decent meals. Hardly a gourmet, but he considered himself a creditable cook. Wednesday evening, Alana would be coming over, and he planned to serve his own variation of *Bolognese e Tagliatelle*—unlike the actual Italian, very spicy—which they both enjoyed. He frequently prepared dinners when he and Phil got together in the evenings (though *that* would soon change, at least as it had been for many years). And he served a formidable array of *tapas* once or twice a year, when he and a handful of other faculty members gathered for a semi-regular social event they called The Beckham College Super Supper Flub. (The "Flub" would have been a "Club" had Dr. Parthemos, the Political Science department head, not poisoned the group with bad shrimp on his debut as host.)

Martin had lamb chops, mint, and a few fresh vegetables on hand. Whip up some Tzatziki and dinner would be set.

A long mirror ran along the back of the upper bar shelf, and as he took a sip of his drink, his eye went to his reflection, half-obscured and distorted by the array of tumblers and wine glasses on the shelf. At once, his vision blurred, the room lighting dimmed, and his reflection in the glass became a silhouette. A brief sensation of movement.

It lasted only a moment. Then his vision, his perceptions, returned to normal.

But he had felt *it* coming on—the beginning of one of his "episodes," in which his vision somehow phased from his actual surroundings to a dark, narrow road twisting and turning before him, the sensation of movement as real as if he were behind the wheel, speeding through the darkness.

This one hadn't fully unfolded.

He threw back the tall shot of scotch and poured another. Wandered away from the bar, considered turning on the television so the house wouldn't be dead silent.

Something isn't right. Something inside my brain.

Surely, not a stroke or neurological damage. Clearly, not a migraine. He took no drugs, certainly no hallucinogens. He doubted he'd consumed enough alcohol in his entire life to trigger such peculiar and vivid sensory impressions.

Still, this episode hadn't progressed beyond its nebulous first stage.

He downed the scotch. Poured another.

He'd never considered—not seriously—the prospect of developing any kind of debilitating condition, something chronic, untreatable. He'd *learned* about countless illnesses, disorders, aberrations, so many things that could and did go wrong inside the human body. Somehow, despite his innate pessimism, he'd never taken to heart the possibility that *he* might succumb to any of them.

How very unrealistic—and uncharacteristic—of him.

His grandmother on his mother's side had suffered from early-onset dementia. And even his mom, now only in her late sixties, had memory issues that, in his considered opinion, went beyond age-related forgetfulness. Dementia came in many forms; memory loss was only one manifestation. Hallucinations and behavioral abnormalities oftentimes accompanied its onset. What if *he*—?

"And now, the overreacting sets in."

Third scotch, down and away. That was enough. Really enough.

He felt it in his system, warming, spreading, mellowing, smoothing the rough edges. It felt good. It would be a few more minutes before the full effect of the drink set in, and that would last a considerable time. This wasn't enough to intoxicate him. He found it simply comfortable.

He could function without fear of blowing over the limit. He could drive safely.

Why even think about driving?

The idea might be stupid, bordering on not sane, but it had gripped him. Nothing about driving frightened him. But whatever was causing him to experience the images and sensations of driving on the dark road *did* frighten him. He knew full well this impulse was the alcohol breaking down his inhibitions, spurring him to indulge in ill-considered whims. At the same time, he discerned some perverse logic in the idea.

The idea of challenging these damned hallucinations.

Drive the road for real.

He knew Old Beckham Road well enough. And he'd been out there with Phil only a short while earlier.

But....

What if he wasn't challenging anything? This evening's occurrence never reached the point of visualization. Barely of sensation. What if he wasn't confronting this aberration but *succumbing* to it?

Attempting to moderate an internal debate always ended in frustration, so there was nothing for it but to do or don't do whatever he intended.

He had hung his car keys on the dragon-shaped iron hook beside the front door. He plucked them from their place, grabbed his jacket from the coatrack, and stepped out the door. The night air had turned chilly, and the stars appeared clear and bright. Apart from the streetlight on the corner, no lights glowed on Knollwood Court. All his neighbors must be out and about.

He started for his vehicle, an older-model Nissan Rogue, parked under the carport beside the house. Then he paused. If he went through with this, he'd end up having a very late dinner. He scoffed to himself.

So be it.

He slid into the driver's seat, buckled up, and started the engine.

Once he'd backed out of the driveway and aimed the small SUV toward the main road, a pair of headlights rounded the corner ahead. As he drew close enough to enough to identify the car—a Toyota Corolla—he confirmed it was Dr. Bremer, math prof, probably on his way home from working late. They both waved as their vehicles passed, but Martin felt an inexplicable twinge of discomfort, almost a pang of guilt, as if someone else witnessing him leaving—and identifying him—posed some kind of danger.

Ridiculous. Every bit of this.

But he wasn't going back.

He turned right onto Starling Drive, the main road in and out of his neighborhood. It curled through a succession of large, brightly lit homes, all far more expensive than his. Thirty-some years ago, before the furniture and textile industries fled the country in search of fewer regulations and dirt-cheap labor, Aiken Mill boasted more millionaires per square mile than any other comparable-sized community in the United States. His parents had been a part of that boom, although they'd never achieved millionaire status. This little hub of wealth was one of the scattered remnants of the town's old money. A fair amount of it still floated around, and thank God for that, or Aiken Mill would be a ghost town.

Martin had always expected his mom and dad to reside in Aiken Mill for the rest of their lives. However, a few years ago they'd moved to Virginia Beach because...well...the beach. They *really* liked the beach.

At the intersection of Starling and Old Beckham Road, he turned right, toward the little town of Beckham and the college. He didn't plan to go that far. Just until it felt *right*. Inasmuch as that might be possible.

To get to work, he usually took Virginia Route 21, the newer Beckham Highway, mainly because it was so much faster. Once in a while, if he felt no rush, he headed home via the old road for its more appealing scenery. Right now, it was just dark. His headlights gleamed on the ribbon of unlined asphalt, which curved first left and then right. For several miles yet, Old Beckham Road paralleled the Camden River, which hid in the darkness several hundred feet to his left. Eventually, the road would veer away from the river, ascend sharply, and begin to wind around the lower slope of Copper Peak.

To either side, the lights from scattered houses glowed in the darkness, though these soon gave way to long stretches of mostly unbroken woodland, pitch black beyond the bright path cut by his headlights. Then his tires clattered onto the aged, increasingly rickety suspension bridge over High Rock Creek, its skeletal framework scrawled with mostly illegible graffiti. Past the bridge, a silvery snake of guardrail here and there, the distant glow of a few farmhouse windows, and a handful of road signs that shimmered in his headlight beams before sliding past him.

Everything seemed—felt—normal enough. Still, he rarely drove this road at night, and he couldn't deny a certain sense of isolation that wasn't altogether comfortable. Cell service dropped out here and there, though for the most part, coverage between Aiken Mill and Beckham remained mostly reliable. Still, this certainly wasn't a place to have car trouble.

And these old woods. Despite having outgrown the caprices of his youthful imagination, he retained a sense of dark wonder about the miles and miles of old forest that occupied a huge percentage of the county. Many old stories still existed about frightening, even horrific goings-on out here, attributed to everything from mad, murderous moonshiners, to unearthly creatures from shadowy netherworlds, to ghostly apparitions that haunted every little graveyard that hid in countless forest glades.

Five miles out of town, the dark road assumed a new character, if only in his mind. He'd reached the series of tight curves that had filled his vision and sent him swaying during those peculiar sensory episodes. He slowed down to negotiate the curves, feeling the same tug of physical forces that his body had experienced even while motionless, miles away from here.

He'd chosen this course, to experience the actual drive, as if doing so could somehow *cure* his strange, illusory sensations. An odd choice, but he understood it. It was an impetuous flight of fancy, and he had indulged it.

"One scotch over the line," he muttered.

A mile ahead, Black Tooth Pond lurked in the woods. As did that crumbling old structure—the House of Caviness. A house of secrets, he thought, remembering the ancient pile of mailed news clippings and anonymous letters declaring that hell was on its way. Real poison-pen letters, he thought. They *had* felt like poison to him.

And he remembered the sound of whippoorwills. Particularly, that singular shrill, damn-near-deafening cry he had first perceived as mimicry. Like an imitation of his brother's voice imitating a whippoorwill.

In the comfort of his home, behind the bastion of his intellect, he'd dismissed his initial disquiet. Out here, those rationalizations felt less assured.

Was this all part and parcel of his hallucinations? Maybe the same alcohol-induced flight of fancy that had compelled him to drive out here?

He slowed down as he approached the all-but-hidden turn-in that led to the pond. He scanned the left edge of the road, seeking that break in the trees that would reveal a narrow dirt driveway. There. A hundred feet ahead. The shadows deepened there. The entrance.

Slowing the vehicle to a creep, he turned in and drove cautiously forward, knowing there were old ruts deep enough to bottom out if he went too fast. He hadn't planned on coming in here. But here he was. He supposed that, simply by driving this road, he had confronted whatever he'd intended to confront.

But he had proven nothing. Conquered nothing.

Could he really have hoped to?

A waste, he thought with a twinge of bitterness.

The trees to either side of the narrow driveway ended, and ahead, beyond the reach of his headlights, he saw only an expanse of unbroken blackness. The pond.

Before him, in the relatively soft earth, more than one set of tire tracks extended toward the water's edge. He hadn't really noticed any when he'd ridden in with Phil, but they'd probably been talking, their attention on other things. At least one set of tracks no doubt belonged to Phil's truck, though there was a narrower set that Phil's had partially effaced. His brother and he clearly weren't the only people who came out here.

On a whim, he switched off the engine and opened his door, though he left the headlights on. Then he slid out of his seat and stood beside the open door, listening to the near silence of a very dark night. A few tree frogs peeped from around the pond, and a couple of soft splashes issued from the distance. He'd never seen any ducks or geese out here. Probably just fish or turtles plopping in the water.

He reached inside and turned off the headlights. Total darkness fell over him, and for a few seconds, he went as blind as if he'd fallen into a deep cavern. Then, as his eyes adjusted, he made out the star-speckled sky, and the silhouettes of a few nearby trees against the blue-black awning above. There was no moon.

Now, he felt no apprehension or discomfort. Just a mild curiosity about what the fuck he was doing here.

"Don't ask me," he said with a sigh. "I'm just the driver."

He stood and listened for a full minute.

He expected to hear the whippoorwill call.

But none came.

He went around the front of the vehicle, opened the passenger door, and, from his glove compartment, withdrew his heavy-duty 1,500-lumen LED flashlight. He flicked it on and fired its narrow white beam into the darkness. To the right and ahead, the glossy surface of the water rippled lazily within the brilliant circle. As he swung the flashlight farther right, its beam crept into the dark crevices between the tall pines, poplars, and sycamores to reveal only deep, empty woods.

He shifted the light to the left and saw the start of the path that curled around the edge of the pond. He and Phil had walked it only, what, a couple of hours earlier?

There was nothing in the darkness that wasn't there during daylight. So people liked to reassure themselves.

Not necessarily so. Plenty of nocturnal critters lived out here, though mostly harmless. Mostly. Bears aplenty roamed the woods of Sylvan County, though in his life he had seen only one, almost a decade ago, and that from the safety of his car. Copperheads might still be out and about, though they tended to flee rather than bite you—and they'd be sluggish now with temperatures in the low 50s. Coyotes, definitely, but they too tended to shy away from humans. Deer, foxes, opossums, beavers, otters, bats, these would be the most likely critter encounters anyone might have in the woods.

So, not *too* much to be concerned about.

Whippoorwills?

Just little noisy birds that loved to holler in remote woods. Nothing more.

He needed to walk. And now he knew what he needed to go after. He went back around his vehicle, opened the rear door, and grabbed one of the canvas grocery bags he kept behind the backseat.

Did he *really* mean to do this?

He closed up the SUV and locked the doors. Aimed his flashlight at the path ahead. And with his grocery bag folded and tucked under his arm, set out walking.

The woods were quiet, if not silent. A few rustles amid the trees, a whisper of breeze stirring the branches. He had camped out in the woods many times in his life, particularly as a Boy Scout in his early teens. Day or night, he'd never felt uncomfortable in the woods. But he had never been on an errand such as this before. And he did see this now as an *errand*.

He traipsed on until he came to the huge, fallen poplar that marked the start of the path to the House of Caviness. This, he thought, represented his point of no return. Go back now, fix dinner, enjoy the warmth and comfort of his home. Or move forward and indulge in this mad—yes, truly *mad*—whim.

He stepped through the break in the fallen trunk and continued onto the side path. The night remained quiet and still. No whippoorwill cries. No bird calls at all. After a few hundred feet, the trees thinned and his flashlight beam fell on the dense clusters of scrub that preceded the site of the old house. Now as he walked, he heard—or felt—a humming vibration at the back of his skull. His pulse increased slightly. It was neither excitement nor apprehension. More a vague, indefinable anticipation.

His beam fell on the base of the magnolia that loomed like a crouching giant in front of the house. He angled the flashlight toward the top of tree, half-expecting to see a pair of huge eyes open to regard him with cold disdain. No such visage appeared, but the dark, towering bulk struck him as strangely sentient, and the slight swaying of its tendril-like branches and leaves seemed somehow deliberate.

A few steps farther, and there it was: the angular silhouette of the overgrown structure, the clawlike branches of the tree that reached for the sky through the jagged hole in the roof. The flashlight beam striking the windows painted images of dull, murky ghosts on the grimy glass. The peeling door hung slightly ajar, just as he and his brother had left it.

The tricky part would be fighting his way through thirty feet of briers and brambles. But as he moved forward, he found that he and Phil had earlier trampled enough of the growth to cut a relatively easy path. He avoided getting as entangled as on his first time through and so reached the door with only a few tiny scratches here and there. Before pushing his way inside, he shined his light through the opening, not *quite* taking it on faith that nothing and no one lurked in the pure darkness on the other side.

This *was* mad.

He pushed hard against the door. It groaned and scuffed its way open.

And now he stood on the threshold of the House of Caviness. A place of secrets, a storage facility for what someone must have meant to be a chronicle of the rise of hell on Earth. It was this chronicle, which he'd initially perceived as poison, that drew him to return.

"I am fucking mad."

He remembered having seen holes in the floor, but far enough inside that they didn't concern him as he stepped across the threshold. Still, he chose his footing with care, as creating a brand-new hole and ending up lying injured in some dark, filthy cellar hardly fit with his plans. Leading with the flashlight, he shuffled toward the coffee table in the center of the room. The mountain of yellowed papers and envelopes waited there for him, as innocuous in appearance as its contents were dismal.

Dismal and fascinating.

Insanely fascinating.

He set his flashlight on the coffee table with its beam highlighting the pile. Then he unfolded his grocery bag, spread its mouth wide, and scooped the pile of papers into it. There must have been fifty or more individual envelopes and loose sheets, and once full, the bag felt heavy and awkward.

Now, having acquired the material for which he had gone to such ludicrous lengths, the urge to leave hit him with sudden force. As he grabbed his flashlight and started for the door, the softest, subtlest whisper of movement from somewhere in the darkness above tickled his eardrums.

He hesitated. Then swung the light beam toward the staircase that ascended into shadow at the far end of the living room. From this angle, the light didn't reach all the way to the top.

Earlier, he'd seen a moving gray *streak* in one of the holes in the floor. An animal, he'd concluded, most likely an opossum. It must have made its way upstairs to explore whatever places opossums liked to explore. Before, the movement in the house had unnerved him. This time, he decided to ignore it, take his bag and himself out of there, and return to his car. His empty stomach was starting to complain, and the prospect of finally having dinner spurred him to move.

He'd barely taken a step when a strong, vile smell assaulted his olfactories. Sour, putrid. Like something dead, maybe, yet *worse*.

The whispery sound from above came again, this time louder and more distinct.

And then again.

"Come. Upstairs."

No, no, no. He could *not* have heard *that*!

Without looking back, and heedless of the risk, he bolted across the floor and out through the still-open door. He didn't bother to close it behind him but lit into the brambles with no thought of retracing his steps, only putting distance between himself and that god-awful house.

There could *not* have been anyone at the top of the stairs. Or anywhere in that old house.

Another hallucination, this one auditory?

Small comfort.

Call it none.

He maintained his footing amid the yielding vines and creepers, but now legions of briers reached for him, tore into his skin and clothing. Somehow, he kept a firm grip on both his flashlight and the bag full of mail. At last, his feet found the flattened, leaf-covered surface of the old path.

No, that "voice" hadn't been a hallucination. Just some random sound from an animal moving about on the upstairs floor, mistranslated by his brain. And that horrible smell? Surely something dead and rotting. He'd simply heard some scavenger feeding on the corpse, and its movement had sent the odor wafting downstairs. As on his earlier outing, he'd attributed deliberation—malevolence, even—to perfectly natural sights, sounds, and smells. Whatever was going on in his brain had not only scrambled his sensory impressions but his analytical abilities. And awakened the dormant remnants of his morbid, youthful imagination.

He didn't run but kept a swift pace back toward his car. He might know better than to take his perceptions at face value, but the farther from the old house he went, the less shaken he felt. Within five minutes' time, the beam of his flashlight reflected on the metal surfaces of the Rogue, and when he slid into the seat behind the wheel, his confidence in simple *misperception* felt firm.

It was the root cause of that misperception that caused him some alarm.

Because the root cause was almost certainly the source of his hallucinations—and his inexplicable new obsession with the House of Caviness.

His venture out here had been specifically to grab those old letters and papers. Which he understood…well…not at all. He had no emotional or intellectual connection to that material other than a passing curiosity. And the sense that it was somehow poisonous.

Venomous.

He started the engine, reversed, and swung the Rogue around until it faced back the way he'd come. As he started forward, he refused to speed over the ruts and bumps. Nothing was after him, and he wasn't about to risk damaging his vehicle.

As soon as he turned onto the main road in the direction of Aiken Mill, headlights appeared not far behind him. He hit the gas so the approaching car wouldn't end up right on his tail. Once he hit cruising speed, the driver behind him maintained a respectful distance, which he appreciated. In a way, he rather welcomed another presence out here on this dark, lonely highway.

He hadn't gone half a mile when he saw headlights approaching. Within seconds, the oncoming car roared past him at high speed, and immediately afterward, blue flashing lights flared into existence behind him. He realized the vehicle on his tail belonged to an officer of the law, probably a sheriff's deputy. The cruiser slowed, made a quick reversal, and sped off in pursuit of whoever was in such a hurry.

Fortunately, he hadn't poured on the speed after his little fright. He didn't need a ticket to bump his humiliation up to the next level.

Another mile closer to home, and a new pair of headlights appeared ahead. He hadn't seen a soul on the road on his drive out to Black Tooth Pond. It seemed Old Beckham Road had suddenly become a busy place.

This car wasn't going fast. As it drew nearer, Martin saw that the oncoming vehicle was a large pickup truck. And as it went past, he felt a twinge of surprise.

No, not surprise. Something bordering on shock.

He hadn't been able to see the driver, but he'd gotten more than a quick glimpse of the truck as it rumbled past. It was an army green

Toyota Tacoma with a distinctive dent in the front left fender.

His brother's truck.

Phil's. It *had* to have been Phil's.

What the hell would Phil be doing out here *now*?

Oh, he knew the answer to that!

Chapter 8

With the Lydell case having taken front and center over the weekend, Sheriff Parrott's more traditional—i.e. administrative—tasks had fallen behind, and, even if the world collapsed into total chaos, hewing away at the never-dwindling pile of bureaucratic bullshit always assumed top priority. On this day, after signing off on countless arrest reports, approving budget updates, and writing performance evaluations, he spent several hours waiting in the wings to occasionally present evidence or offer statements to Judge Marvin Hundley's court. Going back years before he'd become sheriff, he and the judge had enjoyed—as in not at all—a tumultuous, sometimes contentious relationship, and he felt certain that Judge Marvin did everything in his power to waste as much of Parrott's time as possible.

It was just shy of his quitting time when the call came for yet another domestic disturbance at the Draper residence out on Old Beckham Road. Adonis "Donny" Draper and his wife, Florence—or "Pootie," as she was known to her friends—had achieved infamy for engaging in relatively benign arguments over trivial subjects and trading increasingly sharp barbs until their disagreements turned physical. Rather than send Sykes or one of the other available deputies out there—again—Parrott figured he'd go himself, defuse the situation as best he could, and then head home.

Pootie had earned her nickname as a youngster for having achieved a remarkable mastery over the natural act of passing of gas. On this occasion, she had apparently eaten a whole pumpkin pie intended for Donny's diabetic sister, Ida, who'd just come home from the hospital after a toe amputation. Pootie claimed she'd eaten the pie to spare Ida a catastrophic rise in blood sugar (and possibly another amputation), and if Donny had one functioning brain cell in that rotten egg he called a brain, he'd have known that pie for a diabetic was the worst possible get-well gift. Pootie, who weighed in at over 300 pounds and was herself pre-diabetic, had taken it upon herself to dispose of the pie.

Donny had reacted poorly to the waste of such a fine gift.

This evening, Donny's cousin, Earl Shively, had popped by the house to find Pootie in a near-murderous rage, squatting atop her smaller, half-suffocated husband, tormenting him by way of graphically demonstrating how she'd earned her epithet. Unable to budge his cousin's enraged and strategically positioned wife, Earl had phoned the sheriff.

Parrott arrived in time to save Donny from his ultimate fate and, after rebuking both parties for their inappropriate behavior, gently explained that, indeed, pie was a poor choice of gift, but there might have been a better way to dispose of it, especially given Mrs. Draper's own potential health risks. She had been a bit slow to acknowledge her disproportionate response to Donny's invective, but at the end of it all, the couple had kissed and made up.

Until next week.

From there, Parrott started back toward Aiken Mill and home in his Ford Explorer. About a mile from the Draper's place, a long stretch of unbroken woods lined the road, and as he drove through it, to his surprise, he noticed the headlights of a vehicle turning onto the road, seemingly straight out of the dark trees not far ahead. He drew up close enough to determine that it was an older-model Nissan Rogue, though not enough to make out the plate number. As he passed the point where the vehicle had appeared, he realized there was a half-hidden turn-in amid the trees. There were plenty such openings into the woods here and there, the last traces of long-disused logging roads and driveways. These generally passed beneath his notice. Although kids sometimes drove back into the woods to smoke pot and such, with the changes in the laws these days, bothering with recreational users had become anything but high priority.

Still, he had the most hellish unsolved case on his hands, and very, very few clues to go on. Might be prudent to run the plates. The SUV bore a single occupant, and something told him it probably wasn't just a college kid getting high.

The department didn't have the funds for higher end dashcams that could scan plates from a distance, so he still had to rely on his eyeballs for such work. He had just begun to close on the vehicle when a pair of oncoming headlights appeared, these at very high speed. Within seconds, one of the locale's ubiquitous redneck-mobiles zoomed past him, its requisite lack of muffler boosting the engine noise to a painful and illegal level. He jerked his attention away from the SUV, made a quick three-point reversal, and hit the gas to pursue the offender.

Thankfully, as soon as he gained on the vehicle, his overheads flashing, the reckless driver slowed the car—a red Dodge Charger—and drifted to a stop on the narrow gravel shoulder. If he were to tally the car model of every soul in the county he had ticketed in the past decade, he'd bet his pension that the Charger would top the list by an impressive margin. He parked behind the Dodge, quickly reviewed his mental defensive checklist, and exited the Explorer. As he approached the car, he glanced at the license plate to see whether the number rang any alarm bells. It did not.

The driver had already rolled down the window. As Parrott stepped up just behind it, out of long habit, he placed a firm hand on the car's roof to leave his fingerprints on the surface. *Just in case.* When he leaned down and saw the driver, a slap of surprise nearly knocked him backward. He recognized the bespectacled, frizzy-gray-haired driver as Ms. Jenny Stultz, the longtime principal of Bradford Hill Elementary School. Before he could say a word, she was babbling faster than she had been driving.

"I'm so sorry, Sheriff, I know I was going too fast, but my grandson, Charles, he's been down very sick, and I had to run to CVS to pick up a prescription for him, and I need to get this back to him right away. You understand, don't you, Sheriff?" She held up a paper sack bearing the CVS logo and shook it at him.

"This isn't your car, is it, Ms. Jenny?"

"What? No, it's my son's. Mine is in the shop because it needs a new engine, which is why I'm staying at Jeff and Connie's place for a couple of days. Connie is out for the evening, so I went to pick up the prescription so Jeff could stay with Charles."

On anyone else, Parrott would have called bullshit. "It's not far to Jeff and Connie's place, is it?"

"Only about a mile."

"Tell you what. I'm gonna follow you back and make sure you get there safely. You don't fix one bad situation by creating another, you understand?"

"I do."

"I'll stop in and make sure everything's okay with your grandson. Then that'll be it. And I won't write you a ticket."

"I don't care about that. I just want to make sure Gerry is all right."

"You said it was Charles, Ms. Jenny."

"What?"

"You said it was your grandson, Charles, who was down sick."

"Did I say Gerry? No, no, it's Charles. You know, the two of them are so close in age and all, and I admit I'm just flustered. I haven't been pulled over since I taught kindergarten, and that was before you were even out of high school." She paused to take a much-needed breath. Then she gave him a bleak stare. "All right, Sheriff, I lied. The prescription is for me. Go ahead. Write me a ticket."

"Enjoying your son's Charger, are you, ma'am?"

"I guess so."

"You sit tight, and I'll be back in a minute."

She offered him a weak smile. "Sheriff, this really is a nice car."

#

After "escorting" a contrite Ms. Jenny Stultz back to her son's house, Parrott left her with the sternest of warnings about letting her enthusiasm override her good sense (a point she had always emphasized to her students) and pocketed his ticket book without writing her one. He didn't see her as a recidivist, and Jeff, clearly irate about a visit from the sheriff, snatched his Charger keys from his mother on the spot. Parrott kindly warned Jeff that driving his car without a muffler could cost him a hefty sum, and wouldn't it be best if he took care of that situation at the earliest opportunity? A sullen Jeff agreed that, indeed, it would.

Just another day in the life...

He pulled back onto Old Beckham Road and pointed his vehicle toward Aiken Mill. He hadn't gone a quarter mile when his radio chirped, and the familiar voice of Meghan Langley, the evening shift dispatcher, called out, "SC Base One to SC Rover One."

"SC Rover One here."

"Sheriff, I've got the ME on the line for you. She says it's important."

The little alarm bell that inevitably signaled a later night than he expected went off behind his left ear. "Roger that, Meghan, you can patch her through."

"One moment, please." A two-second pause. "All right, Sheriff, you're on."

"This is Sheriff Parrott. What have you got, Mel?"

Doc Crawford's alto voice sounded a step higher than usual. "Bryce, you remember our scattered friend, Mr. Lydell?"

"Yeah. Sure."

"Well...." A very long pause. "It appears that he actually has checked out."

"I don't follow."

"The remains are gone. Disappeared. Poof."

Parrott's brain came up far short of formulating a meaningful response. A long silence.

"I know," Doc Crawford finally said. "That was my first reaction. And I heard from Quantico about the samples I sent. There wasn't anything in the vials. Nothing. Color me shocked, I suppose. So, when I went back to the body this evening, well...." She drew a long breath. "It really is gone. Nothing but some leftover organic residue."

"I'm sure it's safe to assume that no one there just moved the remains elsewhere?"

"That is a very safe assumption, Bryce. We have checked, double-checked, and triple-checked. I suppose you were about to knock off for the evening?"

"That was the plan."

"Yeah, me too. Still, given the tests I've been conducting, this is... well...not altogether unexpected."

"That's not *too* cryptic."

STEPHEN MARK RAINEY

"That's why it's better if you pay me a visit."

"I can be there in fifteen."

"I'll be here."

Parrott signed off the call. He hoped Doc Crawford had put on a fresh pot of Juan Valdez because, in an instant, his already sparse energy reserves had gone bone dry.

As he passed through the long, wooded tunnel—somewhere near the spot he'd earlier seen that SUV—a shrill, warbling cry rang out from the darkness and continued, clear and vibrant, even through the Explorer's closed windows: the sad, eerie voice of a whippoorwill.

"You're not *that* damned sad," Parrott muttered. He didn't feel in any great hurry to get back to work, so he kept to the 55 mile-per-hour speed limit as he drove through the dark passage toward town. Within a couple of seconds, distance had silenced the nightbird's song.

#

Day or night, the little morgue looked the same. With no exterior windows, the combination of overhead fluorescents and various desktop LED lamps provided the only variance in lighting. It was just as well, Parrott thought, because he didn't need darkness peering in to remind him of the hour.

Doc Crawford had opened the sheet-lined drawer that had contained Mr. Lydell's remains. Lurid stains on the fabric drew the suggestive shape of a human figure, but not one of the myriad separate body parts remained.

Despite having had advance warning, shock jolted him like a lightning strike. That the remains of a large, full-grown man could have been reduced to *nothing*—by some substance that registered as *nothing*—bludgeoned every rational thought in his mind. "Hard to fathom," were the only words he could find.

The chemical, disinfectant smell in the room failed to mask an underlying stench. Sour. Fetid. Familiar.

Fried chuck.

His wits required a few minutes to recover.

After a time, Crawford shot him a wary-looking glance. "I have a theory."

"Let's hear it."

"It's a ridiculous theory, and if I share it, you may not want to talk to me anymore."

72

He glanced at his watch. "I don't want to talk to you now."

She drew a bracing breath. "I've learned—or deduced—a few things. This 'Nothing' gel as I'm going to call it. Apparently, after some period of time, it vanishes—evaporates, maybe. This explains why there was nothing left of the samples I sent to Quantico. And why there's none left now. Well, this explains the little 'why,' not the big 'why.' Remember, I had originally thought the gel might be some kind of caustic agent or digestive enzyme, something that broke down the tissues of the body. But given its lack of recognizable chemical properties, that was clearly impossible. Still, somehow, *something* consumed that body."

She turned and, from a shelf next to the open freezer cabinet, retrieved a small test tube rack and placed it on her desk. The rack held four tubes capped with rubber stoppers.

She pointed to the first tube. "Sample one, 2 cc's of Nothing gel swabbed from the body, with no accompanying tissue, taken two hours ago. In less than one hour, it was completely gone."

Parrott leaned close. "Empty tube."

She nodded. "Sample two, two cc's Nothing gel with two cc's agar-agar, also taken two hours ago. Full measure of agar-agar remains, our mystery substance is gone. Now, sample three was two cc's of blood and tissue from the remains with two cc's of Nothing gel, taken two hours ago. Both gel and organic matter, all gone."

He nodded as he began to sense where this was going.

She pointed to the fourth tube. "But this sample—two cc's of gel with two cc's whole blood, not from our remains. The blood is still there, the gel is gone." She paused for effect. "Obviously, I don't know what's happening with this stuff. The Nothing gel taken from our remains appeared to affect tissue *only* from those remains. Not from any other source—at least within the time that I had to work with it. But in the affected tissue, this destructive process, whatever triggered it, must have accelerated over time."

"So, you're telling me that your Nothing ends up becoming Less-Than-Nothing?"

"If this Nothing gel somehow catalyzed the organic material and made it dissolve or evaporate, there should be vapor, residue, some measurable evidence of the transformation of matter in the tubes. But there isn't."

Back in school, Parrott had done well enough in science, but if this went beyond Doc Crawford's understanding, it lost him utterly.

"And now we have nothing left to work with. No body parts, no Nothing. Of course, I have written and recorded notes, photographs, even some video. But I don't even know whether all that amounts to 'something' or not."

She closed the empty freezer cabinet and led Parrott to her office, a glass-enclosed cubicle in the rearmost corner of the room. She sat down at her desk and gestured for him to take the chair opposite her. He slid into the seat with a groan, the aches in his joints sharpened by stress.

"Bryce, have you ever heard of ectoplasm?"

He shrugged. "That's part of a cell, right?"

She nodded. "It's an outer, protective covering for certain cells and single-cell organisms, like amoebas. But here's where we get to the part about you not speaking to me again. There is an alternative definition. Actually, I don't even like dignifying it by calling it a 'definition.' But it does have a usage that relates to paranormal activity. It is—supposedly—a substance that gives form to ghosts or spirits. Some say that spiritists, or mediums, exude ectoplasm from their bodies and that substance takes the shape of whatever spirit they call forth." Her eyes locked on his. "And it supposedly reeks to high heaven."

"Ah! *Ghostbusters*."

She cracked the thinnest smile he had ever seen. "That may be the best example of what it's reputed to be. And this shit sure did smell."

"I am continuing to speak to you only because of what I saw—or didn't see—on that slab. And what you have in those test tubes."

"I appreciate your generosity. As you might guess, there is no empirical evidence that ectoplasm exists. Every claim of its existence that I can find has been thoroughly debunked. Yet, here we have an unknown—very likely dangerous—substance that defies conventional explanation."

"Hence your diversion into the paranormal."

"Bravo. Anyway, even paranormal-wise, this substance doesn't jibe with the theoretical characteristics of ectoplasm. Still, this is a horrifying discovery." She pondered a spot on the ceiling for a time before meeting his gaze again. "So, how many loose ends have you sewed up?"

"So far, none of our queries for additional information about

Lydell have turned up anything. Not from here, not from Providence. No one has come forth to claim the body—now a moot point. Locally, we've managed to keep all this pretty low-key. At least Ben Wyatt from *The Bulletin* hasn't come sniffing around. They've just run with the bare-bones news releases I've given them." He snorted. "Since it was bought out, that newspaper isn't even a ghost of what it used to be."

Crawford smiled and nodded. Then her expression turned grim. "Pinpointing the origin of this is crucial. We don't know if this is the equivalent of a leaked biohazard, some freak event the likes of which we'll never see again, or the beginning of some…ectoplasmic epidemic."

"It's been several days, with no indication that anything else like this has happened, thank God. It's not as if we can quarantine the whole county. Or call in a convenient panel of experts to set things right."

"Believe you me, I've been searching every source I can find for any comparable case." She shook her head. "What about you? Any thoughts on calling for outside help? State? Feds?"

He blew out a long, hot breath. "God help us if it comes to that. We do not need that kind of circus."

"If anything else happens, you may have no choice, Bryce."

"Yeah, I know. But now, we don't have any of your 'Nothing gel' or a body for evidence." His mind zoomed back to his father and his untimely—*unspeakable*—death. There were paranormal overtones to that awful event, although, in the end, no evidence of anything other than an insane, all-too-human murderer. Certainly, nothing like this. "We do live in one of the most legend-haunted areas of a legend-haunted state," he said. "This feels like something straight out of one of them."

"I wonder if our victim was into any kind of occult practice." She gave him an almost apologetic smile. "I know, I'm talking as though I give credence to any of this paranormal business. I don't buy into anything 'supernatural.' If it happens, it's natural. We might not understand it, but there's nothing supernatural about it."

"I reckon that's always been my way of thinking."

"This, though. It's so far beyond anything in science, at least that I know of. It's really fired up my imagination. I'm afraid it's clouding my focus. Preventing me from seeing something that should be obvious."

"Not you, Doc. I think I'd know if you weren't seeing things clearly. You see better than anybody I know."

"I'm going to talk again to my colleague at Quantico. Dr. Bowen.

Patrick Bowen. We worked together in Philadelphia back in the day. If there's any clarity to find, I'd say he's the one to help me find it." She shot him a bemused look. "If nothing else, I'm going to have one hell of a paper to write."

"You know what? We have some pretty smart gourds up at Beckham College. They've helped us out on other cases."

"True."

"Maybe I'll throw out some feelers." He glanced at his watch again. "Tomorrow. Definitely tomorrow."

Chapter 9

If Phil had returned to the House of Caviness hoping to find the mountain of old mail, he had left disappointed, Martin thought.

Because it's all right here.

He felt tempted to call his brother, to ask him bluntly why he had returned to Black Tooth Pond so soon after going home. But that would distract him from the task ahead. He would see Phil tomorrow evening for dinner anyway.

Plus, he already knew why Phil had gone back.

Because *he* had gone back.

He had emptied the bag of mail and assorted papers onto his kitchen table. Rather than prepare the dinner he had intended, he opted for a quick, microwaveable mac & cheese entrée. Generally, coffee after seven p.m. was a bad idea, but he wasn't about to have another scotch, and he knew his head wouldn't be hitting his pillow anytime soon. So, he made a single, large mug on the Keurig machine. Then he sat down at the table, forked down his mac & cheese, and began to sort through the pile of envelopes and assorted papers.

The advertisements he discarded. The bills, late notices, and bank statements he sorted by date and set in their own pile. Then he ordered the envelopes, whether sealed or unsealed, in chronological order and placed them in a new pile. He counted forty-five separate handwritten notes, most of which had clearly come from inside the open envelopes.

"LOOK AT WHAT THEY DONE, NOW ITS ALL ON YOU!"

"LEAVE NOW FOR THE SAKE OF YOUR CHILDREN, HELL IS COMING!!!"

"BEWARE THE DOOM THAT CAME TO EDEN. THE COUNTRY OF THE SNAKE!"

The crude block letters, deep red—almost black—on the yellowing paper might have been scrawled in deep red India ink. Or blood. Many of the oldest sheets had turned brittle enough that pieces of them crumbled in his hand. Tomorrow, he'd grab some plastic page protectors from his office.

He realized this drive to gather and sort these old letters and clippings came from a deeper, more potent source than his innate curiosity. This was a compulsion, a *need*—both intellectual and emotional—to assemble a profile of this family, these individuals, who had inhabited the House of Caviness. To discover their history, their motivations. And to explore, if not solve, the mystery of these anonymous, morbid communications.

He had gone all the way back out there to gather this material. Material to which he had initially felt a profound aversion. No, he did not understand his motivation, yet he felt no inclination to reject it.

Onward, then.

All his focus returned to the Caviness family.

Clarence. Franklin. Harriet. Maxine. Theophilus.

Martin quickly determined that Theophilus—shortened in most cases to Theo—and Maxine were married, the parents of Clarence, Franklin, and Harriet. By examining a series of bank statements— from the now-defunct Piedmont Trust Bank—he deduced that Theo had worked a fair-paying job for its time because, every two weeks, a deposit labeled "SBRF" cleared his account, in amounts ranging from $185 to $488 over a span of years.

Sylvan Blue Ridge Furniture?

From the early twentieth century until the mid-1990s, Sylvan Blue Ridge Furniture—Aiken Mill's single major corporate employer—operated a manufacturing plant on the southern outskirts of town, along the Camden River. That long-closed facility now housed the county jail.

Theo's deposits stopped in June 1973. It wasn't long after that date that the past-due and then collection notices began.

After the earliest of the epistles—the one about the hydrogen bomb test in November 1952—the next was dated December 19, 1952, addressed to both Theo and Maxine. It contained an article clipped from an unidentified newspaper and bore the headline "Fog of Death." The text detailed an event that would become known as the Great Smog of London. Between December 5 and December 9 of that year, a combination of fog, smoke, and other industrial fumes, held close to the ground by a localized high-pressure weather system, resulted in almost 4,000 deaths.

The accompanying note, like the others, was written in dark, blood-red ink. *"DO YOU THINK THIS ACCIDENTAL? NO, GOD SPOKE AND HELL FOLLOW."*

The slightly-better-than-semiliterate writer clearly suffered hyperreligiosity and no small degree of paranoia. *Why* had he sent so much terrible news, along with his own dire messages, to the Caviness family? Was he—Martin assumed the writer was a *he*, given the character of the handwriting—some family member, perhaps estranged? He had discovered nothing in all this material to clarify whether the writer originally came from this area. Had he resided in Sylvan County and then moved to Rhode Island? Or might Theo and Maxine Caviness have lived up north before moving to Virginia?

In May 1964, the addressees on the envelopes began to include Clarence. In the first of these, the news clipping bore a masthead that identified its source as *The Providence Journal*. Well, that was consistent with the postmarks. The article documented the crash of Middle East Airlines Flight 444 in the Persian Gulf after overshooting the runway at Dhahran Airport in Saudi Arabia. All 42 passengers and seven crewmembers died in the disaster. The accompanying handwritten note read, *"THEY RODE THE PALE HORSE."*

In late April 1967, Franklin's name first appeared in the list of addressees. The Cavinesses must have maintained contact with the writer since he clearly knew when a new member of the family came into being. This envelope contained a news story—again from *The Providence Journal*—about a series of tornadoes that had struck several locations in the Midwest and devastated the towns of Oak Lawn and Belvidere, Illinois. However, in this envelope, he found no handwritten note, so he began thumbing through the stack of individual sheets. He had no idea which missive might belong with any given news report, though he had discerned a loose correlation between each story and its accompanying personal message.

One of the messages read, *"THE LORD HAS BLOWED AWAY THE SEATS OF THE DAMNED TO MAKE ROOM FOR HIS THRONE!"* Martin couldn't be certain this was the correct pairing of note and news clipping, but when he couldn't identify a more appropriate match, he placed them together.

Still, if any method to the writer's madness existed, the key eluded him.

Harriet, the youngest of the Caviness siblings, joined the household in July 1969. Inside the first envelope to include her name, he found several articles lauding the Apollo 11 moon landing. Hardly a disaster, Martin thought, more an unparalleled milestone for humankind. However, the writer had also included a page torn from a book, identified by the header as *They Knew Too Much About Flying Saucers*. The text gave a fanciful, if detailed, description of an inhuman creature that "gave off a horrible smell" and "looked worse than Frankenstein." The writer's accompanying note simply said, *"WHAT ARE WE DISTURBING OUT THERE?"*

A quick online search of the book title revealed it had been published in 1967. The author was named Gray Barker.

In frustration, he blew out a long breath.

What the hell happened to the Caviness family?

To his right, a gentle burring vibration rose, and an illuminated rectangle materialized on the table at the edge of his vision. His phone.

The name Phil Pritchett glowed on the screen.

The time read ten-forty. This craziness had occupied his attention far longer than he'd realized.

"Hey, Phil."

"We're still doing dinner tomorrow night, right?"

"Yeah. Sure."

"Carli was going to be with her parents tomorrow night, but those plans fell through. You wouldn't mind if she joins us, would you?"

"No, not at all."

"Why don't you bring Alana? We can make a nice evening of it."

Martin pondered the idea. Couldn't hurt to invite her.

He had *so* wanted to quiz his brother about his return to Black Tooth Pond and the House of Caviness. Yet, now, he felt reluctant to divulge that he, too, had gone back there. He did not want Phil to know about *his* return.

This is messed up.

"Marty?"

"Sure, sure, I'll ask her. Still six-thirty?"

"Yeah. Just let me know. You'll cook for us, right?"

"Haha."

"We're having grilled cheeses and chips, you know."

"I will cook."

"I thought so." He laughed. "You know I'm kidding. I'll grill steaks and chicken. Alana likes chicken, right?"

"She does."

"Hope to see you both."

"Hey," Martin began. "Did you—?"

No, no, no.

"What?"

"Never mind. Nothing. Will see you tomorrow."

Phil hesitated a moment. "Okay. Well, goodnight, then."

"G'night."

Nope. He had already committed to saying nothing to Phil about seeing him on Old Beckham Road. Unless his brother mentioned it, for now, Martin considered it a dead subject.

THE HOUSE AT BLACK TOOTH POND

V. TUESDAY

Chapter 10

Martin had somehow soldiered through his eight and nine-thirty a.m. classes on a single mug of coffee, and—finally—at ten-fifty, he half-staggered up the stairs to his office on the third floor of Reynolds Hall. Immediately, he started brewing a pot. His workspace was about the size of his home's master bathroom, with a single window that overlooked the college's central courtyard, which was walled in by two other academic halls and the main administration building. He envisioned Alana laboring away over there, as occupied with her day's tasks as he was with his. Her office window faced the back of the administration building, so he couldn't see it from here. And that was just as well, because just knowing it was *her* window might prove distracting.

She had no idea about his previous night's activity, and he felt no obligation or inclination to share it with her. Maybe that would change if their relationship deepened over time. He hoped it would.

I'm not in love. No, not me.

Outside, on the crisscrossing walkways between buildings,

students milled and zoomed and plodded like disparate colonies of bugs. In five minutes, the courtyard activity would dwindle to almost nothing until noon, when the Beckham College lunch rush made Times Square look like a pasture of contented sheep.

Daylight plus the overhead fluorescent tubes turned his drab, off-white walls a slightly brighter shade of drab. A few years back, Phil had gifted him a couple of his paintings—stylized but attractive landscapes—so Martin had hung them to face his desk. To his left, a tattered poster for FloydFest, an annual music festival in the county next door, sagged on the same wall it had for the past nine years, unchanged due to inertia. He'd been to only that one 'Fest and found it crowded, energetic, and loud. Enjoyable enough, especially with his date at the time, Leigh Anne Asberry. She had moved away...somewhere...shortly after that. For him, revisiting FloydFest never held much allure.

Forty-some essays on Comparing Theories of Cognitive Development eagerly anticipated his rapt attention, and he'd intended to start reading them during his break between morning and afternoon classes. However, the brain fog that had settled in first thing this morning continued to swirl before his eyes, and finding his focus before his one o'clock class seemed a daunting—possibly unlikely—prospect.

Staying up half the night had been such an awful idea. He'd known this from the start, but the Caviness family rabbit hole ran deep, and pulling out of it had required a heroic effort of will. He had gone through every piece of mail, every sheet of paper, several photographs,· and collated them in as close to chronological order as possible. He had half a notion to build a kind of scrapbook out of the material, though to what end was anyone's guess but his. Now that he'd made such an intimate acquaintance with that relentless negativity, it no longer seemed poisonous. Baffling, yet less malign.

Mostly.

Somewhere in the back of his brain, the shadow of all that terrible history skulked and glowered at him with unknown purpose.

Before his four-cup coffeemaker could utter its final gurgle, he filled his black and gold Beckham College Panthers mug and dumped a packet of raw sugar into it. The machine's sneak-a-cup feature worked only when it felt inclined, and a healthy amount of precious caffeine spurted onto the burner before he could return the pot. The liquid sizzled and hissed for several obnoxious seconds before it evaporated.

His desktop computer screen had gone to sleep, so, with a resigned sigh, he woke it up, opened the folder of essays he'd downloaded from the student submission portal, and gazed at the list without registering the title of a single entry. He was about to bite the bullet and open the first file when a gentle rapping came at his door.

"It's open."

The door opened halfway, and to his surprise, rather than a student dropping in with some lame excuse for why they hadn't completed whatever assignment they were supposed to, the too-cheerful face of College President Jennifer Braxton popped inside. "Hey, Marty. Got a minute?"

He'd never minded friends and family calling him "Marty." Braxton using the more informal moniker grated on his nerves, but he'd let it slide long enough that it was a done deal.

"Always. Well, almost always."

She stepped inside, her lips spread in that damnable, perpetual smile of hers, but her eyes appeared clouded with concern. "You didn't read your email when you got back from class, did you?"

It occurred to him that, no, he had not. Checking his work email was usually as automatic as pouring a drink as soon as he got home. How remiss of him. He concealed the abashed expression that almost overtook his features. "I'm afraid not. I just got in a couple of minutes ago."

"No worries. I'm checking in with most of the faculty. Sheriff Parrott stopped by this morning for a talk. Ever met him?"

Martin's eyebrows arched. He shook his head. "Can't say as I have."

Now her smile appeared a little more relaxed. "Don't look so worried. He's not after anyone here. He's just looking for some help."

"Ah."

"First question. You wouldn't happen to know anyone named Lydell, would you? A Frank Lydell?"

His mental gears whirled for a moment. "Pretty sure I don't. Student?"

She shook her head. "The email I sent has his driver's license photo."

He swiveled to look at his computer screen, opened his email list, and peered at the entries. Braxton's, headed "Request for Assistance," appeared at the top of the list. It had arrived only ten minutes ago. He opened it, barely glanced at the brief text, but peered at the attached image. The muddy photo showed a wide, sagging face with droopy, heavy-lidded eyes, thick lips set in a sullen frown, and thinning black hair. A man in his sixties, Martin guessed.

"No, don't know him."

"I'm afraid he's dead," Braxton said. "The sheriff is looking for information he feels might be helpful. Mr. Lydell wasn't from this area, but he apparently died here. For whatever reason, Sheriff Parrott is trying to keep their investigation low-key."

"Why ask a bunch of college professors?"

Braxton's smile turned quizzical. "Well, he had a few, um, unusual questions. Mostly for the science department. But he was wondering if anyone on the faculty had expertise in the paranormal or the occult."

"Okay, yes, that is somewhat odd."

"Do you?"

He scoffed. "No. Well, no more than anyone who grew up in Sylvan County and had colorful legends served up for dinner every night."

"That's why I came to you, since you're from this area."

"No, I would say I have no expertise in the paranormal." A flash of memory of the Old Beckham Road hallucination hit him with sudden, surprising force. Since he'd gone out there and retrieved that mountain of old mail, he'd experienced no recurrence of those visions.

But those weren't paranormal. Anomalous, inexplicable, and even worrisome, but hardly paranormal.

"Did you think of something?"

He dragged his focus back to the moment. "No. I was just trying to think whether I knew anyone that might fit that description. I don't believe I do."

"If you're sure...?"

"I'm pretty sure."

Braxton's smile went a little crooked. "Well, I can't say I expected to be of much help to the sheriff. But if you think of anyone who might fit the bill, let me know, and I'll pass along the information."

"I will."

"Thanks, Marty."

"Don't mention it."

With a final, almost freakishly wide smile, she slipped out the door and drew it closed behind her. Martin turned back to her email and this time read the body text. It said less than what she had divulged to him—that Sheriff Parrott was seeking assistance from any and all quarters but emphasizing discretion. Braxton indicated she had attached the relevant photo and that she'd be speaking to some of the faculty individually.

And that was that.

It occurred to him that the absence of hallucinations, which had hit him in such startling succession over the past couple of days, now seemed somehow strange, although very, very welcome.

Almost as if his admittedly fanciful "cure" for them had somehow done the trick.

#

Brother Phil owned a tiny, two-bedroom, one bath ranch-style house that hid in a little wooded corner situated at the eastern edge of Aiken Mill's historic downtown district. Unless they were old-timers, few people who drove past the lot even realized that the barrier of lush red cedar trees concealed a dwelling of any sort. This camouflage worked both ways, for Phil rarely saw or heard any traffic on Church Street, only fifty feet from his front door. Not long after he'd started working at Studio 253, most of a decade ago, he had purchased the place as a fixer-upper, for a dollar amount that barely exceeded its original 1970s price. Best of all, from here, he could walk to work in less than five minutes.

Seated next to Phil on his aging, secondhand couch, Carli Vaughan held a near-empty glass of French Chardonnay from the bottle she and Alana had shared during dinner. Martin and Alana sat next to each other in matching wooden rocking chairs they'd moved from either side of the living room fireplace to face the couch along the adjacent wall. Like much of Phil's furniture—and some of Martin's, for that matter—the chairs had belonged to their parents until they moved to Virginia Beach. Since this was Alana's first time visiting his home, before dinner, Phil had given her the grand tour, such as it was.

She'd been very polite.

Carli sent Martin a gracious smile. "Thanks for grilling the chicken, Marty. It was delicious."

"My pleasure."

Phil scowled. "It wasn't my fault I had to go back to the store."

Carli snickered. "You let Rufus eat your steaks from the countertop, you ding-dong."

Alana nudged Martin. "She called him a 'ding-dong.'" He smiled his approval.

Phil's scowl darkened. "He's almost nine years old, and in all this time, he's never stolen dinner before."

"That could have just as easily been *my* dinner, you know," Carli said.

"Ah. Now we know what's important here. Anyway, I'm sure it's because he didn't get his walkies in today."

She laughed. "That dog is not *very* spoiled."

Carli Vaughan hailed from one of Aiken Mill's oldest and wealthiest families. Late thirties, married nine years, divorced for the past three. She owned Vaughan Realty, the town's oldest and largest real estate agency, having inherited the business from her father when he retired at age fifty-two. A devoted patron of the arts, she also owned a share of Studio 253. Somehow, she had taken a liking to Phil's artwork and then to Phil himself.

Poor, deluded woman.

Still, despite her "elite" credentials, Carli struck Martin as down-to-earth and anything but pretentious—except when her business called for a display of snootiness, as it sometimes did. On those occasions, she would flip the necessary switch to the "on" position until the need passed. She could play snob with the best of them, though Martin knew she disdained the role. He most admired the fact that she volunteered considerable time and energy to worthy causes, and that she had proven herself sensitive to the needs of Aiken Mill's many less-than-affluent residents.

But Phil? Phillip Pritchett? Really, Carli?

Both he and Phil held empty wine glasses, so he glanced at Alana and then at Carli. Both had finished their Chardonnay. He cleared his throat. "I brought a bottle of very decent Claret, if either of you would care to switch to red."

Goddamn, that was probably as snooty as anything Carli had ever uttered.

"Sounds lovely," Carli said.

Alana nodded. "Sure."

To Phil, he said, "I *know* you want some red."

"Hell, if you're pouring, I'll drink fuckin' Pabst Blue Ribbon."

Carli sent Phil a sour smile. "How gauche."

Martin stood up, touched Alana's shoulder, and said, "Be right back." He headed for the kitchen, which adjoined the combination living room-dining room. Phil followed him inside.

"Thanks for taking up the slack cooking ," he said with a little frown. "I'm feeling kind of out of it this evening. Couldn't sleep last night, so I stayed up painting."

"I didn't sleep well either, now you mention it." Martin almost opened his mouth to mention the House of Caviness, but he bit it back. He grabbed the corkscrew and wine bottle from the countertop, trimmed the foil around the cork, and proceeded to open the bottle. "I lived on caffeine all afternoon. It ought to keep me going the rest of the evening, but I may end up crashing hard when the time comes."

"I feel bad not taking Rufus out for his walk this afternoon. He seemed really keen on going out."

"You didn't take him around the block before we got here?"

Phil shook his head. "Nah. Time was short. And I really do prefer going out to the old pond with him. Especially since we found that house. I want to take another look at it."

"Yeah. I guess I do too." Martin realized he meant it.

Yet, last night, he'd damn near fled the place in panic.

"Come. Upstairs...."

Just a misperception.

Phil lowered his head but glanced up at him. "I have kind of a confession."

"Yeah?"

He gave a weak grin. "I started early, wine-wise."

"I thought as much."

Phil's expression then turned more thoughtful. "But that's not really it. What I wanted to...what I mean is...I went out to the pond again last night. I didn't stay, though. I didn't have a good flashlight, and I didn't want to go stumbling around out there in the dark."

"That's a strange confession, Phil." Martin did not look him in the eye. "So, you just turned around and came home?"

He nodded. "Yeah. I did. I don't even know why I went out there, really. But I tell you, it was kind of an exciting feeling. Now that I know that house is back there, I mean."

Without elaborating, Martin said, "I think I understand."

"Well, Rufus is gonna need his walkies. Want to go out there tomorrow after work?"

"Maybe. Depends on how much I get done between classes tomorrow. I'm a little behind."

Phil nodded in understanding, though he looked crestfallen. "Sure. I'll give you a shout beforehand."

Martin carried the bottle of wine back into the living room and poured a healthy quantity into each glass, though slightly less for Phil. As he sat down beside Alana, he watched his brother settle next to Carli. Although Phil looked happy enough, his body appeared stooped and a little shaky. Not just older but *aged*.

Nonsense. It was just too much drink. Or Martin projecting his own fatigue from lack of sleep. Since he'd spoken of it with Phil, his sleep shortage seemed on the verge of catching up with him.

He and Alana lifted their glasses and touched them together before taking their first sips. Happily, he found the wine delicious.

Then, to his surprise, he heard Phil say to Carli, "Hey, do you happen to know a place called Black Tooth Pond?"

Martin almost sloshed his wine on the hardwood floor.

"No, I don't think so. Why?"

"It's just a small pond back in the woods between here and Beckham. Back in college, I used to hang out there."

"Oh. I know how you used to 'hang out.' You're not 'hanging out' anymore, are you?"

He laughed. "No, no. Sometimes, I take Rufus for walks out there. In fact, Marty sometimes goes with me. We went out there yesterday. I was just wondering who owns that land."

"Why?" She gave him a long, searching look. "You're not actually looking to buy land or anything, are you?"

"God, no." He laughed again. "Just curious."

"Well, we should be able to find out easily enough. Is your laptop handy?"

"Yeah." He set his wine glass on the end table, drew himself back up from the couch, and disappeared down the short hall that led to his bedroom and home studio. Moments later, he reappeared carrying his computer. As he sat back down, he opened it and powered it up. "So, you can just look up the owner?"

"Pretty much. I can check the GIS map of the area." She glanced at Phil. "It doesn't work well on my phone, though. That's why I needed the computer."

"What is GIS?"

"Geographic Information System. It has an interactive local map, so you just click on whatever tract you want to see, and it brings up a card with all the relevant property information. Including the owner." She smiled. "In my business, it can come in handy."

Phil sat with his laptop at the ready. "Okay, where do we go?"

"May I?"

"Sure." Phil slid the laptop over to her.

Curious, Martin rose from his chair and went over to watch. Alana followed and stood at his side.

A moment later, the screen displayed a detailed, multicolored map of Sylvan County. As Carli zoomed in, town limits, districts, zones, roads, railroad tracks, lakes, and streams all became clear. At the next zoom level, every property boundary and even outlines of structures appeared in the visible field.

Phil leaned closer to Carli and pointed to a network of roads that abutted Aiken Mill's central business district. "There's my neighborhood."

"Yep," Carli said. She moved the cursor to a specific lot on Church Street, clicked on it, and its gray outlines turned blue. In a column on the screen's left-hand side, an information field displayed the property address, its dimensions, tax value, the year the house was built, and more, including the current owner's name: Pritchett, Phillip Michael. At the bottom of the column, the previous owners' names appeared: Shelton, Duane Prentiss & Shelton, Kelley Pace.

"Aha!" Phil pointed to the names. "So those are the fucking assholes who painted the bedrooms lime green."

"That's why Phil painted murals of trains on the walls," Martin explained to Alana.

She lowered her voice. "I thought those looked kind of like trains."

Phil beamed. "I showed them!"

"Indeed." Carli shot him a sardonic look. "But you're probably going to want something more neutral when you put this place up for sale."

"Yeah, yeah."

Martin knew that Phil and Carli planned to purchase a new home before their wedding. After her divorce, she had kept the upscale,

Country Club Drive house where she'd lived with her ex-husband, but both she and Phil preferred to move elsewhere. They had their eye on a house with room to spare in the nearby historic district, with a price so far beyond Phil's individual range that he needed a telescope to see it. Still, neither he nor his fiancé appeared to have any qualms about the cash outlay. Martin hoped the difference in their incomes would not create problems farther down the road.

They're grownups. Their choices.

"So," Carli said. "Where is the pond you want to look up?"

"Off Old Beckham Road, about halfway between Aiken Mill and Beckham." He hovered his finger over the screen to follow the movement of the map as she scrolled. "Right up here," he said and pointed to a tiny body of water a short distance west of the curvy thread that represented Old Beckham Road. "That's it."

The small, pale-green oblong occupied a spot near the center of a much larger, irregular polygon outlined in gray, which represented the property boundary. Carli clicked on the polygon and its outline turned blue.

Martin noticed that no sign of a structure appeared anywhere on the property, although the boundaries clearly encompassed the house's location. Too old, maybe.

Carli ran her finger down to the field with the name of the current owner. "Niemand. Hm. That's all it says. Previous owner, Caviness, Theophilus. Never heard of a company or person named 'Niemand.' But whoever or whatever Niemand is, they've owned the property since 1975." She started to look away and then did a double take. "Wait. The owner prior to Caviness is also listed as Niemand. How odd!"

"Niemand," Martin repeated. "In German, that means 'no one.'"

Alana's deep brown eyes caught Martin's. "Do you speak German?"

"No. But in my field, I run across a lot of German words, so I learn bits and pieces here and there. Mostly, I thank Google."

"I see."

Carli exited the GIS map and ran a search for "Niemand," along with various modifiers. None brought up any relevant entries. "A mystery," she said at last. "Sorry, Phil."

Phil put on a slightly alcohol-tinged smile. "As I suspected. No one owns that property."

This evening, Martin didn't feel humor taking very deep root.

"You're a funny man. Except not very."

"I'd give him one point out of five," Carli said, her face somber.

She handed the laptop back to Phil. He gave her an almost good-natured sneer, tucked the computer under one arm, and started back down the hall. Then he stopped, turned back to them, and lifted one hand, one finger raised to the sky. "It just occurred to me that I have something that'll show you people what for." He cast a stern eye at Martin. "And you, my errant brother, are going to say, 'Phillip, I have doubted you without cause.'" He turned and marched down the hall to the back room that passed for his studio. A few seconds later, he returned, carrying a large canvas—three by four feet, Martin reckoned—with its blank, back side facing outward. Once standing before them all, he lifted it and flipped it around to reveal the image it bore.

"Viola! Er, *voilà*."

Martin would never have recognized the painting as his brother's. The portrait depicted a stocky, dignified-looking gentleman with kindly features in a wide, cherub-like face. The slightly hooded, hazel eyes appeared lifelike. The lines, brush strokes, fields of color, all were rough-hewn, loose but disciplined. God knew why (well, no, leeching as much money as possible from students was *always* the why) but art history had been among the seemingly random courses required for entry into Beckham's Psychology program. To his surprise, he'd enjoyed delving into certain movements in modern art, and even now, all these years later, he remembered a number of artists whose work had impressed him. This painting of Phil's, more impressionistic than expressionistic, recalled the work of Frédéric Bazille or Mary Cassatt.

Carli drew an audible breath "That is amazing, Phil. That's Councilman Edmiston."

Alana leaned forward to study the painting. "Yes, I recognize him. Phil, that really is a great painting."

With a low bow of his head, Martin said softly, "Brother Phil, I have often doubted you with just cause. But not this time."

"I forgive you. Mostly."

"You are a wise and magnanimous brother."

Phil's eyes narrowed. "Why are you lying to me?"

"You owe me for two filets."

Chapter 11

Seated across the desk from Sheriff Parrott, Deputies Sykes and Beamer both had their notepads in hand as they summarized their findings from the past twenty-four hours. So far, they'd offered a boatload of nada. Not that Parrott could reasonably expect otherwise.

Deputy Dan did most of the talking. "The lab in Roanoke hasn't gotten to the mud samples from Lydell's car yet, but we are checking out low-lying areas nearby that tend to stay muddy. Fishing spots, Wildlife Management Areas, trailheads. As you can imagine, that's a lot of territory. So far, we haven't found any sign of matching tire tracks or footprints."

"I know you said it's not even a longshot," Beamer said, "but I talked to the plant managers at Prillaman Paint & Solvents and the county waste treatment plant. They said there's nothing close to any substance matching the parameters you wrote up. Mr. Enwright at Prillaman company said whoever put this information together must have failed basic chemistry."

"That's why I sent you instead of going myself."

Beamer looked hurt. "Well, damn, Sheriff."

Sykes's straight face looked ready to crumble, so Parrott told them to get lost. They still had a lot of ground to cover. And he had a call to make.

Talking to the folks at Beckham College had netted little to no useful information, particularly from the science department. Again, not that he expected otherwise. He had, though, acquired the phone number of a retired history professor who reputedly knew a great deal about Sylvan County's history, including its legends and folklore. Last name of Scales. He glanced at his notepad. Professor Shelton "Shelly" Scales. Parrott had attempted to reach him yesterday evening, but the professor hadn't been available. The woman he'd spoken to, presumably Mrs. Scales, had suggested he call back mid-morning today.

Well, it was mid-morning and it was today.

He dialed the number on his desk phone. After a couple of rings, a scratchy-voiced man answered.

"Good morning, sir. This is Sylvan County Sheriff Bryce Parrott calling. Have I reached Professor Shelton Scales?"

"Yes, sir, you have."

"Professor Scales, I am calling you because my department is investigating an unusual—I might actually call it a bizarre—case that involves a deceased individual, and it's my understanding that you are knowledgeable about...let's call it the darker side of Sylvan County's history."

"You must be George Parrott's son."

"Yes, sir, I am."

"I knew him, at least in passing. I recall him being a fine lawman. A true gentleman."

"I appreciate that."

"So, you say you have a dead body?"

Parrott hesitated a moment. "Well, this was more a body in pieces. And those pieces have since vanished, for want of a better word. And I don't mean removed or stolen. Over a couple of days, by way of some unknown process, they physically disintegrated. What we have, sir, is actually more than a single problem. When we found this body, it had been mutilated. As in torn apart by something unknown. We haven't been able to identify whether it was human or otherwise. But this is the even more remarkable part. The remains of the body were covered in a clear, viscous substance that exhibited...unknown properties. We don't know whether this substance was responsible for destroying the remains or if it was some kind of byproduct."

"'Remarkable properties,' you say. Can you elaborate?"

"It defied every attempt at analysis. By every measurable criteria, this substance did not exist."

"It sounds like you have an unusual science problem."

Parrott chuckled. "That we do, sir."

"May I ask why you thought I might be of help? It doesn't sound like this is my field at all."

"To be honest, Professor, I'm really not sure. The main reason, I guess, is your familiarity with this area's, uh, unconventional history. What some people might call ghostly. Or supernatural, I suppose."

"Well, I am familiar with a lot of local folklore. My family's been in this area since before Virginia was even a state. Still, what you're describing doesn't sound like anything I'd be familiar with. At all."

"During our investigation, the medical examiner used the word 'ectoplasm' as a possible name for the substance we discovered. Does that term mean anything to you?"

Scales grunted a laugh. "You hear about it in connection with ghostly events and such, but as you probably already know, there's no evidence that it exists. And as far as folklore goes, I can't think of anything at all relevant to your case."

"I understand. Now, don't get me wrong, sir. I don't have any belief in the supernatural, or anything like that. But something unexplainable has happened here, and we are desperately looking for any precedent, anything that's happened in this area—or elsewhere, for that matter—that might help us figure out what we're dealing with."

"I suppose that makes sense enough. You grew up in Sylvan County, right?"

"I did."

"Then you probably heard a lot of those old stories that used to go around. These days, though...well, they're moribund. I'm seventy-eight years old. It's a different world, even from a relatively few years ago. I bet no more than a handful of people in this area remember the stories about the Fugue Devil, or the Wampus Cat, or the Yck, or the Bigfoot. You know, every rural community has its Bigfoot, or some variation. And of course, we've had ghosts aplenty. Every little graveyard or abandoned house in the county has had some ghost story connected with it. Remember the Madison Arms building? That was probably our best-known haunting until they tore the place down a few years back. As far as I know, nobody's reported a ghost on that land ever since."

"Yes, I do remember that. Now, the Ick, you said? What is that?"

"Oh, you never heard the stories about the Yck? It's spelled Y-C-K. Goes back to the days before the white man. Nobody remembers what the Indians called it, but early explorers gave it the name 'Yck,' and it stuck."

"So, what was it?"

"Supposedly, some kind of indescribable beast that wandered the woods, always hungry. If its path and yours ever crossed, well, that would be bad. Ever hear of the Wendigo? To my mind, it was the local version of that."

"Heard of it. Don't know anything about it."

"The Wendigo legend most likely originated with the Algonquin Indians. Canadian wilderness, far northern U.S. states. A long way from here. But even those stories tended to migrate as commerce increased around the country in the nineteenth century. Still, none of this seems to have anything to do with what you're looking for."

"I suppose you're right, although there's plenty of 'ick' to go along with his case. It's not for the squeamish."

"I don't envy your work."

"It's not for everyone." He chuckled. "Well, Professor, I do hope I'm not bothering you. I felt I needed to take the chance, even if it was remote."

"I don't mind at all, Mr. Parrott." He paused for several seconds. "You know, you said you're not a believer in the supernatural. Trust me, neither am I. But Aiken Mill and Sylvan County have a long, haunted history. You know the woods around here. They're old and deep, and most of them have never been developed. I know there's been some recent timbering out past Mt. Signal, but ever since the furniture industry left, there's been no appreciable ingress into the forests. You know, I still go walking in the woods as much as I'm able, and I can tell you, it always feels…different. I might even call it spooky." He laughed. "I'd also be the first to tell you that I've always had a vivid imagination. Probably goes back to my summer camp days over in Barren Creek. The camp counselors would scare the bejeezus out of us kids. But I credit them with sparking my interest in history and folklore. It's made for a nice living."

Parrott laughed as well. "I went to camp at Barren Creek too. That was where I first heard of the Wampus Cat. And maybe even the Fugue Devil. I'd call those fun times." He went silent for a moment. "Well, I won't keep you any longer, Professor Scales. Work does call. I appreciate your time."

"It was my pleasure, Sheriff. Best of luck sorting out this case of yours. It sounds like a terrible situation. But at the end of the day, I expect you'll find some logical explanation."

"I'm certainly hoping for that."

"I'll say goodbye then."

"Goodbye, Professor."

Parrott hung up and, as often happened when stress began eating at him, he thought of his father. George Parrott certainly would have gone through periods of extreme frustration, of impatience, of grave doubts in his choices, his conclusions. But where his profession was concerned, he always seemed level-headed, thoughtful, methodical. He never gave into despair or apathy. A more courageous man Bryce had never known.

He doubted, though, that his father had ever encountered any situation comparable to this one. Of course, whatever happened during that last case of his—the one involving the murderer named Ren—it ended up killing him.

Whatever it takes, that is NOT going to happen to me.

He glanced over at his coffeemaker and groaned. Yet again, Juan Valdez lay stone dead.

THE HOUSE AT BLACK TOOTH POND

VI. WEDNESDAY

Chapter 12

"*H*ELL IS COMING! HELL IS COMING FOR YOU!*"
The words rang through corridors of his brain as if a sharp, malevolent voice had shouted them into his ears. But no one had spoken.

A colorless swatch of moonlight seeped through the grimy window to illuminate the lowest risers of the rickety staircase, which ascended into an inverted well of pure darkness. Halfway up, a pale, angular framework—the broken banister—tilted crazily outward from the edge of the stairs, ready to topple to the living room floor at the slightest touch. He ambled toward the stairs but paused at the bottom and peered into the lightless void above. The rapid, repeated *thud-thumping* of his heart drowned the soft susurrus of the breeze outside the open door.

A gray shape—nothing more than a rapid, shifting wisp—appeared and disappeared in the upstairs darkness.

Then it came: the eerie, mournful cry of a whippoorwill.

But, no—not a whippoorwill.

Brother Phil's imitation of a whippoorwill.

\#

"**M**arty?"

Phil's voice on the phone drew him back to the fluorescent-lit confines of his office. Outside the window, the sky appeared gunmetal, the sun a weak, quicksilver blob behind a barrier of low-hanging clouds.

It had happened again. The same hallucination, or rather, the same type of hallucination. The sense of being somewhere else. Of *feeling* somewhere else. But now the vision had shifted to the interior of the House of Caviness.

His heart sank.

"Hey, Marty. Did I lose you?"

"No, I'm here." He could not, *would* not, explain to Phil what had happened—or was still happening—to his senses. "Service must have cut out there for a second."

It seemed some kind of logical progression. From driving on Old Beckham Road to standing inside the old house.

"I did it again, Marty. This time, I took my flashlight. I prepared for it."

"What?"

"I said, I went back to the old house. I went inside."

"You went again—when? Last night?"

"Yeah. After everyone left. It was late. Nearly midnight."

"Why would you do that?"

Was Phil hallucinating too? How could they both be? Maybe some medical issue, something they had both been exposed to?

"I just wanted to. That place, there's something about it. It's like it never leaves my mind. So, I just up and went."

"What did you do there?"

"I went through the rooms." He gave a weak laugh. "Carefully, of course. You know where that big tree is growing up through the roof? That's the kitchen. Not much left of it. Appliances are smashed up. There's a bunch of old mason jars full of some evil crud, unopened canned goods, and stuff all over the place. Two bedrooms on the main floor. Couple of moldy beds, old clothes scattered everywhere, broken up furniture. And I can't even describe what was left of that bathroom."

"Did it help? I mean, did going back satisfy whatever urge took you there?"

This was what he wanted—*needed*—to know.

"I'm not sure. Maybe. But here's something strange, Marty. You know all that mail that was piled in the living room? It was gone."

And there it was. What could he say? He knew Phil was being honest with him. Could he be equally honest?

Why not?

He drew a long, steadying breath. "Okay. Yeah. I went back there myself. I took it all out." His brother said nothing for a long moment, so he continued. "You know how I'd first thought about taking it with me and then changed my mind? Well, I changed it again."

"When?"

"Night before last. Same night we first went into the place."

"Wow. Just...wow."

He wasn't sure how to take Phil's monotone response. "In fact, I think I saw you on your way back there. Out on Old Beckham Road."

"I guess you did." Phil paused. "So, what did you do with the mail?"

"I went through it. Got rid of what was clearly trash. Kept all the news clippings and personal notes and such. Put them more or less in order."

"And did that do anything for you? Did it help?"

He gave a wry laugh. "I don't know. Maybe. I just couldn't say no to going back for it. So, we seem to have that in common."

"You didn't mention it to me, though."

"Sorry. Somehow, I guess, it didn't seem like the right thing. The right time."

Or for talking about the visions that drove me there. Or what happened only a few minutes ago.

After a moment, Phil said, "Fuck it. It's not like we're obligated to tell all or anything." He paused again. "But here's why I really called. When I was there, I went upstairs."

A ripple of anxiety quivered up Martin's spine. "Shit, Phil. From the looks of it, that was damned dangerous. That whole staircase could have come apart under you. Not to mention the upstairs floor."

"*Come. Upstairs....*"

No, no, no!

"Believe it or not, the stairs are sturdy. The banister is busted up, but I had no problem. But here's the thing, Marty. Once I got up there, I don't remember anything."

"Say what?"

"It's all a blank. I remember getting to the top, seeing a long, dark space, and shining my flashlight into it. Next thing I know, I'm walking back to my car. So, I just went back home and sat up painting again."

Martin thought for a moment. "You know, you did drink quite a bit."

"Oh, come on. That was out of my system before I even headed out there."

"I wouldn't be too sure about that."

"Even if I did, I've never lost a minute of time before. This was different."

And I have never hallucinated until the past couple of days.

Phil continued. "I know there's all kinds of mold and stuff in that house. It makes me wonder. Do you think exposure to it could cause any kind of physical effect? Anything…like this?"

"If you were sensitive to mold, you'd probably just have a typical allergic reaction. You know, sneezing, headache, that kind of thing. It would take more exposure than visiting the house a couple of times before you'd suffer any neurological effects. So, I'd say no. Not a factor."

Certainly not for him. Martin's hallucinations had begun shortly *before* they'd discovered the House of Caviness.

"That's kind of what I thought. Still. It made me wonder."

"There's a lot of things more dangerous in that house than mold. It might be better not to go back inside." The moment he said it, he felt a sudden, sharp stab, like a hornet's sting directly to his brain. He realized he was as intent on convincing himself as his brother that going back into the house was a bad idea. His brain did not appreciate it.

"Well, if it doesn't dump rain this afternoon, I plan to take Rufus out to the pond, at least." He paused. "So, what do you think? You want to come with me?"

Martin looked at his computer screen. All those essays to read and grade. Plus, prep for next week's lectures and a major test to put together.

"I don't think I'm going to have time. I'm up to my ears in alligators."

A long silence. "If you're sure. You know you're always welcome to join me."

"I do. And I will. Maybe next time."

"Okay. I guess I'll talk to you later."

"Yeah. Later."

He hung up.

Jesus, Phil.

Whatever had gripped his own mind, something was also happening with his brother. He wanted to pass it off as Phil having consumed a glass or two too many last night, but how could he? As far as he knew, it was true; Phil had never blacked out or lost time due to drinking. Or even from sampling more mind-altering substances than Martin had any idea existed, back when he did that sort of thing. With both of them suffering these aberrations concurrently, how could he chalk this up to coincidence?

Because that's what his rational mind did. Or attempted to. Because the alternative was neither rational nor comprehensible.

He'd made mental excuses to himself to avoid meeting Phil later today. None of the items on his to-do list, other than the essays, presented any appreciable challenges to his schedule. But, my God, this thing in his head, in his mind, he'd considered it over and done with. This *had* to be something physiological.

Didn't it?

To the best of his knowledge, his family had no history of severe mental or physical afflictions, such as schizophrenia, bipolar disorder, Parkinsons, or Alzheimer's, any of which could account for hallucinations. Not that this meant anything conclusively; heredity could play a significant role in the onset of such conditions, but sometimes, the universe simply selected a person at random to strike with a lightning bolt.

A soft *burring* drew him from his musings, and for a moment, he wondered if Phil might be calling him back. Then he realized it was his office phone. The caller ID window displayed Alana's name. He picked up the receiver. "Hey there."

"Want to go to lunch?"

They usually met for lunch once or twice a week, but none so far this week. So much for working on those essays—or commencing his foray into the causes of certain sensory anomalies.

"You mean with you? I don't know."

"Isn't this Dean Stermer? Oh, I may have dialed the wrong number."

"What the hell have you got going on with Stermer?"

She laughed. "Oh, it's you. I guess I could postpone my date with the dean."

"Frith's?"

"Sure. Meet me out front of Admin?"

"Give me five minutes."

#

Within its town limits, Beckham boasted three restaurants, two of which adjoined the campus. Occasionally, Martin and Alana hit the nearby Subway, but they favored the food, ambiance, and almost criminally low prices of the ever-so-imaginatively named Frith's Restaurant. Since 1968, Frith's had been a Beckham institution, their burgers, hot dogs, and fried chicken legendary for hundreds of yards in every direction. Faithfully patronized by students and faculty alike, on weekdays during the academic year, between the hours of eleven-thirty and one o'clock, the little joint—seating capacity sixty-five—became a madhouse. Thankfully, much of the lunchtime rush was for takeout. As if perpetually reserved for them, a cozy corner booth for two, with a window that overlooked the lazy Camden River, remained forever empty, so it had become Martin and Alana's regular table of choice.

Decades' worth of scribbles, etchings, and coats of varnish covered the dining room's wood-paneled walls. Courtesy of some unknown artist, from the lord knew how many years ago, an intricately inked rendering of Godzilla, complete with atomic heat ray gushing from his gaping mouth, adorned the wall beside Martin's seat. Over time, he and the venerable kaiju had become friendly, familiar dining partners.

Alana sat across from him, fingers fidgeting as if to keep herself from taking his hand in hers. Between them, their glasses of iced tea—his sweet, hers unsweet—sweated water droplets onto the dull green Formica tabletop. He took a drink of his, thinking that no one, even the stodgy old Dr. Sinclair, Advanced Math, who sat two tables over, would look askance at them should her fingers and his make contact. He knew of no fewer than four married couples on the faculty, all of whom had met during their employment.

Not that anything like marriage loomed in *their* foreseeable future. Still, for the college's sake, propriety in all things.

"So, are you going to talk about what's bothering you?" Alana's tone was tinged with concern.

"Why do you think something is bothering me?"

"I think anyone could see that you've got something weighing on your mind. Last night, Phil was pretty heavy into the drink, don't you think? Something between you two?"

Nope, not a chance in hell would he share anything about his current internal struggle. Not with her, certainly not now. What would she think if he were to reveal his recent, uncanny experiences? He and Alana hadn't yet reached *that* point of intimacy. "My brother goes in spells with that kind of thing. Once you get to know him, you'll understand. It's his artist's temperament. Or something."

"'I'm not reticent, I just don't talk much.'"

"What?"

"Your exact words a while back." Her smile held a trace of worry. "You go straight to talking about Phil rather than yourself."

"He's easy to talk about. Not always nicely." He grinned. "And I'm sure I never said that."

"Yes, you did."

"Hmm. I did, didn't I?" He appreciated that she felt genuine concern for him. At the same time, he hated having to deflect a conversation because starting into it would lead to places he didn't care to go. "Yes, I'm a little nervous about Phil and me, with his marriage coming up and all." Martin hoped none of this sounded lame. "As I've told you, he can be kind of erratic. He and I have been very close in recent years, and his getting married is going to change our relationship, at least to some degree. I'll admit that I find that a little discouraging."

From her expression, she was debating whether to buy it. "Okay. Well, you know I was always close with Julia. She got married three years before I did, so I had some anxiety about how things would change. Things did, of course, especially the time we got to spend together, but it didn't really affect our relationship. I think it became more special. You'll miss his company, I'm sure, but at least you'll still be living near each other."

He knew her older sister, Julia, and her husband had moved from Orlando to somewhere—he didn't remember where—well before Alana had come to Aiken Mill. She had mentioned how tight they'd been, and that she disliked how far apart they now lived. Of course, everything he'd said about Phil was true, though hardly the source of his deepest anxiety.

When he didn't answer right away, she must have picked up on that fact.

"So, that's not the whole story, is it?"

"It's close enough."

"Is it?"

Before he even realized it, he snapped, "Damn it, this is a real issue for me, and I don't need or want to try dredge up something that isn't there."

Her eyes widened, and she drew back in her seat.

Reason and conscience immediately rebuked him. He slid a hand across the table toward her. "I'm sorry. That was awful of me." He swallowed hard. "I will tell you; work is piled up to here, I've been sleeping like shit, and I'm exhausted. I didn't mean to be short with you. I apologize."

She studied his face, her expression neutral. "Okay. I didn't mean to touch a nerve there."

"I know you didn't."

He could hardly believe he'd reacted like that. She didn't deserve even an ounce of his ire. For the first time in he couldn't remember how long, his own behavior appalled him.

"I didn't feel like I was overstepping my bounds," she said. "Not where we are in our relationship."

"You didn't." He tried to bring up a smile that didn't look forced. "I suppose now is a good time to warn you that I have been known to be needlessly temperamental. It's rare. But I guess it happens."

"I hope it's very rare."

"Yeah," he said in a barely audible voice. "Me too."

She didn't speak for a moment, obviously uncomfortable. He didn't like that at all, especially because this was his fault. At last, she said, "You're still fine for us getting together on Friday night, I hope?"

"Of course." He put on his most reassuring smile. "Okay, here's a thought. I'd love for us to get away from this area for a change. Take a weekend trip. Probably not for this weekend but sometime soon. How would that sound to you?"

She nodded. "I'd like that."

"Hey, have you ever been up to DC? Georgetown, specifically?"

"No."

"When I was at VCU, my roommate was from Northern Virginia.

We spent a lot of time in Georgetown. It's a beautiful place, with lots to see and do. Plus, there's always the standard DC stuff nearby. The Capitol, the memorials, the Smithsonian, all that—if such things appeal to you."

"Yes. I would really like to do this." Her smile became warm again.

"Well. How about we start plotting on Friday evening?"

She lowered her voice. "Plotting sounds perfectly wicked."

Their server, a young woman named Denise, who knew them well enough as regulars, appeared with their food. For him, a bleu cheese burger and fries, and for Alana, a chef's salad that came in a bowl the size of a deep-sea diver's helmet. He knew that, as per her custom, she'd take at least half of that with her when they left.

"Thanks, Denise," he said. She nodded and promised to return shortly to refill their drinks. His burger smelled delicious, and he realized he now felt ravenous.

Before he could take a bite, a stray glance out the window fell on a large, dark figure slogging through the shallow, slow-moving river beyond a screen of small beech trees. Fishermen frequented the river along here, so he thought little of it, until he realized the big man carried no rod or tackle.

He appeared to be dressed in a black suit of some kind. Not at all the kind of clothes in which one would go fishing. Or wading.

Tall and husky, with dark, thick hair. The man's eyes, bright and wide beneath a heavy brow, appeared to focus directly on Martin.

Bullshit.

He pulled his gaze away from the oncoming figure, took a bite of his cheeseburger, and slowly, deliberately chewed it. Then he looked back out the window.

The large man was gone. No sign of any human figure out there at all.

Bullshit. Times two.

#

They walked back across the campus mostly in silence. But the silence felt comfortable again, or mostly so. Despite a sincere urge to apologize again, he held it back because that would take them right back to the most uncomfortable moment they had ever experienced together. Just before they reached the Admin building entrance, he said, "So, you've never been to DC?"

"Nope."

"Well, I would definitely love to get away from Aiken Mill, from Beckham, everything, even for a few days. Maybe right after Thanksgiving? Things will be looking festive for the holidays by then."

Now her laugh seemed stress-free—her normal, happy Alana laugh. "I'd say let's go for it. I could stand to get away too."

"Then I will talk to you later." He gave her shoulder a discreet squeeze, and she turned to go up the stairs to the building's front door. As she opened it, she looked back and gave him a quick wave. Then she disappeared inside.

"You are one stupid son of a bitch," he muttered as he started toward Reynolds Hall, across the courtyard.

Classes would begin in less than ten minutes, and the courtyard teemed with bustling figures. As he sauntered toward Reynolds Hall, mostly looking at his feet, he heard a deep, booming voice rising above the soft student babble around him. It shouted, "Sinners, take heed! The end times are near! Take heed, all of ye!"

Oh, hell. One of the endless supply of proselytizers that targeted the campus more and more frequently. They'd always been around, maybe even more so back in his university days, but there seemed to have been a recent explosion of obtuse zealots.

When he finally looked up, he realized that the voice came from a huge, black-suited man, with wide, glittering eyes beneath a heavy brow.

Good God....

The man stood on the walkway just shy of the stairs to Reynolds Hall. Unless Martin diverted to the side door, he would pass directly in front of the fellow. As he drew nearer, he saw that, indeed, water dripped from the cuffs of the man's otherwise well-cut and presumably expensive suit trousers. His black leather shoes glistened with moisture.

In one hand, the man held a thick sheaf of papers. Flyers or tracts, no doubt. None of the students passing nearby appeared to take even the vaguest notice of him.

Good for them.

He chose to bite the bullet and walk past the man without paying him any more mind than the seemingly oblivious students. He made no eye contact as he approached, and he walked by without the fellow appearing to take any special notice of him.

Until he reached the stairs of his building. And the deep voice bellowed, "Beware, Dr. Pritchett, of the doom that came to Eden, the country of the snake!"

Martin whirled around, incredulous, and saw the figure standing on the walkway with one arm outstretched, pointing directly at him.

"Do you not know what you have disturbed, Dr. Pritchett? Yes, you!"

Martin took a few steps toward the towering figure. How could he know his name? As far as he knew, he'd never seen the man before, though *something* about those features—the thick hair, the widely spaced eyes—struck him as familiar. Maybe a former student?

No.

But his words. Martin knew those words. They came from the pages he'd taken from the House of Caviness. Yet, no one besides his brother could be privy to what he'd done. No one else could have been out there to see him. Who could possibly know what was written on those pages?

No one!

He fought his way through the waves of apprehension that threatened to batter him backward and approached the man without flinching. "Who are you?"

"No one of concern," the voice rumbled. "But I have a message for you."

One huge, unadorned, well-manicured hand reached into the sheaf of papers he carried. He blindly drew one and held it out to Martin, who took it in fingers that somehow remained steady.

He held it up before his eyes and read the words, printed in the same blood-red blocky letters he'd seen on those pages taken from the old house.

"*YOUR NAME IS INSCRIBED IN BLOOD IN THE BOOK OF THE DOOMED.*"

Martin lowered the paper and peered into the deep brown, almost black irises that floated in the centers of the extraordinarily bright whites, both unmarred by any blood vessels or discolorations. "Who the hell are you?"

Thin lips pulled back to reveal perfect, very white teeth. The smile froze on the oversize face, and the man spoke no more.

After a moment, the face appeared to shrink from him, and Martin realized that the man was backing steadily away. Almost as a reflex, he reached into his back pocket for his phone and tapped the camera icon. He tried to punch the button to begin a video recording, but his fingers fumbled and closed the app. With a bark of frustration, he reopened the camera and began snapping still photos.

The man wasn't simply backing away. His rigid body was receding, like a statue mounted on rails, drawn backward by some unseen force. The man dwindled in the distance, passing through the narrow space between Reynolds Hall and the Administration Building. Then he vanished in the wooded shadows beyond.

"No, no, no, no."

He raised his phone, opened the gallery, and selected the most recent photograph.

In the image, the man, distant but recognizable, stood there, facing the camera, though the movement had blurred his features. In the second photo, he appeared closer, face still too indistinct to be recognizable. The third one—the first Martin took—was blurriest of all, no doubt from his scrambling to take the photo. But he had proof the fucker had actually been there. Until he saw the photos, he had begun to doubt his senses, his grasp on reality.

"I got you. Right there in the picture, you vile fuck."

An airy voice piped from behind him. "Are you all right, Dr. Pritchett?"

He turned and saw Bridgette Kolodny, one of his PSYC 301 students—the class to which he was supposedly heading right now. Tiny enough to be called "elfin," the young blonde stared at him, curiosity gleaming in her magnified, bespectacled blue eyes.

"I'm fine," he said, his voice a razor. Then he held out his phone to show her the photograph. "Did you see this man?"

"You mean the preacher? Yes, sir."

"You saw him disappear, right?"

She pointed toward the Admin building. "He wandered off that way."

"He wandered off?"

She nodded, though wariness crept into her curious gaze. "I guess he gave up, since his audience disappeared."

Martin realized the courtyard had nearly emptied, and he had about one minute to get to class. For Bridgette's benefit, he put on his stern professor face and jerked a thumb at Reynolds Hall. "You have about one minute to get to class, Ms. Kolodny."

"Yes, sir, I'm just on my way."

"Tell everyone I'll be there shortly."

She started walking but paused to shoot him a bemused look. "I'll do that."

"Thank you."

As she headed for the building, he took several deep, calming breaths. "Wandered off?" Hardly what he would call it. Now, though, when he looked back at the images, he realized they revealed the man standing not straight-on but half-turned, as if he had paused to glance back at Martin as he made his way out of the courtyard.

That was *not* what he had seen!

Another hallucination? If so, it was very different from the others he'd experienced.

Still, the man had addressed him as only someone who possessed shared knowledge could have. Martin still clutched the scrawled sheet of paper, which proved that, whatever aberrations his mind had suffered, something in the *real* world was also happening. How the hell could he stand in front of his class and lecture as if he'd experienced nothing extraordinary? He feared he lacked sufficient physical and mental reserves to stay on his feet—or think with anything resembling clarity—for the next few hours.

As his eyes and mind absorbed every stroke of the jagged, deep-red letters in the ominous message, he had no idea whether he had reason to hope or fall into despair.

Chapter 13

The homeless population in Aiken Mill hardly rivaled that of the larger communities in the region, such as Roanoke or Danville, but in the past five years or so, the number of individuals living on the street had increased by what most locals considered an alarming degree. All too many of these unfortunate folks suffered mental issues, and Sheriff Parrott found himself dealing with more complaints, altercations, and even break-ins than ever in his experience. The reasons for the increase were manifold, but at the end of the day, the responsibility for public safety, regardless of any individual's status, fell upon the sheriff.

He'd gone to his usual Wednesday lunch at Willy's Downtown Tavern and was on his way back to the station when Francine Harris's voice rang out from his Explorer's radio. "SC Base One to SC Rover One. You there, Sheriff?"

"I'm here, Francine."

"Got a ten-sixty-six over on Church Street, near the intersection at Bondurant. Received a couple of calls reporting a suspicious-looking white male, late twenties to early thirties, said he's been walking back and forth on the street all the morning, and now's he's causing some kind of ruckus. Hollering, and all."

"I'm two minutes away. Consider it covered."

"Roger that, Sheriff. Barbecue plate for lunch?"

"You know it."

"Don't suppose you picked me up an extra corn on the cob?"

"Not today, Francine."

He heard a heavy sigh. "Next week, maybe?"

"Maybe so."

"Thank you, Sheriff. SC Base One out."

A couple of years ago, he had ended up with an extra corn on the cob from Willy's and offered it to Francine. Since then, she'd come to expect corn almost every Wednesday. He hated to disappoint her, though he frequently did. Happily, they had both adjusted to the routine, Francine to regular frustration on Wednesdays, and he to the subsequent chastising.

When he pulled up to the curb at the corner of Church and Bondurant, he saw a couple of older women, one of them holding a dog—a Snickerdoodle, or whatever they called those tall, poofy critters—on a leash, standing on the sidewalk by a row of lush, red cedar trees, which concealed a small ranch-style house. Along the length of the row, a tall, wiry-looking man wearing a maroon hoodie and dirty gray sweatpants was stomping back and forth, his head angled toward the trees, one hand gesturing madly at someone who was not there.

The dogless woman strode toward him as he tugged on his wide-brimmed campaign hat and slid out of the Explorer. She looked familiar, though he couldn't place her. Tall, with wispy silver hair and lots of makeup. She wore a stylish, lightweight turquoise jacket, black slacks, and an incongruous pair of well-worn Skechers running shoes.

"Thank you for getting here quickly, Sheriff." She pointed to the stomping man and then toward the cedars. "He's been roaming the sidewalks all morning. Every now and then, he stops and pokes his head into those trees, looking toward the house. A little while ago, he took to hollering and then ran off for a bit. We figured he was gone, so Cheryl and I came out for a walk. But then he came back, and he's been like that ever since."

"What's your name, ma'am?"

"Janice Edmonds." She nodded toward the woman behind her. "That's Cheryl Piper. She's my next-door neighbor. Right down there on Bondurant."

He recognized the name Edmonds. That was it. She'd been the manager of the Wells Fargo Bank down near his office. Now retired.

"Ms. Edmonds, has this man threatened you or your friend at all?"

"Not directly. Sounds like he's mighty upset with someone, though."

He motioned for her to move back to where she was standing. "If you'll both stay put, I'll see what we've got."

She nodded and returned to her place by the woman with the dog. With slow, cautious steps, he approached the man now stomping toward him. The figure's half-obscured gaze remained fixed on the trees, and he did not appear to register the sheriff's presence.

"Sir, I'm going to ask you to remain where you are. I'd like to have a few words with you."

For the first time, the man looked at him. Beneath the hood, scraggly black hair hung over a pair of blazing eyes—dark irises floating in twin pools of bright white. His bony, grime-smeared face twisted into an angry grimace. "Those motherfuckers," he growled, jabbing a thumb toward the cedar trees. He did not move any closer, though his booted feet shuffled in place. "I'll cut them motherfuckers to pieces, I swear I will."

Parrott slid his right hand down to touch the handle of the taser holstered behind his pistol. "Are you armed, sir?"

The wild eyes seemed to find their focus for a moment, and the young man shrugged.

"What's your name, my friend?"

"Fuck you, I'm not your friend. I saw what I saw."

Parrott took several slow steps forward and stopped ten feet shy of the fellow, who continued to shuffle in place. "Sir, can you tell me what you saw?"

He shook his head and glanced back at the trees. His expression turned fearful. "No!"

"All right. I'm going to ask you to stand still and put your hands out at your sides."

"He was here, I swear he was. And it's all their fault. Them in that house!" Again, he gestured toward the house behind the cedars. "Don't you know what they have done? They've fucked me over.

Them! This would never have happened to me in Chatham!"

"Is that's where you're from? Chatham?"

"Used to be."

"Would you please tell me your name, sir?"

"Fuck. You."

"Have you been drinking or taking any drugs, sir?"

"FUCK! YOU!"

This felt all too familiar. The last call he'd answered that involved a street person had unfolded on an almost identical note. "All right, sir. I'm going to ask you one more time to stand still and put your arms out at your sides. It's the last time I'm going to."

Again, the young man's eyes phased from wild to clear, or damn near, anyway. "Listen to me. He came back because of them. He came back! And that'll be it for me. That'll be it!"

"Who came back, sir?"

Face a belligerent mask, he glared at Parrott for a long, silent spell. When he spoke, it was a gruff whisper. "My father."

"Your father? Really?"

"Don't you get it? Don't you?"

"I'm afraid not, sir."

"My father is dead!"

Parrott felt a little jolt of surprise. "Maybe you saw someone who looked like your father?"

The man shook his head violently. "I know my own father, you fuckhead."

Beyond the fidgeting figure, out on Church Street, Parrott glimpsed a familiar vehicle approaching from the east. Sykes and Beamer.

Good timing, gentlemen.

Finally, some of the fire seemed to go out of the young man. In a softer, almost sad voice, he whined, "He was there, right by these trees. You should have seen him. I *saw* him! He went into those trees, right there. Right the fuck there!"

On the street, Sykes's cruiser rolled past and turned right onto Bondurant Street.

Parrott took a couple of steps forward and firmed his grip on the taser handle. "Sir, I need to know you're not armed. I want you to stand still. And get those arms out."

"Fuck you!" The voice remained defiant yet now sounded tearful. Frightened.

The sound of car doors closing echoed from a short distance behind him. And in seconds, Deputy Dan appeared on his left, Deputy Beamer on his right.

"Howdy, Sheriff." Sykes sent him a grim smile. "Heard the call. We weren't far away."

"Glad to see you." Parrott kept his voice low. "I don't know whether he's armed. He's unpredictable, possibly delusional. We need to get him under control."

"Say no more." Sykes moved toward the man and didn't stop until he was almost in touching distance. Two seconds behind him, Beamer stepped up as well.

The young man's feet stopped shuffling. "Leave me alone, or I'll cut you to pieces!"

"Let's get the arms out at your sides." Parrott's voice turned sharp. "Spread 'em out. Now!"

"Fuck you!" The man's right hand dropped toward his hoodie pocket. As he thrust it inside, Sykes struck with the speed of viper, grabbed the arm, and jerked the hand from the pocket. The man's right foot slid back to brace his weight, and he tugged hard to pull himself free of Sykes's grip. In a flash, Beamer was on him, and the smaller man toppled. Beamer went down with him, pinioning him with iron arms, leaving the other to thrash with impotent rage. Sykes knelt, leaned forward, and reached into the hoodie's right-hand pocket. When he withdrew his hand, a closed, five-inch folding knife came with it. Sykes tossed it onto the sidewalk out of harm's way and grabbed his handcuffs from the holder on his belt.

A moment later, with Beamer now tugging the man's arms behind his back, Sykes cuffed his wrists.

"Fuck you! Fuck you!" Spittle sprayed from the bellowing mouth with every outburst. "It's not me. Not me! It's all *them* people's fault!"

Between them, Sykes and Beamer managed to drag the young man to his feet. Beamer kept a firm grip on his right bicep to keep him from either toppling or attempting to flee.

Parrott gave Beamer an approving smile. "Not bad. Now I see why we've kept you, since you can't shoot worth a lick."

"Aww, Sheriff!"

The deputies tugged the distraught, now slumped figure toward Parrott's vehicle, and with one firm hand, Beamer pressed the man's upper body against the rear passenger door while Sykes ran his hands quickly and expertly over his clothing and body.

He shook his head. "Nothing. No ID on him. You want us to take him in?"

Parrott gazed at the now cowed-looking young man, pondering his options. The poor fucker was a mess. The small hospital in Aiken Mill was equipped to handle only so many mental cases, especially if they might prove dangerous. He knew, almost for a fact, they would not accept this one. Same story for the sole homeless shelter in town, which he knew to be sadly, perpetually full.

"Please do." His voice came out a low, dour grumble. "The fellow said he comes from Chatham." The little town lay about an hour away to the east. "Let's find out if he has any local connections or if we need to send him…somewhere else."

"Are we charging him?" Sykes asked.

"Disorderly conduct. We'll ignore him pulling the knife, but take it in and check it out. Just in case."

"Gotcha."

He left the deputies to haul the young man to their cruiser and trudged back toward the two women, who had watched the incident as if it had been an episode of their favorite TV crime drama.

"Ms. Edmonds. Ms. Piper." He nodded and touched the downward-slanting brim of his hat. "I gather neither of y'all have seen that man before."

"No, sir," Ms. Edmonds said. Ms. Piper, several inches shorter and a few pounds heavier than her friend, equally well dressed, shook her head.

Ms. Piper pointed to the poofy, orange-brown dog that sat on the sidewalk, watching him with big coffee-colored eyes and pink tongue hanging out. "Scared Tawny half to death."

Tawny. Mmm-hmm.

"So, no clue as to the man's identity?"

"No, sir," the women said in unison.

Parrott glanced back toward the mostly hidden house. "Did you see anyone else around here? Over by those trees, maybe?"

Ms. Edmonds smiled thinly. "Not at all. We haven't seen a soul here except that scary man."

"Do you know the folks who live in that house?"

Ms. Piper threw up her hand like a student who knew the answer to a verbal pop quiz. "Oh, that's Mr. Pritchett. Phillip Pritchett, I believe. Lives by himself." Her demeanor turned haughty. "Well, he has a dog. A big Golden Retriever. Seems to be good-natured, except he doesn't like Tawny." Now her face became a sour lemon. "If Mr. Pritchett walks his dog at the same time I do, my Tawny and I go the other way." Her face relaxed. "Most of the time, he walks his dog somewhere else."

"Is Mr. Prichett an older man?"

"Not at all. About forty, I'd say."

Again, he looked back at the Pritchett house. "Well, this young gentleman didn't appear to be casing the house or anything. Still, be sure and keep your doors locked, and please don't hesitate to report any suspicious activity you might see. Do you know whether Mr. Pritchett might be at home?"

"Oh, no, he works during the day."

"I see. Well, it doesn't look like anything untoward occurred on his property. I'll just give the place a quick glance on my way out."

"Thank you again, Sheriff," Ms. Edmonds said. "It's always nice to know we can count on you."

"That's my job, ma'am." He nodded again, touched the brim of his hat, and glanced at the dog, who yawned and looked away. "Have a nice walk, Tawny."

Tawny. Mmm-hmm.

He walked a short distance down the sidewalk, toward the dense wall of red cedars between the sidewalk and Mr. Pritchett's house. He found a small gap in the greenery and poked his head through. The house was smaller than most that bordered the historical district. He remembered that this one had replaced a much older and larger structure that had burned down back in the 1970s. He saw no car parked in the driveway, which curled from the front of the house to the far end of the cedars, where it connected with the street, just beyond his view.

He might yet want to speak to Mr. Pritchett, although he felt certain this was a random incident with a mentally disturbed young man. Parrott's problem now was figuring out just whose problem that son of a bitch was about to become.

Well, he thought, surely this situation would prove less baffling than his disappearing remains. The body parts might have vanished, but the mystery certainly hadn't.

ॐ

Chapter 14

"Dopamine, or DA, is a neurotransmitter and hormone, produced in the substantia nigra, the ventral tegmental area, and the hypothalamus. DA acts specifically on the brain's pleasure centers. Now, with Attention Deficit Hyperactive Disorder, there are numerous factors involved between the body's hormones, neurotransmitters, and the brain. Most researchers agree that a deficit of DA, or a problem with the brain processing it, is among the most significant."

True to form, fourteen of the fifteen faces in the small classroom appeared attentive. Also true to form, the one that didn't was turned toward the window that looked out on the four student dormitories, staggered like stairsteps up the green, red, and gold slope of the wooded ridge that ran the length of the campus's northwestern border.

"Mr. Sigmon, I'm fairly certain you don't suffer from ADHD, so I gather you're looking for smoke signals from your friends?"

The scruffy, black-bearded face turned on a slow swivel toward him. "Oh. Sorry, Dr. Pritchett."

A shameless creature of habit, young Mr. Sigmon had smelled of pot smoke, detectable all the way across the room, when he made his customary five-minute late entry to class.

Martin had preceded Mr. Sigmon by only a minute, which for him was the epitome of uncustomary. He glanced at Ms. Kolodny, whose disconcerting stare from the first row of desks had not shifted since the beginning of class. Although he was under no obligation to explain himself to a student, he felt a peculiar urge to offer some reason, not necessarily an honest one, for his tardiness, mainly so she might dim the intensity of those bright, magnified blue eyes. Although his demeanor prior to class might have appeared baffling to others—with good reason—he did not appreciate such intense scrutiny. Unfortunately, his stumbling over a few words during his lecture only heightened the young woman's curiosity. Thank God no one else in class appeared to be aware that something had rattled him. As it was, he had a tough enough time maintaining his composed facade, and this would-be inquisitor's gaze made it all the more difficult.

"Dopamine is only a part of the ADHD puzzle. DA works hand-in-hand with Norepinephrine, or NET, also a neurotransmitter and hormone, which activates the brain's fight-or-flight response. So, low levels of NET in the brain, or the brain's inability to process it—"

"*Come. Upstairs….*"

"—can cause an inappropriate response—"

A pale, blue sheen flickered into existence around the figures seated before him, and his voice became an alien-sounding crackle from somewhere outside him. At some point, he became dimly aware that he was no longer speaking.

From some vast distance, a whippoorwill's echoing voice warbled its eerie song.

"Dr. Pritchett?" It was the blue-eyed menace.

"*YOUR NAME IS INSCRIBED IN BLOOD IN THE BOOK OF THE DOOMED.*" A deep, deafening not-quite-a-voice.

"Dr. Pritchett?" Now from a chorus.

He felt his hand rise as if to ward away unseen attackers. "I think… I'm having a migraine." It was the first excuse his taut-stretched mind could formulate.

This is no migraine.

"Dr. Pritchett, I've got some pills…." He had no idea who was speaking.

The electric glow in his field of vision softened and vanished. He could see his classroom again. The fourteen concerned faces peering at him from around the room, the fifteenth gazing out the window at the ridge.

"Mr. Sigmon," he heard himself say. "You're still not paying attention. You know, either you or your parents are paying good money for you to come to class and learn. I hate to see money wasted. Especially your parents'." It was his rote reprimand for indifferent students.

"Sorry, Dr. Pritchett."

Bridgette Kolodny had risen to her feet, her eyes as big and bright as the illegal xenon headlights on his next-door neighbor's pickup truck. "Dr. Pritchett," she said, "I feel like you might need medical attention."

Maybe he did. But not now—not in the middle of class. If experience was any teacher, it assured him that, once these episodes passed, he would return to himself in short order. Unsettled, maybe, but still *himself*.

Until the next time.

"Sometimes," he managed, "a migraine starts up, hits hard, and then peters out." This, at any rate, he knew to be true. Years ago, he'd suffered them on occasion, but none since his twenties. "I'll be fine."

No. I WANT to be fine.

I might not be fine.

"Let's move on," he said, forcing the memory of that barrage of images and sensations to the dark internal depths where he shoved unwanted experiences, anything that interfered with his current priorities. "You may sit down, Ms. Kolodny. I appreciate your concern."

The bright eyes had not dimmed. "Are you sure, sir?"

"Quite sure." He forced a little smile that he hoped might convey gratitude. "Thank you, Bridgette."

"You're in denial," Alana would say. And she would be right.

Ms. Kolodny nodded and, with obvious reluctance, sat back down at her desk.

"All right, now. Moving on...."

#

Martin had never cared much for Dr. Larry Hoffman, head of Beckham College's psychology department. Smug, frequently condescending, he grated on nerves with every threshold he darkened.

No one alive knew more about every subject on Earth than Larry Hoffman, with the possible exceptions of President Braxton and Dean Stermer, in whose company he turned obsequious. As professionals, Martin and Hoffman maintained a superficially cordial relationship, although their every conversation held an undercurrent of mutual exasperation.

Hoffman had surely painted the expression of neighborly concern onto his drooping, thick-jowled face moments before entering Martin's office.

"I'm told you suffered—what, a migraine?—in the middle of class." His frown hinted more of disapproval than compassion. "You sure you're all right, Martin?"

"I used to get them with some regularity. It's been a long time, so it took me by surprise. They can be…unsettling."

Hoffman leaned across the desk to study Martin's face for a moment. "You do look a bit peaked."

"I haven't been sleeping that well lately. Stress, I suppose. But it's nothing to worry about."

"Things going all right with your classes?"

"They're fine. But you know how some of these kids get, especially the ones whose parents are paying for their eventual enlightenment."

"Not to mention our salaries."

"Admittedly."

Martin glimpsed a flicker of envy in Hoffman's eyes. "Your students all seem to like you. Especially that young woman who spoke to me after your class. She seemed very flustered when she thought you might be ill."

"What can I say? I'm just that lovable."

"Not too lovable, I hope."

Martin's voice turned sharp. "Don't even think about going there, Larry. I know you've had to deal with that kind of issue before, but if you don't know me better than that…."

Christ, he'd almost said, "…if you don't *fucking* know me…." Good that he didn't.

Hoffman held up an almost placating hand. "I know, I'm sorry. But to stay on the subject of your lovability, I gather you and Ms. Mendes are still, um, serious?"

"I'd say things are fairly serious."

"Good. That's good." The older man's slow delivery indicated he absolutely did not approve. He stared at the FloydFest poster on the wall while his mental machinery clanked and clunked. "Martin, your students have always maintained very good grade averages. But they've slipped a bit this quarter, haven't they?"

"A fraction. Hardly anything to worry about."

"I'm sure it's not." Hoffman's throat sounded like a buzzsaw as he drew a deep breath. "You know, it is my job to make sure everyone on my staff is performing at their peak. Beckham is a small college, and this isn't a very wealthy area anymore. You know how hard we all need to work to keep our accredited status."

"I don't think that's a problem, Larry. Certainly not for our department."

Hoffman's tone turned harsh. "That's top priority for every department. Look, I'm not here to be judgmental, or even uncomplimentary. You've put in a lot of years of fine work. I only want to make sure you're in tip-top shape." He leaned across the desk again. "You *are* all right, aren't you?"

"How much pressure are they putting on you, Larry?"

He scoffed. "You know this administration isn't pressuring me. I always take the long view, my friend. It's the only way to ensure that our work is a substantial and consistent benefit to this college."

"The selfless wonder, as always, Larry."

Hoffman's eyes narrowed. "I don't appreciate flippancy, Martin."

"Sorry." He sighed. "As I said, I'm a bit fatigued. But you have nothing to worry about. I'd hate to see you nursing another ulcer for no reason."

Hoffman stepped back from the desk and nodded to himself, satisfied he'd said what he came to say and had received something akin to the answers he wanted. His eyes rose to the two paintings on the wall. "Somebody painted those, right? Your brother, was it?"

"My brother, yes."

The small, pursed mouth opened and closed a couple of times before issuing any words. "Never had much use for artists. Not the modern ones, anyway."

Martin forced a little humor into his tone. "An odd lot, I suppose." He pointed to the paintings. "That one, I can safely say, is a bit odd."

Hoffman's spreading smile looked damn near affable. "You're a different sort, Martin. I hope you really are fine. We count on you a lot, you know."

"Thank you, Larry."

The smile faded and the narrow eyes lingered on him for a moment, as if the man feared he might have said something entirely too complimentary. Then he shrugged away his misgivings, turned, and walked out the door without another word. He closed it ungently behind him.

"Moron."

Oh, shit, that might have come out a little loud.

When Hoffman didn't reappear, Martin breathed a tad easier. He felt he might actually owe the man some measure of gratitude because, at last, his mind felt clear, his anxiety dispelled. Well, mostly. By diverting his attention to ordinary business, though hardly pleasant, Hoffman had helped recenter Martin's focus. And it was holding. He knew Alana was right—or would be, if she had any inkling of the severity of the episodes he'd suffered—that he was in denial. Anytime something in his life went severely wrong, denial became his first response.

For the love of God, he *knew* what conditions could cause hallucinations. He studied such things, taught such things, lived and breathed the fucking science.

No, he could not accept that it might be a brain tumor. Or schizoaffective disorder. Or that drugs or alcohol might come into play. The latter *could* not. Not drugs, anyway.

Focus on work. On his relationship with Alana. On his brother's upcoming wedding.

He made up his mind. At the onset of those sensory abnormalities, he had indulged them, not just allowed them to play out in the real world but forced them to. Now, he knew he needed to stay away from the House of Caviness. To ignore—or even throw out—all that mail he'd taken from the place. He would tell Phil he had too much work piled up to accompany him to Black Tooth Pond. Today, tomorrow, whenever.

And what the hell was playing out with Phil? Something similar, yet not the same.

Coincidence.

That was it.

That *had* to be it.

#

Phil hadn't answered Martin's call, which he made shortly after his brother's quitting time, so he left a voice mail indicating he would not be coming along for Rufus's afternoon walk.

After the nerve-shattering events of the day, the calm, clear-headed state he found himself enjoying now seemed unshakeable. The anxiety, while not entirely gone, occupied the lowest level of his consciousness, deep enough for his balanced, orderly state of mind to dwell at the forefront. He experienced a moment of pause when he gathered the stack of ancient pages, over which he'd labored so diligently, and placed them in a drawer of the filing cabinet in his tiny den at the back of the house. Upon viewing the news clipping that announced the explosion of the first hydrogen bomb, he felt a quick twinge of dismay and—what? Anger? As if the news story itself sparked a rush of negative emotion.

After he closed the file drawer, a powerful impulse to retrieve the pages commandeered his muscles, but only for a few seconds. With no small effort, he forced back the urge, withdrew from the den, and closed the door, at which moment his more serene, untroubled state returned.

There is nothing wrong in my brain.

NOTHING.

He had considered calling his brother again to ask whether he'd seen, heard, or done anything peculiar this afternoon at Black Tooth Pond, but he dismissed the idea. If Phil wanted to talk, he'd call back, since he didn't exactly share Martin's dubious gift of reticence. Above all, though, Martin had no desire to initiate a conversation that might disrupt his inner calm.

He made dinner for himself—the lamb chops he had originally planned for a couple of nights ago. Settled on the living room couch with his tablet, he read and graded several of the student essays, enough that he'd need only another two- to three-hour session to complete them. By the time he finished, he more than half-believed he *had* suffered a migraine during his afternoon class. Maybe it was indeed the answer to all his unsettling experiences of the past couple of days. He had initially discounted the possibility and held to that opinion, yet it might have been premature. Migraines could affect one's vision, the capacity to formulate coherent thoughts, even one's ability to speak intelligibly. They didn't always bring on headaches; sometimes, it was confusion, disorientation, optical distortion, and other disagreeable manifestations.

No. Beneath these increasingly desperate rationalizations, he knew these sensory anomalies he'd endured were *not* characteristic of migraines.

His rationalizations were characteristic of denial.

Still, he refused to dwell on the unknowns, to allow the stress of uncertainty to reassert itself and set him off-kilter.

He closed out the essay files. As he sometimes did in the evening, he switched over to his couple of social media accounts to take a brief look at the world and at least certain people outside of Aiken Mill. He wasn't very active online, but he did enjoy occasionally catching up with folks he'd known at school or otherwise, mostly from Richmond, plus a few old friends from his high school days. Between his accounts, he maintained a couple of hundred friends and followers. He did make a point to avoid interacting with any of his current students because *that*, he feared, could lead to complications that neither he nor they desired or needed.

Tonight, he had no intention of posting anything, only browsing. To his surprise, he noticed his friends' list had dwindled by a significant number since his last login, a few days ago. Rather than the familiar, more personal posts his "regular" friends generally put up, his feed displayed one saga of distressing news after another. Severe illnesses—COVID-19 in a few cases. Lost jobs. A deadly automobile accident. Jesus Christ, a suicide, even. And the actual news posts offered nothing more uplifting. Deadly fires in California. A plane crash near Chicago that killed all 137 passengers and crew aboard. Yet another school shooting. Not that the news ever offered much positive, but all this put together struck him as extreme.

How the hell did he lose almost a quarter of the individuals on his friends list in such a short time? He certainly hadn't posted anything that should have offended, insulted, or otherwise put off any of the folks he typically interacted with.

Feeling annoyed, he put his tablet to sleep and considered watching a movie. He hadn't done that in ages, and he probably had time to get through one before calling Alana. On nights they didn't get together, they had adopted the practice of talking on the phone, punctually at ten o'clock, for a half-hour or so. Even when they saw each other for lunch or at some other time during the day, that hardly counted for quality time. He always looked forward to the late-evening talks and getting to know her better. Tonight, more than ever.

He preferred serious films to comedies, although he had the idea that, after today, ninety minutes or so of mindless humor might be his best option. He turned on the big-screen TV he almost never used and was about to search for some apt movie selections when, on the end table next to him, his phone burred softly. Probably Phil, he thought, but then he realized it wasn't the custom ringtone he'd programmed for his brother. He didn't recognize the number, though it appeared to be local. This hardly ruled out a scam call, which was why he rarely answered if he didn't recognize the caller. But some vague, intuitive sense prompted him to take it.

"Hello?"

"Marty? Hi. This is Carli."

A tremor of apprehension shook him to full alertness. "Hey, what's up?"

"Sorry to bother you, but Phil gave me your number a while back. He isn't with you, is he?"

"No. I haven't talked to him all evening."

"Oh, I see." She sounded disappointed. Worried. "So, you didn't go out walking with him."

"No. What's going on?"

"I tried calling him a while ago, and the first couple of times, he didn't answer. But then it sounded like he did pick up. I could hear some noise in the background, but he didn't say anything. I know service can be sketchy out where he walks, so I didn't worry too much. But he's been gone so long, I finally came over to his house. Here's the weird thing. Rufus is still here. It looks like he didn't even take his dog with him."

"Really?" Martin felt the unwelcome, prickly fingers of anxiety creeping out from the back of his mind. "Well, maybe he came home and then went back out for something. The grocery store, maybe?"

"In that case, you'd think he'd answer his phone."

"Yeah, you would. I could try calling him. Maybe I'll have better luck."

"If you wouldn't mind."

"Not at all. One of us will be getting back to you shortly."

"Thank you, Marty. I do hate to bother you like this."

"No worries. Stand by, all right?"

"Okay. Bye."

Thunder rolled in his ears, and he realized it was the pounding of his heart. *Damn, damn, damn.* What the hell was going on now? He punched Phil's number and listened to the rings purr from his phone speaker.

After four, the rings stopped, followed by a hollow sound and then a faint scratching and scraping. Sounds of movement, he thought. Then Phil's low voice echoed from what seemed a vast distance.

"Hello, Marty."

"Phil." He swallowed hard. "Where are you?"

"I am here."

"At the old house?"

A long silence. "It's so beautiful. So unreal. You need to see this."

Son of a bitch, that was it. Phil was doing drugs again. Lord knew what variety.

"Carli's been trying to reach you. Is everything all right?"

"I'm not sure where I am now. But it's beautiful, I tell you. There's a long hallway, and it's lit with blue and gold. It goes on and on."

"Did you take something? Acid, maybe?"

For a long moment, his brother didn't speak. "I'm hearing something now. It's kinda strange."

"Phil. You are on something. What did you take?"

The scratching and rasping in the background grew louder. Phil's voice came again, but the other noises rendered his words unintelligible.

Then it came. His brother's unique and certainly peculiar vocalization: the cry of a whippoorwill. Almost deafening over the speaker. Again. And again.

"God damn, Phil!"

The cries stopped, and a series of low scuffling sounds murmured from the speaker. Those too faded. Then the resonant hollowness that meant the call was connected dulled and died. Phil's number vanished from the glowing display.

"Son of a bitch," he muttered to the air. "What the fuck is wrong with you, Phil?"

I should talk.

He switched to his call log and touched the previous entry to reconnect with Carli. She answered after the first ring.

"Hey, Marty."

"I got through briefly, but we were disconnected." The last thing he wanted to do now was to tell her that her fiancé was fucked up on something. That news would not sit well with her, and *he* would end up the proverbial messenger that people loved to shoot. "I think he's fine, but it sounds like he's still out at the pond."

"Are you sure he's all right?"

Think fast.

"You know, when he and I were talking the other day, I could tell he's got some jitters. Nothing serious, but you know how he overthinks things. Kind of like his older brother." He grunted something like a laugh. "He's been a loner for a long time, you know, and I think he's just sanding down those last rough edges in his mind about, uh, let's say, his change of status."

Liar, liar.

She sighed. "I understand what you're saying, but I thought he was long past anything like that." She sounded annoyed. "So, you think that's all it is?"

"Pretty sure."

Pants on fire.

"Should I go out there?"

"God, no," he said, too quickly. "But maybe I should."

"Wait. You *are* worried about him, aren't you? Should I be worried?"

"Actually…." He trailed off. "Let's not either of us jump the gun. It might do more harm than good to intervene, to intrude on him. Are you willing to give him a little more time?"

"Maybe. I don't mind saying that this makes me very uncomfortable."

"I understand."

A long silence. Martin knew he was merely buying time. If Phil were really tripping on something, it might be hours before he came out of it. And out in that environment, he could seriously injure himself. "If you're sure," she said at last. "I really do want to talk to him. If he's having reservations, we can't put off dealing with them."

"I know. Look, I don't believe this is an issue. I know how he feels about you."

"He's been so distant these past few days. Locking himself away painting. Going out to that place. But I've still trusted that he loves me."

"He does."

"All right, Martin. If you hear anything from him, please get him to call me. Or come home. Otherwise, please, please call me."

"I will."

"Thank you."

"Anytime, Carli."

They hung up at the same time. Well, so much for a movie, so much for anything resembling peace of mind, and so much for *not* going out to Black Tooth Pond and the House of Caviness.

The way he saw it, he had no choice.

Chapter 15

O nce he'd pulled off Old Beckham Road and driven a short distance down the bumpy dirt track toward Black Tooth Pond, Martin's headlight beams flashed on a metallic surface. There it was, Phil's truck, parked in its customary spot close to the edge of the pond, which now hid behind a veil of unbroken darkness. He rolled his SUV to a stop behind the Tacoma and shut off the engine. He left the headlights on, reluctant to allow the night to swallow him quite yet. On his first nighttime excursion here, the darkness had not intimidated him, at least initially. He was accustomed to darkness, felt comfortable with it. After sunset, it surrounded his home, cloaking the woods behind his house like a solid, seamless mantle.

Since that first night here, though, his world had changed. Now, the darkness felt like a sentient, secretive entity, watching and calculating, its intent anything but benign.

Still, he could hardly have refused this task, this mission: to bring his brother back, physically and, hopefully, mentally. Phil had almost certainly dropped acid, his compound of choice for taking trips back in the day. Martin couldn't deny his disappointment, even anger, that he had believed his brother without qualm when he said he no longer partook of such mind-altering chemicals. Yet, even now, some small doubt nagged at him, insisted that Phil had indeed told him the truth. But this was not a reasonable prospect. Better to accept that Phil had lied, for if he hadn't, it meant Martin must accept and face something not sane.

He knew he would find his brother inside the House of Caviness. And damn Phil to hell for forcing him to violate his resolution to stay away from this place on the very night he had made it. He had reluctantly texted Alana to let her know that Phil was having "issues," and he might be late calling her if he could manage it at all. He hated to put her off, but at least she understood his concern for his brother, if not the actual reasons for it. He'd promised to call as soon as he could. She told him to please call at any hour.

Jesus, the idea of anything undermining the solid relationship they were building burned like virulent acid in his guts. She might understand, even empathize with his desire to help his brother, but this was not solely Phil's "issue."

He flicked off the headlights and heavy, oppressive darkness fell over him. He reached for his flashlight on the passenger seat, and the moment his fingers closed around it, he switched it on. The beam hit the windshield and dispersed, brightening the Rogue's interior without revealing much beyond the glass. He heaved the door open, slid out of the seat, and sent the beam roaming around the immediate area. To his right, the circle of brilliance fell on a thin barrier of tall reeds and, beyond it, the slightly rippling surface of the pond. When he shifted the light to his left, it revealed only an impenetrable wall of trees and tangled brush.

He ambled around Phil's truck, and the beam illuminated the path they had trodden together many times, neither ever considering that this location might become the backdrop for some psychological crisis that encompassed them both. And why would they? How *could* they? As he set out on the path, the chill in the nighttime air seemed to presage more than the mere maturing of the season. More than anything, he wished his flashlight beam would reveal his brother approaching from the depths of the woods, healthy, sober, and appropriately contrite.

Not a bet on which to stake a fortune.

He trudged on for a time; reached the huge, fallen poplar and the flattened saplings; moved past them onto the narrower, winding path that led toward the house. No sound other than the crunching and clumping of his footsteps issued from the woods. Soon enough, the close-pressing trees on either side of the path thinned, and he came to an expanse of dense black that his light could barely penetrate. He paused to make sure of his bearings. Yes, a short distance ahead and to the left, his beam crawled over a veritable wall of glistening, green-black leaves, and he knew he stood before the massive magnolia that rose like a glowering, cyclopean sentry at the threshold of the House of Caviness.

And there it was, a short distance beyond the big tree: the web of tangled, knotted vines and creepers that clung to the walls and sharply angled roof of the old structure. The trunk of the huge sycamore that had forced its way through rafters and shingles to reach the sky. The splintered wooden siding and grimy windows, which stared back like dark, devious eyes. The gaping doorway through which he and his brother had made their ingress on their previous explorations. He switched off his flashlight long enough for his eyes to adjust to the darkness. Not so much as a glimmer anywhere inside the old house. He flicked the flashlight back on and started toward the door.

As he navigated the now well-trodden path through the brambles, his first impulse was to call his brother's name, but the silent night seemed inimical to such a brazen transgression. If Phil were prowling around in that old hulk, wouldn't at least a glimmer from his flashlight betray his presence, either in the windows or the open doorway?

No light. No sound of movement.

But his brother was here. He *had* to be here.

Martin reached the yawning doorway and thrust his flashlight inside. The beam swept over the dust-coated floorboards, the decrepit furnishings, the cracked plaster walls. The sharp odor of age and mildew wafted from within and seeped into his nostrils. He took a deep, bracing breath and, with a silent growl of mental protest, stepped inside.

He moved farther inside and aimed his flashlight into the open door at the room's far end. It fell upon the pale gray trunk of the invading sycamore. He turned the light toward the ascending staircase with its cracked, tilted banister. Phil said he had gone upstairs previously. If he was up there now, surely, even a slight movement would betray his presence by way of groaning, creaking floorboards.

Now, he couldn't hold back his voice.

"Phil! Where the hell are you?"

Nothing.

"I'm kinda mad at you."

Something up there popped, like a loose floorboard snapping into place. A soft, whispery, sliding sound followed. More likely a critter than his brother, he thought with dismay.

But then came a rough, heavy lumbering noise, moving across a wide space. Floorboards groaning, not directly above him but to his left, near the old fireplace at the far end of the living room. He took a few more steps forward and aimed his light toward the top of the stairwell. From this angle, it didn't reach all the way up. He advanced one more step, wary of the gaping holes in the floor to his right. Now, his beam lit the stained, gray paneling of a perpendicular wall. Apparently, this flight led to a small landing, and there the stairs turned left.

Somewhere—whether inside or outside the house, he couldn't tell—something made a soft warbling sound.

A whippoorwill?

It sounded *almost* like the opening notes of a whippoorwill's song, but they stopped short of a full verse.

Phil working on his birdcall?

He did not hold back. "Phillip fucking Pritchett, where are you, and what are you doing?"

The echo of his voice rang through the house like the cry of a wounded animal.

Won't do that again!

The last time he'd stood in this room, he had fled, nerves shaken, senses confused, imagination triggered by what he'd perceived as a beckoning voice.

"Come. Upstairs...."

Damn all that. Damn the hallucinations. Damn everything but finding Phil and getting the fuck back home.

No further warbling noise, no creaks, no slithers.

Silence.

He placed one foot on the lowest stair and started up. Slow, careful steps, wary of any sudden shifts of weight. Hands off the banister, for even slight pressure might topple it. With each step higher, a hot, sour smell grew and curled around him like questing, ethereal tendrils. He couldn't identify either what or where the odor came from. Not something dead.

This was something different.

At the landing, he tested the floorboards several times before risking his full weight upon them. Phil had indicated the stairs had been sturdy.

So far, so good.

He took the last three steps to the top, where his light revealed a hallway that extended out of sight. Just ahead, another hall turned to the right. Past the opening to the adjacent hall, he saw on either side of the corridor a series of doors, all closed. Somehow, his light did not reach the far end. The passage stretched before him for some unknown distance before vanishing into a lightless void.

What?

The entire house could not be *that* long. Hell, in pitch darkness, if he stood at one end of a football field, his flashlight could illuminate the goalposts at the far end. He glanced back down the stairs to check his bearings. Yes, unless he completely misjudged the length of the house from outside, the hallway before him should end no more than twenty feet ahead. By all rights, his light *should* illuminate the length of the hallway, not die in a field of unbroken darkness.

He turned the beam down the intersecting corridor to his right. Here, too, the light groped its way a short distance before darkness swallowed it.

"What in God's name?"

Wait. Am I—?

Hallucinating again!

It *had* to be the answer. Physics didn't simply take a holiday. During his prior episodes, despite seeing and feeling the false sensations his brain concocted, somewhere deep inside, he'd maintained some tenuous grip on reality. This was not the same.

At all.

He recalled Phil's words from earlier this evening, while they were speaking on the phone: "I'm not sure where I am now." He'd been *here*. Upstairs, in this house.

He knew that he and Phil did not—*could not*—suffer Shared Psychotic Disorder, a rare condition where two individuals in a close relationship shared identical delusions, induced by the dominant partner.

No. This was reality.

He felt his respiration increasing, his pulse beginning to race. Since the hallucinations had begun, he'd felt unsettled, apprehensive, anxious.

Disbelieving.

Now, he was terrified. He tried to cling to the single rational reason for his presence here: to find his brother. It was his anchor to sanity. But where could Phil be? No matter what his eyes told him, this house could only be so big.

Damnation. He had ignored what might be the simplest solution of all. He reached for his phone in his back pocket. Dialed Phil's number. If nothing else, he might hear the other phone ringing somewhere in the house.

At first, the speaker issued a few clicks and hisses, as if his phone were attempting to connect. Then he heard a single, muted ring before his phone dropped the call. With a wordless snarl, he redialed the number. An identical disconnection. Not a hint of sound—or light— in the surrounding darkness to indicate that Phil's phone might be anywhere nearby.

His leg muscles quivered, as if they intended on carrying him of their own volition back downstairs and to his SUV. Now more than ever, he wanted to be free of this place and, once gone, abide by his resolution to never revisit it. But he couldn't do that. Phil might be an adult, responsible for his own welfare, but after all that had happened, Martin could not consider abandoning him.

This was his mission.

The strong, sour odor on this floor caused his stomach to flutter. He tried breathing through his mouth to spare his nostrils the worst of the stench. It helped a little. Forcing his muscles into action, he started down the seemingly endless hallway toward the series of doors, leading with his flashlight, picking each step carefully in case the floor should prove less solid than it appeared.

After a few feet, he switched off the light, scanned the darkness for any flicker, any hint of a light that might belong to his brother. Failing to see such a sign, he turned the light back on and continued his slow progress deeper and deeper into the unknown depths of a darkness that should not, *could* not exist. Not in any sane world.

At the first door on his right, he reached for the doorknob and tested it. Locked.

Same with the door across the hall.

Fuck this.

Then....

Did he hear something? Not an echo. He stopped walking, held his breath, and listened. At first, he wondered if he'd mistaken the thudding of his heart for some external sound because, for a very long moment, no other sound reached him. But then he detected, fainter than a distant whisper, a low, repetitive murmur.

Wait. Was that the warble of a whippoorwill? Almost, but no. More like a mumbling human voice, at the farthest edge of his hearing.

Several steps farther, and he came to two more doors, where he paused to listen, but he didn't bother rattling the knobs. No, the sound drifted from somewhere still farther ahead—inside that well of pitch-black nothing, which his light could not penetrate. The floor remained sturdy beneath his feet, so he picked up his pace a little. Again, he switched the flashlight off. This time, far ahead in the impossible distance, he thought—*maybe*—his eyes had discerned some vague, bluish glimmer.

"*There's a long hallway, and it's lit with blue and gold. It goes on and on.*"

Yes. A small sphere of bluish radiance, God knew how far away.

Light back on, he turned and peered back in the direction he had come.

"No. No way."

He saw the top of the stairs he had ascended only a few yards away, as if in the past several minutes he had taken no more than a dozen steps into this hallway.

Despite fighting like a tiger against it, he had already abandoned his lifelong notion that reality was an immutable, rock-solid companion. Yet, faced with the impossibility before him, his muscles became gelatin, and his body sagged until his knees impacted firm, immovable floorboards with an audible crunch. The infiltration of hellish fumes burned his lungs. And now, with the bitterness of despair, he began to believe that his thundering heartbeat, the rush of blood in his veins, the workings of his nervous system, *these* were the hallucination, and all this other—the insane, the impossible, the intolerable—had become his only reality.

"Bless this house. Bless it, and those within, with all your grace."

Distant but comprehensible words. Faraway, yet deep and resonant.

He thought he recognized the voice. He drew himself back to his feet, and after a couple of steadying breaths, resumed his slow trek toward the island of light that might be some yards or a hundred miles away.

More distant mumbling, and then the louder, clearer voice again. "Bless this house. Bless these souls. Bless all who enter in."

Within the field of dim, electric blue, he detected movement. Nothing more than indistinct shadows, but he felt a little surge of hope that, ahead, he might find his brother. That sphere of light appeared larger now, and his feet moved faster of their own accord. But then he paused, swung his flashlight around toward the stairs, and glanced back.

Still, the distance had not increased.

He felt he must be traversing *different* space, a dimension that both occupied the house and somehow remained *apart* from it. Theoretically, philosophically, he might find this concept fascinating—from his classroom, from his office, from home—but not here, inside the heart of an incomprehensible domain.

Some remaining shred of sense prompted him to reach into his pocket, retrieve his phone, and begin recording a video.

Phone in one hand, flashlight in the other, he continued his forward progress, such as it was. Now he saw what looked like veins or rivulets of hot gold streaming down and around the edges of the increasingly large blue sphere, drawing a brilliant boundary that separated the illuminated field from the surrounding blackness.

"The blue and the gold," he whispered.

Then, with one step more, the blue field expanded and enveloped him. The intense radiance burned his retinas, forced his eyes to close.

The smell. Jesus Christ, that sickening smell!

The odor, so hot, so scorching, seemed to surge through his skull and into his entire body. Then, almost immediately, it dissipated, and he smelled…nothing.

Beyond his eyelids, he sensed a diminishing of the brilliance and opened them as far as a narrow squint. Nothing burned his eyes, so—after a moment to prepare his mind for some unfathomable, unknown sight—he risked opening them wide.

The icy blue hue had blended with a touch of violet, which softened its intensity. The light emanated from some unseen source, with no visible center. The color tinted the walls and furnishings of a room somewhat smaller than the house's living room, but as dilapidated as any space inside the House of Caviness: a warped, dusty floor; peeling, cracked walls; furnishings in various states of disrepair.

This room was occupied.

Was it?

Martin's vision seemed blurred, hazy. It was hard to make out anything clearly. He panned the camera lens around, so maybe it would capture what his eyes would not.

Seven figures stood at various points around the room. One of them was Phil. He leaned against the wall in the far corner to Martin's right, arms at his sides, head slightly tilted to regard his brother, the newcomer. The light painted his face a pale, corpselike gray-blue. A half-smile formed on his lips, and he said without inflection, "Hi, Marty."

The other recognizable figure was the big, black-suited man he had seen the other day at lunchtime—first at the river, from the restaurant windows, and then in the college's courtyard, where he had spouted his dire proclamations and handed Martin the scrawled sheet that read, *"YOUR NAME IS INSCRIBED IN BLOOD IN THE BOOK OF THE DOOMED."*

It was his voice Martin had heard back in that space-defying corridor.

The widely spaced, huge eyes regarded him without expression, as if Martin's presence meant nothing to him.

The other five figures—if figures they were—baffled Martin's senses. They resembled human bodies, or they almost did: dark, hazy, *insubstantial*, like shadows that had half-assumed some kind of substance. Motionless and featureless, they might have been molded from smoke that somehow held its shape.

Ghosts.

Five of them.

The Caviness family?

He stared at Phil, wondering whether his brother understood what was happening. He must, at least on some level, for he had visited here before. But words fell short of reaching his lips, as if some disconnect existed between his mind and his vocal cords. With supreme determination and effort, he managed, "Where are we?" His voice sounded like a frog croaking.

Phil shifted his eyes and pointed to the black-suited figure. "I don't know. It belongs to him, I think."

The smoke figures wavered in and out of focus, as if whatever force that held them together waxed and waned every few seconds.

Martin glared at the man in the black suit. Again, forcing out words required near-painful effort. "Who are you?"

As when Martin had encountered the man in the courtyard, one hand rose to point at him. This time, the deep voice boomed, "Look what is rising around you. Do you see? *Can* you see?" The pointing hand moved to cover the man's heart. "There are things you should not disturb, but you, the heedless, pay no mind!"

Phil spoke again. "He does that a lot, says things like that. I don't think he's really here, though. He's more like some kind of projection, I think."

The wide eyes continued to stare at Martin, but the man did not move or speak again.

Again, he felt a vague sense of recognition. Yes. The man's eyes. The dark, widely spaced *Caviness* eyes.

"Where are we, Phil?" He made a sweeping gesture with his phone hand around the blue-lit room. "Where is *here*?" He took a cautious step toward the nearest smoke figure. It wavered in and out of focus but otherwise did not move. He focused his camera lens directly on it. "Are these Caviness ghosts?"

"I don't think they're ghosts." Phil stared with dreamy eyes at one of the figures. "If you look at them long enough, you'll see things. Faraway things. Incredible things."

Martin focused on the nearby shape, traced its contours, peered into its slowly swirling and shifting essence. After a moment, he felt a disagreeable, swimmy sensation in his head, as if he were falling from a great height, and he tore his eyes away.

"It might be uncomfortable at first. You can see…places. Like no places you've ever seen before."

"This feels dangerous."

Phil shrugged. "It's incredible."

Martin heard what sounded like a train rumbling in the distance. At first, faint with a hollow echo. Then it grew louder, less like a train than an approaching tornado. A sharp scratching at the back of his neck warned of danger.

"What is that?" he whispered.

"Don't look at it."

"At what? Where?"

Sound and shadow swept over him like a cataract. Cold—*frigid*—air gripped him, and he felt a force, almost a wind but not quite, batter him and set him off balance. The blue-lit room rippled and came apart like a reflection on a pond's surface disturbed by a tossed rock. Shapeless bands of light and shadow blended, separated, and whirled past his field of vision.

For a moment, he swore that his brain, his *mind*, tore itself from his physical body, came apart at the seams, and, propelled by an unearthly cyclone, dispersed into the farthest, darkest reaches of outer space.

#

The night air had grown chilly indeed.

"Carli wanted me to—" For a moment, Martin wasn't sure what he meant to say. Something in his mind clicked, yet remained unclear. "Goddamn, what the fuck just happened?"

His brother walked a few steps behind him on the trail that led back to the pond. "Something. It was beautiful, wasn't it?"

He stopped, turned around, and faced Phil. In the LED light, his brother's face resembled a shimmering ghost's. He realized he held his phone in his one hand. He didn't remember taking it out either. He slipped it back into his pocket. "What are you talking about?"

Phil shrugged. "Colors. Shapes. Inside that house. Pretty damned weird, huh?"

"I don't understand what you mean."

"I don't get it either."

Phil seemed way too out of it. What had Martin thought earlier? That his brother had dropped acid? That seemed right.

"Correct," not *"right."*

"You need to get back home. Carli's going to be livid."

For the first time, Phil exhibited genuine, appropriate emotion. "Jesus. Yeah, I do not want to fuck this up. Tell me, I haven't fucked up. Please."

"I don't know. But you owe her a responsible, grown-up husband, not a well-past-college-age delinquent."

"I'm not sure what's happening, Marty. You know, you've been a little off too."

"*I only want to make sure you're in tip-top shape. You ARE all right, aren't you?*"

Yeah, Larry Fucking Hoffman, I'm fine.

"Don't worry about me," he said. "I'm not the one getting married. That's where your focus needs to be."

"Thanks, Dad."

It was not worth a retort, though he probably *had* sounded too much like their father. And, yes, he did have his relationship with Alana to think about. At least he had alerted her to the possibility that he might be late talking with her tonight. It was already almost ten o'clock.

That didn't seem right.

Ahead, beyond a cluster of spindly cedar trees, Martin's flashlight beam glinted on the front end of Phil's Tacoma.

"You want me to follow you back to your place?" he asked.

"Nah, that's way out of your way. I'm fine. How the hell did it get this late?"

Martin turned and gazed past Phil, back in the direction of the House of Caviness. No specific images would form in his mind. A blue light, maybe? Other people besides the two of them? Inside his mind, something twisted and turned.

Where the living fuck HAD all that time gone?

He swallowed hard as the realization of how much time he—and his brother—had lost settled on him. "That is exactly what I would like to know."

THE HOUSE AT BLACK TOOTH POND
VII. THURSDAY

Chapter 16

Sheriff Parrott didn't like to bring interviewees into the interrogation room—a.k.a. The Lounge—in handcuffs unless he suspected the individual might harm himself or others. Once their newest John Doe had cooled off overnight in a cell, he seemed not only less belligerent but damned near docile. Alcohol and drug tests had come back negative. And, almost surprisingly, a search for matching fingerprints returned no results. Nothing about his folding knife indicated it had been used in any crime. With a reasonable semblance of competence, John had waived his right to an attorney. So, at 0900, Deputy Beamer escorted the uncuffed man to the Lounge, saw him seated comfortably, or reasonably so, at the small table in center of the sterile, fluorescent-lit room, and promised that the sheriff would attend to him shortly.

Dr. Julianne "Jules" Cheung, Parrott's go-to psychiatrist for cases that involved possible mental issues, was the closest thing to a criminal psychologist Aiken Mill had to offer. Happily for him, she had been available this morning to help facilitate a productive interrogation. A short, stocky, well-dressed, and perpetually harried woman of fifty-something, she accompanied the sheriff to The Lounge carrying her briefcase and a Styrofoam cup of steaming black coffee from the coffeemaker in his office, not the diesel fuel that Farley MacBane made for everyone else.

"Short and simple questions," Cheung warned. "The less you rile him, the quicker and easier you'll get results."

"Indeed," he said as he led the way into the room. It was the same advice she gave every time she attended an interrogation. He closed the door behind them.

John Doe's widely spaced, almost-black eyes focused on them, his face a wary frown. Parrott sat down in the cushioned wooden chair directly across from him, while Cheung seated herself at the end of the table so she could face them both. She popped her briefcase open and withdrew a spiral notebook and a pen. John's eyes stared holes in the two-way glass window next to the door, which suggested to Parrott that, despite no fingerprint evidence, he might have spent time in similar environments before. These days, the little room on the other side of the glass remained mostly unoccupied, the proceedings in The Lounge recorded by an unobtrusive little camera above the door.

Sheriff Parrott had determined that, a couple of weeks ago, John had spent a few nights at the homeless shelter over on Bridge Street before they'd booted him for unacceptable behavior. No one down there could offer any insight about either his origins or his subsequent whereabouts.

"Good morning, sir. I'm hoping we might have a little talk now," Parrott said to the man. "My friend here is Dr. Cheung. She's here to listen and, if necessary, offer medical opinions. That's all. She cannot provide you with any legal advice. I understand you waived your right to an attorney. Is that correct?"

A desultory nod as the dark eyes locked on Cheung's.

"I take that as a yes?"

"Yuh."

"All right, sir. Would you mind telling me your name?"

The stare shifted to Parrott and lingered for a long, silent spell. At last, he said, "Robert."

"Okay, Robert. What about a last name?"

He shook his head.

Parrott's eyes shifted to Cheung, who glanced downward and

then at him. "All right. We'll not worry about that just now. Yesterday, you said you came from Chatham. That's Chatham, Virginia, right?"

After appearing to consider the question for a long moment, he nodded.

"What brings you to Aiken Mill?"

Parrott now expected the long silence before the response. "Family," Robert mumbled.

"Your family lives in Aiken Mill?"

"Some did."

"Did? Not anymore?"

Robert gave a little shrug and glared at the ceiling.

"Have you ever lived in Aiken Mill?"

A slow shake of the head.

"When did you arrive from Chatham?"

His gaze swung back to meet Parrott's. "I dunno. Pretty good while ago."

"Days? Weeks?"

"I dunno, Pretty good while ago."

Parrott passed on the question. "Do you have a car? Did you drive here?"

He shook his head. "Walked. Rode with people. I think. I dunno."

"But you felt it was important to come to Aiken Mill?"

"Hadda go somewhere."

"Where in Aiken Mill are you staying?"

The sound he made was almost a snicker. "Wherever the fuck I want."

"Manners, please, Robert. Now, you said your father is dead. But you saw him yesterday?"

Robert's eyes darted back and forth several times. The pupils appeared huge and black. "Dead. Yeah. But he come back."

Cheung pursed her lips to indicate Parrott should tread carefully. He gave her a subtle nod and looked back at the young man. "Did your father live in Aiken Mill?"

"Long time ago."

In a flash, an idea struck him. "How about Rhode Island?"

"I dunno."

"Are you sure? Maybe Providence, Rhode Island?"

"I dunno."

"So, you don't know where he lived last?"

Robert shrugged.

"How did your father die?"

"I dunno."

"But he died in Aiken Mill?"

"Yuh. I think so."

"You think so? Robert, are you certain your father is dead?"

The black marble eyes widened and again rolled back and forth. The fingers of one hand, which rested on the table, twitched a few times. He said nothing.

"Robert?"

No response.

Parrott decided to try something else. "All right. Would you please tell me your father's name?"

Now, a vehement shake of the head.

Parrott noticed that Cheung folded her hands together, so he sat back in his chair and let the younger man simmer down for a minute or so. She took the opportunity to scribble some notes on her pad. Once Robert appeared somewhat less agitated, Parrott asked, "Is your last name Lydell?"

For a time, Parrott didn't think he was going to answer. The opaque eyes now appeared worn out, lifeless. "Not my name," he finally said.

Cheung raised one eyebrow, which meant he might try digging a little deeper. "Do you know anyone named Lydell?"

Robert's jaw dropped as if he intended to speak, but nothing came out.

"Are you all right?"

The man's blank stare remained fixed on the wall behind Parrott. Then, in a low, hoarse voice, he said, "He wanted to find out if it was over."

Parrott leaned in close, his curiosity aroused. "Find out if what was over?"

The eyes never shifted. "The slipping away."

After that, Robert refused to speak again.

Parrott heard Cheung whisper, "I think he's done."

"I think he is." He took a long, appraising look at the defeated-looking figure. Then, exhaling something between a sigh and a groan, he scooted his chair back and stood up.

She offered him a faint smile. "You're getting better at these interviews."

"And after only decades of practice."

Cheung rose, gathered her belongings, and followed him out the door. Deputy Beamer was waiting in the hallway and, without prompting, headed into The Lounge to take Robert back to his cell. Parrott continued toward his office with Cheung in tow.

Before he sat down at his desk, he poured himself a fresh mug of Juan Valdez. He held up the nearly empty pot. "You want to kill this?"

She shook her head. "I don't need a case of the jitters." She tossed her empty cup in the green metal trash can next to his desk.

"More for me." He sat down and took a long sip from his mug. "Figuring out what to do with our new friend Robert ought to be fun. As in not at all."

She remained standing. "From what you'd told me, I was surprised to see him so subdued."

He nodded. "Yesterday, my deputies stopped him just as he was about to go full slice-and-dice."

"No drugs in his system?"

"None that we test for."

"He didn't blow up on us, although it looked like he wanted to a couple of times." She glanced at her notepad. "After what you told me about yesterday, my first thought was Intermittent Explosive Disorder, but if that were the case and something set him off, he'd *really* go off. He does seem to be delusional regarding his father. It'll take more observation to work up a diagnosis. He should be hospitalized. You might want to work on getting a court order to do so before you end up with an emergency."

Parrott nodded. "My thought exactly. Anyway, without going into dull detail, I have a feeling about this guy. Might relate to another case that's giving me a headache. Then again, it might not. Don't know which I'd find more frustrating."

"You asked him about the name Lydell."

Parrott nodded.

"That's not very vague."

"Best I can do right now."

"Bryce, I'm late for another appointment. I so appreciate you adding to my workload. Again." She stashed her notepad and pen back in her briefcase, rose from her chair, and started for his office door.

He sent her a wry smile. "You're worth every penny, you know."

"You're not the one who pays me."

"I'll leave you positive feedback."

She didn't look at him as she made her exit. He took another swallow of coffee and was about to call Farley MacBane at the front desk to inquire whether Northeastern Labs in Roanoke had returned his call about the mud samples from Mr. Lydell's vehicle when his office phone rang. He picked it up and answered, "Sheriff Parrott here."

Fortuitous timing. It was MacBane. "Sheriff, Northeastern Labs called back. They said it's still going to be a few more days before they get to your samples. Quote: 'We're overworked and understaffed, and we have several high-priority cases. You're not that far down the queue, so be patient.' Unquote. The lady sounded snippy."

"Well, I kind of hate that."

"I didn't like it either."

"Thank you, Farley."

"No problem."

Well, *quelle surprise.* He had labeled the samples "URGENT," but in the world outside of Aiken Mill, anything *from* Aiken Mill unfailingly moved to the end of the order of operations.

Once cleared of that distraction, his mind zoomed back a few minutes. Robert's final statement had stuck in his memory like a magnet to cast iron.

"'The slipping away.'" He whispered it to his office and heard it echo inside his skull.

Whatever might be going on—or not—inside Robert's head, the man had been surprisingly forthcoming on several counts. Far less so on others. He had remained adamantly silent regarding his family's name. Parrott wasn't entirely sure why he'd made any connection between Robert and the very vanished Frank Lydell, but now that he had, he couldn't—and wouldn't—let it go. Intuition had always served him well, much like his father's intuition had served him.

Pity that it hadn't at the very end. Or maybe it had, but for his father, duty always came first.

What a difference in Robert's demeanor since yesterday. Certain questions riled him, but at no time did Parrott sense that he might become violent, as he had on the previous day. As Jules Cheung had said, he should get a court order so his department could legally hospitalize the man, since he was mentally incapable and they had no way to contact relatives or any other legal representative.

Robert had said his last name wasn't Lydell. Parrott couldn't be certain that their vanished victim's name was, either.

Chapter 17

Most of the time, Robert's thoughts, memories, and ideas were like messages emblazoned on the cars of a moving freight train, viewed by an impatient driver stuck at a railroad crossing. Just as he began to process the information from one car, it passed out of view, to be replaced by another and then another. If several successive cars bore identical messages, they might resolve into clear focus for a time. Regardless, once the cars had passed, his ability to hold onto whatever concept his brain had pieced together lingered only briefly.

Lately, with increasing frequency, a new train, its cars bearing cryptic or unclear information, roared through as if on elevated tracks above the first train. This further muddled his perceptions and made him angry.

Very, very angry.

Angry enough to hurt people. Because people had hurt him. At some time or another, *everyone* had hurt him. But his grasp of time and place felt shaky. Occasionally, he could pinpoint events, locations, and even people—their faces and sometimes their names—with precision, but more often, such memory data appeared to be tacked onto the fastest-moving train cars, which left him disoriented and fatigued.

He didn't remember how long ago he'd left whatever place he came from. He had no idea when he'd last seen his father, although something in the shady recesses upstairs hinted that it was a long, long time ago.

Yet, somehow, he knew beyond a doubt that his father was dead.

That notion—that *fact*—he had plucked it from the jumble of messages hurtling by on that new train, the one that had appeared out of nowhere. He *almost* remembered what his father looked like, and he knew, by way of some thread he'd snagged from that speeding procession, that he and his father must have once shared something like happiness.

Long, long ago. Probably.

Words spoken by his father, or maybe someone else, appeared as blocky, blood-red letters on the side of a boxcar and rolled past his mind's eye: "We are all slipping away."

A deep, booming echo: "*Slip. Slip away.*"

"We are not who we used to be. We can never be who were."

"*Be. Be who we were.*"

"Do not look for me."

"*Look. Look for me.*"

A rising and falling series of whirring vibrations—a recent memory—drifted to him. The vibrations formed words.

"How about a last name?"

His father's words again: "We can never be who we were."

"*Be who we were.*"

New, fragmented images appeared on the cars. He made out a structure—an ancient, crumbling house—with a big tree growing out of its roof. Next to the house, another big tree, different, deep green, fucking huge. He knew the place. He had been there.

And then it was gone from his mind.

From pure darkness, weird noises rang out. Loud, rhythmic, *alien*: a screech, a warble, an eerie echo. A song.

Now gone.

A room lit by electric blue. Five columns of smoke in the shape of human beings. He reached out to touch one of them.

Ice!

Electric shock!

Another and another.

Oh, God, pain.

PAIN!

He tore himself away from the sensations and images, retreated into the well of darkness that always surrounded the railroad crossing. Still, clarity hovered at its threshold.

Clarity.

He desired it. Desperate, he reached for it, clutched it, and held on.

The old house. The smoke figures. The light. The pain. So much pain.

THESE are why I am the way I am….

A memory. Old, but real.

A single track of speeding train cars had returned and replaced the image of the blue-lit room. Now he saw the end of the train, and something—a word, a moment in time, or a feeling—dangled like a tattered banner from the final car. He knew that, once it was gone, it was gone forever. Desperate, he reached for it, clutched it, and held onto whatever moment he had captured.

Then, that *other* train roared into existence on elevated tracks, and as if a hooked arm had extended from it, something reached down, snatched his prize from his grip, and sped away. He tried to run after it, to take back what it had stolen, but the train picked up speed. Still, a split-second before it raced out of existence, he managed to snag something that dangled like a tattered banner from the final car.

It was a word he was holding. When the word's meaning became clear, he began to scream. And he screamed and screamed and screamed.

Chapter 18

Martin had gotten through his classes without incident. No hallucinations, no brain hiccups, no behavior sufficiently out of character to draw the unwelcome attention of Ms. Bridgette Kolodny. No visits from Larry Hoffman, President Braxton, Dean Stermer, or anyone else he preferred not to see. The only drop-in was Nadine Hobart, a PSYC 301 student, who came begging him to allow her a make-up test despite an unexcused absence, which he typically did not do. Still, he considered her an otherwise fine student, and she had appeared sincerely repentant for having overslept the test period, due to a heavy course load and two outside jobs. So, he had decided to give her the benefit of the doubt, plus a stern warning to share her unique good fortune with no living soul, on pain of a big fat zero. Retroactively, if necessary.

Not that the curious goings-on in his brain had magically departed or even softened their insistent beckoning for his attention, especially now that he, like his brother, had experienced a period of lost time. Regardless, an odd, low-level euphoria, much as he had experienced last night prior to Carli's call, had settled into the forefront of his consciousness. As best he knew how, he relegated all else to that tenuous isolation ward at the back of his mind.

A short-term solution, but under the circumstances, what else was there?

Last night, he had managed a mercifully brief conversation with Alana. Somehow, he had concealed his own near panic at having experienced a significant amount of time slipping into oblivion. To cover it, he'd offered a few sketchy details about trying to help Phil through a crisis of conscience. She'd sounded concerned about his clearly overwhelmed state of mind, but she didn't pry too deeply. Right now, he appreciated that more than she could know.

Today, though, they hadn't managed to see each other, as she had been too busy to take off for lunch. Eventually, he knew the truth would come out. If he could only resolve this situation before *it* drew *her* in. Because, whatever the true nature of this "situation," for right or wrong, he had begun to view it as having sprung from something sentient—*intelligent*—and nothing less than cruel.

Once settled in his office, remembering his earlier consternation over his social media accounts, he logged in and discovered only more dire news, a continuation of yesterday's online debacle. A few more friends gone.

Jesus.

He did some work in his office until a half-hour before Phil's quitting time and then drove straight to his house. They had agreed that, after last night, it behooved them to talk in depth, in part regarding Martin's conversation with Carli—not that he had a single reason to feel guilt or remorse for the impromptu excuses he'd made on Phil's behalf. He assumed his brother knew this.

Westward, the late afternoon sun had retreated beyond the distant hump of Copper Peak, and the increasing chill portended a cold evening. Still, when Martin turned into the driveway, he saw Phil waiting for him in one of the two outdoor chairs on his small front porch.

Martin exited the Rogue, shoved the door shut, and went down the walkway toward the porch. A bottle of scotch and two tumblers rested on the small, glass-topped table between the chairs. He didn't bother taking off his jacket before he settled into the vacant seat. "Well, it doesn't look like she killed you too much."

Phil poured a double shot into each glass and handed one to him. "I think she's okay. And I guess I'm okay. She did tell me what you said last night. It upset her a bit."

"It wasn't me who put me in that position. You know that."

"Oh, no, don't get me wrong, brother. I want to thank you. Your covering for me was masterful." He took a sip of his drink. "Still. With what I've been going through—and you too, you know—straight honesty isn't the world's best idea ever. I don't even know, honestly, what is going on with me. With either of us." He shifted his gaze from the cedars at the edge of the yard to Martin. "Do you know what is going on?"

"You know I don't. All along, though, I'd thought that you and I had two distinct sets of issues. That they involved Black Tooth Pond and the old house was coincidence. Weird, but coincidence. Now I'm convinced it's all part of the same thing—whatever that 'thing' is. And it's definitely not all up here." He tapped his forehead with his forefinger. "It manifests itself up here. But that's not where it originates. It comes from somewhere else."

"Um, so, you *do* think it's something external—but not mold or anything we talked about before? How the hell does that work?"

Martin exhaled a lungful of vexation. "Well, there are rare instances of shared psychoses, but this situation doesn't fit any of the criteria. With all my education, all my training, I can't find any workable, rational explanation." He looked at the deepening blue sky as if some momentous message might rain down from it. "That doesn't mean there isn't one. I just don't know it. Whatever its source, this *thing* has stolen time and memories from us. Maybe if we had some inkling of what we were doing during that missing time. What we saw or felt. All we know is that we went back into that house. I can recall a few dissociated fragments. A strange light, I think. Moving shapes. It's less clear to me now than when we left last night."

Phil took a long pull on his scotch, swallowed hard, and puffed scorched air through his lips. Water brimmed in his eyes, and he drew a cooling breath. "You know, I *so* want to tell Carli about this. I want to be honest with her. But I'm afraid she might walk away from me. She'd think I was lying to cover up something. I mean, even *you* believed I was lying about doing acid."

Martin offered him an apologetic smile. "Well, it was pretty easy for me to jump to that conclusion."

"Yeah, I guess so. Still, I think you sell me short sometimes. When I tell you I don't do drugs anymore, I'm telling you the truth. And I don't want Carli to think otherwise."

"I understand, Phil. I apologize for doubting you."

He accepted Martin's admission with a slow nod. "You know, yes, I am aware that Carli and I come from very different backgrounds. She's looking for something that my life offers her, something she's never had in hers. Whatever you may think, neither of us are jumping into this deal half-cocked. This is not the work of Phil the Impulsive or Carli the Capricious." A little rumble came out of his throat that sounded like Rufus when he saw a squirrel through the window. "But now, there's this...thing. I don't mind telling you, it didn't really frighten me before. The sensations. Experiencing something new and different. It was more fascinating than worrisome. It *was* almost like the allure of acid, I'll admit. But now, it scares the hell out of me. It's stealing hours of my life. And it might be stealing the best thing that's ever happened to me. I'm more scared of what it might mean for Carli and me than...well, more than anything."

"I get you. Just last night, I'd made up my mind to stay away from there. For good. But then, when Carli called...well, you know what happened. Not that I blame you. I get why you went out there. These hallucinations I've had, they're more than just visual or sensory. They're like some kind of mental pull. A *tugging*, if you take my meaning."

"So, our experiences aren't that different. More our reactions, at least our initial ones."

"So it would seem."

Martin took a long swallow of his drink. He felt water coming to his eyes as well. "I might mention that you could stand to buy a better brand of scotch."

"That shit's expensive, you fucking snob."

"Carli may have more expensive tastes than I do. Keep that in mind."

Phil smiled, and then his expression turned thoughtful. "Once she and I talked, I think we left things on a positive note. At first, she thought I was messed up on something—acid or whatever. I assured her that I wasn't, but I couldn't tell her about...well, you know. Anyway, I think she's confident that I'm all in with her. And I'm certain she is with me." He laughed bitterly. "As long as I don't throw something absolutely insane in her face before we've reached the starting line."

Martin appreciated his brother's candor. Opening up emotionally had always been easier for Phil than for him. "I'm glad you're both on the same page. But now I have to wonder how I might approach Alana about all this. We're nowhere near the place you and Carli are. I guess I'll burn that bridge when I get to it."

"That's not really the right expression."

"No, but it's true enough."

"Heh, yeah." Phil stared at the sky for a time. Then he looked back at Martin. "This is an abrupt change of course, but here's something kinda weird. You know I do all kinds of digital creation and promotion on social media, right? The last couple of days, things have been completely fucked up."

Martin's ears perked up. "How so?"

"Lost followers, gotten all kinds of angry messages—none of which relate to anything I've done. This could really hurt my business. I don't think I've been hacked or anything. I mean, I've got security apps up to here, and I sure as hell haven't fallen for any scams. It's just a mess."

"That sounds familiar." Martin related what had happened on his accounts. Phil listened with evident dismay.

"After what we've been through, maybe it's trivial. Doesn't feel like it, though." He laughed without humor. "I think it started when you brought back that load of mail from Caviness House. All that bad news."

Now, his mind went running toward an absurd destination. "Son of a bitch. There does seem to be a parallel, doesn't there?"

Phil started to reply when something in the distance caught his attention. He leaned forward and pointed toward the road. A car on Church Street had slowed down and was now turning into his driveway. "Hello," he said. "Holy shit, it's the law."

Indeed, the car was a black, white, and silver Chevrolet Caprice bearing the bold "Sylvan County Sheriff's Department" logo on the side doors. It rolled slowly up the driveway and parked behind Martin's SUV. The driver's door opened, and a tall, fit-looking man of about forty got out, tugged his wide-brimmed hat over his blond crown, and sauntered toward them, a manila folder in one hand. His trim uniform might have been tailored. He offered them a perfunctory smile.

"Good evening," he said in a low, measured voice. "Would one of you be Mr. Phillip Pritchett?"

Phil lifted a hand. "That's me. This is my brother, Martin. What can I do for you?"

"Don't be concerned, there's no problem. My name is Deputy Sykes. I just wanted to ask you a question or two if you don't mind. We had a disturbance out here yesterday morning. A fellow got violent on the sidewalk out in front of your house. Scared a couple of folks."

Phil gave the deputy a quizzical look. "This is the first I've heard about it."

"I stopped by yesterday evening, but no one was home." He drew a large glossy photograph from the manila folder and held it up for Phil to view. "I mainly wanted to find out if you might have seen this gentleman before."

It was a mug shot, with both front and profile views of a feral-looking man with unkempt black hair, a long, curling tendril of which hung down into his face; widely spaced, onyx eyes; grime-streaked, bony cheeks; and a thin, jagged gash for a mouth. Phil gave the image a long, thoughtful appraisal and then shook his head.

"No, sir, I've never seen him before."

"He seemed to have some interest in your property. He is in custody, but we're trying to establish his identity. Said his first name is Robert, but he either can't or won't give us his full name."

Martin leaned forward to get a better look at the photograph. The man's staring eyes—the intense focus on something beyond the camera lens—piqued his interest. Strictly professional, he thought at first, but then he realized it went beyond that. The expression struck him as *haunted*.

"Do you recognize him, sir?" Deputy Sykes's eyes searched Martin's with an almost predatory gleam. A man who enjoyed his work, no doubt.

He shook his head. "No, I'm sorry."

No, not sorry that he didn't know the man. Something about the eyes. He did not *want* to know this man. Ever.

"Would anyone else have been in your house who might have seen this individual at the time, Mr. Pritchett?" Sykes asked.

"Just my dog, Rufus, and he didn't mention anything."

Sykes flashed Phil a look of distaste. Clearly, not one to appreciate frivolity.

"As I said, the gentleman is in custody, so you don't need to be concerned about him coming around again." A thoughtful frown crossed the deputy's face, and he shifted his focus to Martin. "Sir, you seemed to take a special interest in the photo. You're certain you don't know the man?" He held up the image again for Martin's benefit.

"Very certain." Martin forced a smile. "For the record, I teach Psychology at Beckham College. It's second nature for me to guess what might be going on in a person's mind by their appearance. By their expressions. That's all."

Sykes gave him a half-satisfied nod. "I see. Well, this appeared to be an isolated incident, and we don't believe anyone else is involved. All the same, you might want to keep your doors locked, especially when you're not home. And don't hesitate to call us if you witness any suspicious activity."

Deputy Sykes's stilted delivery suggested he was working from a script, Martin thought. All part of the job, no doubt.

"I appreciate you letting us know," Phil said. "If I see anyone more suspicious than my brother, I'll call."

"Please do." Sykes glanced at Martin and, for the first time, cracked a little smile. "Remember, brothers tend to be the most suspicious of all."

Phil smiled. "The voice of experience."

"Twice over." Sykes offered them a polite nod. From his shirt pocket, he produced a business-sized card and handed it to Phil. "Just in case. You can contact me at this number or email. Thank you again, and I'll wish you gentlemen a good afternoon." He gave the brim of his hat a little tug, turned, and headed back to his car.

Phil slipped the card into his jacket pocket and watched the Caprice back slowly out of the driveway, turn eastward on Church Street, and disappear beyond the cedar trees. Then he gave Martin a look that indicated his bullshit detector had pinged. "Evaluating people by their facial expressions is second nature? Since when?"

"Well, it was only half bullshit. This guy…." He paused to consider his words. "Those eyes. It's like I recognized the eyes, not the face itself. But there *was* something there that struck me."

Phil crossed his arms as if to create a bulwark against the creeping chill. His gaze turned inward. "You know, it didn't hit me when I first looked at the photo. But I think I get what you're saying."

"About fucking time."

"You are funny, but not in the way you think." Phil's smile faded quickly. "Does it relate to the old house?"

"The house." Martin's thoughts swirled into a tightening spiral, as if to close in on some image, some memory. "Photographs. There were some old photographs in the house. That much I remember."

"Photographs. You think that's it? Someone in a photograph in the house?"

Martin nodded. "The eyes. Yes. The eyes of someone in a photograph in the House of Caviness."

And the more he thought about it, the more he thought he *might* have seen someone else with Caviness eyes.

#

Phil might have been creative as hell, but his passion for creating did not extend into the culinary field. He'd offered to feed Martin dinner, which meant pizza delivery. Thanks, probably, to his fiancée's influence, he'd had the decency to pay for it without asking Martin to chip in. Not that Martin had anything against pizza. He loved the stuff, especially the deluxe garbage pizza from Najjar's Pizza Haven, which Phil had so kindly ordered for them. It featured all the meats, more delicious fungi than a man had a right to enjoy, a community garden's worth of veggies, with both black and green olives.

After they'd killed the pizza, Martin left Phil to gather up his heart and his wits in preparation for an evening with Carli. After he had bid his brother goodbye and headed out the door, he noticed a short, somewhat portly, gray-haired woman standing at the end of Phil's driveway, caught in the glow of the nearby streetlight. Oblivious to his presence, she appeared to be studying the nearest of the cedar trees. He watched her for a minute or so, but when she didn't show any sign of moving on, he meandered down the driveway toward her. He'd come within a dozen feet of her before she realized he was there.

Behind her thick, wire-rimmed glasses, her dark eyes widened when she realized she was no longer alone. "Oh, hello." Her voice came out low and husky. "I'm sorry, I didn't mean to trespass or anything."

"May I help you?"

She gave him a quick look up and down. Her expression turned wary. "You're not Mr. Pritchett. *Are* you Mr. Pritchett?"

He offered her a thin smile. "This is my brother's place. I'm Martin Pritchett."

"Oh, I see." The smile she returned held a hint of relief. "I am Mrs. Piper. Cheryl Piper. I live right around the corner on Bondurant Street. I'm sorry for coming into your...er...your brother's property, but I was very curious about something here."

"Yes?"

"Well, it was such a pretty evening that I stepped out on the back porch for a little while so Tawny—that's my dog—could run in the yard for a bit. I heard something coming from over here, and I just had to find out if I was really hearing what I thought I was hearing."

"Okay." He tapped his foot once.

"Oh, well, yes. You see, I thought I heard a whippoorwill!"

Martin felt an icy stab in his skull. "A whippoorwill?"

She nodded with exaggerated enthusiasm. "Oh, yes. I haven't heard a whippoorwill since I was a little girl, and I so loved hearing their songs back then. It seemed unusual that a whippoorwill might be calling from anywhere around here, especially so close to downtown, and in this season! Sure enough, though, it seemed to be coming from right here. Right here in these trees!"

"A whippoorwill." Martin's brain seemed to resist processing this information. "My brother and I were inside the house. We didn't hear anything. So, this was...what? Just a few minutes ago?"

"That's right. I walked right over here, and I could hear it calling until I was almost right here at your driveway. Of course, I didn't really think I'd be able to see it or anything. They're just little birds. But I absolutely had to come to look and listen."

"I see."

"Have you heard a whippoorwill before, Mr. Pritchett?"

He nodded. "Quite recently, as a matter of fact, but not near here." He looked up into the trees. If there had been a whippoorwill, the woman's arrival probably scared it away.

Why here, though? Why now?

"I suppose it's gone now." She put on a disappointed frown, but her face soon brightened with a hopeful smile. "Maybe it'll come back. It probably won't sing if people are around. What a lovely song, though."

Martin felt no inclination to explain his less favorable impression of the whippoorwill's song. Especially now. "Yes," he said in a low, neutral tone. "I believe it's gone."

Mrs. Piper's expression switched to abashed. "I should go right back home, shouldn't I? I am so sorry to have trespassed."

He gave her a reassuring smile. "No harm done."

She walked out of the driveway, and just before starting down the sidewalk toward Bondurant Street, she paused and said, "It was nice to meet you, Mister—umm—other Pritchett."

"You too, Mrs. Piper."

As she moved on, he stepped out to the sidewalk and watched her until she reached the end of the cedar row, turned right onto Bondurant Street, and passed out of his line of sight. For a time, he stood there, his mind churning over what, at any other time, would seem an innocuous incident. There was almost no traffic on this section of Church Street, although a couple of hundred yards farther on, several cars were stopped for the traffic light at the Market Street intersection. Beyond that, in downtown proper, vehicle and foot traffic appeared a bit brisker than usual. His eyes registered all this, but his mind remained focused on something else: the question of why a whippoorwill might visit this specific location. And whether it was a *real* whippoorwill.

In his experience, no whippoorwills ever came closer to town than the lowest slopes of the three surrounding mountains. And once Mrs. Piper had mentioned it, he realized that, indeed, this late in the year, most of the local birds—whippoorwills included—would have migrated south.

How odd that he and Phil would not have heard the typically loud bird song, even from inside the house. The two of them weren't exactly hollering up a storm, and the house's relatively thin insulation hardly enclosed them in a cone of silence. Still, something had drawn the older woman to check out the sound. Given his own recent experiences with whippoorwill voices, he felt a sudden surge of nerves.

He started back up the driveway toward his car. He had taken only a few steps when a loud rustling erupted from the cedar boughs behind him. Swiveling to face them, he caught a quick motion in the glow of the streetlight—the lower branches of the endmost tree swishing back and forth as if something large had passed through them. Then he saw, on the sidewalk between that last cedar and the driveway, a long shadow slowly extending from somewhere on the other side of the trees to the midpoint of the entrance, a distance of about fifteen feet. The shadow appeared vaguely man-shaped, though it struck him as unnaturally tall and elongated.

It wasn't the streetlight casting the shadow, for it hovered almost directly above the tree beside the driveway. Only some other source of illumination, lower and farther up the sidewalk, could cast the shadow of a person in such a way. He also saw that the warm, yellow-tinged glow from the streetlight now mingled with another hue: a cool, electric blue. It was the blue light, steady and unblinking, that cast the long shadow.

The color brought back some half-remembered feeling of discomfort, of bewilderment, but he couldn't place its source.

It unsettled him again. Now, as he watched, the shadow shifted, its contours changing from human-shaped to an amorphous, swirling cloud, which vanished within a few seconds.

The blue light faded and disappeared.

Hallucination? He didn't think so, not this time. He had no idea what he'd seen, but still, he could hardly attribute this to anything unnatural or unwholesome. If his nerves hadn't been shaken so many times recently, he might not have noticed it at all. Or, if he had, wouldn't have cared even a little.

Regardless, when he returned to his car and settled into the driver's seat, he quickly closed the door, locked it, and started the engine. He pulled out of the driveway onto Church Street, where he confirmed that the street and sidewalk were empty in the direction from which the shadow had appeared.

He'd driven most of the way back to his house before his heart stopped thundering like the falls over the old hydroelectric dam on the Camden River.

No wonder he continued to feel so worn down.

This shit is never going to end, is it?

Chapter 19

Martin had gone out to the back deck, which faced the vast expanse of woods behind his house. Apart from his phone, the only light was a feeble glow from his den lamp that spilled from the backdoor window. A few stars glimmered through the gap in the treetops directly above the house. Despite the cold night air, he'd felt drawn to the familiar, tranquil darkness of his outdoor surroundings, and after his drive home from Phil's, he needed tranquility.

"I missed seeing you today." Alana's voice over the speaker sounded warm. "I hope it was better than the past few."

The truth, the whole truth, and nothing but the truth would not, *could* not fly. Partial honesty was the best he could manage. "It was productive. I spent some quality time with Phil this evening."

"My magnanimous me wants to tell you that you're a very good brother. Pragmatic me wishes you'd let him sort things out for himself."

"I appreciate you both."

"Are he and Carli all right?"

He wasn't about to elaborate but so much. "I think so. But as I've told you, Phil can get overly emotional sometimes. He's going through a spell."

"For you, saying 'This stoplight annoys me' is overly emotional, so your definition and mine might differ."

"Methinks you exaggerate."

She laughed. "Maybe a little."

"Maybe a lot."

Her serious voice returned. "Okay, here's the thing. Carli asked me to be a bridesmaid."

"Really? That sounds nice. I think."

"Well, I barely know her. I guess she wants me to be in the wedding party since you're Phil's best man."

"That makes sense. She knows just about everyone in Aiken Mill, so I'm not sure who else is going to be in the bridal party except for Robin Hall. That's her best friend."

"What about Phil's party? Do you know them?"

"A little. Bryon Bushnell and Tony Garcia, his best friends from college. They've stayed close over the years. And Chuck Hill, one of the local artists. I've met Chuck a couple of times. Nice fellow, I guess. Has more hair than you do, owns one pair of pants and one T-shirt, both about twenty years old. Smokes like a chimney, keeps a cigarette behind his ear at all times."

"Ah. My kind of man."

"I'll try not to be jealous."

"Oh, you can be jealous."

"Most appreciated."

"I do feel a little nervous about this whole thing."

"Like I said, Chuck is nice enough."

She half-snorted. "That's not what I meant. You'll be the only one I really know." She paused. "I know you're not a Catholic—thank God. What about your brother? And Carli?"

"Not at all. Phil's not a churchgoer. Now, I think Carli is—or maybe was—a Methodist. But the service and reception are at Asberry Vineyards with a non-denominational rent-a-pastor."

She breathed an audible sigh of relief. "As a recovered Catholic, I can tell you that Catholic weddings are *not* my thing."

"Carli must not have given you many details."

"No. She texted me, said she'd love for me to be in the wedding,

STEPHEN MARK RAINEY

and asked if I would like to be a bridesmaid. I told her I was honored, and I'd seriously consider it. It's barely four weeks away, though."

"Are you asking for my opinion? Well, yes, I would love for you to be in the bridal party. But if you'd rather not, I can always spend the evening with Robin Hall."

"Do you think you're funny? You are not."

"Phil said something along those lines earlier tonight." He decided to broach another subject, possibly related. "At the risk of getting very personal, you seemed to have some animosity toward Catholicism."

A lengthy silence followed. "Where I come from, almost everyone is Catholic, and there were some in my life who...." Again, she fell silent. "They could be terrible. I'll call it what it was. Abusive. Not physically. Psychologically. Well, mostly."

He felt a little shudder. "Family?"

"No, not at all. But I will say that my parents, all my relatives, they tried very hard to persuade me to share in their beliefs. But I couldn't. It wasn't me. So, Mom and Dad sent me to a Catholic school, and when I didn't fall in line with their doctrines—their dogma—it got pretty bad. All that guilt they put on me. When I was fifteen, I truly wanted to die. But I was bound to go to hell, pure and simple."

"I'm sorry, Alana."

"Like I said, my parents were not abusive. But I think they were willing to turn a blind eye to my pain because it was 'for my own good.'"

"That in itself can constitute abuse, you know."

"Marty, my mother and father were not—are not—bad people. It's just that they were doing what they thought was best, within the confines of their faith. Eventually, I ended up living a lie to keep the peace, to avoid hurting them. But when I married outside the faith, to them, I became an outsider." She heaved a deep sigh. "So, my parents and I are no longer close. And you know how things turned out with Andrew."

"So, he wasn't Catholic."

"No, ostensibly Presbyterian, though he was no more religious than I am. With him, the struggle was entirely different. No less profound, but it was more about the real world, about his issues with being controlling. Manipulative. Preying on my emotions."

"I'd say you've taken control of your life in the best way possible. You're a very strong person."

She fell silent for a few moments. "Thank you. I'll admit that it was hard opening up to you—at least, at first. You're not exactly forthcoming with your feelings, as I may have mentioned. At least not with me. That's why I've always been a little cautious with you."

"I understand that. But I want you to know that anytime you feel the need to unload, you can always talk to me."

"Well, I appreciate that. I've had a lot of time to reconcile my feelings, my beliefs. I will never go back, and I will never embrace my parents' beliefs." She paused. "Or let myself be run over by a man. Or anyone. For a long time, I wanted to cut ties with those parts of my past. With where I came from. That's one of the reasons I'm here. In Virginia. I admit that I occasionally still stress about having made this break, but overall, I'm okay."

"That's good. I really do appreciate you for who you are, here and now. Although I am a little perturbed about your lack of appreciation for dead cow cooked medium rare."

She laughed, her mood brightening. "Are we still getting together tomorrow evening?"

"Absolutely."

"No last-minute going off with your brother or anything, right?"

"That I promise."

He meant that. He refused to let recent events—even those that had somehow slipped out of his memory—interfere with this blossoming relationship. If it came down to it, Phil would need to fend for himself.

"Will you be cooking?" she asked.

"I will."

"No dead cow, right?"

"Nope. How does mahi-mahi sound? With lemon and garlic?"

"That sounds very good."

"So, my place after work?"

"I shall look forward to this." He could hear the smile in her voice. "Until tomorrow, then."

"Until tomorrow."

"Goodnight, Marty."

"Goodnight, Alana."

He hesitated before ending the call. She remained on the line, also silent.

He whispered, "Goodnight." Then he pressed the end-call button and slipped his phone into his pocket.

That subtle sense of euphoria had returned, if for entirely different reasons than before. His conversation with Alana had driven away almost every trace of that fluctuating but constant current of anxiety, helped restore his confidence, his sense of balance.

Maybe he *was* falling in love.

Ha! In his experience, falling in love meant being perpetually off-balance.

He spoke into the darkness. "Well, sometimes, life is stranger than shit."

For an unexpected, less-than-amusing moment, he perceived that the dark woods might be having a laugh at his expense. No, that couldn't be right. These were *his* woods. He considered them a sanctuary of sorts. He'd spent countless hours out there, walking under the towering beeches, pines, and poplars, exploring and connecting with nature. Several years ago, he'd discovered a perfect little clearing a few hundred yards from the house and set up a campsite, complete with a firepit he fashioned out of rocks from a nearby stream. It had been a long time since—at least five years— but on numerous occasions, he'd slept out there beneath the guardian trees. Those experiences always revitalized his body and spirit.

From a far corner of his mind, the memory surfaced that, on his camping outings, he always took his gun along. Well, despite his familiarity with nature, he acknowledged the reality that it was not always kind.

Until moments ago, even in darkness, the woods *had* felt kind. Now, as if something cold and antagonistic had stirred somewhere out there, he felt a chilly, *slimy* current oozing from the darkness to caress his body with vile, questing fingers. A distant glow—blue, tinged with violet—shimmered into existence and backlit the myriad columns of trees that filled the intervening space.

From where he stood, his mind's eye drew a straight line to the tiny, illuminated sphere in the distance. The end point lay many, many miles from here, but he knew the line passed through hills and trees, crossed roads, and bisected countless structures to connect with the house at Black Tooth Pond.

He recognized the light—its color, its *ghostliness*. He'd seen it at his brother's place earlier this evening. Along with an unknown shadow.

Another hallucination?

Of course it was! Another sensory attack, a continuation of the series he had suffered for days. And, yes, these were *attacks*, for they hit with such evident deliberation that he could no longer believe they were anything but orchestrated. Still, even aware of their essential unreality, he failed time and again to vanquish these psychic intrusions, to mitigate their influence on his will, his grip on *time*.

"Not real," he whispered, struggling to mine his deepest reserves of willpower. "This is not real. *You* are not real."

The blue glow did not diminish. Instead, other images insinuated themselves into his consciousness, as if they *desired* to reveal themselves. Shadows of human beings—smoky, insubstantial—wavering before a nebulous, electric-blue backdrop.

Five of them.

Jesus, ARE they ghosts?

Then it came: the faraway, eerie song of the whippoorwill. Drifting across impossible miles to reach his ears.

He drew his phone from his pocket, aimed its camera lens at the blue glimmer in the darkness, and began recording a video. He let it run for a full minute before shutting it off.

The moment he did, the whippoorwill song waned and fell silent. The glow vanished. Pure darkness again blanketed the woods. And now, the air felt icy, as if the temperature had plummeted below freezing in less than a minute.

On his phone, he selected the video and started it playing.

Unbroken darkness appeared on the screen. A soft whisper rose and fell from the speakers; mere background noise the microphone had picked up. Nothing he had seen or heard registered on the recording.

Not real.

It was only when he closed out the video that he realized there was an earlier video in his gallery, the preview pane showing only a field of solid black. When he selected it and checked the accompanying info screen, his heart jumped. Based on the time, he had taken it last night—while he and Phil had been at Black Tooth Pond.

"Jesus!"

It ran only twenty-three seconds. With a trembling finger, he pressed the play button.

Well, shit.

Only blackness appeared on the screen, although random bumping and scraping sounds echoed from the speaker. He must have butt-recorded it. Wouldn't have been the first time. Still, he watched all twenty-three seconds twice, and he was just about to shut it off and put his phone away when he thought he detected a voice—a soft, whispered voice—on the video's soundtrack. He ran it back, turned the volume up all the way, and played the last few seconds again with the speaker held to his ear.

It did sound like a voice, distant, distorted by swooshing background noise. He *thought* the voice said, "The blue and the gold."

He played it again. He couldn't be any more certain than before. Just a whispered sound that might or might not actually have been a voice. Maybe the recording had picked up his voice, or Phil's. But he remembered Phil describing one of his hallucinations, of having seen blue and gold colors in an otherwise dark space.

Again: "The blue and the gold."

No, it was too unclear. His brain was forcing meaning upon murky, indecipherable syllables. Some random statement one of them had made, barely picked up by the phone's mic.

A whole lot of nothing.

Regardless, he sensed *something* building in the air, something as tangible as the time-ravaged House of Caviness itself. His episodes had begun with images and sensations that had spurred him to follow the path they'd laid. First, out Old Beckham Road to Black Tooth Pond, then into the house, and finally, to its upstairs floor, where both he and Phil had experienced some event—or encounter, perhaps—that neither of them could fully remember. He now suspected this external influence, whatever it might be, intended for him to follow a new path, one he couldn't yet identify.

All of this ran counter to his every instinct, his intellect, his education. An individual brain might fabricate incredible false realities and drive a person to follow an illusory path, sometimes a broken one, even a dangerous one. The blanket term for this was *psychosis*. He knew full well that neither he nor Phil had experienced true psychotic episodes, and certainly not some shared psychosis.

He closed the gallery screen but did not delete the video.

With the passing of his near-euphoric state, anger and frustration rushed in to replace it.

Shivering with the seemingly unnatural cold, he stepped back into his lamplit den and closed the door behind him. He didn't bother taking off his jacket because the bitter chill had worked into his bones. On a whim, he went to the file cabinet in the corner of the room and withdrew the stack of pages from the House of Caviness, which he'd spent such a ludicrous amount of time and effort organizing. He remembered his first reaction to them—that they had seemed toxic— and touching them now, the paper felt cool and viscous. Abhorrent.

Had the original recipients reacted the same way? Why had they kept so many years' worth of dreadful news and ominous personal notes? Why had *he* kept them? He should shove the pile into the living room fireplace and light it up. He'd surely feel better for it.

No. He wouldn't.

Why not? All that material couldn't have been a catalyst for his hallucinations—could it? He'd discovered the stack of mail on his first visit to the house, but he hadn't retrieved it until the next. And by the time he set about organizing the pages, the hallucinations were already well under way. With a sigh of disgust, he dropped the stack on his desktop, again took his phone from his pocket, and opened his social media apps.

His feeds consisted of nothing but shared news stories, all distressing. A terrorist bombing in Israel that had killed over a hundred people, many of them children. An oil spill in the Gulf of Mexico with the potential to rival the 2010 Deepwater Horizon disaster. The umpteenth mass shooting of the year, with seven dead and twelve wounded, at a library in Kennesaw, Georgia. An endless stream of equally heinous events followed. The same shit show one might read on any given day, only presented in a tidy package shared by someone bearing the moniker "No-One-1." Martin didn't know or follow anyone who went by that name, so why the hell was he seeing their posts? When he attempted to view the individual's profile, his app indicated no such user existed.

He now suspected the earlier barrage of terrible news he'd seen had come by way of No-One-1, and he simply hadn't noticed at the time. Somehow, this struck him as all too similar to the piles of bad news to which the Caviness family had been subjected in their day. All these years apart, their anonymous sender and his seemed equally mysterious.

He tried blocking No-One-1, but the app had no mechanism to block an account that apparently did not exist.

"Fucker," Martin muttered. Triggered by his angry mood, he wandered into the dining area to his bar, its multicolored LEDs glowing cheerfully, and poured himself a double shot of scotch. After his conversation with Alana, he'd felt better than he had for days, but it had only taken a few minutes for his spirits to plummet and anxiety to resurface. If these episodes truly originated from *out there* rather than from inside himself, their purpose seemed to be to wreak psychological havoc on him.

Assuming such an unknown psychic force existed, had it specifically targeted him—and Phil—or were they simply targets of opportunity? How could he identify its origin? What was the key? Maybe it was buried in those old notes and news clippings. In the shared bundles of social media posts that served no purpose other than to overwhelm and dishearten him. Or perhaps in the imagery and sensations of the hallucinations themselves.

He desperately needed to discover some means of not just blunting but dismantling these assaults, maybe for his brother's sake as well. Every salvo launched at his psyche struck with damaging force. He could only hold out so long before these blows shattered something crucial in the foundations of his mind, and his sanity— even his sense of self—began to come apart at the seams.

The clock was ticking.

Chapter 20

Loud, querulous voices from the two other occupied cells and a dim but flickering overhead fluorescent tube, which provided the only light beyond the metal bars, had prevented Robert from shutting out the world and getting some sleep. He had no idea of the hour, not that the time on a clock ever meant much to him. At some point, the noise had quieted down, but the light still hummed and sputtered with seemingly intentional belligerence. His bed—the lower of the two metal-framed bunks in the cell—felt as comfortable as some of the blanket-covered rocks he'd spent many a night upon, but that didn't bother him as much as that fucking fluorescent tube—*flick-flick-bright, flick-flick-dark*—which he wished he could pluck from its mounts and smash over someone's head.

He'd forgotten why he was here, didn't remember who was in those other little chambers down the row, if he'd ever known. Didn't care. What he did remember was his father's face because it kept flashing past on continuous train cars. Once upon a time, his father made things all right. This was not all right, this cramped space he occupied, though he couldn't even guess where he *should* be. Someone had forced him into this place, he knew that much. This was not his fault. What the hell had *he* ever done?

Nothing.

Nothing to bring on the soul-deep hurt that was his only constant companion. *Nothing* to scramble every thought in his head, thus becoming deaf, dumb, and blind in everyone else's world. *Nothing* to sacrifice the essence of the human being he once had been.

Sometimes, he remembered love.

Sometimes.

He remembered his father was dead.

No. No, he's not. He can't be dead. I saw him!

"I want out of here!"

He didn't know whether he'd spoken. It *felt* like he'd spoken.

"YOUR NAME IS INSCRIBED IN BLOOD IN THE BOOK OF THE DOOMED."

It was emblazoned on a passing train car in his mind. A very slow-moving car. It took a long time for it to roll out of his view.

"I want OUT!"

Outside the confining bars, the fluorescent light grew brighter, brighter, brighter, and then—with a final, sharp *buzz*—it went out, thrusting the entire row of cells into darkness.

"I WANT OUT!"

Robert was not aware of the camera that watched the parallel rows of jail cells at all times. Even if he had been, he would not have understood that the sudden darkness had activated the camera's 850nm infrared light, and it continued its vigil in night vision mode. He also could not know that, upstairs, Al Krummeck, the sole deputy on duty inside the station, had drifted off to sleep, his personal cell phone still clutched in one hand, after having scrolled through countless insipid online videos for well over an hour. Thus, he failed to see one of the four camera views displayed on his desktop monitor switch to IR mode.

Within seconds of the light going out, Robert saw a vague blue glow rising from somewhere in the darkness beyond the bars. On Krummeck's screen, the IR view displayed only the pale outlines of the cell bars against a dark backdrop. From Robert's perspective, the blue glow spread slowly from the darkness, seeped through the bars, and crept across the floor to his bunk. A cluster of memories formed in his brain and remained stationary long enough for him to grasp certain images, sounds, and smells.

Particularly the smell.

AWFUL!

Not old memories. Recent.

Very recent.

He slid backward in his bunk and pressed himself against the wall, as if retreating even this far might prevent the encroaching, radiant fingers from reaching him. No. The light washed over him like a cobalt blue–tinted wave, and every muscle in his body began to tingle. Just beyond the bars, a wisp of dark smoke rose out of nowhere, followed by another and then another. The smoke plumes wove together into a thickening coil and very gradually assumed the crude contours of a very tall human being.

He had seen others like this before. Somewhere, sometime.

He remembered pain. Shocking, burning pain.

The sour, puke-like smell grew stronger.

"Go away," he whispered, barely able to form words. "Leave me alone."

"Robert."

It was a deep, croaking voice, the sound that might come from the dry, ruined vocal cords of a reanimated corpse. Still, in its tones, he perceived a trace of familiarity.

"Robert. Do you remember?"

"What? Who?"

"Remember me."

"Remember?"

"Remember me. Before."

"Before," Robert muttered, capable now of only simple repetition.

"Before the slipping away."

The voice. It was his father's. But his father was dead. Wasn't he?

"It is time, Robert."

The swirling, smoke-filled shape lurched forward. Passed through the bars as if they were nothing more than air. One wavering arm rose and moved forward as if to touch him.

"Oh, no. No!"

A blurry, spidery shape, barely recognizable as a hand, lowered and fell to rest upon his shoulder. Vanished *into* his shoulder. An electric current arced into his flesh and bones, turning his body into a blazing livewire.

He screamed more in surprise than pain, for the full agony had not yet registered.

From the far end of the row of jail cells, a groggy voice growled, "Hey! Shut the fuck up!"

Robert didn't hear it. What he heard was his father's voice, now speaking gently. "I'm sorry, son," the voice said. "I found what I was looking for. So will you."

Now, the sizzling current became an onslaught of fiery spears. Piercing. Slicing. Searing.

In his tortured mind's field of vision, that endless line of train cars roared into existence and whizzed past, carrying his thoughts and memories into oblivion. Then the elevated train, the *evil* train, appeared above the other, this one slower, more defined. The side of each car bore a name, written in what looked like blood.

Each one a name he knew.

The awful smell ripped into his sinuses and wriggled deep into his brain. The magma in his veins drew his awareness away from the images of the train cars, his only relief the screams that now rang from his gaping mouth.

"I said shut the fuck up!"

The shout from the darkness beyond his bars meant nothing. He wanted release. He wanted out—wherever *out* was, whatever *out* meant. He *had* to find the way *out*.

#

Upstairs, the ruckus in the cells below finally penetrated the mantle of sleep that had settled over Deputy Krummeck, and after some clumsy recalibrating, his dulled senses *almost* identified the sounds. Once his eyes had opened and found their focus, he noticed that the camera downstairs had switched to night vision mode. He saw nothing happening on the screen, but the howling and shouting that hammered its way through the closed door at the top of the stairs assured him that *something* down there required his attention.

He tore himself from his seat and trudged to the door, which he pushed open far enough to poke his head through and listen. An ear-shattering scream rang from below, followed by a loud, heavy banging against metal bars. Indeed, no hint of light gleamed down there. He flipped up the middle of the five switches at the top of the stairs to turn on the second set of fluorescents, which typically remained off at night. Below, from the corridor beyond the stairwell, a pale light came on, bright enough to guide him down. He verified his baton, taser, and firearm were secured at his belt, and with a grumble of reluctant resignation, he started down the stairs. Before he reached the landing where the stairway turned to the left, a horrible smell hit him, so overwhelming he drew a deep breath and held it until he reached the bottom and faced the two rows of twelve cells—tonight, mostly empty—on either side of the corridor. Another series of harsh screams erupted from the far end of the right-hand row, apparently from John "Robert" Doe, who had seemed almost catatonic since Krummeck had begun his shift at eight.

His lungs felt ready to explode, so he exhaled and drew a new breath.

It took supreme effort to hold back the stream of vomit that *so* wanted to gush up from his stomach and spew out his mouth.

"Hey, you!" came a shout from one of the occupied cells. "You wanna do something about the noise and the reek down here? Talk about fuckin' cruel and unusual."

"Yeah," came a second voice. "It's violating my constitution."

Krummeck ignored the complaints and made his way toward the end-most cell, where he made out a thrashing shadow on the other side of the bars. The screams from in there sounded increasingly frantic, unhinged. He lowered his hand to his baton, gulped the tiniest amount of air possible to refresh his lungs, and made his final approach with more caution than an obviously locked cell probably warranted.

"Holy shit," he whispered when he saw the figure inside the cell twisting and writhing as if flames engulfed his body. Again and again, the man hurled himself against the barred door, whether hoping to break it down or simply escape from some hellish internal torment, Krummeck had no idea. Then, pushing off the door with his hands, the man propelled himself backward, slammed into the cinder block wall, and began bashing his head against the unyielding surface.

"Hey, hey!" Krummeck yelled. "Sir, you need to stop that. Sir, you're going to injure yourself!"

His "No great loss" remained unspoken, for that was not how this job worked. As it was, the only voice Robert seemed to hear was in his head, and his fits continued unabated. All too aware of his duty to prevent the man from losing a devastating contest with the wall,

Krummeck unlocked the barred door.

It wasn't until he had stepped inside the cell that his still sleep-addled brain understood the foolish move he'd made. Dammit, he should have called for backup before putting himself in here with such an unbalanced, violent individual. Krummeck might have been the only deputy inside the building at this hour, but he was hardly the only one working. One of the other four deputies—or even the local EMTs—could have been on the scene within five minutes.

Yeah, but in five minutes, the son of a bitch would probably be dead.

He grabbed the smaller man by the shoulders and, with no little difficulty, managed to press his body face-first against the cinder blocks. However, his attempt to restrain the flailing arms failed miserably. Like a writhing snake, the wiry figure twisted, jerked his elbows forward, and freed his wrists in only a couple of seconds. The next thing Deputy Krummeck knew, a bunch of rock-hard knuckles smashed into the bridge of his nose. He heard a *crunch* and felt pain spread like wildfire into his sinuses, through his cheeks, and even into the back of his throat.

The fucker had broken his nose!

Then the heel of Robert's right palm arced upward and caught Krummeck under his jaw, the force of the blow lifting his body several inches off the floor. This time, pain exploded in the deputy's skull as if a hand grenade had gone off in his mouth. He sank first to his knees and then, after swaying back and forth a couple of times, onto his back. The world around him spun like a top for a few seconds before going darker than a sealed cavern. He could still hear—he wasn't fully unconscious—but his body felt like some faraway hunk of deadweight over which he had no control.

The screaming that had reverberated through his brain now receded, and he realized that Robert had fled his cell and run for the stairwell. In a moment of terrible clarity, Krummeck realized that, in his haste to reach the screaming man, he *might* not have pushed the upstairs door all the way shut. In its old age, that damned latch needed a good, solid shove.

From one of the occupied cells, an enthusiastic voice cheered, "Go, dawg, go, go, go!" Then came the rapid, uneven clatter of footsteps on the stairs. A metallic groan echoed down the stairwell, followed by a smooth, hydraulic hiss. There was no final *click*, since the lock didn't engage without physical assistance, and when Robert's feverish screaming became a distant, muted mumble, Krummeck wondered no longer whether he'd secured the upstairs door.

A dim but unfocused light took shape in his field of vision, and an all-encompassing pain throbbed through his face and jaw. Jesus, what a mess! No telling where the rabid fucker might go once outside the building. Right now, Krummeck knew only two things for certain: one, that he needed medical attention; two, that tonight had been the last shift he would ever work for the Sylvan County Sheriff's Department.

Sometime later, as feeling began to creep back into the leaden mass below his shoulders, he managed to roll onto his left side and explore the sensations his brain deigned to register. Nothing from the neck down seemed to be broken, but his internal signals still seemed to be scrambled. When he tried to move his right arm, it lay there stupidly for a few seconds before obeying his command. After a while longer, by sheer effort of will, he managed to heave his body into a sitting position, pull the dizzily spinning world back into reasonable focus, and take a quick inventory of his equipment.

Thank God Robert hadn't grabbed anything off him that would further complicate his already bleak future. From the rapid cessation of the screaming upstairs, he gathered the tormented man had fled the premises without pausing to hunt for weapons or any other useful items for the fugitive on the run, be he sane or otherwise.

At last, Krummeck made it to his feet and hobbled toward the stairs. Priority number one—*oh Jesus oh Jesus oh Jesus*—was to notify Sheriff Parrott of the situation. After that, he could busy himself contemplating the lightning-fast termination of his employment. For all he knew, after this debacle, the department might consider itself less than obliged to cover his medical expenses. Or would it? Wasn't it the sheriff's job to make sure every nut and bolt in the station was functioning properly—including the upstairs door lock?

Ah, fuck it. There'd be no passing the buck here. This was every bit his own damned fault. He just hoped the county wouldn't cancel his insurance before he could get to the Urgent Care out on Highway 21.

"Yo, dawg," came a familiar voice from among the incarcerated. "Not looking so good there, are you?"

"Yeah," came the second voice. "Just toss us the keys, and you can say that other dawg took 'em and let us out. Can't be any worse than what you got comin'."

Double guffaws rang from the cells. Krummeck shut out the voices and half-staggered up the stairs, trying to figure out how to make himself appear marginally less the idiot that he suspected he truly was.

Had it mattered, it wouldn't have helped his case that he completely missed seeing several lengthy splatters of clear, viscous fluid on the floor and stairs, which any reasonable observer could only conclude had been left by the man fleeing the open jail cell below.

By the time Sheriff Parrott and Chief Deputy Sykes arrived on the scene, a good half-hour later, all traces of the unknown substance had vanished.

THE HOUSE AT BLACK TOOTH POND

VIII. FRIDAY

Chapter 21

Sheriff Parrott had never had to deal with an escapee from his jail, but if he'd been asked to bet on the instigator of this inaugural event, Deputy Krummeck would have been at the top of his list. The young man had trained well enough and demonstrated a positive attitude, but he'd proven himself easily distracted and prone to the inevitable early-thirty-something's propensity for losing himself in technology at inopportune times. Not all that long ago, Parrott had mentioned this latter point to him, and by all appearances, he had shaped right up.

Appearances deceived.

Of course, the final responsibility for such a fiasco lay with the sheriff. As his dad used to remark, that was one of the laws of the Medes and the Persians.

Krummeck had started with the department at the same time as Deputy Beamer. In general, he'd seemed more self-assured than Beamer, if somewhat impetuous—not unlike Sykes—though until now, Krummeck's self-discipline had not been rigorously field tested.

He did not test well.

Parrott would have to suspend him until all the facts were in, though to his mind, the situation appeared cut and dry. Deputy puts personal interest ahead of his duty, gets caught with his pants down, forgets his training and discipline, and ends up hurt.

So, Parrott now had a potentially dangerous fugitive on the loose. Out there. Somewhere.

He had called in a dozen deputies to scour every conceivable area that friend Robert might have reached on foot in the time since his escape. It was barely past 0600, and Parrott felt as if he'd been trying to herd cats for the past hour. Aiken Mill's early risers and first-shift workers on their way into downtown might notice a significant number of law enforcement personnel engaged in all kinds of law enforcement activities this morning. Best-case scenario was Robert making as much noise as when he'd run out of the station so Parrott's men could follow the sound and haul him back in. Or, next-best case, that someone else would hear him and call in a report—preferably without any physical interaction, since that might turn out ugly. So far, no such call.

"I think we've got everyone we can get coming on duty," Deputy Dan said as he slid into Parrott's office through the partially open door. "Suzan has sent out a blue alert and posted notices on all social media. I thought I might check out that house our man was so interested in the other day. It's only a couple of miles from here."

"I had that on my mind as well. Let's both ride over that way. What was the owner's name? Pickett? Prickett? Pitchfork? Something such?"

"Pritchett. Phillip Pritchett."

"Right. I'll have Farley mind the store." He rolled his chair back from his desk and heaved himself to his feet. "We can take my car. I'll meet you out front."

Sykes nodded and headed out the door. Parrott grabbed his hat from the rack behind him, then paused to put his computer to sleep and make sure he hadn't forgotten to address any messages or notes that had come in since last night. Nope, nothing pressing, all good.

No word from Krummeck or the ER yet. He knew the man had a broken nose and probably a concussion. Maybe a fractured jaw.

The last thing he wanted was for some civilian to suffer any similar—or worse—misfortune. On its own, that would be bad enough, but it galled him even more that he had to hold someone from his department responsible. And by extension, himself.

After closing up his office, he stopped at the front desk, where Farley MacBane had just ended a call and was scribbling something on his notepad. "Got anything, Farley?"

The young man shook his head. "Nothing on Robert. But if you'd care to detour over to the McDonalds on Northside Drive...." He checked his note. "Ms. Eleanor Clifton, of 104 Lakemont Court, would like to press charges because they are out of Egg McMuffins."

"How the hell can McDonalds be out of McMuffins?"

"That's what she wants you to find out."

"I'll be stopping there when we're done. Farley, you have the con."

MacBane heaved an exaggerated sigh. "And on such a relaxing morning."

"Call me only if you're desperate. Scratch that. If you're desperate, call Beamer. He needs the practice."

"Ten-four, Sheriff."

Parrott tugged his hat onto his head and headed out the front door. To the left, looking east down Main Street, the first pale rays of daylight streamed between the downtown buildings. Hardly anyone, either on foot or in vehicles, appeared out and about yet. He turned right on the walkway to the parking lot, where Sykes stood waiting next to the Explorer, parked in first space next to the building. He unlocked the doors with his key fob. "Let's mount up."

Once they were out of the parking lot and cruising east on Main Street, Parrott glanced at Sykes. "You said Mr. Pritchett claimed to know nothing about Robert. Was he telling the truth?"

Sykes nodded. "I'm certain he was. Now, his brother—Martin Pritchett's his name—seemed to take special interest in Robert's mugshot. He indicated it was entirely 'professional,' since he teaches psychology."

"Do you buy 'professional interest'?"

Sykes gave a little shrug. "Maybe. Well, probably. I never quite know what to make of those college professor types."

"Any idea where his residence is?"

"Not offhand."

At Walnut Street, Parrott turned right for the short, block-long jog down to Church Street. Here, several small shops and other buildings lined either side of the street. His eyes automatically scanned every alcove, every shadowed space that might conceal someone trying not to be seen. He doubted Robert would have kept so close to the station, but as unstable as he was, he *might* try to find a nearby hiding place and hole up there for a time.

Next, he turned left onto Church Street and continued eastward through the main business district. It was too early for pedestrians, other than a scant handful of folks on their ways into work. Many of the buildings stood empty, since the old, family-run businesses that once occupied them had closed in the past two to three decades, the structures left to slowly deteriorate. Over on the left, Goldman's—the last remaining downtown department store—still clung to some semblance of life, though Parrott had no complimentary words for the crew who'd owned and managed the store since Mr. Goldman's death in the early 1990s. As he drove slowly past the building, his eyes focused on the alley between it and the brooding hulk of the First United Methodist Church to its right. He glimpsed what appeared to be a human figure silhouetted in that narrow space.

Reflexes drove his foot to the brake. There were no cars behind him, so he shifted into reverse and rolled back far enough to peer into the alley again.

Indeed, there was person back there. Rather than attempting to duck out of sight, the individual—it appeared to be a large male—stood erect and motionless in the center of the alley, facing Parrott's vehicle.

"What've you got, Sheriff?" Sykes asked.

"Someone back there. I don't think it's our man, though."

Sykes leaned forward to peer around Parrott. "Nope. Too large."

The figure advanced until Parrott could make out a tall, heavyset figure with thick, dark hair and deep-set, shadowed eyes that stared at him without blinking. He wore a black suit, black shoes, even a black shirt. Parrott's first impression was that he was too well-dressed to be a street person. From the outfit, he might be a clergyman, though certainly not from the Methodist Church. Parrott knew its pastor, a woman named Marianne Lockett, as well as her associate, a young fellow named Jonathan Bartee. This fellow was neither of them.

"You want me to get out and talk to him?" Sykes asked. "Find out if he's seen Robert, maybe?"

Parrott continued to gaze at the man, waiting for those staring eyes to blink. When they didn't, he steered the Explorer into an empty parallel parking spot next to the sidewalk. "Yeah. Let's see what he's about."

Once he'd turned off the engine, he swiveled out of the driver's seat, and started toward the alley, with Sykes close behind him. As he approached the opening between the two buildings, to his surprise, the black-clad figure turned and strode back into the shadows. Parrott hustled the last few steps to peer into the long, dark space, only to find it gaping back at him—empty.

Sykes came up behind him. "What the hell?"

Parrott walked a dozen yards into the alley, examined the walls on either side. There were no doors or windows here. Only solid brick siding to both left and right. And no manhole or grating in the concrete floor through which a person might descend into some underground culvert. A series of channel drains lined both sides of the alley, but there wasn't a single opening large enough to allow human access.

"If that don't beat all," Parrott grumbled as he returned to the sidewalk.

"He must have hauled ass all the way through to Main Street."

"He didn't have time to get half that distance without us seeing him."

"True. Rex Fisher couldn't run that fast," Sykes said, referring to Aiken Mill High School's star quarterback. "Still. He must have. He sure as hell didn't come out this way."

"No. He did not."

Sykes ventured down the alley, examined both walls, stepped out at the far end, and looked both ways on Main Street. On his return trip, he checked the walls yet again to verify he hadn't missed some hidden access.

"Nope, there's no way in and out of there except at each end."

"I trust he didn't up and vanish like our Mr. Lydell down at the morgue," Parrott said. "I think one of those is more than plenty."

Sykes stared down the long, empty passage, his expression grim. "Call me mystified."

"Well, that man wasn't Robert. And the longer we take, the farther he may go." He motioned toward the Explorer.

They trudged back to the vehicle and, once inside, Parrott drove them the mile or so down Church Street to the Pritchett residence. Just past the wall of red cedar trees that concealed the house, he turned into the driveway and parked next to a gleaming white BMW iX SUV in the wide turnaround in front of the porch. To the right, an older Toyota pickup dozed on a short concrete extension to the driveway. The modest, ranch-style structure struck Parrott as out of place, for he remembered the grand, two-story Southern Colonial that had occupied this lot when he was a child.

Neither Parrott nor Sykes spoke as they got out of the Explorer and approached the front door. Sykes, with a copy of Robert's mugshot in hand, pressed the doorbell button, and took two steps back to stand next to the sheriff. A shuffling noise came from inside, and a distorted, half-visible face—a woman's—appeared on the other side of the three cut-glass panes in the upper panel. The door drew partway open, and the face, which belonged to a blonde, thirty-something woman, peeked around it. She didn't open the glass storm door.

"Hello," she said, voice slightly muffled. "What can I do for you?"

Parrott took one step forward. It took him a moment, but he recognized the woman from a few face-to-face meetings at town council meetings as well as her glamor shot on innumerable "For Sale" signs in yards around town. "Good morning, ma'am. Sorry to disturb you, but we'd like to speak to Mr. Phillip Pritchett, if he's available."

She now pulled the front door wide and opened the storm door to address them. "Ah, Sheriff Parrott. I'm Carli Vaughan. We've met before, if you'll remember."

"I do remember."

"I'm afraid Mr. Pritchett isn't in just now. He's out walking his dog. May I help you?"

"He must get out and about early."

She laughed. "Only on very rare occasions. He went this morning because it's supposed to rain later. But you need to see him about…?"

Sykes produced Robert's mugshot and handed it to her. "Ma'am, we're looking for this man, who escaped our custody early this morning. He was seen in front of this property two days ago, and I questioned Mr. Pritchett and his brother about him yesterday. We wanted to check back in case the man might have returned to this area."

She gave the photo a thoughtful look. "No, I've never seen him. Phil didn't mention you'd been here before." She shot Parrott an annoyed glance. "Or that there'd been any kind of trouble."

Parrott cleared his throat. "You're not a resident here, are you, Ms. Vaughan? At this house, I mean?"

"Oh, no. Mr. Pritchett is my fiancé. We're getting married next month."

"I see. Well, congarters to you both."

She snickered. "Thank you."

"You said Mr. Pritchett is out walking his dog. Do you know where he might be walking?"

She stepped out to the porch, wearing an expensive, blue satin dressing gown and slippers. She glanced both left and right, and Parrott noticed that she appeared relieved to see the pickup truck in the driveway. "He usually drives out to the country to walk Rufus in the afternoon, but he sometimes walks in the neighborhood in the morning. He's likely on one of the side streets off Starling Avenue. He's got to be at work by nine. Would you like me to call him?"

"That might be a good idea," Parrott said.

"Give me a moment." She turned and disappeared back inside the house. When she returned a minute later, she had her cell phone pressed to her ear. After another few moments, she shook her head. "He's not answering. I'm sure he took his phone with him. He turns the ringer off at night and probably hasn't turned it back up. He does that a lot."

"Where does he work, ma'am?" Deputy Sykes asked.

"Studio 253, downtown." Ms. Vaughan's face shadowed with concern. "Is there more to worry about than you're telling me, Sheriff?"

"We don't think so," Parrott said in his most reassuring voice. "We just don't like to leave any stone unturned."

Her expression suggested that she found his answer unsatisfactory. "Does this have anything to do specifically with Phil—Mr. Pritchett?"

"Not that we know of. This was probably a random incident, but we don't want to take chances with people's safety. I trust you understand."

"I can appreciate that."

"Would you try calling him one more time, please?"

She nodded, lifted her phone, and punched Phil's number again. Still no answer. Clearly frustrated, she shook her head. "I'll text him. If nothing else, you could come back in a little while. I'm sure he'll be back by eight."

"Do text him, if you would. I hate to ask, Ms. Vaughan, but would you mind if we took a quick look around the property?"

"Seriously?" The apprehension in her eyes increased. "Well, if you must, I'm sure Phil won't mind."

"Thank you. We'll only be a short time. But you might want to lock your doors until we get back."

Her face went a shade paler. "Sheriff, you're making this sound more and more ominous."

"Just a routine precaution."

With a sigh of resignation, she started back into the house. "I'll make sure all the doors are locked, and I'll text Phil. I'll even keep calling."

"Once we're done, I'll come back and knock. Maybe by then you'll have reached him."

With a frown of clear displeasure, she closed the front door. He heard the click of the lock.

"You may have just lost one of your supporters," Sykes said with a wry laugh.

Parrott "hmmpf'd" as vague discomfort spread through his bones. "I don't know, Dan. There is some weird shit going on in this town, and I don't like the feeling I'm getting right now."

"You don't mean from Ms. Vaughan, do you?"

He shook his head, stepped off the porch, and started around the right side of the house. He gave the pickup truck a look up and down. Splotches of mud covered the tires and fenders. "Around this place," he said. "This house. Something's got my hackles up."

Around back, freshly fallen leaves from a pair of huge white oaks littered the yard. A line of red cedars, like those along the road, separated Pritchett's backyard from the lot directly behind it. A couple of dozen little white flags ringed the yard's perimeter, evidently to mark the boundaries of an invisible fence. Sykes wandered down to the lush evergreens and made a full circuit, eyeing every shadow with a critical eye. A large wooden storage shed, elevated on cinder blocks, occupied a space just behind the house on the left. A padlock sealed the door, which Parrott verified was locked. He lowered himself onto one knee and peered into the darkness beneath the shed. A grown man could have barely squeezed into that space. Apart from a couple of old bags of fertilizer, it appeared empty.

He saw no footprints, no paths of disturbed leaves, nothing to indicate that anyone—or even the dog—might have trodden in this yard in the past few hours. Sykes had walked the full perimeter and scanned the adjacent yards. He wandered back with a shake of his head.

"Looks all clear."

"That it does." The sheriff gave the backyard a long last gaze. "Well, let's see if Ms. Vaughan has had any success reaching Mr. Pritchett."

They went back around to the front of the house, and Parrott rapped on the door. Within seconds, Ms. Vaughan reappeared wearing a dejected expression.

"I'm sorry, I haven't been able to reach him," she said in a soft voice. "I did text him, though. Is everything all right here?"

Parrott nodded. "No sign of anything amiss."

"As soon as I get in touch with Phil, I can have him contact you."

"Please do."

"Oh, by the way." From her dressing gown pocket, she drew the now-crumpled mugshot. "Does this man have a name?"

"Robert. That's all we know. I'll be candid, Ms. Vaughan, this gentleman is unstable and has shown himself to be violent. If you do happen to see him, do not engage him in any way. Call us immediately. Will you do that?"

"Of course I will."

He gave her a genuine, appreciative smile. "I'm sure everything is fine here. But I wouldn't be doing my job if we didn't cover all our bases. I'll look forward to hearing from your fiancé."

She nodded and, with a wave of dismissal, closed herself inside the house.

As they climbed back into the Explorer, Parrott said, "Our man is somewhere close. You know what I'm going to do? I'm going to put two deputies on bicycles for a continuous patrol on Church Street from Bondurant to the old Liberty Mall. You and Carter are good on bikes, and that'll keep you close to the Pritchett residence. How do you like that idea, Deputy Dan?"

"I like it, Sheriff."

"I'm so glad."

"You really think Robert has his eye on that place, don't you?"

Parrott bit his lip, not entirely sure why this conviction had rooted itself so deeply. "I do. And there's no one I'd trust more than you to take him down."

Sykes shot him an approving smile. "Sometimes, Sheriff, you're all right."

"Sometimes."

"Yeah. But sometimes...."

ॐ

Chapter 22

The pain came and went. When it came, it was agony, as if scores of red-hot irons, wielded by powerful, unseen hands, rose and fell with devastating force upon his flesh and bones. Yet, this torture brought with it an unexpected clarity, a stability of thought, as if the smashing and burning also served to focus his senses on his internal torment. But with every pause in the hellish onslaught, his mind again became a whirl of disconnected ideas and images, bereft of coherence or sensation.

The pain was a conscious entity, actively—deliberately—forcing his mind to comprehend its depth, its cruelty.

At first, Robert had run and run, desperate to escape his physical and mental anguish. Yet, even with the clutching talons of agony ripping at him, he understood that he must avoid being seen or heard, or he'd be caught and probably killed by those looking for him. Yet, how could he hold back his screams? Vocalizing his anguish brought his only relief, and that only a little.

He left the sidewalks he'd been running on, made his way into woods, yards, and culverts, avoiding people, animals, anyone and anything that might become aware of his presence. He didn't know where he was going, only that he must keep moving. Every step carried him farther and farther from the source of this horror.

Didn't it?

Then the pain eased, and he suddenly had no idea where he was, or what he was doing. The sights his eyes beheld, the images his brain processed, all now shattered like paintings on glass panes blasted by buckshot. Then the slow, rolling train began again, and every concept, every memory, every sensation his brain attempted to grasp slipped away as if the train's engineer had gleefully firewalled the throttle.

Then searing heat crept back into his veins and coursed through his body like molten iron. He remembered his father's face. A kind, loving face. Had his dad experienced this same torture? Oh, yes! He remembered now! His father had told him he planned to come here, to this place, and Robert had followed, hoping to find him, *needing* to find him.

His father. Now only a ghost.

"The slipping away...."

Yes. Robert knew he was slipping away. Everything he had ever known, had ever been, was leaving. All of it, a little at a time. Sometimes faster, sometimes slower. But it *was* leaving.

Slipping away.

"Oh, no. Please, don't take my daddy."

Too late.

Shit! In the grip of rising pain, he realized he had left the cover of a copse of trees, and now he saw unbroken daylight.

Bad. This is bad!

Something made a loud noise. Startled him. A familiar sound, yet unknown. A warning? A dangerous sound?

A dog. A dog had barked.

At him.

Then he heard: "You! What the fuck do you want?"

At first, the utterance had no meaning, a mish-mosh of syllables in some unintelligible language. But then, like a self-solving puzzle, the syllables shifted, assumed shape and then depth. They conveyed recognition. He didn't know the person before him, but he somehow identified *with* this person. He felt something, *smelled* something.

It was a man. A man holding a dog on a leash. A big, golden-red dog with dark eyes that bored into his as if it could read him, *feel* him. He knew the animal could hurt him.

Whatever had touched him, it had also touched this man.

Somewhere they had both been.

Where his father had been!

Around the man, swirling wisps of smoke began to rise, curling plumes that sometimes rolled over and obscured his face, sometimes seemed to *be* his face.

Robert could smell the smoke.

"They tried to burn it," he mumbled. "Tried to burn everything."

"What the hell are you talking about?"

These were memories, yes. But not *his* memories.

"Long time ago."

The man and dog before him appeared now only as wavering, wispy silhouettes. He'd seen figures like this before. Did *they* create this pain, this torture?

A deep, menacing growl rumbled in his eardrums.

"Easy, Rufus." The low voice drifted out of the smoke.

"Looking for my father." Robert barely heard his own voice. "He's slipped away."

"I saw some of the sheriff's men a few minutes ago. I bet they're looking for you. How about I call them?"

No! He must not let himself be caught again. *They* could not help him. *They* would only harm him, inflict even more torment on him.

The dog's growl grew deeper.

"Jesus, there's something really wrong with you." The man's voice now seemed very far away. Hard to understand.

"Slipping...."

The alarmed voice had receded farther, now barely more than a whisper. "You are a fucking mess, man."

A spike of white-hot iron drove into Robert's brain, sent fire coursing through his body. He had to escape this, but how? *How?* With a desperate cry, he spun away from the smoke man with the smoke dog and bolted into the nearest cluster of shadow: a tangle of bushes and spindly trees off the edge of the sidewalk. He tore through the barrier of foliage, picked up speed, and ran blindly forward, into a chiaroscuro of wild colors and textures. He stumbled, fell, and rose again, but now his feet carried him over some dark edge. Then he was falling, tumbling into a crevasse of rushing green, onyx, and brown.

He hit bottom with a splash and realized he'd fallen into frigid, moving water.

A creek.

Through a mist of red, he saw a circular black maw, rimmed with weathered, uneven bricks, yawning before him. A mouth large enough to swallow him whole.

A steady stream of water poured from the opening, and its near-freezing touch cooled the fire in his blood without stealing his thoughts or his vision. He struggled upright and slogged through the almost knee-deep stream until he reached the gaping, brick-lined mouth. Inside, unbroken darkness leered at him. But the water felt like a welcome balm for the inferno inside him. Maybe he could conceal himself here, at least for a while.

He stepped into the tunnel, and blackness, like a living, beckoning thing, drew him deeper and deeper into its gullet. The sound of his sloshing footsteps echoed into unknown depths.

So tired. So exhausted. And still, hot pain wove through his body like fiery threads manipulated by unseen hands. From his tangled hair, water dripped into his eyes, fragmenting the darkness. He wiped his face with the back of his hand. When he drew it away, something thick and slippery covered his fingers.

"Whut?"

He ran one hand over his other arm, felt more slick warmth.

"Agh, God!"

He twisted around to face the tunnel's entrance, which admitted just enough light to cast a pale tint over his body. Some shiny, clear substance coated his arms, oozed down his neck, even dribbled from a corner of his mouth. Jesus, it was leaking from his ears!

Was he fucking *melting*?

From behind him, a new light seeped into his field of vision. He swung back around to face the dark passage, found the curved walls around him brightening with some bluish hue, a wash of luminous color that seemed to creep out of the distance. But it was a reflection without a source, for there was nothing down there that could cast such rays onto the cold stone.

But wait. Something *was* there, moving, coming toward him. Something so black it stood out against the pure darkness like a beacon, radiating waves of electric blue that washed over and surrounded him.

As it moved closer, the black thing assumed the shape of a man. A very large man who splashed his way toward Robert with dreadful purpose evident in his stride, if not his half-seen face.

He knew this figure. He didn't know *how* he knew. But, somehow, he did.

From that deep-shadowed face, a pair of wide, gleaming eyes stared at him without blinking.

"You," Robert muttered. "Whut?"

A weird, warbling cry rose and rang through the culvert, almost deafening him.

Some kind of bird?

An explosion of agony hit him, so powerful it rendered the fire inside him meaningless, nothing more than a little prickle of heat.

A scream tore its way from his lungs, erupted from his mouth, and rang into the dark depths like the howl of a tortured lion. Something splashed into the water beside him.

His arm.

Oh, my, Jesus! My fucking arm!

Another birdlike cry came, but far too loud to *be* a bird. Pressure built inside his skull, and then his eardrums blew out, spewing blood and clear, viscous fluid into the stream. The crack of thunder that accompanied the burst died instantly, and sound became nothing more than a painful, drilling vibration that first filled his skull and then zoomed like a current through his body.

He dropped to his knees, but then his left leg collapsed, and he toppled onto his side with a splash. Something seemed to be clawing at every inch of his flesh and bone, and in the electric glow, he saw his lower left leg twist around, the booted foot jerking itself free to spiral into the water and disappear with a silent splash. His screams pealed through the tunnel, his memory of sound making them *almost* real to his dying senses.

The unseen and unheard attacker clawed, ripped, and tore until Robert felt everything inside him fleeing—blood, bone, mind, memory. *Life.* In otherworldly silence, he saw what might have been flashes of electricity popping all around the thrashing remnants of his physical body.

The face of the figure standing in the tunnel appeared dull and lifeless but for the eyes, which might have been twin black suns blazing in the void of outer space. Under that unfathomable gaze began the final dissolution of Robert John Caviness, the only child of Franklin Lydell Caviness, thus ending forever that family's tenure in the world of the living.

Chapter 23

"**Y**ou saw who?" Martin asked, not sure whether he'd heard his brother correctly.

"I think it was the man in the mugshot," came Phil's slow, weary-sounding voice over Martin's cellphone. "You know, the one the deputy brought by yesterday. The one you had bullshit to say about."

"Are you sure?"

Phil seemed to think for a moment. "Pretty sure. Same wild hair and eyes. Like the guy in the photo."

"Where did you see him?"

"Over on Pine Street. I couldn't sleep for shit, so I got up early and took Rufus for a walk. He just came out of nowhere, hollering and acting crazy."

"I thought he was in jail."

"Apparently, he broke out last night. That's what Carli told me. The sheriff and that deputy came to the house while Rufus and I were walking."

"So, what happened?"

199

"Huh?"

"What happened? What did he do?"

"Oh. He babbled a lot. Couldn't make out much. Then he just ran away."

"Did you call the sheriff?"

"What?"

"Did. You. Call. The. Sheriff?"

"Oh. Yeah, I did. Well, I talked to Deputy Sykes, told him where I saw the guy. He said they'd check it out right away."

"I'll be damned." Martin leaned back in his office chair, glanced out the window. It had begun to rain a short while ago and was now coming down in sheets so heavy he couldn't see the courtyard below. He realized he had been damn near shouting to hear himself over the torrents that battered the glass panes. He lowered his voice a little. "So, I gather you're all right?"

A long pause. "Yeah."

"Are you sure? Is anything wrong, Phil?"

"Huh? What?"

"That, right there. You sound very out of it."

Another pause. "I'm just tired. Having a hard time focusing."

"Are you at your studio?"

"Yeah. Not getting much work done. Got an administrative meeting after lunch. Not looking forward to it."

"Sorry to hear it. Anyway, about this man. What did you think? Did he have the eyes? The Caviness eyes?"

A very long pause. "I don't know."

"Damn, Phil. You seemed pretty convinced last night. We both did."

"Well, it was hard to tell in person. He was kind of a mess, you know."

"What do you mean?"

"I mean he was filthy dirty, like he'd been crawling in mud and shit. Had all kinds of nasty-looking goop on him. I didn't get very close."

"Did the deputy say anything else? Other than they'd check things out?"

"No." He drew a long breath. "Nothing."

"I just wonder if they intend to talk to you again."

"Didn't say anything about it. I expect they were busy as hell at the time."

"I guess they were." Martin glanced at the clock. He had five minutes to get to his eleven o'clock class. "If they talk to you again, it might be worth bringing up his resemblance to the people in the photos at the old house."

"Why?"

"Could be a clue. They were trying to establish his identity."

"Robert. His first name's Robert, right?"

"Yeah, I believe so."

Phil sounded like he was on the verge of saying something, but he did not.

"Well?"

"I don't know." A pause. "No. I wouldn't say anything about it. Don't see that it would help any."

Martin wanted to disagree. Logic and reason insisted that he disagree. But then....

No.

"All right, Phil, I've got to get to class. I'll be out of here at three, and Alana's coming over tonight. But give me a call if anything else happens."

"What do you mean 'happens'?"

"What the hell do you think I mean? If you see that man again. If the sheriff comes back around. If you actually think of anything worth saying."

"Oh. All right."

"Maybe you should go home and get some sleep, brother. You sound like shit."

"Yeah. Maybe I will."

"We'll talk later."

Silence. Finally, "Okay."

"Bye, Phil."

Dead silence. Phil was gone.

"Shit," Martin muttered. Phil sounded beyond lethargic, which worried him a little. Especially given that he had encountered this "Robert" on the street—and after the man had created a disturbance in front of his house a couple of days before. And why the hell not tell the sheriff about the possible resemblance between Robert and the members of the Caviness family they'd seen in the old photographs?

Why did *he* not want to?

He opened his phone's photo gallery and selected the clearest of the photos he had taken of the preacher on campus—the man who had zoomed away from him as if on a rail and then vanished.

Were those Caviness eyes as well?

The image was too blurry to tell for certain. But he saw that face in his memory. Dark, thick hair. And those damn-near black, widely spaced eyes.

The things he said. The message he'd given him. He fucking *had* to be a Caviness!

Martin had three minutes to get to class.

His notes, briefcase, tablet, all still down there. He knew he should never leave any class materials behind like that, but he hadn't thought to grab them before coming up to his office, fifteen minutes ago. He started to put his phone away when a whisper crept out of nowhere.

"The blue and the gold."

Now, he stood facing a long, dark passage that stretched ahead for some unfathomable distance. A tiny sphere of electric blue hovered like a shimmering star in the field of dense black.

"Jesus Christ, not this!"

A warm, golden gleam rose around the blue, like the sun's corona during a total eclipse. He felt himself moving toward it in steady if not rapid strides, though he did not will the movement. It was automatic. *Programmed.* A deep voice—one that would boom in his ears once he drew nearer—enunciated syllables that surely formed words, though his ears and brain could not yet apprehend them. The blue light brightened, the ring of gold sharpened, and the voice became clearer.

"They lasted years, not days," came the oratorial voice. "Their suffering slow and sweet, their time hath served the others well. But as these others hath flourished, so shall ye bear witness and service them in *their* time. Mark ye these words!"

Martin nearly stumbled, as if he'd been in mid-step, when his office reappeared in his field of vision and he saw the clock on the wall in front of his desk.

Two minutes to get downstairs to his classroom.

The vision seemed to have lasted much longer. That darkness, the colors, all familiar to him, though he could not place where he'd seen them. And he knew the voice. Without a doubt, it belonged to that preacher.

He still held his phone, and the screen still displayed the image of the mystery man.

"Who the hell are you? What do you want?"

He closed the gallery image and slid the phone back into his pocket. How in the hell could he function with these endless delusions taking him by surprise, striking at random times and with overwhelming power? He needed a fucking doctor. Holding some willful outside force responsible for them was not sane.

No! That willful force originated at the House of Caviness. It absolutely *did*.

One minute.

"And now I am going downstairs to teach college students how to research aberrant mental conditions." As he started out the door, he almost laughed. "Behold exhibit number one."

#

As planned, he made dinner for Alana. It turned out damned good, if Martin might say so himself. They accompanied the Mahi Mahi with a bottle of excellent Gewürztraminer, which he knew would be insufficient to brace him for what he intended to share with her, so he had preceded her arrival with a double Martytini. Between the cocktail and the wine, he felt almost adequately braced.

They had anticipated spending the evening plotting their trip to Northern Virginia. However, this morning's hallucination had felt like the last straw. He argued long and hard with himself about the wisdom of relating select details about his experiences over the past week. Even as of last night, he had resolved to say nothing about these issues to her. Yet now, he felt forced to acknowledge that honesty—well, maybe not *total* honesty—was necessary if this relationship had any hope of progressing to true, mutual commitment. What if one of these hallucinations struck in her presence? There could be no concealing it, and Alana learning that he had kept something so significant from her would spell the end of everything.

He could not, would not, abide that eventuality. So, during dinner, he'd forewarned her that he needed to broach a potentially uncomfortable subject with her.

Heavy rain still rattled against the roof, though he felt grateful for their ears' sake that the relentless thunder had stopped a couple of hours ago. They settled on the loveseat adjacent to his couch, facing the television, which streamed smooth jazz at barely enough volume to be heard over the rain. A scrolling series of picturesque scenes from Europe accompanied the music. He'd poured them both a glass of Cockburn's 20-year-aged Tawny Port to make sure they were both well-fortified once he worked up the nerve to open his mouth.

Alana gave him a searching look as he took a long swallow. "All right," she said. "You've been very mysterious, but I gather this is important. I think we can rule out a marriage proposal, since neither of us have any desire to go down that road." Her face shadowed. "That's still true, yes?"

"Still very true," he said with a nervous laugh. Then he turned somber. "But yes, I would call this serious because it involves some truly weird events and situations. I know I've told you a little about my brother going through some peculiar experiences."

"You've mostly spelled out how your brother is a peculiar individual."

"This too is true. But he isn't the only one to experience the things I am about to tell you. I have too. And I think it's fair to say that they're beyond my understanding."

"I'm listening."

He hadn't wanted to launch into his account in college professor mode, but now on the spot, it felt like the only way to keep from sounding like a babbling twit. So, he thought, follow the sequence of events. Don't get rattled. Pretend you've made notes.

"Okay. You know Phil and I sometimes go out to that little pond off Old Beckham Road to walk his dog, right?"

She nodded.

"Well, a week or so ago, we discovered an old house out there. A real ruin. Phil and I have gone exploring in there a few times. I've even been into it on my own. We've found some very unusual things."

"Old houses are fascinating," she said in an understanding tone. "I've done that kind of thing too—when I was a youngster, anyway."

"Well, from the time we found it, I became fixated on that place. So did Phil. Even before we found the house itself, I had a...." He paused to select the proper words. "Maybe you'd call it a premonition. Some very strong feeling that drew me out to Black Tooth Pond. And it's kept on drawing me there." He stopped again, knowing he wasn't painting her an accurate picture. "No. This was a true hallucination. Not just sight and sound. A full sensory experience. They have continued for several days now, getting more and more vivid. And influential."

He now had her rapt attention. At least she did not appear disturbed. More curious. Intrigued.

"What do you mean 'influential'?"

"I mean that, when they happen, there's usually a kind of sequence to them. A progression. One builds on another, and I've felt compelled to follow where they lead." He swallowed hard. "They've influenced me to go out to that house. And just the other night, I lost time out there. I mean, hours gone. Again, so did Phil. Both of us. A long spell that neither of us can remember. He's had even more of these episodes than I have. They're wearing him down, I think. Hell, I think I'm feeling it myself."

Alana's gaze turned inward for a moment. "How would you account for this happening to both of you?"

"Well, as you might guess, the first thing I considered was basic science. Something in the environment. Not inside the house itself, though. Remember, these all started prior to us even finding the house. But maybe something at the pond—chemicals, something organic. But I don't think it's anything environmental. It's just too unlikely."

"Are you sure? Shouldn't you see a doctor? Both you and Phil? What if it's some condition or susceptibility running in your family? Something congenital, even."

"I've thought about all that. In depth. But I can't buy the coincidental timing for anything like that. So no, I do not believe a doctor is the answer here."

"Okay. How about some of the professors at Beckham? All these departments we've got. Chemistry, Biology, Zoology, Environmental Science. I'd say Psychology, but something tells me you might have already consulted with someone in that field." She gave him a weak smile.

"Very sensible. But before I say anything else, I want to show you something." No, he *didn't* want to show her, but he had come this far without retreating. He rose from his seat, went to his den, and retrieved the bound stack of papers from the House of Caviness. Once seated again, he said, "These are from the house. I call it the House of Caviness, by the way. This is why." He pointed out the names on the addressed envelopes. "I've been through these over and over. Look at the notes. I'm pretty sure they were written in blood."

She studied several of the pages, thumbed through the envelopes. Once she'd examined a fair sampling of them, she gave him a contemplative frown. "I'd say someone was mentally disturbed."

He nodded, removed a few of the news clippings from the envelopes, and gave her a summary of their contents. "I'd call these a catalog of some of the world's worst events from those years. And now, I've been getting a barrage of contemporary news in the same vein, all shared from an online account that, by all indications, doesn't even exist. Phil's getting them too. Now." He flipped to the bottom of the stack, withdrew the last page, and handed it to her.

"'Your name is inscribed in blood in the book of the doomed.'" She gave a disgusted snort. "Southern Baptist, I'd say."

He cracked a smile for a half-second. "But would you say it's exactly the same as the others?"

She looked at a few of the other notes, then held up the sheet. "This paper is newer."

He nodded. "I received it just the other day. In fact, it was on Wednesday, after we had lunch at Frith's. A man on campus, looked and acted a lot like a preacher. He gave it to me." He did not mention the phenomenon he had witnessed, the man seeming to *glide* away from him. Or having seen him walking across the river at lunchtime. Or his appearance in Martin's hallucinations. But he took his phone from his pocket, opened his image gallery, and selected one of the photos he had taken. "This is the man. He called me by name."

She regarded the figure for a few moments. "Striking."

"What are the chances of coincidence here? That someone would know my name and give me a message like this—hell, it's one of the exact same lines—in the very same writing as these old, old pages?"

For the first time, Alana's eyes reflected a hint of apprehension. "Not very likely."

"And unless I'm very much mistaken, he resembles the people in the photos at the house. He's got to be related." He pointed to the pile of paper. "For what it's worth, I don't think any one of these notes or clippings stands out as especially significant. My feeling is that they were meant to have a cumulative effect on that family. On their collective psyche, one might say."

"Why?"

"To depress them, wear them down, I don't know for sure. Maybe out of spite or resentment."

She breathed a sigh of frustration. "Okay, Marty. Once you've eliminated the implausible, if not the impossible, and put all the rest together, what do you come up with?"

This was the moment for which he had fortified himself. He should have sunk at least one more glass of port.

"An assault. A deliberate attack, both physical and psychological. Not only on me, but on my brother."

She spoke in a flat tone. "An assault by whom? Or what?"

He tried to swallow, but his throat felt so parched it burned. To say the words took more effort, more courage, than anything he'd ever said in his life. "I believe this is a psychic attack by...something. Some force that is beyond my understanding."

This is it. This is where she either stays or leaves.

She did not leave but stared at him as if he were a stranger who'd directed an obscene remark at her. Then, after an excruciating few moments, her eyes took on a gleam of what might have been humor.

"Martin Pritchett. Did you just admit to me that you believe in ghosts? Or maybe demons?"

She's still here. She stayed.

"I don't know what to believe anymore. A week ago, I would never have believed any of this."

She slid one hand over to rest on top of his. "This has tortured you. I'm sorry, Marty. But if I had known...."

"I wasn't even going to tell you tonight. But then this morning, I had one of those hallucinations. Even 'hallucination' is an inadequate word. It's more a state of total sensory experience, even if I'm rationally aware it's not really happening. But at least I remember these. Out at the house...." He shook his head.

"All right, Marty. This is what we're going to do. You're going to take me out to this pond. And to this house. I want to see it for myself."

He felt a hot blade stab the back of his skull. "No. No way. I'm not going to let you be subjected to whatever this is. That's where all this comes from, Alana. Out there."

"You believe there's something there. Obviously, strange things have been happening. But you of all people know the power of *belief*. Believing in something doesn't make something real."

"I didn't believe it to start with. I don't think even I believed it until I said those words to you just now. Alana, belief didn't start this or perpetuate it. If I have belief, it's a direct result of all this."

"Still, you've shared your feelings and experiences with your brother, is that right? But until now, you haven't shared any of this with me." She squeezed his hand. "We're going out there. Or, if you can't bring yourself to go, I'll go myself. But I intend to see this place."

"I'll show you the photos I've taken. There are quite a lot."

She shook her head. "That's not even close to experiencing the place itself."

His nerves jangled like windchimes in a violent gale. "You don't understand what might happen. If it follows the same pattern...."

Her gaze was incontestable. "We can't go tonight, obviously. The weather's supposed to clear up overnight, though. Tomorrow morning, I have to go into the office. No way out of that, but I'll be done by lunchtime. So tomorrow afternoon, either you will take me out there, or I will go alone."

"You're not going alone. No way."

"Well, then. It's settled."

Martin hated the idea of Alana going out to that house, possibly—maybe even likely—to be victimized by the same psychic force that had overwhelmed him. Yet, despite his mind rebelling violently against the prospect, he realized now that he could desire no experience, no treasure, no anything, more than he desired to return to the House of Caviness.

THE HOUSE AT BLACK TOOTH POND

IX. SATURDAY

Chapter 24

Northeastern Labs in Roanoke had emailed the test results of the mud from Frank Lydell's car late Friday afternoon. Sheriff Parrott didn't see the email until Saturday morning, not that those few off-duty hours impacted the investigation's progress—or lack thereof. The analysis report included charts and graphs that detailed Soil pH, Nutrient Concentration, Organic Matter Concentration, and other such categories, none of which meant diddly to him. What mattered was the comments section at the end, which read, "Soil content indicates sample originated from low-lying wetlands area, of primarily deciduous forest, most consistent with characteristics of northwestern Sylvan County. Small amounts of petroleum and other synthetic materials suggest no significant motor vehicle presence. Trace amount of charcoal and a minimal nutrient material, likely due to a long period of high erosion, suggest occurrence of high-intensity forest fire, dating as far back as a century."

Soil samples were like fingerprints, for every locale possessed unique identifying characteristics. So, in this case, the clues led to northwestern Sylvan County, a remote wetland area, and an old forest fire. Parrott's brain stored a fair amount of the county's history, but mostly from his lifetime, and more about its people and their businesses than places and events. He surmised the location in question lay somewhere off Old Beckham Road, likely closer to Beckham than Aiken Mill.

His men had focused their search efforts for Robert on the southeastern corner of the county, near Lake Charity along the Camden River, because if you wanted to wrestle with mud, you'd find swamps and marshlands aplenty out that way. And a lot of moonshine, which meant networks of little-known, mostly hidden roads into and through the woods.

He had no idea if the mud on that car had even the slightest connection to Lydell's grisly death—and his remains' subsequent vanishing. For all Parrott knew, Lydell had gone fishing or something and driven through a sizable puddle. And after yesterday, he knew, there would be lots and lots of new puddles—damn near lakes— out there. For that matter, yesterday's gullywashers had sure as hell complicated his team's search for Robert.

Well, if one were going to grasp at straws, might as well grasp even the tiniest of them. Especially when straws were all you had left.

God knew how many forest fires had burned through Sylvan County over the years. The only one he could recall for certain was a big one out east, beyond Mount Signal, in the late 1970s. If anyone in the department could claim to be well-versed in county history, it would be Francine Harris. She knew a little about a lot, though not necessarily vice-versa. She was off duty today, though.

But wait. He had spoken with an expert in local history a few days ago, and he still had Professor Scales's phone number stuck to his desktop blotter. Worth a try, he supposed.

He called the number and, after a couple of rings, the professor's familiar voice answered.

"Good morning, Professor Scales. This is Sheriff Parrott again. I hope I'm not intruding on your time."

"What can I do for you, Sheriff?" Scales's voice sounded cheerful enough.

"I was hoping to pick your brain again about that case we discussed the other day. I've received an analysis of some mud samples that may help lead us to a location of interest. I'm looking for a location in northwestern Sylvan County. There would have been a forest fire there, maybe a century ago, give or take a couple of decades. Would that ring a bell for you?"

"Well, there've been plenty of forest fires in this area over the years. Up toward Beckham you're saying?"

"That is correct."

"The biggest one out that way was around 1930. Supposedly arson. I can't say I know much about it, though. I know it was big and hot enough to burn through a bunch of marsh land."

"I expect that's the one."

"Ever hear of a spot called Black Tooth Pond? It's out that way, not far off Old Beckham Road."

"I may have. It's never really been on my radar, officially or otherwise."

"Of course, that area's all grown back up, but it's roughly where the big fire started. The most commonly accepted story is that feuding moonshiners started it. Who knows whether that's actually true." He laughed. "It's quite coincidental, but do you remember I mentioned the legend of the Yck the other day?"

"I do remember."

"That's one of the areas the Yck supposedly haunted. Of course, it had a wide area of influence, so to speak, but the Native Americans—the Tutelo tribe in this region—believed it lived in those woods. I told you that they didn't call it the 'Yck.' That was a later appellation, not that it would matter to you. I just find it interesting."

"Indeed. Well, I'll figure out where to find Black Tooth Pond and take it from there."

"It's on local maps, though not labeled with any name. Tell you what, if you'd like, I can email you a screenshot of the area map. That ought to put you where you need to be."

"That might be very helpful. Just out of curiosity, have you ever been to Black Tooth Pond yourself?"

"A long time ago, when I was a youngster. My family lived a couple of miles from there. Used to go fishing at the pond from time to time—or I tried to. The fishing there was never much good. And in those days, there was a house or two nearby, and I got run off one too many times. Of course, after all the jobs went away, that area just died out. Far as I know, no one's lived on that land for forty, fifty years."

"Did you know the people who lived there at the time? The ones who ran you off?"

"I think the name was Cavanaugh or Cabinets, or something to that effect." He laughed. "Didn't know them at all, and they clearly didn't care to know me."

"I gather you don't still live out that way?"

"Oh, no. I've lived in Forest Park at Lake Charity ever since I retired. And when I taught at Beckham, I lived just off campus."

"Once again, you've been very helpful, and I appreciate it."

"Well, I can't imagine I provided you much help when you called before. But if you'll give me your email, I'll drop you a shot of the map."

Parrott and Scales exchanged email addresses. "Thank you again, sir. I've enjoyed our conversations."

"Likewise. And I do hope you'll crack this case, Sheriff. You have a hard job."

"It can be that. Let's talk again sometime when circumstances are better."

"I'd like that."

"Until then."

"Bye, now."

Two minutes later, Professor Scales's email arrived with an attached screenshot from Google Maps. Sure enough, the image showed a small body of water a short distance west of Old Beckham Road, several miles north of Aiken Mill. The sheriff traveled that road regularly, so he would have passed the pond countless times essentially unawares. Now that he thought about it, it lay near the spot—in fact, it might be *the* spot—where he'd seen that SUV pull out of the woods a few nights ago, after he'd made his semi-regular house call to the Draper place. Once he'd turned around to pursue the hooligan school principal, Ms. Stultz, his sighting of the SUV had all but vanished from his mind.

Again today, Chief Deputy Sykes had his team out in the field to hunt down their jailbreaker. This was Beamer's Saturday to be on duty. Surely, the young deputy would enjoy going for a drive in the country, so Parrott called him on the radio.

"Where are you?"

"Out on Highway 21, Sheriff."

"How much money have you made us?"

A moment of abashed silence. "Do I have to answer that, Sheriff?"

"Not immediately. Can you be back here in ten?"

"Not without breaking laws."

"Try for as soon as you can without having to write yourself a ticket."

Another long silence. "I expect that'll take fifteen."

"You're a prince. See you then."

#

The rain had stopped early this morning, though the day remained overcast. Numerous deep pools of water had formed in several low-lying areas along Old Beckham Road. When he turned the Explorer into the damn-near hidden entrance to the woods, the first thing Parrott saw was what appeared to be a small lake about fifteen feet in. He had to park his Explorer with its front tires at the edge of the water to prevent its tail end hanging out in the road. After yesterday and last night, he might have expected this. Unfortunately, it did not bode well for gathering any of the clues he'd hoped to find.

Between the weatherman and the slowpoke bastards at South-eastern Labs, he felt an uncharacteristic hankering to slap some folks in jail and let them stew for a very long time.

Alas.

In any event, based on his recollection, he felt certain this was, in fact, the spot from which that SUV had turned onto the road the other night.

He had looked up the owner of the property that encompassed Black Tooth Pond, which was listed as an individual or business called Niemand. No clarifying information came up on his subsequent search, so he'd follow up on it when he had a spare moment. If the mystery owner had any issue with the sheriff's warrantless incursion, they could take it up with him later. As it was, he more than half-suspected the records simply hadn't been updated and the county now owned the land due to this "Niemand" failing to pay property taxes. Hardly an infrequent occurrence in Sylvan County.

He and Beamer got out of the Explorer and picked their way along the edge of what had clearly been, until last night, a narrow, rutted road. By sticking to the slightly elevated, root-choked shoulder on its left, they were able to avoid the worst of the deep water. Still, their boots sank up to their ankles as they made their way into the shadows beneath the towering beeches, ironwoods, poplars, and sycamores. Out here, the air held the agreeable scent of petrichor and loam, although he detected some harsher, sour odor lurking behind it. A short distance farther on, they came to the edge of a dark, oblong body of water, its banks choked by reeds, tangled vines, and piles of old, rotting brush. Sure enough, at the far end of the pond, several broken, blackened stumps jutted from the murky water. Black Tooth Pond indeed. If these represented the last, weathered remnants of that ages-old fire, then at one time, it must have been a spectacular array of jagged black tusks that sprouted from the pond.

Parrott heard no sound, not even a whisper of breeze. No birds calling, no frogs croaking or peeping, no splashing of fish, not even any scrambling squirrels to make their presence known. No doubt, the maturing season accounted for the lack of active fauna, but the overbearing stillness struck him as unusual. Uncomfortable, even.

"It's a pretty enough place," Beamer said, staring at the distant, truncated wooden towers. "Kinda sad and lonely, though."

Parrott nodded. "I think you're right."

This far in, the pooled water wasn't as deep, but if there had been any distinguishable tracks here, they were gone now. His heart sank even farther.

Then Carli Vaughan's statement about her fiancé, Phillip Pritchett, slipped out from one of his brain's recent creases.

"He usually drives out to the country to walk Rufus in the afternoon...."

Well, that probably meant nothing. Given that the better part of Sylvan County constituted "the country," the odds didn't favor this place. Yet, if he squinted, some of the little puzzle pieces he'd collected seemed to have interlocking edges. Given the information Professor Scales had shared with him, he felt more than half-certain that Frank Lydell had set foot on this very ground. Earlier, Parrott had intuited some link between Lydell and their mentally disturbed friend, Robert. Friend Robert had shown specific interest in Phillip Pritchett's property. And Phillip Pritchett liked to come out to the country to walk his dog.

True, these puzzle pieces had yet to form anything that resembled a solid image, and chances were that none of them connected at all. Still, one ignored even the slimmest evidence at one's own peril.

So, here we are.

Finding a narrow ridge of only half-submerged earth, Beamer stepped onto it and treaded cautiously toward the pond. An alarm

215

bell sounded in Parrott's head. "Do me a favor, Vince. Don't get too close to the bank there. Assuming our friend Mr. Lydell did come out here, this could be where he ran into what got him."

Beamer shot the sheriff a look of surprise. "You think something in the water?"

"No idea. But better safe than sorry."

Beamer backtracked, picking his steps carefully. His face became a thoughtful frown. "You know, it's a long way from here to that Druid Hills apartment."

"Granted. But assuming Lydell's trail leads here, then following it is what we do."

"True that." Beamer looked around and pointed to the pond's left bank. "Looks like a path over there, Sheriff."

Parrott saw it. A break in the thick foliage revealed a ribbon of flattened, soaked earth that led to slightly higher ground and into the deeper woods. His right hand automatically slid down to touch the handle of his holstered Glock 19. On the path itself, although trampled leaves, grass, and brush suggested human passage, if there had been any individual footprints before yesterday, they didn't exist anymore.

Their footsteps squishing in the mud, he led the way for a hundred yards or so without seeing anything that struck him as out of place or even unusual. As they rounded a long curve, they came to a broad pool of muddy water and saw, on the far side of it, a huge fallen poplar blocking the path. Parrott drew up short of the water, gave the woods to either side a quick scan, and peered beyond the fallen tree at the continuing path, which curled to the right and out of sight around the pond.

"Well, no red flags that I can see. Not to here, anyway. Just a lot of mud and water."

Beamer agreed. "Woods is woods. Very, very wet woods."

Somewhere beyond the reeds and brush that obscured their view of the pond, something splashed. A heavy, solid *ker-blump*—like the sound of a man doing a cannonball off a high diving board, Parrott thought. Far too big to be a fish or duck or beaver. After a moment, he detected a rapid, rhythmic splashing, like someone swimming fast and hard across the pond.

"What do you make of that?" Beamer asked.

Parrott kept his voice low. "There was an open space a ways back. Let's check it out from there."

He wandered back thirty or forty feet, with Beamer in tow, until they came to an opening between two gnarled ironwood trees that framed the long view of the pond. From here, maybe a hundred yards out, a long, rippling streamer, like a motorboat's wake, moved steadily from right to left across the pond's breadth. In the murky brown water, he couldn't discern what created the disturbance—no shape, no shadow, no nothing at the streamer's leading edge. Once it reached a point roughly at the pond's center, the movement ceased, and the ripples trailed away until the water again appeared still.

For a full two minutes, both men's gazes zoomed from point to point around the pond, seeking a sign of any further movement out there. None came.

"No way that could have been a man, could it?" Beamer asked at last.

"Only if he had an aqualung."

"It must have been pretty big, though. A bear?"

Parrott shook his head. "I don't think so. Bears don't usually stay underwater like that."

Beamer's eyes continued to rove around the pond and its banks. "If it breathes air, it's got to come back up. Somewhere."

Two more minutes, and no further sound or movement. The stillness in both the water and the air felt absolute.

Parrott folded his arms and pondered his next move. He hardly felt ready to suggest, even to himself, that whatever had *almost* appeared out there might have been responsible for Frank Lydell's death and mutilation. Still, he knew the region's forest and aquatic animals well enough to respect the little tickle in those sensitive nerves that told him something wasn't right.

Professor Scales's "Yck," perhaps?

He was just about to suggest that he and Beamer return to the Explorer when he again heard a heavy splash in the water, this time to his right, only a few feet beyond the nearest ironwood and the layers of tangled creepers that impeded his view of the water. Continued splashing, which grew steadily louder, told him that something was moving toward them at a clip.

Another sound rose from the other side of the creepers, loud and shocking, which Parrott could not reconcile with the oncoming splashing noise. This was a shrill yet voluminous "*WHIPP-WHIPP-WHIPP*," which he recognized as the opening notes of a whippoorwill cry, repeated over and over but never swelling into a full song.

But this could be no bird. It was too *big*. Too coarse. Not to mention the whippoorwill was a small nightbird. A nightbird that, as far as he knew, did not swim.

Beamer looked at him with barely concealed trepidation, and one hand slid toward his gun. "I'm gonna check it out, Sheriff."

"Hold on. We'll do it together. I'll move around to the right."

Beamer positioned himself on the left side of the nearest ironwood as Parrott maneuvered to its right through a cluster of twisted vines that dangled from its long, splayed branches. Once a couple of feet from the water's edge, he drew his Glock, motioned for Beamer to do the same. All he had to do now was take two steps to his right, tug away a thick tangle of creepers, and he'd have a clear view of the pond.

He whispered, "On three, Vince."

The splashing drew still nearer.

"One. Two. Three."

He made his move and found his right foot sinking deep into water and soft mud. Still, with a reasonably smooth motion, he managed to complete his two-step shift, pull back the long creepers as if they were curtains, and aim his gun at the point where he predicted he'd see *something*.

Nothing.

Five yards to his left, on the other side of the ironwood, Beamer materialized amid the creepers, pistol also outstretched. When his eyes registered the same thing as Parrott's, he gaped in bewilderment.

Nothing but empty, muddy water. The only ripples on the surface were those spreading from where the sheriff's foot had splashed down.

Parrott scanned every knot of vines, every jumble of undergrowth, even the gnarled branches of the nearest trees, mostly ironwoods, which arched out over the water in their quests for sunlight.

Not one damn thing out of the ordinary. A tiny frog jumping into the water would have made more of a disturbance.

"Vince," he called out.

"Yes, sir?"

"I think we're going to head back to the barn. Then I will return home and start the day over again. I will not be coming into work."

"Sounds like a good plan."

"Not for you. Somebody's got to mind the store."

Beamer glanced at him with hopeful eyes. "Does that make me

the boss?"

"Not really, no."

"Oh."

Despite his unperturbed tone, Parrott's nerves felt like taut springs. Both he and Beamer had seen something out in the middle of the pond, and they'd both heard the odd, incongruous sounds only a few feet from the bank. Then to find themselves faced with nothing?

Really?

Once recouped and regrouped, they started back toward the Explorer, again treading carefully along the raised, root-choked edge of the road to avoid the deep water. In the time they'd been here, some of the most extensive puddles had already run off via little gurgling waterfalls into the lower-lying wooded area to the right of the road, which had overnight become a bona fide swamp. Still, even with no further rainfall, it might be days or weeks before this morass dried up.

As they reached the Explorer, Parrott said to Beamer, "Grab a mud sample, Vince. The least we can do is to confirm that it matches the shit from Lydell's truck."

Beamer nodded, opened the back door, and rummaged through one of the large, lock & lock-style evidence kits to find an apt sample jar. As Beamer set about collecting a good sample, Parrott took his place behind the wheel, started the engine, and radioed the dispatcher—Meghan Langley this morning—to let her know that he and Beamer would be back within twenty minutes.

"Meghan, I don't suppose there's any word about Robert, our escapee, is there?"

"Afraid not, Sheriff. You know you'll be the first to hear."

"Roger that. It would just be nice to see somebody besides Beamer making a little progress. He wrote two tickets this morning."

A little pause while Meghan snickered to herself. "Remember, Sheriff, it takes time and effort to come up in the world."

"Here is wisdom. Look, Meghan, I want you to holler at Deputy Dan. I don't care what he's doing or where he is with his search, I want him in my office in an hour."

"Urgent, is it, Sheriff?"

"Serious."

"Roger that."

"Parrott, out."

The passenger door opened and Beamer climbed in. He held up

his sample jar as if it were a prized trophy. "I'm done here."

"All right, then." Parrott shifted the vehicle into reverse, backed into the road, and then pulled up along the shoulder. "Hold on for a short minute, Vince."

Beamer gave him curious look. "Okay."

The sheriff slid out of his seat, went around back, and, upon opening the door, grabbed a roll of yellow tape. Two tall, sturdy poplar trees rose on either side of the road's entrance, so he unrolled a length of tape, wrapped one end around the trunk on the left, and tied it securely in place. He drew the tape across the space between the trees, pulled it semi-tight, and tied it in place to cordon off the entrance to the little road.

For now, it would have to do.

He tossed the tape roll back into the Explorer, closed the rear door, and pulled himself into the driver's seat. He gave Beamer a thoughtful glance.

"Good work back there, Vince. You're all right."

Beamer's look of surprise appeared genuine. "Well, thanks, Sheriff. That being my job, and all."

"Do me a favor."

"What's that?"

"Don't tell Deputy Dan I complimented you. If you say a word, I will fire your ass."

Beamer's face grew five miles long. "Aww, Sheriff."

#

Sheriff Bryce Parrott would never know that, as he drove his Explorer back toward Aiken Mill, at Black Tooth Pond, a massive shadow, cast by nothing, spread itself over the water's surface. Slowly at first, and then with increasing speed, the shadow swirled into motion, gradually transforming into a massive, seething cyclone from which an array of vaporous black arms sprouted and swept a huge circle through the surrounding forest with the roar of a tornado. Within a minute, the arms retreated into the dark cyclone, which slowed, shrank, and vanished as if it had never existed.

A handful of residents within a couple miles of the location, including Donnie and Pootie Draper, heard a deep, rising roar that peaked and trailed away after a short time. Sound carried in curious ways through the ridges and valleys between Copper Peak, Mount

Signal, and Thunder Knob, and local people were long accustomed to such phenomena. Trains, jet planes, thunder, even work at the old quarry way up near Barren Creek could set up a reverberation that might be heard for miles in every direction.

No one ever paid such sounds any mind.

Chapter 25

Alana didn't arrive at Martin's place until well after one o'clock. He had spent the earlier part of the day struggling to focus on grading student tests but mostly fretting. He contemplated alternative methods of shifting her resolve, including but not limited to buying her a couple of kittens, or, should she prefer them, hedgehogs. And, for reasons he did not attempt to pinpoint, he pored over the notes and news clippings from the House of Caviness yet again. He'd consumed enough coffee to wire the population of a small city, yet keeping that mug in hand and the hot java flowing steadied his jangling nerves.

Old habits.

Thank God, he had suffered no hallucinations today, although, given their upcoming venture, he more than halfway anticipated any variety of sensory aberrations to assail him before it was all over with. He prayed that, if so, they might strike him alone and Alana not at all.

She came to his door dressed in a ragged flannel shirt over a turtleneck sweater, well-weathered jeans, and muddy hiking boots, with a canvas, water-resistant jacket tucked under one arm. Her eyes glinted with pleasure to see him, though her expression appeared solemn.

"We're going to do this together, right?"

"Hello to you too."

She smiled, hinting at an apology, and slid her arms around his neck. They kissed for a long, pleasurable moment. When she drew back, she said, "I won't come inside wearing these boots. I'm not ready to incur that kind of wrath."

He pointed to his already booted feet. He'd made sure his old Timberlands were mud-free before putting them on inside the house. "Mine are going to look like that as soon as I step off the porch."

"Are you ready to go?"

He placed a firm hand on her shoulder. "I'm going to ask you one more time...."

"No."

"Alana. With everything I've told you...."

She shook her head. "Marty, I know you've experienced strange things. And I can't explain everything you've described. You know I have great faith in your judgment. But I absolutely cannot believe your interpretation of *why* they've happened. I just can't."

He nodded, already having resigned himself to this undertaking. "I know. I've said my piece, and you've made your decision. So, we're going to do this."

"Yes, we are."

"One moment, and we'll go." He turned back inside and grabbed his leather bomber jacket and Beckham Panthers baseball cap from the rack behind the door. Like her, he had dressed for chilly, possibly damp weather. It wasn't supposed to rain again, but the sky had remained overcast all day, and gray, low-hanging clouds smothered the surrounding mountains. He kept two high-powered LED flashlights in his car, but for good measure, he grabbed a smaller one from the closet adjacent to the front door and tucked it into his jeans pocket. He slid into the jacket and tugged the cap onto his head.

He didn't mention it to Alana, but he'd stashed his Smith & Wesson M&P9 pistol in his inner jacket pocket. He knew she had no aversion to handguns, as she had at least one of her own, but he couldn't be sure how she'd feel about him carrying it out to the old house with them. Not that he had any realistic hope that it could offer protection against the force that he believed originated there.

Regardless, some intuitive sense had urged him to take the gun with him. He had chosen to heed it.

He glanced back to verify he'd turned out the living room lights, stepped out to the porch, and pulled the door closed behind him. Sure enough, his gravel driveway was awash with mud, so their boots crunched, squished, and splashed as they made their way to his Rogue. Once they had settled themselves inside it, Martin said to Alana, "It's going to be a mess out there. I'll have to park close to the road, or we might end up stuck. But it's not too far a walk back to the old house."

"That's okay. I didn't dress for a fancy dinner." She offered him a faint smile. "I did put extra clothes in my car, just in case."

Off they went. The main roads, at least, had begun to dry out. Martin drove without speaking, for he could scarcely articulate the thoughts and feelings that scrabbled around in his brain. He dreaded going out to the house, *dreaded* it, more for Alana's sake than his own. Somewhere in that chaos upstairs, he feared the idea that she might be right, that he had fabricated a fantasy as a defense against some fault in his mind, whether psychological or physiological. On the other hand, if his conclusions proved correct—or landed somewhere close to the truth—then he might be driving her to a terrible outcome, a potentially crushing assault on her mind and spirit. Yet, *she* had decided on this course. How could he deny her, even if for her protection, and still hope to continue an intimate relationship with her? She would not tolerate being forbidden, and rightly so.

At the same time, the prospect of returning to the house exhilarated him, like the anticipation he'd felt before his one and only skydiving experience, almost a decade ago. Hardly a comparable endeavor, though the consequences of unforeseen complications felt as dire for this as had the other.

"I know you don't like this," Alana said, as they threaded their way along Old Beckham Road. "I am sorry, Marty. I guess I feel like I have something to prove here. You know I went through psychological hell getting past the guilt and stress of trying to believe in some supernatural 'thing' when I was part of the church. I was never a Catholic for *me*. it was for my parents. They wanted— maybe needed—for me to believe as they did, to accept something that, when it came down to it, I absolutely could not. And this...." Her voice trailed away before continuing. "I hope you know I am not trivializing something you believe in. I know you believe it because you feel it's based on evidence. And maybe there's something to it, I don't know. But if there is—if you're right that there's some deliberate, outside force at work—it means that my conclusions, all my logic, everything I've reconciled myself to believing, are wrong. If it comes down to faith, then my faith is that I am *not* wrong."

Martin understood her view. It was hardly different from his own. Or what had been his own, barely more than a week ago. "But what if there is a cost to you? Maybe to your own sanity?"

"As I said, I don't need you to do this with me. Stay in the car. Take a walk down the road. I can and will do this alone."

"No. I don't want you to do it alone. I don't want you to do it at all, but I respect how important it is for you. I'm sorry I've put you in this position."

"No. You didn't. All you've done was make me realize that I've never built my house on a rock, so to speak. Maybe *I* need to do this."

"Alana, if—hypothetically—something should happen to you, if you start going through things like I have, how do I manage that guilt? I really was not going to tell you about any of this. Not until I realized that keeping it from you could kill our relationship if you did find out."

Her conflict burned in her eyes. Very softly, she said, "I'm being selfish. That's not my intention, Marty. Do you truly want to stop? If your belief in this is so strong...."

"No." He took his eyes off the road for a perilous spell to gaze at her in what he felt must be absolute love. "No. I don't know what I believe. I know what I *think*, not what I believe. So, we do this together. Right?"

Her relief spread like a palpable wave. "Together."

"You realize that, now that we've had this discussion, we'll go out there and see a decaying, crumbling old house, and that will be it. And one of us will leave feeling very foolish. And profoundly relieved."

"I've always liked decaying, crumbling old houses. You know that. I find them fascinating."

"We're almost there."

Her gaze turned sober again. "Together?"

He nodded. "Consider us duct taped."

She smiled. "Maybe later."

He saw the opening in the trees ahead and slowed the vehicle, aware that a veritable sea of mud might lie in wait for them just off the road. As he made the turn, to his surprise, he saw a narrow, almost smooth expanse before him, barely even wet. The other day, deep tracks had rutted the narrow road, from his brother's truck if not other vehicles. Once he'd pulled in a short distance, he saw that a few vague tracks marred the mud, but there must have been enough rain to wash them mostly away. At least he didn't have to worry about his SUV getting stuck out here.

"Wow," he said, eyeing the way ahead. "It must not have stormed here the way it did back home."

She smiled. "I remember one time it was dumping rain in my front yard and dry as a bone in the back."

He drove in about thirty feet or so, leaving space in front and behind so that he could make a three-point turn if necessary. Almost shocking, he thought, to find so little water pooled in this low-lying area. Last night, he'd been damn near surprised that the rain hadn't battered its way into his living room.

"Well," he said. "This is the place." He drew a deep, fortifying breath when he realized his heart had begun to race.

Alana looked first at him and then at the surrounding woods. "I'm ready."

He reached into the center console, withdrew his two flashlights, and handed of them to her. "We'll need these."

She slid the flashlight into her inner jacket pocket. Then they opened their doors and slid out of the SUV. Alana walked to the pond's edge, stopped next to a gnarled ironwood tree, and peered into the gray distance. At the far end of the pond, the old broken trunks jutted from a layer of mist like the spears of an ancient, ghostly army. He stepped to her side.

She pointed. "The black teeth, I gather."

"Yep. Been there a very long time, apparently. Those are all that's left."

"It's a lovely place. So quiet and still." She scanned the banks and the nearby trees. "Which way is the house?"

He pointed to the left, in the general direction of their destination. "Out that way. Maybe a ten-minute walk."

"Well, shall we?"

He had managed to force down his simmering fear and led the

way to the path without hesitating. As they passed through the close-pressing foliage, displaced water droplets fell and rattled to the ground. So far, the path, though muddy, had been free of standing water. *Small favors, at least.* Alana appeared to be enjoying the scenery with no outward sign of anxiety. Was she really as calm as all that inside?

Ahead, he saw the big, fallen poplar across the trail and, as they approached it, the smashed saplings splayed beneath the heavy bole. Once they'd made their way through the gap in the shattered trunk, he paused and pointed to the left. "Back in there. That's the trail to the house."

She peered into the shadows beneath the trees. "I see it."

On they went into the deeper woods, and now Martin's heart rate increased again. When, five minutes later, he caught sight of a dark, hulking silhouette—the massive magnolia in front of the house—a sharp drone rose behind his ears, like a swarm of abruptly roused bees. He drew to a stop with Alana at his side.

They were standing at the edge of his nightmares, he thought. Yet, along with rising apprehension, exhilaration blossomed in equal measure.

"Straight ahead," he said to Alana. "It's on the other side of *that*."

"That's one huge tree." Her voice held a hint of awe.

They walked past the magnolia until they faced the house's crumbling, vine-choked façade, with its array of grime-streaked windows and the gaping front door, which revealed a well of pitch darkness. The branches of the ghostly gray sycamore that had clawed its way through the crooked, broken roof spread over it like a crown.

Alana gazed at him with wide eyes. "You went in there alone after dark?"

"I'm afraid I did."

"You're either very brave, very stupid, or both."

"Guilty."

"Weird happenings aside, you know you could have been killed, right? That is not a sturdy-looking structure."

"It's held up this long. It's ugly but pretty solid inside. Strong bones."

"If you say so."

"Are you backing out? If you don't care to go in there...."

Her eyes turned defensive. "No, I am not backing out."

He nodded and started toward the door on the path of crushed brambles he and his brother had made. By now, water soaked his boots and pants legs up to his knees, and a chill had begun to work into his bones. Alana no doubt felt the same, though she showed no sign of discomfort. At least it should be marginally drier inside the house.

At the door, he stopped and drew his flashlight, gesturing for her to do the same. He switched it on and aimed its beam into the wide, dark gap between the rickety door and doorframe. No sense in going through all this and getting caught unawares by some rabid or otherwise aggressive critter that might have taken up residence here since his last visit. Hardly any daylight filtered in through the pair of filth-layered windows. His flashlight beam revealed the floor littered with debris and broken knick-knacks, the moldy couch, the dust-smothered coffee table, and the shattered remains of the ancient television set. He almost felt a moment of surprise that the pile of old mail no longer occupied the coffee table. He took his first cautious step into the dark interior, playing the light around every corner of the living room. It all looked the same as before. The smell of mildew and the sick, sour odor he'd noticed before lingered but seemed far less potent. As he made his way toward the staircase that led to the second floor, behind him, Alana stepped inside the House of Caviness.

Her flashlight beam joined his roving around the room. Neither of them spoke for a time.

At last, she said, "It feels...."

"What?"

"Off. Strange."

He aimed his light at the holes in the floor to the right of the stairs. "Mind those. They go deep."

She nodded her acknowledgment. He held the light on one of the openings, remembering that moment when something—some smoke-gray smudge—slid through the darkness in there, and he'd heard what sounded like whippoorwill cry.

Brother Phil's mimicry of a whippoorwill cry.

But it wasn't his brother.

As he swung his light back through the living room, the beam fell on a few of the old, framed photographs that littered the floor around the couch. Now he took a moment to study the images behind the cracked, dingy glass panes, and his eyes homed in on one of them. Very carefully, he lifted the frame and held it up to inspect the photograph it enclosed.

"Oh, Jesus."

"What, Marty?"

It was a horizontal shot of three individuals, all probably around age forty, standing side by side in front of the doors of a white, wooden church building. A sign above the door identified it as "Providence Church of the Seven Stars." Martin's eyes locked on the middle of the three men, a large, dark-haired man wearing the traditional black garb of a clergyman. The photo had never been a professional-quality portrait, and now, old, faded, and obscured behind dusty, dingy glass, its details appeared muddy, difficult to make out. Still, the very tall, husky man with dark, widely spaced eyes beneath a prominent brow *was* the spitting image of the preacher he'd seen on campus.

Except this *could not be* the same individual.

"Would you hold this for me?" He handed Alana his flashlight. She took it and kept both its beam and hers aimed at the photo. A rectangle of thick, warped cardboard secured by four metal clips secured the photo in the wooden frame. With trembling fingers, he nudged the clips open and drew the photo from the crooked frame, which he dropped onto one of the couch's moldy seat cushions.

There could be no doubt.

He pointed to the clergyman. "I know this man."

"How could you?"

"The preacher I told you about. The one I saw on campus the other day, the one who called me by name. This is him."

She scoffed. "No way. How old is this picture."

On a whim, he flipped the photo around and found, scrawled in faded black ink, "William Bouldin, assoc.; Lawrence Caviness, pastor; Eugene Blake, choir dir. September, 1951."

Now he knew: this man, this Lawrence Caviness, from Providence, Rhode Island, had been the sender of all those dire missives. A relative—Theo's brother, perhaps.

"That man has got to be long dead," Alana said.

Martin drew his phone from his pocket, opened the photo gallery, and brought up the best of the photos he had taken of the preacher. "This is him."

She studied the image for a time. "Definitely looks like him. But he must be a relative. Just a strong family resemblance."

"But what he said. The quotes from those old notes."

"Carrying on a long family tradition?"

Frustrated, Martin shook his head. He put his phone away. Then, without folding it, he slid the photograph inside his shirt. "Shall we keep looking?"

Alana nodded and handed his flashlight back.

He took it, stood there for another long moment of reflection, and then, at last, turned his light to the stairway and its broken, hanging banister. Alana stepped toward the bottom stair, but then aimed her flashlight beam across the room and through the opening that led to the kitchen. The light bathed the trunk of the sycamore that had tenaciously pushed its way through every intervening surface between earth and sky.

"This is something," she whispered. "Wonder how it could grow like that?"

"Indomitable nature."

She swung the light around and aimed it up the stairs. "So, you've been up there?"

"*Come. Upstairs....*"

He felt a cold, bony finger on the back of his neck. *That* he remembered. It had sounded like a voice. He nodded. "Phil and I both, and every memory of what we did up there is gone. More than an hour. For both of us."

Her eyes shifted between his and the stairs. And back to his. For the first time, she appeared nervous. In this environment, her rationality was proving itself a less substantial bulwark against the inexplicable than she had believed. He felt a sudden rush of warmth, of empathy, for no one could relate to her quandary better than he.

"Those are not exactly solid-looking stairs, Marty."

Was her nervousness more about the danger to life and limb here? *No.* Her reaction to his lost time revealed everything. She had begun to understand.

"They're okay. Just don't grab the railing, and you'll be fine."

"We've got to go up there, don't we?"

"I don't know any other way." He drew his phone back out of his pocket. "What I propose is this. Once we go up, we shoot videos. This may be the best way to pick up something definitive."

"And if nothing happens?"

"Then we're back to square one."

Her smile appeared strained yet genuine. She held up her phone. "All right, then. Lead on."

With flashlight in one hand, phone in the other, Martin started up the stairs, slow and steady, hugging the left-hand wall to make sure he didn't inadvertently shift, bump into the dangling banister, and possibly send both it and him plummeting to the floor below. Alana followed close behind, picking her steps with care, not trusting the stairs to be any sturdier than they appeared.

At the top, Martin stopped and looked around. Here, he saw a single, circular window, so filthy and overgrown with vines on the outside that it admitted no appreciable daylight. He aimed his flashlight beam into the hallway ahead, which extended maybe twenty feet, with a couple of closed doors on either side. The hall ended at another closed door. To his right, a perpendicular corridor vanished in darkness. Swiveling his flashlight, he saw that it too ended at a closed door, with one door on either side, both closed. The floorboards throughout were stained and bowed but looked sound enough. All this seemed consistent with his memory, although he knew *something* about this layout also had been different.

Or had *become* different.

He held up his phone, turned on the camera flash, and shot a several-second video of both hallways. Then he played it back to verify it matched what his eyes saw. The video image appeared crisp and clear.

"Do you want me to take photos?" Alana asked.

"Sure. Can't hurt."

From somewhere in the house, a long, slow creak, like a stubborn door opening, broke through the silence. They both froze and listened. The sound didn't repeat, but Martin felt something different now. No. *Smelled* something different. It was the subsequent cold chill he had felt.

That sour odor they'd smelled, now stronger and blended with something scorched, almost like burnt sulfur. It swirled into his nostrils like a fetid wind and seeped through his sinuses, past the barrier of bone, and into his brain. He turned to look at Alana, five feet away, and from her shocked expression, he knew she was experiencing the same sensations.

Her gaze shifted to meet his. "What is this?"

Rather than the pale white illumination from their flashlights, a new, bluish tint painted her forehead and cheeks. Another source of light, he realized, one that originated from the main hall at top of the stairs. He turned to peer toward its far end.

No longer a twenty-foot hallway ending at a closed door, the corridor had become a shaft of pure black—a vast void broken only by a small circle of electric blue that hovered in its center, some unimaginable distance away. Shifting, organic splashes of color—blue, violet, and magenta—bathed their bodies, each hue phasing from one to another in random cycles. Those colors touched no other surface. Not the floor, not the walls, not the doors. Only *them*.

No hallucination. No illusion. This is as real as real gets.

"Jesus." He held up his camera in trembling fingers and in a hoarse voice called, "Alana, video it!"

At the same moment, both their camera flashes fired to life, but—like their flashlights, Martin realized—neither penetrated the intervening darkness. He switched off both his flashlight and flash, wondering whether the camera might pick up that distant, luminous sphere more clearly without the interference of the other lights.

"Alana, switch your lights off. See if it makes any difference."

She did not speak, but her flashlight and camera light both went dark.

He looked back at his camera screen. No. The absence of those lights had made no difference. The image on the screen appeared exactly the same. He saw only that tiny, brilliant orb, devoid of definition.

He stopped the video and played it back.

"Oh, no."

Nothing there. No distant light to be seen. Only total darkness and a soft, random swishing sound—the recording of his own tiny movements. On the live camera screen, he could see that little bluish orb, its edges vibrating, hazy. But in the video, it did not appear.

"Alana," he said, his voice a defeated whisper. "Check yours."

Her video turned out the same.

Nothing there.

She moved closer to him until their shoulders touched. Her voice quavered. "Marty. You were never hallucinating. Not unless I am hallucinating right now."

"No. You're not."

Fragments of memory clawed their way up from the depths of his mind. He remembered seeing this abyss before. That distant light. On that previous occasion, he had moved toward it, traveled the distance of that black shaft to reach the shining orb.

And found what lay at its center.

"Oh, my God. My God."

Then Martin's ears pricked. A sound from somewhere below tore his attention from those materializing memories. A scrape and a groan rose from downstairs. Definitely a door, he thought. A solid *thump* followed, and then another. And another. Stumbling, unsteady footsteps, he thought. Moving toward the stairs.

No doubt about it. Someone else had entered the House of Caviness.

Chapter 26

Martin pocketed his phone, and his right hand reflexively slipped inside his jacket to touch the handle of his Smith & Wesson. He did not draw it, not yet, although his first suspicion—he had no idea why—was that the newcomer must be Robert, the unhinged man who had showed up outside of Phil's house. He took a couple of steps toward the head of the stairs. Alana stuck close to him, one hand gripping his right bicep. The irregular footsteps moved closer to the staircase.

"You weren't expecting company, were you?" Alana whispered.

He shook his head, though she probably couldn't see it in the darkness. When he heard the first footstep clump on the lowest stair, his left hand throttled his flashlight, his middle finger hovering over the little rubber button that switched it on. He slid his hand forward and aimed the flashlight at the little landing three stairs down. As soon as the new arrival reached the landing, he'd hit them with the beam.

He had all but forgotten the unreal scene behind him.

Something back there—in that long, dark shaft—went *boom*.

Faraway, but very heavy, it reverberated like a wrecking ball falling on an iron surface.

All the air seemed to rush from his lungs. He drew his hand from his jacket and touched Alana's shoulder. He spoke in his softest whisper. "Can you see anything back there?"

"No. Nothing."

Again, small favors, he thought.

Whoever was coming up the stairs, they seemed to be having a hard time maintaining balance. The footsteps thunked and thudded in an irregular rhythm, yet they still grew steadily louder. In moments, their visitor would appear at the landing. Martin's hand slid back to touch the gun.

The vaguest shadow appeared in the darkness before him, and Martin switched on his flashlight. A sharp cry came from the figure that now stood with one foot on the landing. Martin immediately recognized him—only not quite.

"Phil?"

Yes, it was his brother. But what the hell was wrong with him?

Phillip Pritchett's eyes bulged like huge marbles, his face paler than milky quartz in the flashlight's beam. His clothes hung on a stooped, emaciated frame. Then Martin realized that Phil's skin, wherever it was exposed, appeared wet and rubbery. Some kind of transparent goo covered his skin and clothing.

"Phil! What the hell?"

His brother stumbled onto the landing and almost toppled forward. He caught himself by throwing out a clawlike hand at the wall. His eyes rolled toward Martin's.

"Marty. I'm done. I am done."

He slid toward the floor, and both Martin and Alana moved in an instant to support him. Martin knelt and helped Phil sit down on the uppermost stair. Martin choked when he realized how weak and frail his brother had become—and so suddenly. "What in God's name happened?"

"Jesus," Alana said, realizing that globs of the jellylike substance now coated her hands. With an expression of disgust, she wiped them on her jeans and then turned her attention back to Phil. "Can you tell us what's happened?"

"It gets you from inside." Phil's voice came out a ragged whisper. "And it won't let you go."

Behind Martin, another *boom* echoed from the distance. This one sounded closer. He threw a quick glance behind him, but his eyes barely registered the faraway sphere of light. But now he realized that the myriad colors reflected on Phil as well. A spotlight of shifting hues that encompassed only their three bodies.

One of Phil's hands rose and swept at the air. "Oh, I see...it's like a train. Moving. Moving."

"This is unbelievable," Martin whispered. "Phil, please."

His brother's gaze appeared locked on something in the distance, and for a time, he couldn't or wouldn't speak. Then his lips drew back in a sudden rictus. "Oh, God, that hurts. Oh, Jesus. God!"

One of Phil's hands rose and flailed at the air. Martin caught it and drew it toward him. "Phil, please, talk to us."

The pain-bright eyes rolled toward Martin's face. "Listen. Time is short." He drew several rasping breaths. "There's something here. Once it touches you, it gets inside you. And that's it. That's it."

Alana touched Martin's shoulder. "We need to get him to the hospital. Right now."

He nodded and squeezed Phil's hand. His brother's grip was so weak that even a little pressure almost crushed it. He ignored the glistening gel that spread from Phil's hand to his as if it were alive. "We're going to get you out of here. You're going to be okay."

A little strength returned to his brother's hand. "Too late. Listen, while I can think." He grimaced for a long moment, until Martin thought he wasn't going to speak again. Then: "It's been here a very long time. They tried to burn it." He moaned and fell silent again.

Alana clutched Martin's shoulder. "Marty, we've got to get out. I don't know what it is, but something's moving back there. Let's get Phil downstairs, and we'll take him to the hospital."

Another *boom* resounded from the corridor, still louder than before.

Phil cried out in agony. As the pain seemed to pass, he peered at Martin again. "It's too late, brother. It's got us now."

"Come on." Martin slid his right arm around Phil's left shoulder and under his right arm. "We're going to get you to the hospital. You're going to be okay."

But Phil cried out as Martin tried to lift him. "No! Just wanna rest. I'll be gone soon." His eyes blazed like flares. "So will you."

Martin shook his head. "No, no." He sharpened his tone. "Come on. We're getting out of here." His arms encircling Phil's upper body, he started to rise, lifting with as much care as he could. Halfway to his feet, he realized that the stairwell behind his brother had gone pitch dark. As dark as the corridor that led to that orb of blue.

Alana saw the new darkness at the same time. "What the hell, Marty? It's still daylight outside."

"We do what we said. We get Phil downstairs and to the car."

He pivoted so he was behind Phil and began backing down the three stairs to the landing. Now Alana positioned herself on the stair just above, crouched to lower her center of gravity, and gripped Phil's forearms. "We've got him."

As Martin started downward, he felt an odd pressure at his back. He shifted all his strength to his right leg and tried to force it down to the next stair.

He could not.

"What the fuck?"

Phil groaned. "It's too late, Marty. I'm slipping. Slipping away."

Martin turned his head and saw that, behind him, blackness formed a solid, impenetrable veil, an absolute barrier to both his sight and his person. He shoved his entire weight into it. He might as well have attempted to power his way through a concrete wall.

His spirit, as if it were corporeal, sagged in defeat. "I can't get through."

Phil's voice came out as a whisper. "Just let me rest, please, Marty. It hurts so bad. But once it stops...."

His brother's body lurched in his arms. Again and again, until it began thrashing. Phil cried out in agony, and his voice rose even higher. "Here it comes!"

As if a giant hand had grabbed his brother's body, *something* jerked Phil free of Martin's encircling arms, nearly dragging him down the stairs as well. A heavy thumping followed as Phil's body vanished into the impenetrable darkness below.

Then Phil screamed. A heart-rending cry of absolute pain and terror, of both surprise and resignation. Martin pushed, shoved, *leaped* with every ounce of strength in his body in an attempt to break through the black barrier and reach his brother.

Immovable.

"Phil!" he cried. "Please come back. Please, Phil."

A series of awful, wet, ripping sounds rose from below. But Phil no longer cried out.

His brother was gone.

"Oh, God, no." His brain struggled to process what had just happened. Somewhere inside, he understood it. But the truth was *not* coming home to him. No, what he'd seen, felt, heard....

None of it could be true.

Hallucination.

That was it. Yes, this was *all* hallucination. Nothing that had happened here was real.

"Marty." From behind him, Alana's hands settled on his shoulders. "Marty. He's gone."

No. This is real.

"Phil, please don't go. Please don't go."

"Marty." Her voice was more urgent. "Something's in that corridor. It's coming this way."

On his shoulders, her fingers turned to steel. The pain brought him back to the moment, if not to acceptance.

"What's back there?" he whispered.

"I can't tell. A weird silhouette. Wait. No, I think it's a man."

He could hardly bring himself to turn around and face the impossible abyss—which he now recalled he'd termed "different space" the first time he'd encountered it. But he did it. Grasping Alana's bicep, he drew himself upright and peered into the mad void. At the electric blue sphere far, far away.

Yes, against the distant glow, he saw a featureless silhouette, which might or might not have been moving. Hard to tell against the backdrop of vibrant blue. He realized that a low whooshing sound seeped through the corridor toward them. It grew louder until it became a rumble.

A roar.

He'd heard this sound before. The last time here, the noise, accompanied by a furious rush of wind, was the last thing he and Phil experienced before they found themselves back outside. Maybe this was it.

Please be it.

"Take us out of here," he whispered. "Alana, hold tight." He pulled her toward him and locked his arm around her waist. She pressed close to him as if aware of what must be coming.

Then it struck: the wind. A thunderous crash and a massive gust like a sledgehammer blow that nearly lifted them off their feet. Martin felt his perceptions reeling, a sense of dislocation—as if his body and mind were somehow being *stretched* and drawn to some other place.

It all passed in an instant.

As his surroundings swam back into focus, his every hope died, dashed like a fragile raft against a rocky shore.

He and Alana stood together inside a small, dilapidated room, which he now remembered, lit by a slowly pulsing blue-violet hue that emanated from everywhere and nowhere. Seven wavering figures—silhouettes composed of swirling smoke—hovered before them in a semicircle. Last time, there had been five.

From behind, Marty heard a low *thump*, like a heavy footstep. Together, he and Alana spun to find themselves facing a large, black-suited figure, which Martin immediately recognized.

The "preacher" he had seen before. At Frith's Restaurant. On campus. And *here*.

The *ghost* of Lawrence Caviness?

The man stood like a stone statue before them. The widely spaced eyes in the expressionless face stared at them, and when Alana shifted nervously backward, they followed her movement. He did not speak.

A clump of gravel clogged Martin's throat. "Who are you?"

"Niemand." The slow, deep voice seemed to drift from much farther away.

"Not Lawrence Caviness?"

"Niemand."

He heard Alana's rapid, shallow breathing. Her eyes were wide, disbelieving. She must be near panic, he thought, but she didn't appear ready to bolt. She remained in control of her faculties, her emotions.

How much longer he could maintain his own grip, he didn't know. *Not very.*

Grief. Confusion. Anger. A tsunami of emotions swept over him, and he tried—desperately—to cling to *anger*, for it felt like his only bulwark, the sole emotional pillar that might not crack.

"You killed my brother."

The piercing stare did not soften or deviate.

"What was the meaning of all those notes? The news articles?"

The thick-lipped mouth widened in something like a grin. It did not open to speak.

Then the room began to change. The light shifted to a more

natural hue, like dim daylight. Then one of the smoky figures *slid* across the floor in his direction. It stopped several feet short of him. A wavering arm rose and extended toward him. Longer and longer, far beyond the proportion of any human arm, until its hazy tip almost brushed his face.

"Marty," Alana whispered, tugging on his arm. "Don't let it touch you!"

It was too late. He felt an icy dagger penetrate his forehead. And a host of moving images exploded in his mind, as if his brain had instantly downloaded a movie. No—an *experience*. Or a series of them.

He could perceive no individual frame, no coherent combination of images. But this psychic infusion had generated something like a tapestry, or a puzzle. No, it was a map—a *timeline!*—of people, places, and events from long ago, one that slid past his mind's eye at varying rates, never pausing long enough for him to piece together a coherent whole.

But as this lurid patchwork wormed through his brain, a little at a time, he began to understand the crux of this invading, deadly horror.

Yes, the Caviness family had built and lived in this house, but something else owned the ground beneath it. Something *old*. Something that earlier inhabitants of the land had tried to destroy with fire.

Those dire news stories, the warning notes—these represented only a small part of a pervasive negative energy field, like a power grid, constructed to unsettle the family, steep them in turmoil, anxiety, and distrust. Because that was what *it* relished. It allowed them to coexist with it because their perpetual psychic distress nourished it.

Until it was done with them.

And then it rested. At least, until one of them—the last living member of that family—had returned and disturbed it.

Now the thing was ravenous. No more coexisting. By coming back here, that last Caviness had opened the door to a frenzy of fear, anxiety, and horror. It had swept up Phil. And—good God, yes!—that man, Robert. He, too, was a Caviness. One of the sons of the original family, Franklin Lydell Caviness, who had escaped before it was too late for him.

Yet, for reasons of his own, he had returned, and it cost him everything.

Now it has us.

Martin grasped these snippets as if they had been imprinted on a moving surface. Slow, but never stopping. And as they moved on, each piece became increasingly difficult to capture and retain.

Train cars appearing and then pulling away from him.

Oh, God, no.

He understood what Phil had experienced before he died. Now, it was his turn.

Oh, Jesus, Phil.

"Marty!" Alana's voice drifted to him from miles away, tinny and thin.

He heard her, but her urgency failed to register. A new train car was sliding into view, and he had to catch its meaning quickly.

An image of the black-suited preacher. Yes. He—or some incarnation of him—had sent all that mail, over so many years, from Providence, Rhode Island, to the Caviness family here, in Sylvan County.

"Marty!"

Good Christ, what about Alana?

With all the strength he could summon, he tore himself free from the mesmerizing progression of images, words, and sounds. Still, he became only vaguely aware of the luminous blue-violet field that once again shimmered around him, and the frigid, unblinking stare of the black-suited man before him.

Niemand?

No One.

No-One-1.

Alana was tugging his right bicep with one hand, her lips close to his ear. "Martin Pritchett. Come out of it! Now!"

Full cognizance hit him like whiplash, and sharp pain slashed through his head and neck. As it began to abate, he lifted a hand to acknowledge her presence. His voice sounded like sandpaper on rough wood. "I'm here."

"We've got to get out. There must be a way."

His eyes swept the weirdly illuminated room, beyond the hellish figures that surrounded them. His mind had passed so far beyond disbelief that he now realized only despair. "No door. No windows. Only these walls."

"No door." Niemand's hollow voice might have drifted down from outer space. "Except *my* door."

Terror gleamed in Alana's eyes, but she met the statue-like figure's stare. "Then open it."

The almost-grinning lips spread into a cold smile. "I *will* open it."

A random memory—recent, empowering—brought the horror of their predicament into focus, and Martin's right hand, guided more by impulse than volition, slid into his inner jacket pocket. It might not have been a smooth, expert draw, but in little more than a flash, the Smith & Wesson's barrel had homed in on the smiling, black-suited figure. Martin's hand trembled like a leaf in the wind, but at this close range, it didn't matter. When he pulled the trigger, the sound of the discharge erupted in his ears with exaggerated clarity, so sharp and piercing that his eyelids clenched tight and his jaw snapped shut, sending waves of pain radiating through his skull.

It hurt so badly, for so long, he feared his eyes must have welded themselves shut.

Chapter 27

Sykes entered the sheriff's office holding a bagged object that resembled a piece of human anatomy closely enough to give Parrott a start. It took him a moment to realize that it was a boot. A soaking wet boot.

"Foot fetish, Dan?"

"Visual aid. Found this in Henry Creek, a ways past East Church. Pretty certain it's Robert's."

Parrott took the boot from Sykes and examined it through the clear plastic evidence bag. The worn-out tread and partially separated sole cinched it for him. "Yeah. It's Robert's." He handed the boot back. Sykes set it on the floor next to the vacant chair across from Parrott's desk and slid into the seat.

"We followed footprints we found in the woods behind Stuart Street. They led down to the creek bank, stopped at a culvert under Lee Terrace. They match up with the boot. That's all we've found, so we moved on downstream to see if we could turn up anything else. Nothing yet." Deputy Dan gave him a curious look. "So, what's so

STEPHEN MARK RAINEY

serious on this end?"

"Come first light tomorrow, I need a team at a place called Black Tooth Pond. It's out Old Beckham Road. Assuming we don't find Robert between now and then, put Carter in charge of your search. I want you with me. I'm taking Beamer and Collins as well."

In a cautious tone, Sykes asked, "Have you checked the weather?"

"Thirty percent chance of rain early. Higher later in the day. I'd prefer to get out there before the next gullywasher."

"Okay." Sykes contemplated Parrott's tie tack for a moment. "With Krummeck out, the crew's gonna be a bit thin. What's going on out there?"

"Beamer and I gave the place a look this afternoon, but I want to check it out in more detail. Nothing definite, but there might be a link to our late Mr. Lydell." He didn't care to elaborate on the day's events, particularly since, at the first opportunity, Beamer would regale everyone with his own colorful account. "It's kind of a strange place, Dan. Remote." He remembered Beamer's words. "Lonely."

"Well, since Robert has already wrecked my Sunday morning, it's only fitting that you take it to the next level."

"Glad you approve. We'll hit the road at 0700. I want at least two cameras out there. More, if we can spare them. Use your phones if necessary."

Sykes cast him a curious gaze. "You're sounding kind of funny about this, Sheriff. Anything I should know?"

"Only what I've told you."

"We have ways of making you talk, Sheriff."

"Yeah?"

"We ask Beamer."

"We have ways of silencing Beamer. You don't want to know them."

"You know, you're a lot nicer on television."

"Who have you got on search duty for the evening?"

"Wilson, Aaron, Rodriguez. That whittles patrol down to Bartholomay and Wright." Sykes leaned forward. "What's going on, Sheriff?"

"Before you knock off for the evening, I want you to grab Beamer and take a quick ride up to Black Tooth Pond. About seven miles out Old Beckham Road. Beamer can show you where. I put tape across the entrance, so you can't miss it."

"And then?"

"Take a quick walk in. It's muddy as hell, so put Beamer out in front if you want. Take your lights with you, give the banks a quick look around. Be cautious."

Sykes's face became a puzzled scowl. "What's this about, Sheriff? Are we supposed to find something?"

Parrott shrugged. "Somehow, I doubt it. But be alert. I'm quite sure Vince will fill you in on every detail and then some."

"I've never known you to be so mysterious."

Parrott laughed softly. "I prefer to think of it as judicious. What I'm really looking for is your impression of the place. As I mentioned before, it's kind of odd. If you disagree—or strongly agree—give me a shout afterward."

"It must be odd, since it seems to have you rattled. I do believe that's a first."

"I prefer to think of it as an opportunity for you to hone your instincts."

"Is that it?"

"Just catalog that boot instead of taking it home with you."

"What about my fetish?"

"Vince keeps his street shoes in his locker. Steal those. Call me tonight if you must." He lifted a hand and made a shooing gesture.

"Have a lovely evening, boss." Sykes rose, grabbed the boot, and left Parrott's office with a final, quick wave.

Parrott drew a long breath. Sykes hadn't been wrong; he *was* rattled. Sending his chief deputy out to the site for a quick look-see felt like a prudent idea. What he didn't care to admit, even to himself, was that, after this afternoon, he wasn't sure he had it in him to go out there after dark on his own.

A sad situation for a man in his position.

Chapter 28

When Martin's eyes finally cracked open, through a thin haze of smoke, he saw the tall, erect figure in black—*Niemand*—still a statue, still bathed in a pale, blue-violet glow, unblinking eyes still staring at him with cold, unreadable purpose. Though he could hardly have expected his gunshot to produce a different result, the air fled from his lungs. Waves of sharp pain arced through his neck and shoulders. His hammering heart pumped hopelessness through his weakening body.

Despite knowing its futility, he kept the gun trained, however unsteadily, on the dark figure. He felt Alana's fingers touch his right shoulder.

"Did you see it?" Her eyes flicked toward his. "Right after you shot?"

He shook his head. "What?"

"I saw...." She paused and swallowed. "He changed to something different, just in that flash."

"What?" he repeated.

"Something behind him. Or maybe part of him." Again, her voice trailed away for a few seconds. "He looked like a hand puppet."

"I didn't see it," he whispered.

Alana's fingers slid away from his shoulder, and he heard her gasp. "Oh, no. Marty."

He saw something glistening on her hands. Then he felt it: a cool, slick caress on both sides of his neck below his ears and down his jaw.

That same gel-like substance that had coated portions of Phil's body. It now oozed and dripped from his ears.

He didn't know what it was, but he knew what it must mean.

"Jesus." He wiped away the dribbling mess. It took herculean effort for him to face the black-suited figure again. He held up one gel-smeared left hand while his right finger tightened on the pistol's trigger. "What is this? And who—*what*—are you?"

The distant, reverberating voice replied, "Niemand. I am the messenger."

Alana squeezed his shoulder. "You said Niemand meant 'no one,' didn't you? In German?"

He nodded.

Then, pealing through the chamber, over and over: "NIEMAND! NIEMAND! NIEMAND!"

The volume of the still-distant voice deafened them, *enveloped* them. When it stopped, its echoes continued for countless ages before swirling into silence.

Now, the preacher's eyes swiveled to regard Alana. The deafening voice blared, "NOW YOUR NAME HAS BEEN INSCRIBED IN BLOOD IN THE BOOK OF THE DOOMED!"

Before Martin could process what was happening, one of the smoke wraiths glided like a swift boat over still water toward Alana. A long armlike appendage rose and extended in her direction.

The Smith & Wesson tumbled to the floor with a *thunk* as he pivoted to intercept the thing. He felt a frigid blade pierce his shoulder, and the smoky arm drove straight through his flesh and bone. Alana cried out, her voice shrill with horror. He spun away from the ethereal figure and reached for her, but the vaporous limb had driven itself into her heart.

"Oh, God," she whispered. Her agonized eyes turned to him. "What does this...?"

She dropped to her knees, her hands closing over her chest.

Martin didn't see the ghostly arm withdraw, but before he knew it, the figure had glided back to its original place a dozen feet away.

"Alana!" He kneeled beside her, his mind numb, scattered. He realized his pain had relented somewhat, but at the same time, his focus faltered, and everything around him seemed to disperse into a jumble of swarming, meaningless impressions. Random images— from the massive magnolia outside the house to faces of people he had known long ago—slid into and out of his mind's eye to the sound of a rumbling freight train. Coherent thought slipped farther and farther from his grasp, and when he gazed at Alana, she might as well have been a stranger. Or a rag doll.

Now, the pain slid away like a final trickle of water over stones in a dead creek. And before his mind's eye, only a meaningless stream of assorted images and sensations, a progression of irrelevant thoughts and memories that drew him so far from his present circumstances that the latter simply dissolved.

Mom, Dad, Phil. All of them together in a living snapshot from his early childhood. He knew he loved them and that they loved him. The sights and sounds of downtown Aiken Mill at Christmas. A party at VCU, with lots of drink, many young people he knew, some he liked, some he didn't. Gia Romano, the first girl to smite his heart at age eleven. Phil at his college graduation ceremony, stoned off his motherfucking ass.

The sound of a whippoorwill.

Louder. Louder.

No, it was *not* a whippoorwill. Something that mimicked the night bird's cry.

His brother's voice. Yeah, Phil. Just smart-ass Phil.

No, not so. Phil is dead.

Tonight. Here, in this house, his brother had died.

Torn apart.

Like Robert Caviness.

Robert John Caviness.

Wait.

How did he know that man's full name? He didn't know Robert's full name. He *couldn't* know.

WHIPP! WHIPP! WHIPP!

Jesus, that sound! So loud, so harsh. With it, pain began to creep back. Jagged shards of glass materialized inside his muscles, cutting, tearing, slicing. Invisible claws ripped at his limbs, slashed his neck and back. Something inside him was moving, twisting, *biting*, as if seeking to escape the envelope of flesh and bone.

Yet, he could think again. He recognized the lurid color of the chamber. Felt the cool, vile gel dripping from his ears—and now from the corner of his left eye. Alana knelt next to him, sobbing in pain and incomprehension. Somehow, he thought, he had to save her, to get her the hell out of here. He hadn't been able to save Phil. He couldn't let her go the same way.

God, no, not like that.

Somehow, they had to find help. How and from whom, he had no idea. No door. No windows. What incredible alteration of space had transported them here? How could he reverse it? Now that these figures, these *beings*, had touched Alana, he didn't know how long either of them had left. Probably not long. They must have *infected* him far, far sooner than he even realized. Maybe back when he'd first trespassed on this ground. Probably before he even became aware of the house itself.

All those hallucinations. They had been intended to lure him out here, to draw him to this house.

And now—oh, God—the pain returned in throbbing waves, each harsher than the one before. How could he stand any more of this?

A random glance to his left, and he saw his gun on the violet-lit floor a yard away. He dropped to one knee, swiped it up, and spun to again aim it at the dark, statue-like figure of the preacher. *Niemand.* A "hand puppet," Alana had said. His brother had called it a "projection." Martin knew his gun couldn't harm the other-worldly inhabitants of this chamber without portals.

Maybe he could make one.

He raised the pistol in his trembling right hand, picked a spot on the wall, and fired. Again, the room amplified the sharp report by some impossible factor, and the agony that scythed through his muscles and bones nearly floored him again. Alana's hands rose to her ears, and her eyes clenched shut. But the shot had opened a quarter-sized hole in the ancient plaster, and, through it, he saw what *might* have been daylight, for it shone warm gold, not ghostly blue or violet.

Aware that he could lose his eardrums, he fired again, and again, trying to hit a series of points that might weaken a section of wall that he might break through. The pain that shot through his skull forced him to release the trigger. The gun again fell from his hand, and he toppled to the warped wooden planks with an agonizing *thud*.

He knew now that he was never going to leave this room.

Not in *this* life.

Neither by way of train cars sliding past his field of vision nor some shifting mosaic of images and sensations, but by a laser-targeted transmission of *truth*, he understood that none of these figures were ghosts, or a conclave of the dead returned to enact some mysterious vengeance on the living. Here, there existed *two* entities: Niemand, a thing that wore the face of a long-dead preacher, Lawrence Caviness, like a mask; and the *other*, almost as old as the first, yet somehow different. Distinct.

The smoke ghosts were nothing more than the *fingers* of the latter.

WHIPP! WHIPP! WHIPP!

"Whippoorwill," he whispered, remembering how its song had unsettled him when he was a child. His brother had learned to mimic the night bird's call, and this *other* simply mimicked his brother's voice.

That was its nature. It had insinuated itself into this world by mimicry. Reaching into human brains, mimicking memories. Images. People. Places.

"WHYCK! WHYCK! WHYCK!"

God, what a sound!

So loud. Brimming with power.

"YYYCK! YYYCK!"

Something moved in Martin's stomach, through his chest. Claws, spikes, fangs, all tearing through his body. This was unbearable. The end *must* be near.

Finish it. Just finish it!

An explosion of sound nearly burst his skull, but the other pains in his body partially subsided. A light flared around him. Its brilliance forced him to clamp his eyelids together, but when he opened them, he saw Alana holding his gun, aiming it at the wall. She fired again, and another hole appeared in the plaster. The golden light from the other side felt like a balm for the internal pyre consuming him.

"Marty, hold on." Her voice was a whisper, but it broke through the roaring in his ears, in his brain. "We'll get out. We'll get help."

Over and over, she fired, each bullet smashing through the ancient plaster and rotten boards. At last, when she pulled the trigger, only a dull click followed. That was it. But including his initial shots, a total of eight 9-millimeter bullet holes, spaced several inches apart in a roughly diagonal line, had wreaked havoc on a portion of the wall. Alana launched herself toward the damaged section and slammed her full weight against it. Again. And again. With each blow, narrow cracks appeared between the holes, and plumes of dust erupted from the crumbling plaster.

None of the smoky figures appeared to react to her movement. Niemand's dark eyes had rolled toward her, and the mouth had become a straight, thin gash, but the black-suited body remained stationary.

Now, half-exhausted, Alana backed away from the wall to catch her breath. Seeing this, Martin forced himself to move. He struggled to his knees, then rose to his feet as far as a crouch. With as much strength as he could muster, he propelled himself forward, leading with his right shoulder, trying to center the impact in the already weakened area. His shoulder slammed against the cracked surface, and he felt the wall give slightly. But that effort nearly finished him, and he again sank to his knees.

He felt a renewed tickling below his ears, and several drops of glistening gel plopped to the floor next to him.

Sick, disgusted, agonized, he shifted his body around so his back faced the wall. Then he shoved with all his strength.

With a loud *crunch*, the surface behind him buckled inward a couple of inches.

Alana moved toward him with outstretched arms and gripped his shoulders. "I'm okay," she said. "Let me."

He nodded and half-slid, half-crabwalked away from the wall to give her some clearance. Now, Alana settled onto her backside facing the wall, lifted her feet, and kicked with all her strength. A yard-long diagonal crack, which mostly followed the line of bullet holes, opened to admit a stream of warm light. Again, she drew her feet back and thrust them forward. Upon impact, a wedge-shaped hunk of plaster the size of a bicycle seat broke away and fell to the floor in a cloud of dust.

The opening revealed a crooked array of wormy wooden boards, with what looked like sunlight streaming through the gaps.

"Again." Martin's voice was a pained groan. But the terrific pain in his body had dwindled, and, for the moment, his mind retained its focus.

Repeatedly, Alana smashed her feet into the yielding plaster, until the weakened, crumbling surface gave way, and a two-foot, oblong section of the interior wall collapsed into rubble. Without hesitating, she scooted forward and began kicking through the hole at the flimsy-looking outer boards. Two of them broke away and tumbled out of sight.

It only took a second for both Martin and Alana to realize that the light streaming through the hole did not come from the sun.

Chapter 29

To the southwest, an array of golden sunbeams blossomed from behind the tortoise-shell hump of Copper Peak, painting a brilliant flower in the deepening blue sky. The shadows of the skeletal trees that arched over the road had softened to murky, wavering smudges on the pitted asphalt. North of Aiken Mill, Old Beckham Road had been all but deserted. Behind the wheel of the Caprice cruiser, Chief Deputy Sykes had seen only a couple of cars heading south toward town, and none traveling in their direction.

Young Mr. Beamer leaned forward in the passenger seat and scanned the trees for an opening. "Should be up on the left."

Sykes slowed the cruiser, alert for any sign of the yellow tape that Sheriff Parrott had secured at the entrance to the pond.

Nothing yet.

Then, a hundred yards ahead, something bright flickered amid the tight row of trees that lined the road. And there it was: a length of yellow barrier tape stretched across a gap in the seemingly endless line of pines and poplars. He braked to a crawl and determined that, indeed, between two thick poplar trunks, a narrow, muddy strip suggested an ingress to the woods.

It looked like just enough room to maneuver the Caprice off the road's edge and park parallel to the tape barrier. He swung wide, made a three-point turn so the car faced back toward town, and, with practiced precision, slid the cruiser into the tight space. People out here tended to haul ass, so he flipped on the overheads, figuring it might reduce the chances of some idiot sideswiping the cruiser. The flashing blues flared into the shadows beneath the trees for a couple of hundred feet. Beamer peered out the passenger window into the woods, and Sykes saw one of his hands curl into a nervous fist.

He couldn't hold back a little smirk. "See something gruesome?"

Beamer shook his head. "Can't see much of anything."

Sykes shut off the engine, shoved the door open, and heaved himself out of the car. Beamer opened the passenger door carefully to keep it from banging into the close-pressing poplar tree. Once out, he and Sykes sidled around the thick trunk to bypass the tape and, from there, proceeded onto the muddy, half-assed excuse for a road, which led into the increasingly dark, skeletal woods. Before them, a set of tire tracks—left earlier today by Sheriff Parrott's Explorer—extended maybe fifteen feet before ending at the edge of a twenty-foot-long pool of opaque, brown water. Intermittent dapples of blue light from the cruiser reflected on its murky surface.

Beamer pointed to the pool. "That's gone down since earlier today, but it's still damned deep." He motioned to the left-hand edge of the road. "Higher ground over there."

Indeed, to the left, the pool petered out before it reached the tangled growth and thick roots that bordered the road's edge. With Beamer in tow, Sykes made his way along the little ridge of drier earth, picking his steps carefully to avoid slipping into the water, which would certainly soak his feet up to his ankles. From its sheath on his belt, he pulled his 1,200-lumen LED flashlight, switched it on, and sent the beam roving through the darkness beneath the trees.

In the mud ahead, a mess of intermingled footprints marked the sheriff's and Beamer's paths—both coming and going—from earlier today. He saw no other tracks, human or animal. The sky had turned deep purple, and it wouldn't be long before full darkness fell over the woods. It felt damned chilly now too; the temperature must have dropped ten degrees since they'd left the station.

He pointed to the tracks in the mud. "Looks like nobody's been here since you left," he said to Beamer.

The younger man nodded. "This does not disappoint me."

Once past the pool, Sykes noticed, to the right and maybe fifty feet ahead, the glimmer of undulating water beyond a barrier of reeds and creepers.

"So, that's Black Tooth Pond, eh?"

"That's it," Beamer said, moving up beside him. "Not a fan. To me, this place still feels funny. Creepy."

As loath as Sykes was to admit it, something about the almost total silence and the shadows, which seemed too dark and too deep here, had set off an uncomfortable tingle at the back of his skull. It was the kind of tingle he felt when he entered a dangerous environment.

But there was nothing out here. *Nothing.*

Hell, if anything had made him uncomfortable, it was listening to Beamer recounting his unsettling experience out here. Three times already. So, he and the sheriff had seen something out in the water and then heard splashing sounds nearby, only to find nothing there. Well, among these hills, ridges, and mountains, sound bounced and carried all over the place. Rationally, he could put no stock in Beamer's weird perceptions. Or, more likely, misperceptions.

This, he thought with a twinge of humor, accounted for his own sense of disquiet. A misperception due to chronic Beamer fatigue.

Now, the younger deputy drew his flashlight, switched it on, and fired its beam toward the dark body of water. "The road ends right up there at the edge," he said. Then he swung his light slightly to the left. "And there's a path that goes around the pond over there. It's pretty well blocked, though. A downed tree and more deep water."

Sykes sighed. "I don't think there's any reason to go roaming around in the dark. The sheriff told us to have a look-see. We've looked, we've seen, and all we've got to show for it is muddy feet."

Beamer raised one dripping boot. "Twice today."

"What a lucky, lucky man."

"Not me. I don't like it. I don't like it at all."

"Vince, to the impartial observer, it is clear that you need to lighten up. You're wound up tighter than my wife watching a Hannibal Lecter movie."

"Aww, Dan."

They were about to turn around and head back to the car when

Beamer reached out and touched his shoulder. "Hey, you hear something?"

Sykes heard nothing more than the faint creak of a few tree branches scraping together in the low, barely noticeable breeze.

"Nah. What did it sound like?"

"I dunno. Kind of a—"

Then, from somewhere in the darkness, a shrill, warbling cry rang out.

A bird, Sykes thought.

A whippoorwill.

He hadn't heard a whippoorwill in a long, long time. Loud, yet it obviously came from a fair distance away.

Powerful lungs, that bird.

"That's too loud for a damn bird in the woods." Beamer's voice quavered a bit. "Don't you think?"

Sykes shook his head. "A bird is a bird, Vince."

The cry came again—this time, so loud and powerful that it shocked his senses. No, he had never heard a bird that sounded like *that.*

"Jesus," Beamer whispered. "You think we oughta stay here?"

"Vince, it is a bird. A loud—very loud—bird."

"Maybe so, but I think we should head out of here. As you said, there ain't nothing to see."

He was beginning to wonder whether that tingle in his skull might have actually meant something. But the sound—it was only a bird. Maybe a fucking weird-sounding bird, but nothing more.

It could *be* nothing more.

"All right, Vince."

He started back toward the car along the elevated edge of the road. But now, absolute silence had fallen over the landscape. No more breeze, no bird calls, not a single sound crept from the woods.

But now, from somewhere in the distance, a low rumble rose, which Sykes at first took to be thunder. They'd had one hell of a storm, but the sky now looked mostly clear. A few stars had begun to glimmer through gaps in the networks of branches above.

The rumble rose to a roar, deep and steady, not rising and falling like thunder. More like an approaching freight train.

"The fuck?" Beamer turned to peer back the way they'd come. "Tornado? Is that a tornado?"

Nope, still no breeze. It couldn't be a tornado.

Could it?

The roar mounted to a deafening crescendo, and then—as quickly as it had risen, fell to a muted rumble. Three seconds later, silence again blanketed the dark woods.

Beamer's eyes gleamed like glossy, dark marbles reflecting flashes of blue. "What the hell? Was that a jet?"

Sykes shook his head. "I know jets. And that wasn't one."

Around them, neither bird nor woodland animal stirred. Not so much as a chirp or splash or other sign of life from the pond.

In the aftermath of that noise, the renewed silence felt *eerie*.

"Vince," Sykes said. "I hate to give you more credit than you're due, but yeah. This is a weird place. I'm not fond of it either."

"Told you."

Above, the last remnants of daylight had vanished, and the cruiser's electric blue lights cast a throbbing, ghostly sheen over the landscape. Once back at the car and behind the wheel, Sykes felt a distinct wave of relief. The admittedly unusual sounds out here had rattled him more than they had any right to. He had only just derided Beamer's hypersensitivity, and now here he was, ready to attribute mysterious, even sinister purpose to what could only be natural noises, distorted and amplified by the unique acoustics of the terrain out here.

The very thing he had tried to explain to Beamer.

Regardless that it flew in the face of all rationality, between the bird noise, the rumbling, roaring sound, and this plain *weird* feeling, he couldn't let go of the idea that something truly out of the ordinary was happening out there. No telling what or even exactly where, but…something.

Out in that darkness around the pond. Yeah. It was from out there, this cold, oppressive dread seeping into his bones.

"I think it's beer time," he said in a flat voice and started the vehicle. He carefully maneuvered the car back onto the road and started back toward town.

They didn't need the overheads anymore, so he reached to flip them off. As he did, he glanced in the rearview mirror and, for the briefest moment, he saw a series of violet-blue flickers and what looked like some huge, oblong, gold-colored object hovering just beyond that gap in the trees.

Nope. Not possible. Not possible at all. They were just there. Right the fuck there!

Still....

He pressed the brakes and craned his neck to peer out the rear window. No more sign of the peculiar glow back there. What he saw now was the headlights of a car in the distance heading in their direction.

"What's the matter?" Beamer asked, casting him a wary eye.

He shook his head, forced to believe—against his will—the flashing blues had simply played some trick on his eyes. No other explanation. He heaved a deep sigh and gave Beamer a frustrated glance.

The young bastard might be more perceptive than he gave him credit for.

"Not a thing," he grumbled. "Not one goddamn thing."

Chapter 30

On the verge of slipping into the expanding opening before her, Alana reached for Martin's arm. He grabbed her hand and, gritting his teeth against the pain ravaging every nerve in his body, managed to drag her back toward him. He fell onto his backside, but she was clear of the opening. He tried to rise, to get back to his feet, but he only got as far as a crouch before the pain doubled him over again. The hole in the wall grew larger and larger as something on the other side tore away the outer boards with a deafening clatter.

Beyond that aperture, the thing radiating hot, golden light was a gigantic, glaring *eye*. A fiery orb hovering in some vast, dark space that might or might not have been their outside world. In the eye's center, a dark pupil whose outer rim spun like a black cyclone encompassed them both with a malignant gaze.

"Oh, God," Alana whispered. "Oh, *God!*"

Now on her knees, facing that blazing, impossible shape, Alana raised a trembling hand and made the sign of the cross over her chest.

The hole had grown taller and wider than Martin's body, and it continued to expand as the thing on the other side tore at its edges. Martin now saw that the eye was part of far, far bigger shape, the same hue and texture as those smoky figures in the chamber with them.

That thing's *fingers*, as he thought of them.

He could not stop himself glancing back at those wavering entities, and—to his renewed horror—he saw that they had begun moving, *gliding*, slowly toward him.

No. Not toward him.

Toward Alana.

He scrambled toward her and reached out to grab an arm, to draw her sideways, away from both the opening and the oncoming shapes from the center of the room. She appeared frozen before the glare of the monstrous eye. Once he had hold of her right bicep, he managed to tug her away from the center of the hole, but the formation of gray, *almost* human-shaped columns shifted direction and continued their gliding approach.

Behind the seven ghostly shapes, from the deep, violet-blue shadows at the room's farthest end, the eyes of the thing that called itself "Niemand" blazed like black light bulbs. He—or it—had not moved since Martin had taken the first shot with his gun. His bullet had not affected the human-looking being but had passed through that body as if it, too, were made of smoke and struck the wall. He couldn't be sure, but something about the figure appeared different than before.

It had not moved, but it had *changed*.

It looked taller. Yes, much taller, for the head now came close to touching the ceiling.

Alana cried out, her voice shrill and laden with panic, drawing Martin's eyes back to her. The smoke figures closed in on her, and as one of them moved forward, it slid *through* his right forearm and hand, which still gripped her upper right arm.

Icy fire shot past his elbow and drove like a spike into his shoulder. He felt her arm slip from his grasp.

"No!"

He threw himself after her, heedless of the seething forms, which now moved in unison to surround her. Like a hand closing around her body, all seven of them curled into a single, roiling mass, all but obscuring her struggling figure from view. Then, in a smooth motion, the gray, semi-solid knot slipped into the opening in the wall, dragging Alana with it. She unleashed a final, piteous scream as she disappeared into that unknown space beyond.

From the opening, a whirling, dark pupil in the center of the massive golden eye now rolled toward *him*.

"Alana!" His voice came out as a croak, no louder than a whisper. Ignoring the fiery glare, he stumbled toward the opening, braced himself with one barely functioning hand, and poked his head through to the other side.

His brain could not process the hellish vista before his eyes.

As gigantic as it appeared, the eye was a comparatively tiny organ at the end of a knotty, twisted stem, which protruded from a cohesive yet endlessly shifting, smoky mass of no definite shape. In a well of seemingly infinite darkness, the thing's fluctuating contours appeared luminous enough to be visible, yet of no color he could describe—other than maybe a gray-blue-pink-orange-violet miasma, no hue more prominent than another at any given moment. Countless tendrils furled and unfurled from those billowing and contracting masses, which he thought might be some kind of plasma.

No sign of Alana anywhere.

A rush of pure hopelessness—of love lost before it could blossom—overwhelmed his heart and mind, extinguished his last remaining spark of defiance.

"Oh, no. No, no."

She was gone. Stolen, he knew, by the same thing that had taken his brother.

The thing already at work inside him, and that would soon take him as well.

Yes, the moment he had set foot in that thing's sphere of influence, some small piece of it had infiltrated his body and mind and begun feeding on him. Even as it fed on him at this moment. All those hallucinations, the scrambling of his thoughts and memories, this ever-increasing agony—every bit the work of that monstrosity consuming him from the inside out.

Just as it had consumed Phil.

And now, beyond that hole in the wall, he faced an abyss of *other* space. This alien-lit room, some closed-off corner of the House of Caviness, must lie on its border—partly in his familiar reality, partly in the other. That nameless horror out there could pass between the disparate realms, alter space, and create bridges into this world to touch human beings. To feast on their energy, physical as well as psychic.

From behind him, a scraping, cracking sound seized his attention, and with a groan of pain, he swiveled to face the violet-lit room. The smoke figures that had taken Alana were gone, but something else—something huge—now occupied the far corner. The entity that had masqueraded as a black-clad preacher and gone by the name "Niemand"—perhaps an alias it had found ironic, amusing—had grown so tall it had folded itself almost in half against the confines of this chamber. This being now arched toward him like a tall, spindly gargoyle, the golden glow from the eye beyond the opening painting a twisted, grotesque shadow on the far wall. The gangling creature only vaguely resembled a man, with skin of polished onyx and jointed, segmented limbs that looked more insectoid than human. From around the narrow, black torso, an array of smoky tendrils, like those of that *other* thing, curled and thrashed with the sound of cracking whips.

The elongated head that hovered above him had no face. Yet he felt its full awareness focused on him.

The voice Martin now heard sounded like a weirdly modulated chainsaw—not in his ears but inside his head.

"ABANDON HOPE."

Then the thing pitched forward onto its upper appendages and began to move, spiderlike, toward the opening in the wall. Several more limbs, which had not existed only an instant before, extended from its sides, hissing and creaking, as the onyx mass heaved itself past him. The oblong, faceless head swiveled toward him as if it possessed invisible eyes, their gaze locked on his frozen body.

Then, with a jolt of agony, Martin felt something tear through his abdomen. A set of smoke-hued talons burst through the flesh of his stomach, and he saw blood erupt like a geyser in the talons' wake. Clear, thick fluid splashed over his entire body, and he could feel it burning, eating away at his flesh. He thought he saw his lower left leg break and twist in two different directions, but his awareness had shattered into so many fragments that he could no longer be certain of anything.

The pain was exquisite, beyond endurance, and yet it remained somehow distant. His mind refused to flee, though he desired it now more than any hope of surviving.

The Faceless One—the Crawling Chaos—thrust itself into the opening, and one massive, jointed appendage swept toward Martin. Its tip, from which a cluster of curved barbs sprang like huge, living treble hooks, slammed into his torso and batted him across the floor into the adjacent wall. He didn't feel the blow. At last, the most merciful part of his brain had begun to shut down the pain receptors in what remained of his body.

That inhuman voice had warned him to abandon hope, but hope refused to depart, and he clung to it with his every reserve of strength. He *hoped* he might yet join with Alana in some distant realm beyond suffering. He *hoped* that he and his brother could again know each other's presence and revel together in the pure joy they had known as children. He *hoped* that the terror, pain, and sorrow that had sprung from the House of Caviness were, in reality, as illusory as those hallucinations that had plagued him, and that a just, orderly universe would sweep all of that away, just as he might have swept away the cobwebs of a nightmare after a fitful sleep.

Gentle, cool waves washed over and through him, soothing his few remaining senses. And when a sharp, shrill keening tore into his waning awareness, he held it at bay by clinging to the tranquility that *hope* afforded him. He could not and would not release his grip.

He recognized the keening sound as a voice. Not a human voice, although a human brain might process it as something akin to a whippoorwill's call. But its volume, timbre, and cadence—and the exultant, alien syllables—belied a connection to any organism ever to have sprung from this earth.

This voice surged from something old enough to have thrived, mutated, and *evolved* over countless millennia. Something from elsewhere.

Something whose essence originated in *other* space.

Martin Pritchett's destroyer.

But this no longer mattered to him. All that mattered now was that he defy that crawling purveyor of madness, the one that had commanded him to abandon hope. The "Messenger." The thing that called itself "Niemand."

And as he slipped away, he held hope close.

It did not abandon him.

Chapter 31

It was going on 1800 hours, and Sheriff Parrott still sat at his desk. He had sworn for the third time that he was done and ready to leave, but as usual, one niggling item after another grabbed his attention before he could motivate himself out of his chair. Most pressing for a late Saturday afternoon—ha-ha—was a call from Town Councilman Edmiston to remind him of Monday night's council meeting, where the sheriff was expected to present ideas for shaving a significant number of dollars from the departmental budget for the upcoming year.

He genuinely liked Councilman Edmiston, who was one of the town's most capable entrepreneurs and one of Parrott's most outspoken proponents. But damn, that man kept no regular business hours, and he *so* liked to talk. Without a breath or other segue, Edmiston could shift from carrying on about the council's budget woes to his daughter's upcoming dance recital at the high school to the imminent downfall of civilization, perfectly heralded by the installation of automated service kiosks at the McDonalds out on Highway 21.

Which reminded Parrott that he'd never gone out there yesterday to determine how the hell they had run out of McMuffins. That, surely, was a far more telling harbinger of the end times than automated kiosks. How on earth would he explain his negligence to Mrs. Eleanor Clifton?

He had been on the verge of leaving—again—when Deputy Sykes called in from the field. Meghan patched the call through to his office phone. He switched on the external speaker.

"Sheriff Parrott here."

"Sykes here. We're heading back from Black Tooth Pond." A long, long silence followed. "Nothing to report."

"Nothing?"

Another silence. "Beamer might have a point when he calls the place 'different.' But yeah. Nothing."

Parrott heard a few unintelligible, grumbled syllables in the background before Sykes clicked off.

"I suppose that's good. We're going to give that whole area a good look-see come morning. Be ready."

"I'll be ready."

That was the most unenthusiastic "I'll be ready" he had ever heard from Sykes. Did they really have nothing to report from out there? If Parrott had officially related this afternoon's experience to himself, *he* might have avoided elaborating in detail. He knew Sykes as too down-to-earth to exaggerate any claims, but after all that had happened recently....

"I did ask for your impressions," he said. "So, it's 'different.' Is that all you've got?"

"Well," Sykes began, "if you—" The speaker crackled and stuttered for a moment. "But I figure—" More crackling. A crash of harsh, electronic noise. A warbling screech.

Static.

"Dan?"

A few sharp hisses. And then: "Something back there. Bright—" And then only a series of scratching and popping sounds. The connection broke.

To Parrott's surprise, he noticed a subtle tingling in his ears. A distant vibration that crept into his auditory canals and then began to scratch like a thrashing insect at his tympanic membranes. From the deepest, almost subliminal bass vibrations to the sharpest, birdlike screeches, a chaotic range of tones assaulted his hearing—not loud, yet potent. Insistent. At first, he thought the noises came from the phone speaker, but it was turned off. Then he realized the sounds were creeping in from somewhere outside.

He rose from his chair and stepped out to the hallway. He saw no one around, so he wandered down the short corridor to the reception area. Farley MacBane had already closed up the front desk for the day, but he was on phone duty till 2100, so he must be around somewhere. Then Parrott noticed movement outside the double glass doors to the parking area, so he pushed his way into the chilly evening air. Out on Main Street, a handful of cars crawled past, and the lights in the attorneys' office across the street indicated somebody else was working a bit late this evening. To his right, on the short walkway to the parking lot, he saw Deputy MacBane pacing slowly back and forth, staring skyward.

At the moment, Parrott didn't hear any odd sounds.

"What's up, Farley?"

The deputy glanced at him. "Thought I heard a racket."

"So did I." He peered up at the stars that had begun to speckle the purple sky. "What did it sound like to you?"

The younger man gave an uncertain shake of his head. "I dunno. Some kind of squalling. Thumping. Maybe some moron screeching his tires somewhere. Just hope he didn't hit something—or someone."

Parrott shrugged. "Maybe. But I don't think that was it."

There! He felt it again. A vibration in his ears, a rough tickling. The impression of some distant screech, and then a faint roll of thunder.

And then it came. A shocking explosion of sound, first shrill and keening, then trailing off like a roll of thunder.

Over and over, it repeated itself, soaring from some unknown distance to peal across the sky.

T'KKK-ELLL-EEE-LIIII!

T'KKK-ELLL-EEE-LIIII!

T'KKK-ELLL-EEE-LIIII!

When the cry—for *cry* he knew it must be—fell silent, his senses felt shocked, numbed.

Around him, the world seemed to have paused. No cars moved on Main Street. Not a breath of breeze stirred the air. No distant sounds of traffic or trains or other human movement.

"Sheriff?" came MacBane's voice at last.

He shook his head and said nothing. He didn't know what had made that noise, but he felt certain he knew *where* it came from.

What the sound meant, he had no idea. Yet, something inside assured him that, sooner or later, he—and perhaps many others—would certainly find out.

THE HOUSE AT BLACK TOOTH POND

X. SUNDAY

Chapter 32

Carli Vaughan hoped—desperately hoped—that she hadn't made a dreadful mistake falling in love with Phil Pritchett.

No, no, no. Neither he nor she had made any mistake about their feelings for each other. It was just that, these past few days, something was going on with him, something *off*, but she did not, could not, believe he might be getting cold feet. Still, his brother, Marty, had said that Phil felt he needed to work out the nuts and bolts of such a major life change in his own mind. That was as may be.

Of course, after the unmitigated disaster of her first marriage, she understood the desire—the need—to be certain.

With Phil, she was. Absolutely.

But how could he have dropped off the map for so long?

Okay, it wasn't *that* long. They'd spoken yesterday afternoon. But last night, this morning, and now this afternoon, he had not answered any calls or texts. Hadn't even looked at the texts, for that matter. She'd spent last night at her mom and dad's in Christiansburg, helping them out with various odds and ends since Dad's COPD had about laid him out these past few days. Damn him and his precious cigarettes, which he'd smoked since age twelve. In the past year, he had "permanently" quit no less than eighty times and was now working his way toward eighty-one.

At this rate, by the time of the wedding, Dad would be lucky if he were still breathing.

Now back home, she'd hoped that Phil would at least answer his damn phone. Nope. She again shut down that little voice warning her that something might have happened, like a car accident, or breaking a leg out in the woods, or—God forbid—something worse. More likely, he had just lost his phone. Lately, he'd had a devil of a time keeping up with it. And just about everything else, for that matter. He seemed to have become absent-minded these past few days. Part and parcel of his ostensible wedding jitters?

She decided to call his brother. They kept close tabs on each other, spent tons of time in each other's company. But when she dialed his number, after several rings, only his voice mail answered. She didn't leave a message, but if she couldn't reach Phil soon, she would try Marty again.

Oh, what the hell, Phil's place was ten minutes away, and she hadn't even taken off her shoes yet. Might as well run over there and see if she could figure out what was up. She'd hung her keys on the hook in the kitchen beside the door to the garage, so she grabbed them back up, took her purse from kitchen tabletop, and headed back out the door. With her key fob, she started the BMW, slid behind the steering wheel, and punched the garage door opener button. Concern and annoyance wrangled with each other as she backed out of the driveway and turned onto Country Club Drive, headed toward town.

If Phil was home and he *hadn't* misplaced his phone, she saw no alternative but to provide him with a free, no-holds-barred lesson in consideration for others, especially her—not that this should even be a thing for him. He might be young at heart, but he was hardly a kid. Until the past few days, he'd never shown her anything *but* consideration, courtesy, and genuine respect. She had admired that about him from the beginning, accepted those qualities as integral parts of his character, not affectations to adopt at whim, which had been Hank's way. Her ex-husband could turn sincerity on and off at will as a means of manipulation, so she had long been hypersensitive to disingenuous attitudes and behavior, particularly from men. Phil's consistent, thoughtful conduct had convinced her that this was not his way.

Well, it had better not be!

But there was that visit from the sheriff the other day about that man who had escaped from jail. She still felt anxious about someone potentially dangerous lurking in the area. Better if Phil had suffered some temporary, stress-induced slip of the brain than come to harm at the hands of some deranged piece of shit. She didn't think she could handle him being hurt or worse, not after she'd survived so much trauma with Hank and then—unexpectedly—discovered so much happiness with Phil. She had almost come to believe that she and happiness were never destined to share the same road.

At Mulberry Road, she turned left, toward downtown and the historic district. There was hardly any traffic at the moment, since the church and lunch crowds had pretty well dispersed for the day. Three minutes later, she pulled up at Phil's place, and the first thing she saw was his empty driveway. No truck.

"Well, shit."

Could he have gone to his brother's place? She drew her phone from her purse and redialed Marty's number. Voice mail again.

Well, maybe he'd taken Rufus out to walk in the country. But couldn't he have let her know what was going on? He knew she would be back this afternoon.

Now, she shut off the engine, got out, and went to the front door. She knocked once but didn't wait to thrust her key into the lock, push the door open, and step inside.

First thing, she heard a rapid *thump-thump-thump*, and here came Rufus tearing through the living room from the kitchen, tail wagging so fast it became a blur. He jumped up and pawed happily at her, which nearly set her off-balance.

"Easy, easy, buddy!" She rubbed his head and scratched behind his ears, which calmed him in short order. "Where's your dad, huh? Did he leave you all by your lonesome?"

Now that he had greeted her with sufficient alacrity, Rufus looked around with wide, questioning eyes and then back at her, as if to ask where his customary human might be.

She headed to the kitchen with the dog hard at her heels. Immediately, she saw his empty food dish and half-empty water bowl in the corner by the refrigerator.

That was not right. Rufus could snarf down some food in a hurry, but he always left a little at the bottom of his bowl. Unless he was *really* starving.

"What the hell, boy?"

Rufus eyed his bowls and gave her an approving glance. The he trotted straight to the back door and scratched at the jamb.

"Gotcha," she said and opened the door for him. He bolted out to the backyard, clearly in need of relief.

She grabbed both bowls, filled one with fresh water from the sink, and set it back on the floor. Phil kept a big bag of kibble in the pantry next to the dining area door, so she pulled it out and dumped a healthy quantity into the food dish, which she placed next to the water bowl.

Moments later, business accomplished, Rufus rushed back to the little porch and pawed again at the storm door. When she opened it, he scooted inside and headed straight for his food. Within moments, he had obliterated the kibble and begun lapping at his water.

Now, a little tremor of apprehension shimmied down her back. Phil would never, ever leave for any length of time without leaving Rufus more than adequate goodies. Yeah, this was beginning to feel more than a little troubling.

Okay. At least a time or two now, Phil had driven out to the country, to his favorite place for walking Rufus, but without the dog. What was up with that? Might he have gone out there again?

She had looked up the property for him the other night on the computer. It was out Old Beckham Road. "Black Tooth Pond" he'd called it. Up toward Beckham, about seven miles.

Should she?

Either that or head back home in defeat with little else to do but to wait for some word from him. She liked that idea least of all.

She refilled both of Rufus's bowls and gave the Retriever's neck a vigorous scratching. "I'm gonna see if I can find your dad, okay? And I think he's going to get a talking to. A very serious one."

Rufus wagged his tail in response but kept his attention on his bowls.

As she headed back out the front door and locked it, she had to fight back another surge of anxiety. Had Phil been gone all night? How could *that* be?

She didn't know exactly where Black Tooth Pond lay, but she

retained a vivid mental image of the GIS map from the other night. She had a pretty good idea where to look and no doubt whatsoever that she could find the place in short order.

#

The afternoon weather forecast called for rain, but so far, it had held off. Vast gray and purple clouds stole across the gunmetal sky, though, and Carli figured she didn't have very long before the bottom fell out. By the time she had driven far enough out Old Beckham Road to start looking for an apt-looking turnoff, her pulse had begun to race and her throat had gone dry. Maybe she was overreacting—in fact, she felt certain of it—but the threat of a storm had heightened her sense of urgency.

As she rounded a long curve and then hit a straightaway through a heavily treed stretch of the road, she noticed a flutter of something yellow not far ahead on the left. Her foot reflexively went to the brake, and when she came to what she recognized as a strip of yellow barrier tape between two tall poplars, she knew she had reached her destination. Just off the pavement, a narrow stretch of mud, marred by countless tire tracks, extended some distance into the woods, now a patchwork of skeletal branches and clusters of brown leaves that clung with desperate tenacity to their hosts.

On the right-hand poplar, above the tied-off end of the yellow tape, what looked like a brand-new "No Trespassing" sign glared out at the road. When she peered down the little mud track, she saw no sign of Phil's truck.

Well, that tore this idea, didn't it? *Was* this the right place? Phil had been coming out here for a long time, and he obviously had never encountered anything to impede his entry. The tape and sign did look new, though, didn't they?

"Shit."

Well, she hadn't come all the way out here to give up on the spot. It made no sense that his truck might be parked somewhere beyond this barrier, yet she couldn't deny a little voice that urged her to venture farther into what Phil considered his "private" realm. Knowing him, if he found the entry to a place he considered "his" to be barred, he'd park somewhere else and go in on foot. You did not deny Phil his personal place in the woods, it was as simple as that.

The print on the tape read, "POLICE LINE – DO NOT CROSS."

Yeah. Like that meant anything around these parts. It certainly wouldn't to Phillip Pritchett.

It took some maneuvering, but she parked the SUV parallel to the road, just this side of the barrier tape. She hadn't exactly dressed for traipsing around in the woods but neither had she worn her best clothes for driving back from her parents'; just a sweatshirt, jeans, and her old, comfy loafers. Still, did she *really* mean to go wandering into some unfamiliar patch of woods, one that had been deliberately cordoned off? And with rain possibly on the way?

Good sense answered with a resounding *no*, but something else, something purely intuitive, pressed her to continue.

Without warning, the name "Niemand" popped into her mind. It took her a moment to place it. Then she recalled that it was the name of the owner of this parcel listed on the GIS information card. She hadn't found anything beyond that single name. No individual, no company, no other reference, anywhere.

Interesting. Maybe troubling.

Moonshiners?

She clambered out of the car, locked the doors, and made her way around the tape onto the muddy track beyond. The plethora of tire tracks had turned the surface into ruts and mounds of what looked like squishy, slippery peanut butter. To the left, though, along the edge of the encroaching brush, a relatively dry ridge appeared to offer more solid footing. She made her way to it and then half-tiptoed along its length, bypassing a menacing-looking pool of murky water in the middle of the narrow excuse for a road.

And then, ahead, there it was. There could be no mistaking Black Tooth Pond. A dark, oblong body of water that extended several hundred yards into the deep woods, where a number of blackened trunks protruded from its surface like long, broken teeth.

So, *this* was Phil's private haven—well, sort of—where he had misspent countless hours of his youth and now regularly brought Rufus to walk, play, and roam. Now that she saw it for herself, she understood its allure for him. Secluded. Quiet. Picturesque in its way. Given his artistic temperament, the place probably inspired his creativity.

But by all indications, he was not here now.

To the left of the pond, what looked like a little deer path extended around the water's edge and into the woods. She saw footprints back here, too. A damned army must have marched through. Overlapping prints of numerous booted feet, here, there, and everywhere.

Wait.

Police?

Indeed, the print on that yellow tape had read "POLICE LINE – DO NOT CROSS." And now she saw, on a tree next to the pond, another new-looking "No Trespassing" sign.

No. These wouldn't have deterred Phil for a minute if he'd set his mind on coming back here.

She continued a short distance onto the path, but there was no telling how far it went. Good sense finally began to reassert itself, and the caprice that had goaded her to wander this far began to feel sillier and sillier.

He was *not* out here.

Overhead, the swollen clouds had turned darker and heavier. She could use a shower, for sure, but she had no desire to get caught in a deluge way out here. Damn that man for leaving her in such a state of uncertainty. No, he didn't *owe* her accountability for every move he made, but neither should he make determining his whereabouts so needlessly difficult.

This definitely meant a conversation.

She turned and started back the way she had come, only to lurch to an immediate halt. A shrill, almost musical sound had warbled from the woods, back in the direction she'd been heading. It sounded like a whippoorwill song.

But it was still daylight. Dull, dim daylight, true, but no matter how cloudy, those birds never began calling before twilight. And she knew this specific call. It wasn't a bird.

It was Phil's voice. That silly little mimic he did. A good mimic, but not quite the real thing.

She turned and peered into the shadows beneath the tangled branches that surrounded the path. What was this? Some kind of ridiculous game?

"Phil?"

At first, no response. Then, from what sounded like a considerable distance, she heard his voice.

"Carli."

Yes, it *was* his voice! But it sounded flat, almost dead. Was he all right?

"Phil? Where are you?"

Then his whippoorwill call again. This time, it sounded more distant.

What the *hell* was this about?

"Phil!"

No response.

She started back in the direction from which the voice had come and then stopped again. What to do, what to do? She knew now that he was out here. But if he were hurt, why would he do his bird call? Maybe he thought the sound would carry farther? His voice sounded so low and flat, as if there were no force behind it.

One more time, she called, "Phil!"

And then, again, the whippoorwill call. The *false* call. It was him all right.

At her fastest pace, she lit into the woods, heading toward the source of the sound.

#

"**O**h, Jesus. Oh, Jesus!"

Carli had emerged from the woods and followed the path into a rough circle of brambles and weeds. Now, she faced a massive, sprawling magnolia tree, its dense boughs almost black beneath the leaden sky. Beyond it, she saw a crumbling, dilapidated structure, covered by creepers and surrounded by close-pressing foliage. The branches of a giant, ghostly sycamore appeared to have burst through the crooked roof to clutch at the glowering clouds above. Grimy, cracked windowpanes leered at her like empty eye sockets, and to her mind, the gaping front door resembled a screaming mouth.

But it wasn't the old house that held her attention.

It was the two vehicles—or what was left of them—that lay amid the brambles between the magnolia tree and the house's front door. There was no mistaking them: Phil's Toyota pickup truck and Marty's Nissan SUV. Both half-flattened, with pieces of wreckage strewn around what had once been a small yard. They both looked as if they had been dropped from hundreds of feet and smashed upon impact.

Impossible. Absolutely impossible.

After gathering what little nerve she had left, she crept toward Phil's truck, the nearer of the pair. The cab was a twisted mass of ruined seats, a crushed steering column, and shreds of insulation from the roof. The warped bed looked as if a giant had twisted each end in opposite directions before discarding it. Only one tire—the front driver's side—remained attached, and it hung at an awkward angle.

Martin Pritchett's SUV looked just as bad.

She felt some faint measure of relief that she saw no blood or other trace of human bodies in either vehicle.

She *had* heard his voice, so he must be alive. And around here somewhere. But she could not draw enough air into her lungs to call his name.

"Carli."

There! Again, his voice, but so low, so lifeless.

It *was* his voice, wasn't it?

Not just the tone, but the character of the voice itself seemed off. For a second, she thought it must be someone mimicking his voice. The way he mimicked the whippoorwill's song.

"Phil?"

A barely audible whisper.

She tried again.

"Phil?"

A little louder. Still, that choked sound wouldn't have carried even as far as the house's front door.

She felt a faint breeze on her exposed skin. The sky appeared as dark as night now, though it was barely past two in the afternoon. Around her, she heard a gentle patter, like raindrops beginning to leak from the clouds. But then, somewhere in her field of vision, a warm light began to glimmer. Pulling her attention away from Phil's truck, she saw a spherical, golden glow rising in one of the house's upper windows. Almost the color of sunlight, she thought.

But in the center of the golden sphere, a circular black spot whirled like a little cyclone.

A pupil!

"No, no. No, no, no."

She took a few steps back, and the sound of pattering grew louder. She didn't feel a single raindrop.

When she dared to turn around, she had no idea what she was seeing. She now faced that huge black magnolia, and from the depths of that crouching hulk, a number of smoky-looking columns appeared to be drifting toward her—ten of them, she thought. The pattering sound rose from the piles of old, dead leaves in the wake of their passage.

The bramble-choked ground before her brightened with a golden glow. The light cast from that upper window, creeping, *oozing* over the ground to encompass her. Her shadow lengthened before her, as if reaching out to the approaching smoke figures.

As they advanced, they seemed to swallow her shadow, somehow absorbing its essence.

Then they began to swallow her.

THE HOUSE AT BLACK TOOTH POND

XI. ONE MONTH LATER—MONDAY

Chapter 33

F BI Special Agent Tyler Kincaid and his forensic team had finally packed up and left, their farewells barely civil, certainly not cordial. For six days, Aiken Mill—specifically, the Flying Dutchman Inn, with its distinctive, towering windmill, out on Highway 21—had been their base of operations, and during that time, Sheriff Parrott had spent more time at the hotel and in the field than in his office. Now that the feds had headed back for Northern Virginia, Parrott had one hell of a report to write, and he hardly knew where to begin.

The hour hand on the clock had just passed five in the afternoon. Dr. Mel Crawford sat directly across from him, in the chair in front of his desk. She looked not unlike a beaten dog, barely able to lick her wounds after the brutal savaging she had endured, primarily by Dr. Nelson Rouse, the FBI team's chief forensic examiner. If he had missed finding fault with a single aspect of her investigation and subsequent conclusions, she was at a loss to recall it.

"Not exactly open-minded, are they?" Parrott said, feeling more than a touch of empathy for her. He had hardly come away from the feds' investigation unscathed.

"I suppose it was to be expected," she said. "I know you were reluctant to bring them in. I shouldn't have insisted."

"Circumstances didn't leave us much choice."

"I guess not."

But what the hell else *could* he have done?

At dawn on that Sunday, four weeks ago, the sheriff and his team had converged on Black Tooth Pond and spent half the day exploring every inch of the property that encompassed the pond and surrounding woods. Not a single indication of anything amiss—other than a recurrence of the "strange feelings" the place seemed to inspire. Regardless, afterward, he'd cordoned off the entrance from the road and posted new "No Trespassing" signs, for all the good any of that would do. Several additional, more extensive searches also turned up nothing, even after they'd learned there *might* be an old dwelling on the property. If so, neither the sheriff's department nor the FBI team could locate it. Nothing back there but deep woods, with virtually no sign of human encroachment since God knew when.

They'd had no success tracking down anyone named "Niemand," the landowner on record, despite property tax payments on that parcel being up to date. According to the county treasurer, as far back as could be recorded, all payments had been made in cash. Parrott had put a watch on the account so he might be notified of any activity, though he held little hope that it might ever offer any clues to the owner's identity.

After the discovery of the now-nonexistent remains of one Franklin Lydell—originally named Franklin Lydell Caviness, he had determined—a bewildering series of disappearances led to Parrott's calling in the FBI. The list of the missing included John "Robert" Doe (now presumed to be Robert John Caviness), itinerant, formerly of Providence, Rhode Island; Phillip Michael Pritchett, commercial artist, of Aiken Mill, Virginia; Martin Ford Pritchett, Ph.D., professor of psychology at Beckham College, of Aiken Mill, Virginia; Alana Gisele Mendes, admissions director at Beckham College, of Aiken Mill, Virginia; and Carli Jennings Vaughan, owner of Vaughan Realty, LLC, of Aiken Mill, Virginia. Vehicles owned by both Pritchett brothers and Ms. Vaughan could not be accounted for. Ms. Mendes' car had been located at Martin Pritchett's home on Knollwood Court in Aiken Mill.

On the Monday following the sheriff's first investigation of the Niemand property, reports came in that both of the Pritchett brothers,

Ms. Mendes, and Ms. Vaughan had failed to show up at their respective places of employment. A search of Dr. Pritchett's home had turned up a cache of very old letters, notes, and news clippings that had been mailed by an unidentified sender from Providence, Rhode Island, to members of the then-local Caviness family at an Aiken Mill post office box. From this material, Parrott had pieced together a timeline, which indicated that, in the early 1950s, Theophilus and Maxine Caviness had moved from Providence to Sylvan County. From then until the mid-1970s, they had owned a portion of the land that included Black Tooth Pond, a fact that Parrott found perplexing, for the family appeared to have resided *at* that property; yet numerous intensive searches had turned up no trace of a dwelling there.

The material in Dr. Pritchett's possession, odd as it was, had been sent by either a Providence-based Caviness family member or an acquaintance. At some point, Franklin Lydell Caviness, son of Theophilus and Maxine, had moved to Rhode Island, the family's original home, and officially dropped the "Caviness" surname. Then, recently, for reasons unknown, Franklin and his son, Robert, of Cleveland, Ohio, had come back to Aiken Mill.

Parrott couldn't begin to say precisely how, but Franklin's return had without question triggered the current crisis.

Photographs and videos taken by the Pritchett brothers and Ms. Mendes, retrieved from their personal cloud accounts, suggested they had found an old dwelling *somewhere*. However, the location tags from those files proved useless; just sets of meaningless numbers rather than valid geographic coordinates. Unfortunately, all of their photos and video files had been of such poor quality that the law enforcement agencies could draw no definitive conclusions from them.

Special Agent Kincaid's insinuation that the sheriff and his deputies might need a refresher course in both local geography and investigative procedure stung Parrott personally. But it was Dr. Rouse, the FBI's lead forensic investigator, who had very nearly earned a good clocking for all but accusing Doc Crawford of not only ineptitude but perpetuating some kind of hoax regarding the disappearance of Franklin Lydell's remains. Her explanation that they had been "consumed" by some unknown chemical agent that left no trace flew in the face of even the most elementary science. No competent forensic investigator could or would give credence to the medical examiner's outlandish "theories."

So, the feds had returned to their black hole of origin, leaving the case open but, Parrott suspected, unlikely to be revisited. As far as those folks were concerned, no solid evidence of foul play existed. Just a series of bungled procedures and opportunities by a force of inept backwoods hicks.

Doc Crawford gave him a long, thoughtful stare. "I don't suppose you're going to let this go, are you?"

"No more than you are."

Her smile was wan. "Yeah. Well. I've got nothing to work with. I can write my paper, but it's a given that it's a lost cause."

"You kept meticulous records."

"Sure. On paper, so to speak. But there's nothing verifiable— or repeatable—in the real world. At the very least, I should have made complete video records. And ordinarily I would, but under the circum- stances, it was so—" She stopped and sighed. "I got ahead of myself."

"You're not saying the FBI guys are right?"

She gave a vigorous shake of her head. "Not at all. Only that if I had it to do over, I'd do it differently. Better. But I don't ever want to experience anything like this again. No one should."

"You're right. No one should."

"So, Bryce. Where do we go from here?"

He glanced at the clock. "How about Willy's?"

Finally, Doc Crawford's face brightened a little. "I could use a belt."

"Shall we?"

"Let's."

He shoved his chair back and rose to his feet. "Let me close up and make sure Deputy Dan hasn't resigned in disgust."

"Meet you outside?"

He nodded. "Meet you outside."

Mel rose, offered him an almost enthusiastic smile, and stepped out the door. For a moment, Parrott gazed into the space she'd vacated. Yeah. Maybe an occasional after-hours belt with her might lead to better places for both of them.

He grabbed his campaign hat from the rack and slapped it on his head. His eyes roved around his office, and he wondered for the umpteenth time if this really, truly was the life he ought to be living.

"Sylvan County," he muttered. "The Cold Case Capital of the World."

Yep. He'd chosen this life, and he would never let anything, not even *this* monster of a case, drag him away from it.

ॐ

STEPHEN MARK RAINEY

XII. TUESDAY

Chapter 34

3:05 p.m.

"Sheriff, we've got something." Deputy Dan stood with his head poked into Parrott's office, regarding him with bemused eyes. "They found it at Studio 253. Something of Phillip Pritchett's."

Parrott felt an ice-cold blade slice through his chest wall. "Well, don't stand there yapping. Let's have it."

Sykes pushed his way through the door, carrying a large rectangular case—an artist's portfolio, Parrott realized—obviously heavy, its canvas sides bulging slightly. It was too wide to fit on the sheriff's desk, so Sykes laid the case on the floor, unzipped it, and pulled it open like a huge book. Inside lay a pile of Masonite boards, at least a half-dozen, all cut into various sizes, mostly oblong or kidney shaped, the largest about two feet in width. Each piece bore colorful images, some on both sides, all painted with crude, thick brush strokes. Some had holes cut or drilled into them. Several cylinders of what looked like cork, each about an inch in diameter and an inch tall, nestled in the bottom of the case.

"What the hell is this?"

"It's gotta be some art project Pritchett was working on."

Parrott rose from his chair and ambled around the desk to regard the portfolio's contents. "How the hell did this just now come to light?"

"It wasn't stored in Pritchett's studio workspace. They found it tucked in a storage room in the building's basement."

"Down there a long time?"

The deputy shook his head. "This is a new case, and the acrylic paint is relatively fresh. Ms. Eggleston—she's the studio manager—said it had to be recent."

"So, maybe Pritchett didn't want other people to see what he was working on?"

"Maybe."

Parrott knelt and studied the loose, almost childlike renderings on the Masonite. When the images they formed crystalized in his mind, he swallowed hard and damn near choked on his own saliva.

The significance of what lay before them appeared to strike Deputy Dan at the same time. His pale blue eyes widened until they gleamed like brilliant sapphires beneath the overhead fluorescent bulbs. "Sheriff?"

Several seconds passed before Parrott's churning thoughts settled enough for him to form coherent words. "I know what we're looking at. But I have no idea what it means."

"What do we do with this? Send it to forensics?"

The sheriff shook his head. "Leave it with me. I have to make a phone call."

#

Professor Shelton "Shelly" Scales looked almost exactly as the sheriff had imagined him from their previous phone conversations. Stocky, almost a head shorter than Parrott, with thinning silver hair, a close-trimmed white beard, and clear, emerald eyes. The face of a sage. When Parrott had described to him the contents of the portfolio that had turned up at Studio 523, Professor Scales agreed to see him, his tone a mix of enthusiasm and grim expectation.

Within moments of ending the call, the sheriff had taken the portfolio and set out for the professor's Forest Park address, following his GPS navigator's directions. The two-story, Georgian-style house, set in a well-tended yard behind a screen of dogwood and crape myrtle trees, appeared smaller but hardly less impressive than most of its neighbors.

Parrott's heart hadn't hammered nonstop like this since the discovery of Franklin Lydell's grisly remains—the incident that had set this entire, ill-fated investigation in motion.

"Good afternoon, Sheriff." Scales wore a warm but cautious smile. His voice was low and measured. "It's nice to meet you in person, but I suppose not for this reason. Please come in."

"Thank you, sir." Parrott crossed the threshold and found himself inside a small foyer with plain white walls and trim. Scales motioned for him to follow and led the way through a tidy, unassuming living room, its furnishings comfortable-looking if not lavish. Almost inevitably, Parrott thought, the sweet aroma of pipe smoke permeated the air. He followed the squat but energetic figure into a smaller adjoining room, its walls predictably lined with bookshelves filled to overflowing. While the living room appeared neat, barely shy of formal, the professor's inner sanctum looked like marginally controlled chaos. A 27-inch iMac monitor and keyboard dominated the surface of his large wooden desk, also littered by stacks of books and several unruly piles of paper. Scales's thin lips spread in a smile as he closed the door behind the sheriff.

"If I'd known you were coming, I'd have dusted." Then his expression darkened, and he pointed to the portfolio case Parrott held in his right hand. "So, this belonged to the late artist you told me about."

"Yes." He glanced around the cluttered room and lifted the case. "Where can I…?"

"Here." Scales motioned to a small wooden table next to his desk, its surface also covered with books. He deftly gathered them into two heavy stacks and transferred them to the floor nearby. "This ought to do."

The professor watched with interest as Parrott set the canvas case on the floor, unzipped it, and opened it to expose its contents. As the sheriff removed the irregularly shaped pieces of Masonite and placed them on the table, Scales's expression grew increasingly bleak.

Parrott glanced at him. "That look tells me that you must know something about this. Did you know Phillip Pritchett?"

"No, I didn't." He let out a soft sigh. "But I'd certainly like to learn more about what you've got there. And I trust you have a few questions of your own."

"Of that, you can be sure."

His gaze shifted from the portfolio's contents to Parrott. "This will have to do with that case you referred to. The one that prompted you to call me in the first place?"

"It would."

Scales nodded, his brain's gears clearly engaged and cranking. He pointed to the painted Masonite pieces. "Mr. Parrott, If I'm going to be of any assistance to you, I need you to tell me everything you know about this. And about the late Phillip Pritchett."

There was no point now in holding anything back. The professor almost certainly knew more than he had shared in their previous conversations—though likely because Parrott hadn't given him enough information to formulate any meaningful conclusions. Whatever the case, Professor Scales was probably the only person, anywhere, who could shed any light on the events that had stymied the sheriff, his entire department, and even the Federal authorities.

And how this "art project" might fit into the mystery.

So, doing his best to keep his focus and leave nothing out, he related the events that had led him to this point, in detail and in chronological order. From the discovery of Franklin Lydell's horrifically ruined body and determination that something beyond extraordinary had both taken his life and then—presumably—consumed the remains; to the incarceration, escape, and apparent death of the man who turned out to be Lydell's son, Robert John Caviness; to the various, inexplicable phenomena at Black Tooth Pond, where the Caviness family had lived long ago; to the Pritchett brothers' apparent connection to that place and possibly the Caviness family itself.

The strange, tall man in town who had vanished in front of Parrott and his chief deputy's eyes. The deafening noise that had roared through the sky from the direction of Black Tooth Pond—a noise Scales had apparently not heard. The disappearance of real estate agent Carli Vaughan, Phillip Pritchett's fiancée. The FBI's inability—or, as Parrott was convinced, its unwillingness—to verify events as the sheriff, the medical examiner, and every deputy in the department had presented them.

Parrott's spirits plummeted deeper with every word of his own recitation.

This was the coldest possible case in the cold case capital of the world.

When he finished speaking, he saw that Scales was not looking at him but at the pieces of Phillip Pritchett's "art project" scattered over the table's surface.

After a long silence, Scales said, "Sheriff, I can't say that I understand everything you've described, but I will tell you that I absolutely accept it. You and I both know that many, many strange things have happened in this town—in these mountains—over the years. The centuries. Even what happened to your father. I recall there was an element of the strange in that. And I'm convinced that everything you just shared is a part of that same 'strange.'" He sent Parrott a thoughtful look. "Maybe even the underlying source."

Parrott pointed to the paintings on the table. "You're saying this somehow makes sense to you?"

"Well, it obviously pinpoints a location. Black Tooth Pond. But it's the other pieces that convey its meaning."

"I'm listening."

Scales began to sort the sections of Masonite like an oversized, oddly shaped deck of cards. The first—the largest piece, a rough, two-foot wide oval—bore what looked like a Van Gogh-esque depiction of outer space. The board's surface was a thick, unevenly blended layer of blue and violet paint, covered with explosions of white, yellow, and orange that might have represented stars. A prominent ring of fiery gold dominated the right side, its center occupied by a black oval. On the left, a smaller black oval overlapped a cluster of star-like shapes.

"On most of these surfaces, there's a mess of overpainting, filled-in holes, and images that have been scraped away," Scales said. "I believe your artist was trying to work out something he could not fully visualize." He held up two smaller oval pieces, which Parrott found the most unsettling: a tall, spindly human figure, rendered entirely in black, with an outstretched oversized hand; and an amorphous, swirling blob of green, white, pink, and gray. What appeared to be a bright gold, cyclopean eye extended from one end of the blob on a wiry-looking stalk. From the base of the stalk, a series of purple tendrils—five of them—sprang forth, each bearing an almost human-shaped figure at its tip. Scales studied the two images for a moment; then he placed them atop the pair of painted ovals on the large board, the black figure on the left, the blob with the eye and tendrils on the right. The pieces fit perfectly in the spaces.

Parrott pointed at the pile of boards on the table. "It's almost like a three-dimensional jigsaw puzzle, isn't it?"

Scales nodded. "More or less. Except I believe it's meant to represent *other* dimensions." He picked up another large oval piece, cut to the precise size of the base piece, and placed it carefully atop the first. This one bore a familiar aspect, for it displayed an expansive, deep green forest that encompassed a blue-green ellipse—a pond— with numerous spiky trees protruding from one end. Two ovals, rendered in a translucent glaze near the lower, curved edge of the board, occupied roughly the same positions as the two enigmatic figures on the layer beneath. On the left, a simple, box-like white house stood amid the trees, with a huge, green-black tree towering above it. A couple of inches to its right, just above the rim of the glazed oval, a rendering of the scribbled figure's black hand hovered amid the splotchy green forest. Above and to its left, another black-painted hand appeared to grope its way out of the forest. A third hand appeared at the rightmost edge of the pond. At both the leftmost edge of the board and in the center of the pond, the artist had cut a hole, each about an inch in diameter.

Parrott felt a little chill. A house in the forest near Black Tooth Pond.

But there had been no house out there.

Scales fitted one of the cork cylinders into the hole on the left. Then, after careful consideration, he selected the next piece: a partial oval with a hole at its left edge, this one displaying only trees and the seemingly ubiquitous black hand. Scales placed the section of board atop the other, fitting the hole over the protruding cork, so that now only forest—and the floating hand—occupied the left side of the weird, stylized construct.

"No house," Parrott whispered, as the puzzle's meaning began to take rough shape in his mind. "The hand from below appears on each level—and three times on the one that shows the house."

"I believe Pritchett intended to convey that this underlying figure reaches up, or out, through various levels of space. And it manipulates space, to some degree." He pointed to the forest-painted section of Masonite that concealed the house. Then, with gentle fingers, he rotated it on the cork, which served as an axis, to again uncover the house. "See, now the hand on this piece aligns with the hand on the board underneath."

"There's one more piece left." Parrott pointed to a circular piece of Masonite, six inches in diameter, also with a hole in its center. This disc bore an odd whirl, almost like a cyclone viewed from above, but with two distinct, black arms radiating from the hole to form a wide "V" shape. The black hand occupied a spot at the outer edge of the disc between the two arms.

There was only one place left where it might fit.

Scales fitted the circular piece on the cork that protruded from the hole in the pond and aligned the hand at its edge with the one on the layer below. For several moments, he appeared bemused. But then, apparently settling on his next move, he grasped the edges of the oval board that depicted the house and rotated it until it revealed the full shape of the amorphous, cyclopean figure on the bottom-most layer.

"How in the hell could someone come up with this?" Parrott muttered. "Was he trying to leave some clue behind?"

Scales studied the construct. "Like I said, I think he wanted to visualize something in three dimensions that his mind couldn't otherwise grasp. Some space or dimension lying outside of ours where these things come from. By manipulating space, they have an entry into our level of reality. And once here, they can warp it." He pointed to several globs of thick, dried paint and rough, scraped areas on the various boards where some image or another had been masked out or effaced. "As you can see, your artist reworked these pieces until he settled on what we see here. Ten will get you one it took him many attempts to accomplish even this much."

"You seemed to grasp it pretty quickly. Faster than I could have."

Scales scratched at his short beard. Then he tapped the image of the cyclopean thing. His eyes swiveled to meet Parrott's. "This is not the first time I've seen something like this."

Parrott felt a stab of surprise. "Go on. Please."

Scales nodded. "Remember that I told you about the legend of the Yck? At the time, I didn't make any connection to your case. Didn't have any reason to. But now I very well might."

He shuffled to a file cabinet in the corner, opened the second drawer from the top, and spent a couple of minutes thumbing through its jam-packed contents. Finally, he drew a manila folder from one of the slots and opened it to reveal several yellowed, photocopied pages, all covered in barely legible scrawl. Parrott noted that the folder was labeled "Batts and Fallam Expedition, 1671." Scales rifled through the thick stack of pages within, drew out a couple, and laid them on his desk.

"Thomas Batts and Robert Fallam are credited with being the first white men to explore this region of Virginia," he said. "They're best known for discovering the New River, not very far from here. They called it the 'Woods' River, after Major General Abraham Woods, who sponsored the expedition. In early September, 1761, they left from what is now Petersburg and would have reached our area about mid-month." He tapped the pages he'd extracted with a fingertip. "From their expedition journal."

On one of the pages, Parrott saw a crude ink rendering of what looked like a bloated grub or thick, stubby caterpillar, but with a single, huge eye and an array of tendrils that curled from its underside. Next to it stood a tiny stick figure.

"Jesus!"

After recovering from the shock of seeing a much earlier representation of the very thing Phillip Pritchett had painted, he read the text on the accompanying page.

#

"Sept. 16. Our guide went from us yesterday and we saw him no more. About ten of the clock we set forward and after we had travelled about ten miles one of our Indians killed us a Deer. Presently afterwards we had sight of a curious River like Apomatack River. Its course here was north, and so we suppose it runs about a certain three mountains we saw westward. Here we set up our quarters, our course having been west. We understand the Mohecan Indians did here formerly live.

"Soon after Sun set did happen a most peculiar experience. First we heard many birds of an unknown breed and haunting cry. Then out of the woods sounded a "YCK-YCK, TIKILI-TIKILI," many times and of surpassing volume. Then did appear a Stranger of peculiar aspect, neither Indian nor Englishman, in black garb of unusual cut. When asked of his name, he did say 'No One' but nothing more. Upon this man departing our quarters, Thomas Preston attempted following but returned in little time, claiming with no slight fear to have seen that herein depicted. This he swore to be at a nearby body of water which we have since failed to locate. Time does not permit forestalling our continued progress westward.

"After a long sleep, Thomas Preston forgot any sight of this

Stranger and claims no recognition of that which he rendered with his very hand."

#

"It fits. That damn well fits." Parrott could hardly croak the words. "But if that blob with the eye is supposed to be the Yck, what about the other? The one that looks human?"

"'No One.'" Scales exhaled slowly. "I would infer that he—or *it*—plays some pivotal role in the other's manifestation. A controller of sorts, maybe."

"'No One.'" Something about this appellation nagged at him, but he found his thoughts racing too fast, too chaotically, to wrap themselves around it. "I think I've seen this person. Or whatever *it* is."

"Is that so?" Scales appeared at once impressed and revolted. "It's a pity your duty prevented you from sharing more details with me sooner, Sheriff. I understand, of course. And, honestly, even if you had, what could it have changed? But I am sorry for all you must have been through."

"That wasn't much, though, was it? Not compared to what must have happened to those others."

Scales pointed to Pritchett's art project. "Is it fair for me to infer that you now believe in these things?"

Parrott didn't answer immediately but stared back at Scales for a time. "Do you?"

The professor shot him a humorless grin. "Sheriff, I never talk about my beliefs. They wouldn't necessarily fly in academic or even social circles around these parts. But regarding this particular 'legend,' I will tell you this. There is at least one other account that might relate to what you've seen here—most notably from the time of the fire around Black Tooth Pond all those years ago. There was a newspaper article from that period—I don't need to find it because I have it up here." He tapped his forehead. "One unnamed witness said, 'They tried to burn it.' He was in shock, and no one ever knew what he was referring to. But certain stories—verbal stories—lingered afterward."

"It would stand to reason that the fire failed."

Scales nodded. "Now, when you and I talked on the phone a while back, we reminisced about our summer camp days, when the counselors tried to scare us kids. For me, the most memorable thing about that Yck story they told concerned its voracious hunger. 'It can lurk like a trapdoor spider, but it also hunts like a shark.'"

"I never knew that one," Parrott said. "But if it and that other thing—'No One'—come from 'somewhere else,' why this area, Professor? Why Black Tooth Pond?"

"Who can answer that? I think perhaps a more apt question is why *not* this area? Shy of certain areas in New England, I'd be hard-pressed to think of a place with a more haunted history."

"Touché. But for me, the real question is...." Parrott paused, reluctant to give voice to his most unsettling thought. "Is this all over? Good God, it needs to be over. At least on my watch."

#

When Parrott opened the front door to his little house on Whittle Road, the first thing he heard was a rapid *thump-thump-thump* from the back of the house, and an instant later, the big Golden Retriever came tearing into the living room, tail whipping back and forth, big brown eyes regarding him with fondness.

"Hello, Rufus. And how are you tonight?"

Rufus's tail became a blur.

When it had become clear that the dog's original owner would almost certainly never return home, Parrott had decided to take him in. He had always loved dogs. Still, at first, he'd been reluctant because he worked such odd hours, and dogs required regular attention. But his next-door neighbors, Fred and Maureen Conroy, who always kept a close eye on his place, promised that they would make sure the Retriever got all the attention he needed whenever the sheriff couldn't provide it himself. They owned four dogs, and Fred assured him that they'd love to have a fifth as a "part-time" charge. So, Parrott opted to go for it and brought the dog home.

He'd learned the Retriever's name was Rufus, and he wasn't about to change it. He was a hell of a good dog, and he responded well to Parrott as his new best buddy.

Still, Rufus occasionally bore an aspect of melancholia, and he frequently stared out the bedroom window into the woods behind Parrott's house. He obviously missed his former owner and no doubt hoped that Phil Pritchett might yet return to him. In those moments, Parrott let him grieve without intruding. Then, he and the dog often cuddled up on the couch or went outside to play or just sat and watched television. The shine in Rufus's eyes told Parrott that while he might remember and feel sad, he had—probably, anyway—reconciled himself to his new life.

Tonight, after getting out of his uniform and into his comfy lounge clothes, Parrott settled on the couch with Rufus, and somehow forced his thoughts away from the afternoon's mind-numbing revelations to Doc Crawford.

The one bright spot in his life that could overcome so much horror.

That first drink at Willy's the other night had numbed their pain a bit, the second had loosened them up, and the third had gotten them laughing and talking. They both knew that, in the face of such a dreadful unknown, they had done the best anyone in their positions could do, and the FBI people's perceptions on the matter meant jack shit.

Yep. Jack. Fucking. Shit.

Doc Crawford—Mel—had agreed to join him for dinner on Friday night at Calaman House, and he couldn't deny that the prospect of spending future quality time with her held more allure than any other prospect in he couldn't count how many ages.

Rufus clearly agreed, for he lay with his hefty body pressed close to Parrott and frequently leaned his face over to offer a consoling nuzzle.

"Thank you, my friend."

At first, he didn't pay much mind when Rufus's ears rose and his attention wandered toward the hall that led to the back rooms. But when the dog slid off the couch and trotted toward the bedroom, his senses came alert, and he sat upright, his muscles shifting from relaxed to taut.

Oh, no.

He felt a prickling at the back of his neck, and he sensed what must be coming.

"It can lurk like a trap-door spider, but it also hunts like a shark."

He rose from the couch and shambled back to his bedroom. Rufus sat in front of the window to the backyard, eyes and ears alert, his breathing rapid. As Parrott entered, the dog gave him a brief glance that read as plainly as if emblazoned on the wall, "I'm here, but I don't like this."

From the woods behind the house, the sound drifted to his ears.

A whippoorwill cry.

Only…it wasn't. Not a bird but some kind of mimic.

Whatever made the noise, it must be right at the edge of the woods.

He remembered that Saturday evening almost exactly a month ago, outside his office, the incredible, blaring siren of a sound that had pealed across the sky. It had the same cadence as a whippoorwill song. A different sound, issued at an impossible volume, yet the *syllables* followed the same pattern.

T'KKK-ELLL-EEE-LIIII!

No, this was not *that* noise. This sounded like a human voice mimicking a whippoorwill's call. But there could be no mistaking the similarities, the commonalities of the sounds. Had all those people who'd vanished heard this noise before they went...gone?

The call came again, so close now he could feel its vibrations.

Rufus whimpered once and then skulked away, into another room.

Parrott knew, now beyond any doubt, that the original owner of the voice out there was dead. And for a moment, he wondered if, by this time tomorrow, the only one alive in his house might be Rufus.

No, it isn't over.

Today's conversation with Professor Scales, the conclusions they had reached, had erased any conceivable doubt. Sheriff Parrott, his officers—the whole damned town—had so far faced the earliest rumbles of some terrible storm, and he feared that storm was ready to break over them all, in full.

A storm that blew from some dimension not of this earth.

– END –

Meet the Author

Stephen Mark Rainey is author of the novels *Balak, Dark Shadows: Dreams of the Dark* (with Elizabeth Massie), *The Nightmare Frontier, Blue Devil Island, The Gods of Moab,* and many others; over 200 published works of short fiction; six short-fiction collections; and a trio of audio dramas for Big Finish Productions based on the *Dark Shadows* TV series, featuring several original cast members. For ten years, he edited the award-winning *Deathrealm* magazine and has edited anthologies for Chaosium, Arkham House, Delirium Books, and Shortwave Publishing. Mark lives in Martinsville, VA, with his wife, Kimberly, and a houseful of precocious house cats. He is an avid geocacher and frequently explores "challenging" settings that most sane individuals would avoid. Visit his website at **www.stephenmarkrainey.com**.

Books by Stephen Mark Rainey

Novels:
Balak
The Lebo Coven
Dark Shadows: Dreams of the Dark (with Elizabeth Massie)
The Nightmare Frontier
Blue Devil Island
The Monarchs

Elizabeth Massie's Ameri-Scares Novels for Young Readers:
West Virginia: Lair of the Mothman
Michigan: The Dragon of Lake Superior
Ohio: Fear the Grassman!
New Hampshire: Ghosts From the Skies
Georgia: The Haunting of Tate's Mill

Novella:
The Gods of Moab

Collections:
Fugue Devil & Other Weird Horrors
The Last Trumpet
Legends of the Night
Other Gods
The Gaki & Other Hungry Spirits
Fugue Devil: Resurgence

Anthologies (edited):
Deathrealms
Song of Cthulhu
Evermore (with James Robert Smith)
Deathrealm: Spirits